# Snakes

# Wolves

A NOVEL

A.V. ARMS

HARPER WOODS PUBLISHING

This book is a work of fiction. References to real people, events, establishments, organizations, or locales are intended only to provide a sense of authenticity and are used fictitiously. All other characters, and all incidents and dialogue, are drawn from the author's imagination and are not to be construed as real.



ISBN : 979-8-9864337-0-7

www.avarmsbooks.com

Also, by A.V. Arms

The Norman Invasion trilogy –

The Dead King

The Pretend King

The Queen's Kings

American Civil War novel –

Shadows

**Friday, May 12, 1447, road to London**

The lightning cracked over Squire Adrian's head, and the thunder rolled across the sky, drowning out the pounding of his horse's hooves as the pair parted the torrential rain. He shivered as the horse moved beneath him, its lather flying, indiscernible from the precipitation. The cold rain soaked his clothes, making his young body quiver. The cold dampness leeched away his warmth before he could even ride from the bailey of Ravenshill. He still wrestled with the horror that sent him flying from the walls of the old Norman castle and racing down the road to London.

***Thursday, May 11, 1447, Ravenshill***

*The screams came from the tower, penetrating the walls of the gatehouse. The ear-splitting cries chilled Adrian. He did not hesitate but dashed into the downpour from his dry shelter. The sound traveled through the old stone walls and across the bailey. It echoed within the enclosure of that inner courtyard, surrounded by its stone walls. Lady Elisabeth's voice rose above the clap of thunder and the driving rain. He darted for the tower. His feet slipped on the wet wood of the narrow bridge that spanned the moat of the old Ravenshill tower. Centuries of sediment filled the moat, creating little more than a small trench the drawbridge spanned. He crossed through the arched doorway and into the lord's hall and halted suddenly. The weather outside threatened to shake the stones loose from the old tower. The young Lord Walter Kirkham lay at the bottom of the long spiraling wooden staircase. Blood collected around the six-year-old's shattered skull. Baron Thomas Kirkham of Ravenshill moved around his son, reaching for him and then drawing away. The boy did not breathe.*

*The house servants gathered, their faces full of shock and tears. The scene of a family tragedy unfolded before them. Adrian could not pull his eyes from Thomas's oldest child, eleven-year-old Elisabeth, who stood at the base of the steps. Her screams fell silent, and her mouth hung open in shock and disbelief. Her blue eyes flowed tears, and he could hear her choking on her sobs. She clutched a wooden sword, and just as the steps disappeared around its first bend lay another, and Adrian pieced the tragedy together. The siblings had been playing swords. Guilt struck Adrian. Walter had asked Adrian to play with him and the wood swords only half an hour before. But Adrian felt he was beyond the age of playing with the toys. For a brief and insane moment, Adrian wondered if the boy died before or after he dropped the sword. Did he die a true warrior with a sword in hand, or was he merely a child who died this night.*

*Elisabeth's terrible screams echoing above the thunder had drawn the small number of servants from their chambers. The shriek picked up again. She screamed her brother's name over and over. It came from Elisabeth's throat, competing with the raging storm outside. Then it was as if it all paused so her father could be heard asking, "Elisabeth, what have you done?"*

*That question stopped her screams. The minutes ticked by, the chasm of silence deep. Then Sir Lincoln Victers stepped into the hall. A level of comfort filled Adrian with the big man standing in the open doorway. As the storm raged behind him, neither God's wrath nor the death of a child could rattle the big knight. The man moved forward, and his eyes assessed while he advanced. He reached a strong hand out and squeezed Adrian on the shoulder with reassurance that he would take control of the situation. By the time Sir Lincoln stood over the child, everyone waited.*

*He crouched by the boy and, reaching a steady hand out, forced the boy's eyelids closed for a final time. "He is gone," Lincoln announced.*

*Lord Thomas's face morphed into a rage so intense it turned his flesh red and his eyes wild. The baron straightened, and thunder that imitated the violence raging outside cracked across his brows. Thomas studied his daughter. Elisabeth trembled as her father's angry strides carried him to her. She lifted her small head and met her father's eyes that mirrored the same pure blue of her own. Lord Thomas raised his hand and smacked her. She stumbled sideways. Her knuckles turned white on the wooden sword, and she landed on her rear. She sat, one hand braced on the floor, the other still holding the sword. Her blond hair hung like a shroud around her face as she stared at the floor beneath her.*

*"My lord," Lincoln's voice broke the heavy silence. To Adrian, it seemed as if the storm began again outside with Lincoln's words.*

*Adrian never saw Elisabeth look so frail and vulnerable as she did in that instant. He wanted to comfort her, but it felt wrong with eyes watching. Everything felt wrong. Not prone to violence, Lord Thomas never hit his children, and Sir Lincoln never hesitated, but he did now. His eyes traveled to Elisabeth before falling back on Lord Thomas. A flurry of motion came from Elisabeth as she jumped to her feet and fled the terrible scene.*

*"My lord," Lincoln said again. The knight's stance grew a little taller and straighter.*

*"My son," Lord Thomas whispered. Then something passed over his face that matched a father's grief. "What shall be done?"*

*"Attend to the boy," Lincoln snapped at the handful of servants that gathered. His voice was not harsh but sharp enough to release the few women and men from their shock.*

*"Lord Thomas," Lincoln said, with a hand indicating he should precede him into the chapel. The baron obediently complied. Not receiving an order of his own, Adrian fell into step with the two men.*

*The door closed behind them, and Adrian would become a part of truths that could make the House of Ravenshill crumble.*

**Saturday, May 13, 1447, road to London**

The storm abated through the night. But it began again early the next day with a steady drizzle until dusk, and then the storm raged again. A flash of lightning so bright it bathed the road and deepened the shadows beneath the trees looming over him. Then lightning struck the tree a few strides ahead with a deafening crack, and it exploded. His horse reared and twisted, terrified. But Sir Lincoln had taught Adrian how to handle horses with the expertise of a knight, and the boy brought the animal back under control. But on her next step, the horse slipped.

The animal lost her purchase, and Adrian shifted his weight to help her stay on her feet, but they flew from beneath her. Adrian kicked free of the stirrups and rolled from the saddle. The horse landed on the ground with a splash. The air in Adrian's chest exploded from him in a grunt. His elbow struck something sharp, sending talons of pain shooting up his arm.

The torrent of rain beat at him. He lay prone on the ground, and it struck his face and surged around him. He rolled from his back, feeling frantic. He scrambled to his feet with a speed that left him woozy. Weighed down by his clothes, water draining from his boots, he took two steps toward the floundering animal. The horse panicked. He made a fruitless lunge toward the horse as it clambered up. His hand reached for the reins, and another shot of lightning struck. The horse bolted past him. She struck him on the shoulder, and he spun, nearly falling. He straightened and saw his horse's heels disappear into the dark storm. With her went his clothes, his blanket, and the money that could buy a child.

Undecided, Adrian stood with the rain pelting him and thunder shaking the Earth. He could chase after the horse and his sword still in its scabbard, strapped to the saddle. But she could run for miles despite having already done so. The boy's exhaustion debilitated him. He did not have the strength to give chase to the horse carrying all his possessions with it. In all probability, he would never see that horse again. Adrian did not know how far ahead London still lay. He knew he now rode the path that led straight to the city, but Sir Lincoln did not tell him how long he would travel before arriving. When the chapel door closed two days before, Adrian learned the importance of his journey. That night plunged him into a world that required all his strength and resilience while testing his loyalty. Adrian turned his feet toward London and began walking. The mud sucked at his boots, and the rain tried to drive him to his knees.

***Thursday, May 11, 1447, Ravenshill***

*Adrian followed Lord Thomas and Lincoln into the room filled with an ominous silence.*

*"It's all gone with my son," Lord Thomas mumbled. Then the man broke down sobbing. He covered his face, and his knees buckled, striking the floor.*

*Lincoln stood his ground, and so did Adrian. Adrian sensed an air of annoyance coming from Lincoln. Then Lord Thomas quieted and looked up at the knight with tears on his cheeks.*

*"We must do what has been done." Grimness filled Lincoln's reluctant words.*

*Lord Thomas bowed his head and nodded. With that, Lincoln turned, and his large body loomed over Adrian. "You will go to London. There you will find a boy who can pass as Lord Walter. You will bring him back."*

*Lincoln's words confused Adrian. "My pardon, sir?"*

*"It must be done," Lincoln said. "The lord I promised my sword to, the man I gave my oath to and forever bound myself to, was ruined years ago. We have nothing, and you would have nothing without your titles. The wolves are knocking at the door, Young Adrian. Lady Elisabeth must marry well, or she will be an impoverished spinster. That my boy will only happen if*

*there is a male heir. No one here would have a pot to piss in without an heir, and Ravenshill will fall from the Kirkham's hands."*

*Then Lincoln grabbed Adrian's arm to focus the boy's chaotic mind. "This will work. It has worked before." Then the big knight lowered his head and made Adrian his confidant. "Lord Walter died with his mother on the birthing bed." Lincoln raised himself to assess the boy's reaction.*

*"But there are witnesses."*

*"I will see to that. There is a man that secures the Dog Hound Brothel, Paul Graham. He can't do much but fight and produce sons. He is a drunk and will sell anything for another drink, including his children. Where I found this Walter, there is another son, a little older. As Walter grew, he resembled that brother a great deal. Go find the boy." Then Lincoln's face softened, and he dropped to a knee in front of Adrian, gripping the boy's shoulders. "I know you can do this. You are a fine, strong lad who is nothing if not loyal. You have learned much here but know what must be done is for Ravenshill and Elisabeth. I do not know what fate would befall her if Lord Thomas were stripped of his title. I will be honest. I do not know what fate will befall me if our secrets are freed."*

*The legend of Sir Lincoln Victors was why the great knight was Adrian's hero. He was a commander with the Teutonic Order of Knights, reclaiming the Vistula River for a short time. Then Lincoln removed himself from wars, settled at Ravenshill, and commanded its defenses. He did not talk about his time in Poland, his victories or defeats there. But Adrian had heard enough stories to make the knight larger than life in Adrian's eyes. He remembered the day his parents told him he would foster with Lincoln at Ravenshill. Disobeying Lincoln now would never enter Adrian's eleven-year-old mind. Adrian nodded. "The secrets of Ravenshill will never pass my lips," he promised.*

*"Good boy," Lincoln said with a smile that did not reach his eyes. "Make haste. Walter will be upon his sickbed until you return."*

*"And the witnesses?"*

*Lincoln stood. "As I said., they will be my concern. In my trunk, you will find a pouch. Take that. I know there is enough money to buy a son of Paul Graham. Now go," Lincoln commanded.*

**Sunday, May 14, 1447, road to London**

So, Adrian had fled into the storm, choking back the fear and disbelief of what rested upon his thin shoulders. As a squire, he thought himself ready for anything. But now, Adrian feared this responsibility was far beyond his capabilities. He never considered where the people of Ravenshill went through the years. Adrian never contemplated why he and Lincoln now stood as the sole defenders of the old Norman castle. He did not know why a force no longer trained and protected the walls of Ravenshill and the village of Kielder. The young Adrian did not understand the magnitude of a house with one knight and a diminishing town. Now he understood it meant poverty. Only a few servants remained. But Lincoln's loyalty lay with Ravenshill and would never waver. In five years, Adrian would return home. Finding another Walter would decide the fate of the household he would one day leave behind.

Exhaustion dragged at Adrian. The rain poured and eased but always fell, forcing him forward despite his desire for rest. Perhaps Lord Thomas deserved a pauper's life, but not Elisabeth. Her breeding should give her the peaceful life of a lady. Adrian paused, now understanding why Elisabeth returned home after fostering for a short time. If Lord Thomas's money ran out, he could not provide the fees needed for Elisabeth's upkeep away from home. Just as Adrian's father paid Lord Thomas for Adrian's stay at Ravenshill.

Adrian needed rest. But the rain made that impossible. He forced himself on, and the thought of Elisabeth filled his mind. She killed her brother. Her father laid that burden on her little shoulders. Elisabeth, the oldest child, protected her younger brother, taught him, and guided him with pride. Did she blame herself? He had not had the time to ask how the accident transpired. Did she recover from her father's slap?

He wished he could be there with her. Without many servants, there were no other children residing at Ravenshill. He, Elisabeth, and Walter were the only children who called Ravenshill home. At the same age, Adrian and Elisabeth depended on one another for play and socializing. They often played the valiant knights rescuing the princess from the tower. Adrian almost laughed out loud, remembering Walter always played the princess. Elisabeth did not want the boys taking all the fun with their wooden swords while she waited, twiddling her thumbs. Elisabeth always got her way. Only because Walter could do nothing but what they told him if he wanted to play with them. And because Adrian would be a knight, he took chivalry very seriously, especially where ladies were concerned.

Adrian had to swallow his grief because the Walter he knew was as close to him as any younger brother could be. An image of Walter's body lying at the foot of the stairs flashed in his mind. A numbness began to spread through Adrian's limbs and settled deep. The true Walter Kirkham died long ago, his corpse long rotted in his grave. Now Walter would be replaced again, and that quest fell to Adrian. He wondered if this new boy would be worthy of Ravenshill.

Adrian dragged his tired feet along the road. No dry place existed on his body. He shivered from his loss of strength, the fear of being alone, the weight of his journey, worry for Elisabeth, and witnessing Walter's death.

The sun rose, and the downpour turned into a drizzle. The thick clouds concealed the sun and gave Adrian very little relief other than he no longer drowned, inhaling the heavy rainfall. Then he saw the first buildings that heralded the metropolis at the end of the road. His legs gave out. He knelt on the road for some time as he fought for his breath and some strength that might move him forward. Then, finally, a small amount of tenacity returned. He stood and moved into the city.

Adrian had never visited London, and seeing it crowded and filthy was intimidating. He feared the brothel would not be as easy to find as he initially thought. Filled with fear, he approached people to ask for directions, but they shooed him away repeatedly. He might be a baron, but he was still only a boy.

His clothes hung from him, ill-suited now that the weight of the rain stretched them. The expensive material sent by his mother no longer looked of fine quality, weighted down with mud. His face and dark hair were saturated with the soil of the road. He looked nothing like a lord.

A hand snaked around his arm and jerked him backward. He stumbled, looking up into the face of a man with craters cutting across his face from pox marks. He sneered down at Adrian. "You will sell well, a big strong lad like you."

Adrian tried to pull away, finding the iron grip did not loosen. But the man holding him firmly could not know Adrian got his training from a great knight. His fighting skills went well beyond what would be expected of a boy his age. The one possession left to him was his knife, hidden so he could pull it quickly and use it effectively. He whipped the blade out and slashed across the arm holding him. The man released him instantly. Adrian fled, and the man let him go.

Adrian raced along the streets, turning corners, racing block after block until the city's bowels enveloped him. Then, out of breath, his legs burning, he stopped. No place could be as intimidating as London in the boy's mind. He could feel people watching him. Those he didn't see, lurking behind dark windows and in deserted alleys, made the hair on the back of his neck stand up.

Starving children held their hands out, hoping anyone who passed would show them mercy. A sad situation in a sad place. He wondered how a boy from here could become a baron. The boy would come from nothing but must convince everyone otherwise.

After searching beyond his capacity, he had to seek shelter before he collapsed. Finally, he found a place to rest until dawn. Cold and wet, he shivered between two barrels beneath an old wooden slab he laid across the top for protection from the drizzle. He lay his head on the damp ground. A putrid odor of piss rose around him, but his exhaustion left him debilitated. His eyes closed, and darkness claimed him.

**Monday, May 15, 1447, London**

The nudge on his leg brought him awake with a start. Adrian sat up, banging his head on the board.

"Get out of here, you filthy cur." The man kicked him harder. He considered asking his question, but instead, he ran.

Adrian did not stop until his legs could carry him no further. London lay like a maze with its labyrinth of roads and buildings. He gathered his courage again and asked some passersby where to find the Dog Hound Brothel. A few ignored him, some stared, and others shrugged. Eventually, he got directions but was still lost in London's streets.

The neighborhood Adrian finally entered housed poverty like he had never witnessed. The brothel stood just as sad with its patched walls and roof. It appeared to have stood for two hundred years without repairs. Despite the early hour, the brothel bustled with activity. The drunk stumbled out, and the randy rushed in. Adrian approached with trepidation. Reaching for the door, someone yanked it open from the other side. Adrian's breath caught, and he took a step back. The boy he came to find stood before him. There would be no other who could look like Walter so precisely.

Adrian jumped into action before he could think. He grabbed the boy and dragged him away from the building. The boy allowed it for a moment, then planted his feet. The money for the boy's father was gone, and it would be hard to convince the boy of the truth in the wild story. But he had to try, and he could not fail.

"I need to talk to you," Adrian said. He turned the boy so they faced each other, but he did not let go of his arm.

"I don't even know you," the boy argued.

"No, you do not." Adrian stepped closer. He saw subtle differences now. The other Walter's full lips differed from this boy's flat ones. They almost sat too straight, making even lines that cut across the boy's square and gaunt face. The eyes contained flecks of gold that the Kirkhams' blue eyes did not possess. This kid grew up starving on the streets. While the other Walter got food and care. Perhaps a cleaning and a haircut could help. But it would not detract from the aura that surrounded the young boy. Even the way he held himself portrayed him as someone other than Walter. A quiet and shy boy would not be found in this child, exuding confidence surprising for one so young and desperate. Would anyone who did not know Ravenshill's secret notice?

"Do you want to get away from here?"

"What if I do?" The boy's voice filled with apprehension.

This Walter looked at him now and frowned. Adrian found it difficult to hide his own breeding. Though the mud-covered him, his speech patterns betrayed him. Even the way he stood over the boy, as the kid butchered his own language, declared him more than he appeared.

"Are you recruiting for the slavers," the boy asked with a great deal of hostility.

"No," Adrian said, but he gained nothing but a skeptical look from this Walter.

"My lord has sent me for a boy who could pass as his son."

The boy stared at him with hesitancy and mistrust. "You lie."

"Why would I lie?" Adrian asked.

"Why does anyone lie? There's something in it for you."

"I am a squire, and all that is in it for me is pleasing my knight and not letting the lordship he has dedicated his life for crumble. There is a great deal more in it for you."

The boy's arms folded over his chest, and his blue eyes roved up and down Adrian. This Walter's eyes would appear faded compared with Elisabeth's. Before, Adrian paid little attention and only knew Walter's eyes to be blue. Perhaps no one spent time looking at the eyes of a little boy more than a moment. "What?" the boy asked after a silence that obviously irritated him.

"You will be a baron with your own land."

The boy perked up. "A title. I will be rich?"

"No," Adrian informed him. "You will be the son of a lord in great debt. You will help keep them from losing everything."

"Who is this lord?" the boy asked.

Adrian shook his head. He did not think it prudent to disclose more information on Lord Thomas or that his younger brother previously served the role. The secret's ramifications could reach far and devastate those Adrian loved. Adrian knew if he could not convince this boy, he could not leave him with those secrets. "You will only learn more if you come with me."

He took a step back. "I don't believe you."

"Then I wish you luck." Adrian's gaze moved over his surroundings. Then, wrinkling his nose, he looked down, showing this kid his place beneath his gaze and his boot if Adrian desired. "You are six?" Adrian asked.

"I am eight," this Walter said before hesitating. "At least, I think I am."

"Then you have more years before you can fight off the slavers." Adrian sneered at him so the boy would see he did not care about his fate. Adrian turned on his heel with quick deliberation. But he did care, and he could not leave this boy here. But there was no time to convince this boy poverty differed with a title and a safe home. Perhaps it would be easier for the kid to traverse poverty without a coveted title attached.

"Wait," the boy called after Adrian took two steps away.

"What will happen if I go with you?"

Adrian turned back around. "We will teach you to be this boy. How to speak like him, carry yourself like him. Then, if we are successful, you will inherit and fix what your father has broken."

"My father," the boy said in a voice low and ashamed. Whatever man sired this kid did not father as one should. "And a mother?" he asked. The tone of his voice, the desire that lurked there, left Adrian uneasy.

"She died birthing you." Adrian almost told him of the first replaced Walter, but he knew it did not matter.

This Walter's face fell. "I never had a mother," the boy said.

"Your father is a kind man," Adrian said, shoving the vision of him slapping Elisabeth from his mind. "You will also have a sister older than you. She is gentle and kind." Adrian wondered how they would silence Elisabeth. Would they silence her like the other witnesses? Would the daughter be sacrificed for the son? Urgency began building, constricting Adrian's chest.

"I will not be rich?" the boy mulled this over. "If you were lying, you would also say I would be rich. I have sisters. What of them?"

"If you come, you will have only one sister. That is the only sister you ever had," Adrian said in a clipped voice. He could not distract himself from the question. With the question, what would happen to Elisabeth if she did not go along with their story?

The boy stepped closer, his face twisted into a menacing stare, "I will go, but if you lie, I will kill you."

A moment ago, Adrian would laugh at the boy, a street urchin, looking up at him, a trained squire, and threatening him. But now tremendous relief washed over him. He could now return and find out Elisabeth's fate. He knew he would think of nothing else until they arrived back at Ravenshill.

A new problem now presented itself. The boys needed horses, or it would take weeks to arrive at Ravenshill. Moreover, no shoes graced this Walter's feet, and his clothes swallowed his small frame.

"Where can I find a horse?"

The boy stepped back. His body grew rigid with renewed distrust. "You are a squire, but yet you have no horse?"

"I lost her last night. She fell in the rain," Adrian said.

Then the new Walter laughed, bending over and slapping his knee. "You do not sound like a good squire if you lost your horse."

Adrian scowled at the boy.

After a moment, the boy sobered enough and asked, "A horse to buy or steal?"

Adrian contemplated this for a moment. He never stole before, but they needed something, even a worn-down nag.

"Do you know where we can steal a horse?"

"I do, Baby Squire," the boy taunted. "Follow me."

Adrian almost didn't. He did not like the boy's ridicule. But, the would-be lord needed something to sell the act, and his confidence and mirth could help.

***Thursday, May 11, 1447, Ravenshill***

Elisabeth's hand lifted, pressing against her stinging cheek. Numbness surrounded her, enveloping her. It shielded her and stopped her tears that brimmed on the precipice, flooding her blue eyes but not falling again. She stared at her brother's blood spreading around him. She did that. Her father asked her what she did, and Elisabeth couldn't answer him. She didn't know. They only played.

The swordplay began when the five-year-old Walter brought their wooden swords as mischief danced in his eyes. He wouldn't stop whacking her leg with his. So she picked up the sword he had brought for her. But the hour turned late, and she did not want to play. Which she told Walter again and again. But once she picked the sword up, it turned into fun.

In her chamber, they cracked their wooden swords together. Laughter filled the room. Elisabeth crossed the threshold from her chamber, backing her brother away. They parried, and Walter's improved skills impressed her. Several times, he put her on the defensive, and their play grew earnest. Elisabeth did not care that Walter was a boy. The oldest should always be the best, especially matching wooden swords. Walter would tire of their wooden swordplay, eventually. He grew, aged, and soon would be a knight ready for real battles.

This filled her mind when Walter slipped. Only then did she become aware of where she stood and where Walter stood. His face registered a moment of surprise. Then he pitched backward, and Elisabeth rushed forward, grabbing for him. She missed the first step but caught herself, gripping her sword, and jolted down onto the second. His head cracked on the wooden steps, and there followed a sickening crunch of bone.

It happened in slow motion. She raced down behind her tumbling brother. The sword flew from his hand just as she reached it. She thought she could stop the chaotic tumble, but Elisabeth couldn't reach him before taking the next step and then the next, chasing his tumbling body down. Then a sickening thud followed as his body stopped on the floor of the lord's hall. It echoed against the quiet stone walls, reverberating, and then silence followed.

Elisabeth stopped in her tracks. The bottom of the steps was so far away. Walter lay there, his body twisted and so very still. She stood over him, screaming. She still held the sword, but she could not release it and could not stop screaming. It echoed and deafened, growing louder and more intense. Torrents of tears flowed down her cheeks.

People gathered. She saw the movement from the corners of her eyes. The tears crashed onto the floor at her feet until her father advanced and smacked her. Her father never struck her. He never raised his voice. She turned and fled through the nearest door and into the chapel. She dropped behind the altar to crouch, then collapsed, drawing her knees against her chest. The golden white of the elder tree's natural wood formed the altar. She pressed her back hard into the wood shrine, hoping God would protect her from the horror she did. She made no sound, contemplating what happened in her upheaved world.

Approaching steps made her start crying again. What did her father do? Why did he slap her? She tried stopping this before it ever began. She still held the wooden toy, evidence of her guilt. The steps of more than one person entered the chapel. She lay the sword down with caution, staring at the straight grain of the sword carved from an ash tree. Its light brown hue made the sword appear incapable of such horrific damage. The door closed, and voices began.

At first, she did not listen. Her mind would not connect with the words. She could only see her brother's body, hear his skull crack, smell the coppery stench, and feel the burn of her father's hand against her cheek. But then Adrian and Lincoln's voices penetrated her sanctuary. With Adrian there, she almost came from her hiding place. But she heard her father's voice and did not think she could face him. What would Elisabeth say? That she was sorry? She was definitely that.

Elisabeth leaned forward. She couldn't hear her father's mumbled words, but Sir Lincoln's carried to her clearly.

"We must do what has been done." Lincoln's voice held a dark threat that made the hair on the back of Elisabeth's neck stand up. Elisabeth sometimes debated which man filled a more prominent role as a father figure. Her dad adored her as much as he loved the woman who birthed her. He never went to court, and not a day of her life went by without her father at her side. Sir Lincoln held her hand through the years, both figurately and literally. He played with her and never turned her away because she was a girl, including her in many of Adrian's and Walter's lessons.

Lincoln always filled her childish fantasies as her knight in shining armor. Though she knew of her betrothal, it did not stop her from dreaming or looking at him upon a pedestal.

Lincoln's voice froze her breath, "You will go to London and find an orphan who can pass as Lord Walter."

She could imagine Adrian's face, an arched brow, a flat line of lips pressed tight. How could Lincoln send him away at a time like this? She needed Adrian's smile, a soft touch on the shoulder, or a hug. He would say the right things that would ease her fear of what happened and what would happen. He could keep her world from tilting so precariously. His numerous techniques of humor and compassion soothed her moods.

"It must be done." Lincoln's voice sounded urgent, near panic, but Lincoln never panicked. Nothing ever rattled Lincoln. "The lord I promised my sword to, the man I gave my oath to and forever bound myself to, was ruined years ago."

Elisabeth shifted but could not rise and demand why Lincoln said these things. Her father said nothing, and that left her anxious.

"We have nothing, and you would have nothing without your titles. The wolves are knocking at the door, Young Adrian. Elisabeth must marry well, or she will be an impoverished spinster. That my boy will only happen if there is a male heir. No one here would have a pot to piss in without an heir, and Ravenshill will fall from the Kirkhams' hands."

Her betrothal guaranteed her a husband, but a dowery would be expected. The betrothal contract stated Elisabeth Kirkham of Ravenshill, who was she without Ravenshill. Indeed, the agreement would not stand if she did not hold that title. The stone floor of the chapel tilted beneath Elisabeth's cold hands. It spun as she slid toward an unknown abyss.

"This will work," Lincoln's voice and the urgency snapped Elisabeth's attention back. "It has worked before."

Elisabeth held her breath. Lincoln's hushed voice said, "Lord Walter died with his mother on the birthing bed."

She tumbled into a dark abyss filled with unease. She caught herself before she cried out.

"But there are witnesses." Elisabeth needed Adrian's assurance everything would be alright. She always believed him when he said it. He always said it with confidence.

"I will see to that. There is a man that secures the Dog Hound Brothel, Paul Graham. He can't do much but fight and produce sons. He is a drunk and will sell anything for another drink, including his son. Where I found this, Walter, there is another son." Elisabeth placed her hands over her ears and squeezed her eyes tightly closed. She prayed this was a nightmare she would wake from. But not even the altar in the chapel could chase away the evil that lurked in the tower that night. She moved her shaking hands from her head.

"I know you can do this. You are a fine, strong lad who is nothing if not loyal." Elisabeth nodded, agreeing with Lincoln's words. Her limbs turned numb. She still did not understand. Everything happened so fast. Her brother wasn't her brother? Would she lose her betrothed too? And something else, something much more sinister than these revelations, filled the room.

"You have learned much here, but know what must be done, must be done for Ravenshill and Elisabeth." Lincoln's voice sounded so sure this would save her and her home. "I do not know what fate would befall her if Lord Thomas did not have his title. But I will be honest. I do not know what fate will befall me if our secrets are freed."

What role did Lincoln play that made these secrets change his fate? Indeed, if he took a vow for the next lord, he could retain his position here.

"The secrets of Ravenshill will never pass my lips." Adrian didn't sound like himself. She leaned forward but stopped herself from peering around the corner. She did not doubt the voice of her friend. But the timbre of his voice changed, and she did not recognize it. The tone said life and death hung in the balance and made it a man's voice.

"Good boy," Lincoln said. *Yes, good boy,* Elisabeth thought, filled with love for her friend. He would reach London and save her—save them all.

"Make haste. Walter will be upon his sickbed until you return." But the storm raged outside, too dangerous for travel. Elisabeth squeezed her eyes shut. Adrian couldn't leave her because she needed his hand. She needed its warmth until this nightmare ended.

"And the witnesses?" Adrian asked.

"As I said, they will be my concern. In my trunk, you will find a pouch. Take that. I know there is enough money there to buy a son of Paul Graham. Now go."

The last word commanded and nearly made Elisabeth jump, with the crash of thunder outside joining it. *Oh Adrian,* she thought, *I am so sorry.* As she crouched behind the altar, she feared for her friend. He only had to go to London because of her. She was the oldest and a girl, and girls didn't play with swords. Girls were made for different things like embroidery and babies, not playing with wooden swords. She should have sent Walter away as a lady of any degree would have. But she hadn't.

Elisabeth shivered behind the altar, and her mind worked at her questions. Walter wasn't her brother? If they could replace her brother, why couldn't they replace their mother too? It would be a different world at Ravenshill with a mother. All of it was a lie—even her own life.

So deep in thought, she did not hear the room empty. When she finally realized she was alone in the chapel, she rose. She circled the altar and dropped to her knees in front of it. "Dear heavenly father, please forgive me for what I have done." She drew in a deep sob. "Please let Father forgive me." She dropped her head, and tears fell on the hands folded in front of her. "But most of all," she whispered, feeling guilty for it, "protect Adrian. Please protect him," she begged the lord she hoped looked down on her and would answer that one prayer. "I will take any punishment for my deeds this night, even if it means Father will hate me forever, but bring Adrian back."

She cried a moment more, drew in a snot-filled sob, and rubbed the back of her sleeve across her face to wipe it away. Elisabeth knew what she had to do. She was Adrian's knight of swords. He could not go to London alone and accomplish such a dangerous task without her at his side. "He needs me as much as I need him right now," she whispered.

She jumped up from the altar and fled the room teamed with lies.

No one lingered in the hall outside the chapel, not even Walter. Then, a giant flash of lightning lit the room and its stone walls. Elisabeth saw the pool of blood at the bottom of the steps and Walter's wooden sword lying just within sight on the curved staircase.

Her slippered feet made little sounds fleeing through the hall and out into the pouring rain. She hesitated there. The heavy clouds blocked the moon and stars. The gate stood open, and she reassured herself it was best if Adrian got a little ahead so he could not make her stay at Ravenshill.

She splashed through the bailey toward the stables. Adrian's young warhorse Achilles welcomed her with a nicker, but his lighter and faster palfrey was gone from her stall. Elisabeth lifted her lightweight saddle and placed it on her horse's back. Her trembling hands slowed her and gave her pause again when thunder rolled overhead, shaking the earth beneath her feet. Her horse, Sasha, had outrun Adrian's larger Bandida once and only by half a length. But that was over a greater distance, and this journey would be about endurance. She had to be bolder than her male counterpart, pushing through the storm quickly and not letting fear slow her. Or she would never catch up to Adrian.

With only three guardsmen at the keep, the walls would be empty on this wicked night. She moved past the gatehouse, her steps quick and quiet, tugging on the reluctant Sasha, forcing her every step of the way. She heard the door to the gatehouse open just as she walked beneath the parapet. She thought for a panicked moment her reluctant animal would be seen, but she came to stand next to Elisabeth, pressing herself against the wall. Soon she heard the heavy hinges of the gate as it closed next to her.

Elisabeth closed her eyes and prayed again. She was drenched to the skin, and lightning burst, cascading the night into a bright flash before falling to darkness again. She shivered and drew Sasha close. She was outside the gates now, and no one would hear her call to be permitted back in if she changed her mind.

Sasha's trot was smooth and fast, carrying her down the hill from the keep, although the animal was reluctant to be outside the stable on such a stormy night. The night was so black Adrian would not be able to go beyond a trot himself. *Be brave*, rang again and again in her head. Reaching the bridge, the horse nearly went to her haunches in refusal. She snapped the whip twice on the horse's hindquarters while fighting her head with the reins in her other hand. Once Sasha stepped onto the bridge, she let the animal pick her own pace on the wet boards. In the darkness below, she heard the angry river churning, shaking the bridge, and she recognized the terror filling her. She could not push it away, but she could steady herself so her already flighty mare wouldn't get spooked by the feel of her rider trembling with fear. Reaching the solid ground, Elisabeth spun Sasha and spurred her south.

They rode beyond breakneck speed on the treacherous ground. The rain and wind beat at her, blinding her. Now that the horse was moving forward, Elisabeth felt her settle into the gate that ate up the road.

The tree exploded next to them, followed by instant thunder deafening her. The forest and road were awash in blinding light. As the night was plunged back beneath its shroud, Sasha shrieked and fought Elisabeth for control of the bit. Sasha lurched from side to side, and with the pop of another lightning bolt nearby, the horse gained her head. The animal bolted forward, far faster than Elisabeth dared to go on such a dark and treacherous road. Elisabeth tried to take control of the horse that was out of her mind. Not breaking stride even when Elisabeth tried to turn her. Sasha did not care if the bit was dragged up between her jaws, through skin and bone, because she was determined to outrun the storm.

Elisabeth clung to the soaked animal, wondering how she could see what lay ahead in the stinging downpour. Suddenly Sasha turned and plunged in a different direction. The branches whipped across her, nearly pulling her from the saddle as they assaulted her from the dark. Elisabeth fought with her horse again, but Sasha screamed and fought back. The girl was no match for the animal. Sasha charged through the forest. Elisabeth saw the trees looming overhead and all around in the lightning flashes, broken only by the narrow path. The ground here was more solid than the well-worn road, and with great care, as the horse ran out of steam, Elisabeth coaxed her back to a walk.

Sasha settled, her sides heaved, and Elisabeth trembled with such terror and relief she sobbed and let out a long-held breath. Elisabeth shook her head. "It's okay," she said out loud, more for herself than Sasha. Elisabeth turned the horse and moved her back in the direction they had come from. What had only been a few minutes racing through the forest turned into eternity, time immeasurable with no moon overhead. She reassured herself it would not be long before they reached the road. But too much time passed, and she could no longer deny she was lost when the small road turned up an incline. The horse hadn't raced down an incline in her dash for safety.

By dawn, she was still lost amidst the maze of trails, some ending frustratingly in game trails. Everything looked different but the same. Tree after tree, big and small, in her panicked mind, she could discern no difference when she tried to backtrack. Then, finally, they found themselves on a better-defined road than Elisabeth had seen in hours. Exhausted, she dismounted and tied Sasha so she could graze on the small tuft of grass beneath the trees. Then Elisabeth fell into an exhausted sleep despite her soaked clothes and the rain pelting and dripping from the leaves overhead. Sometime later, she jolted awake, sitting up so suddenly her head swam for a moment.

A man stood with Sasha's reins in his hand.

"Looky here, James," the man said to another who stood behind her.

Elisabeth stumbled to her feet and turned to stare at the man in rags, a leering smile on his face that made her skin crawl. She wondered if she could take the man holding Sasha by surprise and take her back. But she knew that was wishful thinking.

"Are you alone, sweety?" one man asked, taking a step closer. Dark, beady slits of eyes fixed on her. A chill sped through her, and she took a step back.

"You are soaked to the bone," one of the men said. Their voices sounded sympathetic, but instinct warned her of grave danger.

The man named James began moving around her. She turned and bolted. Slick mud covered the road from the torrential rain. She slipped and slid, and the men charged behind her, doing the same. A limb lay across the path, and she jumped it. Landing, her feet flew from beneath her, and she pitched forward. She landed hard, a ragged breath choked off with the mud.

"I got her," one of the men yelled a moment before a knee slammed into the small of her back. She gagged and sputtered, the mud filling her mouth and nose. The man hauled her up, gripping her arm painfully.

"She is a pretty little thing," James said, stepping forward and lifting a strand of her muddy, rain-soaked blonde hair.

"Clean her up, and she will be great fun," one of the men declared.

"She's young enough, of money too. Look at her."

James stepped forward and covered her breast with his hand. His fingers dug into her skin, searching for a woman's flesh. Elisabeth slapped his hand away, but the man holding her arm squeezed it sharply and yanked up until she rose on her tiptoes. He glared down at her. "Let him touch you," he growled.

"No," the third man said. The man holding her did not release her but let her sink back onto flat feet. James stepped back and turned.

"She is money, and I know where to sell her," he said.

"We get to sample her first, don't we?" James asked.

The man laughed at his companion. "No way. A girl like her is worth big money. Big money, my friends," he declared with confidence that frightened her. Her heart did not cease its wild clamor for an eternity.

"I want to go home." Elisabeth's voice shook. Elisabeth knew humans bought and sold others every day like cattle. She knew that much of the world. The walls of Ravenshill separated her from those poor souls. Unfortunately, they no longer protected her.

"Don't worry, Honey," one of the men said. "We'll take care of you."

Elisabeth tugged against the hand, but the man holding her would not ease his grip.

"I just want to go home," she said. She did not care that she cried in front of them. "Please let me go home." Her voice implored the man gripping her.

He said no word but shook his head before shoving her forward.

# Chapter 3

**Monday, May 15, 1447, London**

"I can get us horses," the boy said earlier. An hour passed, and they still sat. Adrian grew annoyed with every second ticking by. His goal was closer now, but it did little good without coin and a horse. Though Sir Lincoln would never send him from Ravenshill without ensuring he could make it back, Adrian found himself in that situation. The boy kept fidgeting. He could not sit still. Adrian had stopped Walter from telling him his real name. He feared he might forget one day and call him by it. This way, this boy would be forever known to Adrian as Walter.

The Walter jumped to his feet, going toward two riders moving down the narrow street before Adrian could stop him. Adrian followed, keeping a distance. In the back of his mind, he worried one of these men could be the boy's father, and he toyed with Adrian all this time. All so the boy could watch his daddy rip off another little boy's head.

"I'll take your horses to the livery," the boy said, adopting a quick shuffling step. He reached up toward one man, keeping pace with his horse. "For some coin," the boy added.

The men pulled rein. "All right, boy," one of the men said. Then, groaning, he eased from the saddle planting his feet on the ground. The second man dismounted, letting Walter take the reins. "Meet us here at noon tomorrow," the man said.

Adrian nearly pissed himself when the boy waved him forward. Sir Lincoln taught him many things through the years. One was to show bravery despite feeling terror. Now all Adrian could do was stare at the horse's chest, sure the men would see his terror. His grip tightened on the reins, willing his hands not to shake.

"Care for them well," the second man barked. Adrian could feel the man studying him. They stood on the busy street for an eternity under the men's scrutiny. Yet, no time passed before they turned away and headed for the brothel across the street.

"We have our horses." The boy said, his voice full of pride.

Adrian shook his head with disbelief and vigor. "We can't steal these horses," he whispered with urgency. The leather reins burned his hand with his guilt. "They will take our hands or hang us." Again, Adrian shook his head, making up his mind, "Knights do not steal horses."

The boy studied him with a detached seriousness that annoyed Adrian. "At worst, they would take only one hand."

"That doesn't make it better."

"Do you want to make it better, or do you want horses? Besides, we will be long from here by the time they raise their heads from their whores' laps tomorrow."

Sir Lincoln sent him for a new Walter. Adrian accomplished that. Getting Walter back could only be achieved with horses. "Come on," Adrian said, heading toward the road he arrived on.

They led the horses through the streets, Adrian leading the way, street after street, until he could not get them more lost.

"How many times do you want to see that old market?" the boy asked. His tone held a sarcastic barb.

Adrian became aware they passed the market from the other direction at least twice. "It is beautiful," Adrian mumbled. Embarrassment flooded him. He could not even get them out of the city.

"To the north, we go?" the boy asked. "Then it is that direction we need to go," he said, pointing the way.

"Of course," Adrian said. The boy's lips twisted with amusement. Adrian cast him a scathing look. The boy shrugged.

Reaching the outskirts of the city, another problem presented itself. Adrian shortened his stirrups and vaulted into the saddle.

"I can't ride," Walter said.

A long explosive sigh escaped Adrian. "Then why did you take two horses?"

"I think I should learn to ride. Does a lord not ride?"

Adrian fought the sigh of frustration. Like every knight, Walter needed riding skills. At the thought, his friend's loss stabbed his heart again. But, instead of wallowing, he dismounted and moved to the Walter. He shortened his stirrups and then stepped around, giving him a boost.

"Hold her. I can do it from the ground," the boy said.

Adrian grumbled under his breath, moving to hold the horse. The other boy gained the saddle on his second attempt. But the momentum from the climb almost tumbled him off the other side. "What do I need to know?"

The awkward and unsure seat of the other boy would not go ignored. Nothing about this boy proclaimed him a lord of the realm. "Everything," Adrian said. He pulled the reins over the horse's head and showed Walter how to hold them.

Adrian's pace slowed, accommodating Walter and his first time riding a horse. The fearless boy moved the animal through its paces despite his awkward seat. Would the Kirkhams accept this boy as one of their own? Could he accept this new Walter? This Walter took the name of his friend. Friends could not be replaced, not this way. Adrian's mind wandered to Elisabeth again. What must she be going through if he worried about replacing a friend? Her image appeared again, crying, her hand clutching the wooden sword and the devastation of the moment etched in her features.

"What will my father be like?"

Walter's voice snapped Adrian back to the present. For a moment, his mind worked out what the boy asked. "He is lord," Adrian said, shrugging. But he gave the question more thought. Lord Thomas wanted both his children educated to be strong, confident individuals. Because they carried the aristocracy's bloodlines, he expected his children to comport themselves in such a manner. The Kirkham name was all the family had left.

"He is kind to everyone," Adrian said. Lord of Ravenshill had never raised his voice at Adrian since he arrived four years ago. Until he hit Elisabeth, he never saw aggression from the man. That was Sir Lincoln's realm. Things differed at Helmsley, where Adrian's dad ruled with an iron fist. Helmsley's wealth did not mirror Ravenshill's financial troubles.

"He is not a well-schooled man, but he wishes both his children to be," Adrian said.

"What is it like to have a father such as a lord?" the boy asked. Walter concentrated on his horse, mimicking Adrian and looking worse for it.

Adrian snapped at him, growing annoyed at his awkwardness and the possible mistake Adrian had made. "You don't use your stirrups to rise." Adrian snapped at the boy and could not empathize with one not born for the saddle. "Do this." Leaning forward, Adrian stood in the stirrups, resting his hands on the horse's shoulders. "Feel the horse thrust from behind and then roll on his shoulders?" Adrian tried teaching him the rhythm of his horse. Each time one of the horse's hooves struck the ground, Adrian said, "Down." The same foot lifted, and Adrian said, "Up." He spoke with each step of the horse's legs. "Now, when I say down, you let yourself sink into the saddle and let the thrust of his hind legs lift you back up." Frustration filled Adrian. The boy still moved off the pace with the horse. "Move forward with your pelvis, sit a little forward with your shoulders so you're not tugging on the reins, and keep your hands soft."

Adrian picked up the rhythm, so Walter could anticipate the downward motion. He scowled. Adrian admitted there was not much this Walter could do correctly without proper training. "On the flat, you alternate which hoof you rise on, so you don't wear the horse." Picking the conversation back up, Adrian said, "I do not know what it is like. My father sent me to foster at six. The closest thing I believe I have to a real father is my knight. He will teach you your fighting skills so you can be a true lord."

"Can I joust?" Walter asked. But, unfortunately, his excitement made him lose concentration on the horse's steps.

"We do not enter tournaments," Adrian said.

"Why not?"

Adrian readied himself with Sir Lincoln's excuse that it was beneath the dignity of a true knight. A true knight did not battle before an audience with sticks. But Adrian doubted the truth of those words. Did Ravenshill avoid the tournaments because they couldn't pay the entrance fees? Through the years, Sir Lincoln's armor had aged and was never replaced. It would be Lord Thomas's decision to avoid the tournaments. A wise one because tournaments served as a window into a family's coffers.

"He does not allow us to participate because we are needed at Ravenshill. That is where we belong, and we do not need to parade our skills before everyone. They can see them in battle." The well-rehearsed answer now sounded empty.

"It does not matter," the boy said. "Tell me of this sister." The boy synchronized his rise with the horse's step for a couple of beats, but then he lost it.

"You are putting too much thought into it," Adrian said. "Elisabeth and I are eleven. She will not let you step on her. Lord Thomas has educated his children and taught her to have a mind."

The new Walter faltered and nearly tumbled from his horse. "I will learn to read?"

"Yes," Adrian said, annoyed. Reading and arithmetic were his least favorite of all the lessons he received at Ravenshill. "You need to stop fooling around, and let's move," Adrian said. Walter could learn all about Ravenshill upon their arrival. A knot of dread settled in Adrian's stomach and churned. Would they tell this boy he would not do? Would they send him back? They couldn't do that. He knew their secret, so he would not be a witness. Sir Lincoln would guarantee that.

Adrian led them at a hard gallop for a stretch until the new Walter called him back, sore from the saddle. He could pamper himself once he was lord, but for now, they could not waste time. Adrian walked his horse, Walter matched his stride, and they rode abreast.

"Will I have my own horse?"

"Yes," Adrian said. But there stood no horse in Ravenshill's stables for the boy. Adrian thought of his young destroyer, Achilles, a recent gift from his father as he neared the age of knighthood. A beautiful black charger, everything a knight could want.

"What is it like to live in a castle? What's it like to be a boy in one?"

Adrian never thought his life any different than another boy's. His home was always inside a castle. Whether in his younger days at Helmsley or now at Ravenshill. He could not compare Ravenshill to Helmsley. Adrian's home, which he would inherit, consisted of a newer structure with open spaces, high windows, extensive grounds, multiple baileys, and towers. At Ravenshill, only one bailey greeted guests with its one tower and stones so old they showed their age. "It is grand, I guess," he said. "I don't know. It's what I am used to. What was it like for you?"

The boy shrugged. "I am never full. I would imagine there would be plenty of food at a lord's table." The boy grew thoughtful for a minute, then scoffed, "A lord would never want me at his table. No one wanted me around. They didn't want to feed me, I guess. I had to steal my clothes. I had to steal everything. Some overzealous housemaid caught me stealing this shirt and almost sliced my ear off." He turned, showing a small scar just above his ear on the side of his head. Adrian thought it did not look at all like she tried to remove his ear.

"There were always other children, but it was hard dealing with them because we shared. I didn't have enough for me, let alone them. The smaller children liked me because I would try to protect them."

"Protect them from what?" Adrian asked, wishing they would kick up the speed again.

"Donald mostly, but others who wanted to hurt them."

Adrian now wanted to stand behind this Walter even if everyone else at Ravenshill rejected him. Adrian never called his father by his first name. Despite Earl Hagan's strict rules, Adrian loved his father. Adrian could not imagine having to protect his younger brother from him.

The boy grew quiet, then mumbled, "I wish I could have a mother where you are taking me. I have one memory of my ma. She was lying on a bed covered with sweat, coughing. She is reaching for me, but someone pulls me away from her. It is the only memory I have of her. I think it was the last time I saw her. Then we only had Donald. That's what I know. My older sister looked out for me when I was little, but Donald sold her to a brothel."

Adrian suspected this Walter knew nothing of his younger brother also sold. "I think life will be easier for you as a lord," Adrian said. But he might be lying. The entirety of Ravenshill rested on this young boy's shoulders, and Adrian did not have the heart to saddle him with the details.

"Tell me of this knight."

Before yesterday Adrian would enthusiastically tell this Walter of Sir Lincoln and the legends that followed in his wake. But Lincoln hid great secrets and murdered to keep it that way. "He is a great knight," Adrian said, falling silent.

"Then what of you? How did you come to foster at Ravenshill?"

"My parents wanted me to foster with him."

Walter expected more, but not getting it, he stopped his horse. "Do you not like this knight?" the boy asked.

The frail child seemed even smaller on the horse. Adrian could not tell him for sure what kind of life lay before him. Sir Lincoln was not the man he thought. Adrian wanted to follow in his footsteps and become a Teutonic Knight. To Adrian, Lincoln possessed all the chivalry and valor a knight could. But that was not the case.

"He is a great knight, one of the greatest. First, he was a mercenary and then became a knight of the Teutonic Order. Then, he took the Polish river Vistula when no other knights could. Then, when he was captured, he escaped and fought again for the riverway when they tried taking it back."

"So why isn't he there now?" Walter asked.

"The order lost the river again."

"Doesn't sound like a very good knight if he lost the fight."

Suddenly Adrian's opinion of Lincoln changed, and his desire to defend him rose. "He is a great knight. You should be honored to be meeting him."

"I'm sure I will be," the boy replied. His tone, however, contradicted his statement. Adrian gnashed his teeth together. This boy would never pass for the sweet Walter. This boy was course and too skeptical for a boy of five or even seven. His upbringing would tell on him, no matter how much the boys resembled each other. Soon the choice would be taken from him once they made it to Ravenshill. If he was not accepted, he would be killed to protect secrets. He wanted to say this to the boy, but exhaustion pulled at him. He just wanted Ravenshill and the safety of its walls.

# Chapter 4

***Saturday, September 21, 1443, Ravenshill***

*"Little Elisabeth," Lincoln's voice greeted her. The big man took a seat at the table beside her. She played with the figurines Lincoln carved for her. Gifts he gave her each year for her birthday. Six animals now lay on the table, carved from different woods, giving the animals different shades. She now had a horse, cat, dog, squirrel, rabbit, and goat. Even at age six, Elisabeth could appreciate the work put into the creations. The wood was smoothed with a meticulous hand, so no rough edge or splinter would prick her.*

*Lincoln picked up the squirrel and turned it over and over in his hand, studying it before sitting it back down among the rest. He gave her that one when she turned four. She did not remember much from those years, but she remembered Lincoln presented it cradled by his giant hands. He slowly opened them, and there lay the squirrel. It lay on its side, the eyes looking at her, the detail of its little paws held up, gripping a nut was extraordinary. The bushy tail did not look like wood but like the fur on her squirrel-lined cloak. She remembered nothing else but the squirrel and his big hands cupping it.*

*"You will have a new friend coming to Ravenshill," Lincoln said.*

*Eagerness filled her. Finally, a friend. Not many kids lived at Ravenshill. None of the younger ones were older than Walter. The older kids' duties kept them from playing or even befriending Elisabeth. "Who?" she asked.*

*"The young Baron Adrian de Ros of Stokesley, and one day he will be Earl of Helmsley. He is your age and will be my squire."*

*A boy, no older than herself, living at Ravenshill. A boy already holding his own title and property. One of the glories of being born male. Elisabeth did not know Stokesley, but even she knew of Helmsley. So many great knights came from there. Their names resided on the tongues of many who knew more than her about such things.*

*"But you don't want a squire," Elisabeth said. "That's what you have always said." The great Sir Lincoln Victers never took on a squire that Elisabeth knew of, while other knights kept several. Perhaps his greatness precluded him from needing one.*

*Lincoln smiled fondly at her. "I know what I have said. But I think it is time. Besides, it is a promise owed." Then Lincoln winked at her. "The best part is he is your age, and you can have a friend."*

*Elisabeth smiled at him. She could not fathom having someone she could play with. "When will he be here?"*

*"Tomorrow," Lincoln said. "I wonder if you would like to help me prepare a space for him in the barracks. Perhaps you can help make it special so he will not be so homesick."*

*She spent the day with Lincoln. They shuffled cots around so Adrian could be next to the knight. Elisabeth could remember a day the keep of Ravenshill could barely house the population serving it. She remembered the barracks filled with the soldiers residing within the keep. Knights, even those with grander titles, lived with the lowliest foot soldiers. The lords and higher knights got the choicest cots. During the winter months, they slept close to the hearth and moved for the warmer seasons to catch the cool breeze. But they resided together all the same. They served at Ravenshill for Lincoln, their commander. Lincoln trained and protected Ravenshill, sending an abundance of men to King Henry VI in France. Once, there was a constant rotation of men in and out of the regiments of Ravenshill. But she recognized the numbers dwindling. The barracks emptied over time. Though the numerous cots filled the room, only a few held the possessions of knights and their squires. Such things did not concern her.*

*Elisabeth took a rug from her own room and placed it between Adrian's and Lincoln's cots. She told Lincoln it was for both of them, so their feet would be warmer in the colder months. The temperature inside the barracks dropped beneath the onslaught of winter. The one hearth could not chase the chill from the large space. Outranking all the men inside the barracks, she knew Lincoln could take the area near the hearth. But Elisabeth knew he never exercised that right. He always commanded but never held himself in higher regard than his men. What his men suffered, Lincoln suffered as well.*

*"I think he will feel welcome," Lincoln declared after sliding the cots over the rug and sitting down. Elisabeth sat on Adrian's facing him. "I have a gift for you to give him," Lincoln said, reaching into his chest of*

*personal items next to his bed. He pulled out another wooden carving. It was a horse, larger than her horse figurine. This new horse was taller with a broad chest and carved from blackened wood.*

*"It is a destrier," she said, turning the figurine over, marveling at it, and running her fingers over the smooth wood.*

*"Yes," Lincoln said with pride. "After Adrian is shown around the keep, I want you to invite him to play with you. Then I want you to give this to him so he has his own."*

*"Shouldn't you give it to him?" she asked, handing it back.*

*He folded his arms across his chest, refusing it. "Not at all. You give it to him. You are welcome to tell him I carved it. But I want you to give it to him so he knows right away how kind and generous you are."*

*When Elisabeth retired that night, she stood before her floor-length mirror. She offered her reflection curtsy after curtsy until she thought she had perfected the gesture. Then she lay awake long into the night, imagining what this boy coming to Ravenshill might look like and be like. Would he be nice and spend time with her? Or would Lincoln's squire be too busy for a friend?*

*The next morning she stood in the library's window as the men filed into the bailey below. Among them, a child who could be none other than Baron Adrian de Ros of Stokesley." She could tell right away his hair was dark. She recognized the fine fabric of his clothing, not worn or ill-fitting. She knew nothing more of clothing beyond that. Her father told her to stay out of the way until they arrived in the hall. By then, Adrian's tour would be over, and Lincoln would be done with him for the day.*

*The leather soles of Elisabeth's slippers slapped against the wooden floor as she ran for her small chest and the figurines inside. With her arms full, she entered the hall. She placed the animals by the cold hearth, sat beside them, and waited. The large stone hearth would heat the hall from its high ceiling to the stone floor in the winter. But now it lay cold and empty, the doors open on each end, the windows uncovered, letting the warm breeze flow through with fresh air and warmth, pushing back the chill of the coming fall. The tapestries hung over the walls and kept the cold trapped that froze the stone behind them. When spring neared summer, the women removed the tapestries, allowing the stones to breathe. Always cold to the touch, they sweated on the warmest of days.*

*An eternity passed before Lincoln led the boy into the hall. She fidgeted on the edge of the hearth, waiting for Lincoln's signal. But Lincoln kept talking, introducing the boy as people gathered. For his part, Adrian stood without a sound, offering a wary smile here and there while his eyes kept straying around the hall. Then, finally, Lincoln motioned her forward.*

*She jumped up and rushed to Lincoln's side. "Lord Adrian de Ros, this is the Lady Elisabeth Kirkham."*

*Elisabeth offered him her perfected curtsy, and he returned an awkward bow. Though of the same height, something about the scrawny boy made him larger. She liked his eyes which were a perfect mix of blue and gray. "Would you like to come play?" she asked. Adrian glanced up at Lincoln warily.*

*He gave the boy a nod, but still, the boy scanned the hall. He was looking for boys his age and not girls, no doubt. She seized his hand and gripped it. She tugged at him. She was concerned he might prefer the company of the older boys in the village over her. "Come," she encouraged. "I have a gift for you."*

*Finally, Adrian let her lead him. Reaching the hearth, she motioned for him to sit. He did so, hesitating, his eyes still darting about the hall.*

*"There are no children here our age," she told him. She scooted the goat and dog closer to him. He picked up the dog and studied it. Hiding his disappointment. "The closest is my little brother Walter."*

*He sat the dog down, instantly bored.*

*From the fold of her skirt, she pulled out his horse. "Sir Lincoln carved these," she said before sitting the horse down before him. "This is the gift he wanted me to give to you."*

*Adrian scooped it up with a smile on his face. His smile came with ease. A boy who smiled and no doubt laughed often. It lit his face and turned it into the face of a friend and not someone eager to ignore her. "I have one, too," she said. She held her own horse up and danced it in front of him.*

*His eyes fell on the figurine she held, then skittered away and locked eyes with her. He saw her for the first time since he walked into the hall. She smiled at him, and he smiled back.*

*"Can we play with them in the stable?" Adrian asked.*

*"Where else would we play horses?" she asked. She rose quickly and scooped the figurines into her hands. She grabbed the boy's hand, yanking him up and dragging him behind her. They raced for the stable, running beneath the archway and into the outer bailey. Lincoln stepped back with a broad smile and let them pass.*

**Saturday, May 20, 1447, road to Aberdeen, Scotland**

Elisabeth's eyes popped open. She lay quietly and let her exhaustion bring on the rest of the memory. She wondered if Lincoln brought Adrian to Ravenshill for her. The knight swore he would never train his own squire. It was a stand he did not waver from. Then one day, he changed his mind and got a squire her age. She still did not understand the nightmare that unfolded before her with Lincoln at its center. Then the memory of her own terrifying situation returned to her.

Her shoulders ached, tied behind her back. The three men grew tired of her attempts to escape. They retaliated by binding her hands behind her back before tying them to a tree. She could lie down, but she could do little else. She vowed she would try again to escape. There was no other choice if she ever wished to see Ravenshill again.

During the day, she walked with them and prepared their fire and beds for them at night. Sasha, they sold on the first day, and the men bought ale, leaving them without food. It did not matter to them. They cared more about drinking than eating. If the bottle came out before the food, there would be none. The men were selfish, not only to her but to each other. She tried running again. Hiding for hours, she thought herself safe. But she stumbled upon Dwayne when she immerged from her hiding place. It was exceptionally fortunate for the man, not so for her. They beat her with switches so hard she curled into a ball with her hands over her head. They landed blow after blow, leaving welts across her hands and legs where her skirt rode up.

The men did not hurry, often stopping, visiting brothels and alehouses, always leaving someone behind with her. They spent money they were yet to get for selling her. How long would it be for those of Ravenshill to realize she was gone? Would they realize? Would her father care after what she did?

The night wore on, and she wished it could be endless. Exhaustion pulled at her, along with the cold and fear. She got no food or water the day before. Every part of her ached from work and not just the blows. They did not want to sleep on the bare ground but demanded softer beds. Last night, she cut pine bow after pine bow with a giant machete, nearly severing her finger. She lay them each out a bed with these while she slept on the cold ground. Scratches covered her arms, and the sap clung to her fingers. If pine had not grown nearby, she would have had to gather sod or saplings. And still, they did not feed her.

Sleep eluded her, the darkness swallowed her, and she shivered. She awoke with warmth spreading across her legs. At first, confusion slowed her. It made no sense whether at home or with the kidnappers. Then, she opened her eyes, and reality flowed in. James stood over her, urinating on her legs with a smile of sick pleasure pulling at his thin lips.

"Welcome to the other side of slavery, my lady," the man said. His voice held a cold and vicious tone. The men behind him laughed. He stood on her rope, and she couldn't scramble away. She could do nothing but lie beneath his stream of urine, moving upward, landing some in her face, in her eyes, and across her lips. "Get up!" he yelled at her after putting himself away but before stepping off her rope. Then, he kicked her leg bringing forth a terrified sob.

She rose to her knees. Edgar walked behind her, untied her hands, then planted the bottom of his boot against her back and shoved her forward. She landed in the mud created by the urine. The mud mixed with the urine already on her, and she sputtered.

"Get the fire going, you worthless bitch," the man snarled. "We're hungry."

Elisabeth let out a sob. Her stomach ached with her own hunger. She wanted a moment, just a moment, to curl into a ball and mourn. She killed her brother, and yet, he wasn't her brother. She needed time to think, but these cruel men found her, and she was not allowed even a moment.

"Quiet!" the man snarled, and his hand slapped her across the face, sending her sprawling. "If we want your tears, we'll tell you to give them to us," he spat. "Get up!" he screamed at her again.

She did. With her head ringing, her body aching, her skin freezing, and her stomach churning empty, she did what the men told her, their fists driving her on.

The men settled around the fire and ate the rabbit and carrots she cooked for them. "What are you looking at?" Edgar snarled. He tore a piece of meat from the carcass.

"I'm hungry. And I want to go home," Elisabeth said. Her voice sounded so frightened. Hearing it, the way it shook, terrified her more.

"So," James said with indifference.

"Might I have some food?"

James laughed, followed by the other two. She was packing one of the men's supply bags, and he approached her. James yanked the bag from her hands and swung it at her, knocking her onto the ground. Then he stepped over her, stepping on her hand. He pressed the heel of his boot into her palm until she cried out. He kept pushing, and she writhed, pulling at his offending foot with her other hand. Desperation filled her chest and built her fear with its intensity.

"You seem to not understand what it is you are now." He knelt, driving his heel deeper into her hand. "You are lower than the dung on the bottom of my boot. You do not speak. You do not ask. You do what we say. Do you understand?"

"Yes," she cried.

His hand struck her hard on her cheek. She lay stunned.

"Do you understand?"

"Yes," she stammered.

Again, he struck her.

"Do you understand?"

She stared at the legs of the man crouching over her. She dared not move. She dared not make a sound. But she understood. She would do what this man wanted.

Finally, he raised his foot and stepped off her hand.

Their journey north continued the same each day. Elisabeth walked the miles the men forced her feet to swallow. She worked for the men each time they stopped. At night her shivers broke apart her sleep. A new day would dawn, and it all began again. Her hunger grew fierce, weakening her.

There came a point the men's violence could not spur her on. They finally gave her food and water. She grabbed the meager piece of dried fish one of the men offered. She scarfed it down, wishing for more. Unfortunately, the hunger was too great to be assuaged with the small fare.

While James and Edgar wanted to rape her, Dwayne insisted the booty they would get for a virgin would be far better. They fought over this often, and one day the anger spilled over. James and Edgar thought they would overpower Dwayne. They were mistaken, and James came away with a nasty scar down his cheek from Dwayne's wicked knife. Edgar received a dislocated nose and a black eye for his efforts. The men did not stop talking about raping her, but they no longer challenged Dwayne.

**Wednesday, May 17, 1447, Ravenshill**

Dusk cast Ravenshill in shadows as Adrian approached with the boy. A heavy feeling, like the stone walls settling on him. They pulled rein inside the courtyard. Lord Thomas ran to Adrian and pulled him from his horse. "Elisabeth, did she go with you? Is she with you?" The man's frantic blue eyes kept shooting between the two boys while shaking Adrian.

"No, my lord," Adrian said. He shot Walter a fearful glance. This was not what he expected.

Lincoln rested his hands on Lord Thomas's, clinging to Adrian's tunic. Lincoln gave his lord's hands a tug while the knight gripped Adrian on his shoulder and pulled the man and squire apart.

"She has been missing since Walter's accident," Lincoln said, his deep voice taking the edge from Adrian.

"Let's have a look at you, boy," Lincoln said, taking command while Lord Thomas wrung his hands together and shifted from foot to foot.

Lincoln reached Walter, still mounted, peering up at him. Then he reached the boy and pulled him off the horse. The knight suspended the boy in front of him, and they studied one another before Lincoln nodded and sat him on his feet. “He is passable. Adrian put these horses in the field, then find us in Walter’s chamber.”

Releasing the two new horses with the others that shared the field with goats and sheep, Adrian returned to the keep. He found them dressing the new Walter in the other boy’s clothes. The clothes were too large on this Walter, though they were made for a six-year-old, not the older boy. Sir Lincoln and Lord Thomas had begun the new boy’s lessons on how to be Lord Walter Kirkham. He would remain in his chamber until he could pass as the future lord of Ravenshill.

“It is a small enough price, is it not?” Adrian asked. Walter looked at him with pleading blue eyes flecked with gold. More gold shone now that they made it inside Ravenshill’s walls.

“I guess,” the boy said, unconvinced.

“Elisabeth has been missing all this time?” Adrian asked, watching Lord Thomas pacing.

“She knows,” Lincoln said. He used his hands and straightened Walter’s posture. “Young lords don’t slouch.”

“What do you mean she knows?”

“She was hiding in the chapel. We found only her wooden sword when we searched for her. She has taken Sasha, which is why we thought she might have gone with you.”

“Then she has run away,” Lord Thomas said. It confirmed all his worst nightmares.

“We will find her, my lord,” Lincoln said.

“How?” Lord Thomas screamed at him. “I told you to forget replacing my son. We needed to find my daughter. You, Sir Lincoln, said she must have gone with Adrian, but she did not, and now the trail has grown cold."

Lincoln spun on Lord Thomas, and his face twisted with a cold countenance threatening to crack from its iciness. "I got rid of witnesses not once but twice for you to have an heir. Do not question the choices I must now make. You have made poor ones and may yet drag everyone here down with you. As long as I breathe, I will not let that happen. Besides," Lincoln said, taking on a note of challenge as he raised his head a notch, making him even taller. "In weather like that, there was no trail left to follow."

Lord Thomas glared at Lincoln. "She is all I have left of my blood," the lord said. Thomas's eyes landed on Walter with deep sadness. Walter was essential to Ravenshill, but Elisabeth carried the last of her father's blood and that of all their ancestors.

"I will find her," Lincoln assured Lord Thomas. "I have yet to let you down in all my service. I must take Adrian, so gather men to protect the walls while we are gone."

With that, the knight swept from the room. Adrian followed. His place was with Lincoln. He would be of no use here.

Lincoln was already in the barracks, packing a bag. His movements were hurried, his face focused, his mind set on the task at hand.

Adrian's heart pounded with additional bad news to lay at Lincoln's feet. "Sir Lincoln," Adrian began. He was aware his scared voice gave him away. Even being big for his age, taller and broader than most, his young youth still sometimes peeked through the façade of being a man.

Lincoln stopped packing, and his attention swung toward Adrian. "What is it, Adrian?" Lincoln's voice had softened, coaxing Adrian like a frightened child. Adrian knew he was only a boy and everything that had happened since that night left him with near-debilitating fear.

"I lost my horse and my sword." Guilt washed over Adrian for the loss of both. It spoke volumes for the fact he was not ready for knighthood.

Lincoln straightened, peering down at Adrian and making him feel very small.

"When did this happen?" Lincoln's voice held no hint of anger or disappointment.

"During the storm. Lightning struck nearby, and she slipped and fell into the mud. I couldn't catch her, and she ran away with everything. Even your money."

"Everything?" Lincoln asked.

Adrian nodded.

"I see." Lincoln fell silent for a moment, looking down on Adrian with a thousand bees buzzing inside his head, waiting for the fallout of his ineptitude. "You did not lose your life. On the contrary, you brought Walter home, fulfilling your task and bringing honor to yourself. I do not think your old sword and a little money were anything. Your honor and your survival, now that is everything. Besides, you have long outgrown that sword. It is time you take up your father's sword. We will correct that before we leave. Now pack. It will take us time to find her."

Silence fell inside the barracks, Adrian following Lincoln's command. His movements were slow, with little thought but for his father's sword. Since his father had given him the sword, there wasn't a day that passed that he did not heft it and wish for the day he could do so with the strength needed to wield the heavy weapon.

"She knows in which direction you went. I assume she would follow you," Lincoln said with confidence. Adrian could not imagine she would go anywhere but to seek him. Lincoln stuffed the last item into his bag, a small pouch where he kept the pieces of wood he was carving. The fox would be a gift to Elisabeth on her next birthday. He cinched his bag tight, then turned to Adrian's bag and began piling things from the squire's chest. Adrian's packing was slow, unsure what he would need and how long they would be gone. The boy assumed Lincoln knew what he would need for the journey and stepped out of his way. "We will begin with the road to London. Get your sword and ready the horses."

It took long, frustrating days for Lincoln to find what he looked for. Three men had passed through Falstone and tried to snatch a child two days before Walter died. The villagers ran them away, and they went north toward Ravenshill.

Lincoln got the descriptions of the three men. Then he and Adrian turned north away from Ravenshill, at last on her trail. With the story of the three men, Lincoln discovered they now traveled with a young girl. The girl wore a garment notably finer than those of the men. Between the men's behavior and the little girl, the four of them stood out. But Lincoln warned Adrian that the group pulled further away from them. He cautioned it might not even be Elisabeth they chased. But what were the odds the child was not Elisabeth? Still, he feared they chased the wrong people, and Elisabeth would be another poor innocent life swallowed.

Adrian and Lincoln lost another day continuing north when they should have turned east. It took them two villages before Lincoln realized they had lost the trail and had to backtrack to the road leading east.

Adrian's frustration grew, but Lincoln dealt every bump with a level of calm Adrian found hard to understand. Lincoln did not wear down in the week they were gone from Ravenshill, while Adrian was exhausted. Tonight, he lay in the old barn among the musty smell of the long-abandoned structure with its dangerous leaning walls and leaking roof, but it was better than no roof and no walls. Sleep eluded him. He worried for Elisabeth. Did she know he searched for her? Was she afraid? He prayed she would not be scared—that she knew he would come for her. Once, he told her, if she was frightened, to hold his hand, and he would get them through. She didn't have his hand, but he prayed she knew he would get them through some way.

### *Thursday, June 2, 1446, Ravenshill*

*The rains fell around Ravenshill for days. A constant curtain of water falling from the sky. Lincoln and Lord Thomas were in Rochester, where the horse traders were scheduled to pass. Elisabeth talked Adrian into visiting the fair in the village of Kielder. Lincoln and Lord Thomas took them the day before, but Elisabeth had to watch Walter and trailed behind. She cast glances of desire at the tents where she wanted to visit. Adrian would not admit it, but he didn't have much fun either, following the two men around studying the wares he only pretended to be interested in.*

*But Adrian knew it was wrong sneaking away to Kielder. Even if they weren't told they couldn't go, he knew they weren't supposed to. Neither kid could claim otherwise. A fact Elisabeth ignored. No matter how often Adrian tried to convince her of the inappropriateness of her behavior, she persisted. It did not take Elisabeth long to wear him down. She also convinced him if they were discovered away from the keep, they would not get into that much trouble. Perhaps an extra chore, which she convinced him would be worth the risk. They crossed the bridge over the river North Tyne its brown churning waters crashing beneath it.*

*The fair's sights, sounds, and smells greeted them with all its vivid glory. Animals milled about in their makeshift pens. Bleating sheep and crowing chickens competed with the call of goats and the bark of geese. Men shouted, calling to one another. The high-pitched calls of women's voices and laughter filled the air.*

*As they moved deeper, the animals' smells gave way to that of meats cooking over open flames, giant pots bubbled, emitting aromas that made the children's mouths water. Both large and small, booths, tables, and tents filled the space. Many of the tents' sides were tied back, allowing the flow of air while displaying their wares. The road was mud-filled, but the sun fought through the clouds.*

*Adrian used his coin and bought them each a poultry leg and dried fruits they ate walking. Dancing bears and jugglers entertained. They stood outside a tent, watching a play that held their interest for a time before the ax-throwing contest drew them away. Adrian and Elisabeth competed in a foot race but were outrun by a tall, long-legged boy twice their age. The day wore on. Adrian bought them each a sweet pastry filled with berries and covered with sugar.*

*"Let's go to the fortune-teller," Elisabeth said, starting a happy step in the woman's direction.*

*"We should leave," Adrian insisted. The storm clouds gathered overhead. The tent flaps and flags beat against the growing wind.*

*"If you are in such a hurry to slop pigs, I will walk back on my own."*

*"I will stay. But hurry," he complained. He wouldn't leave Elisabeth at the fair alone. After seeing most of what the fair offered, he began to doubt the wisdom of their outing.*

*"I will. Come with me." Then Elisabeth sprinted away, and Adrian followed, having little choice.*

*He stood behind Elisabeth, sitting across from the woman. He leaned over her shoulder and placed a penny on the table. Then he scoffed, the woman was way overpaid, and he wanted to tell them both this. But if Elisabeth wanted to play along with such foolishness, it was her business.*

*The fortune-teller, a middle-aged woman with graying hair and rotten teeth, began shuffling a deck of cards. The thin wooden cards told a tale of extensive use and bending, fading, chipping, and cracking through many readings. The woman shuffled, studying Elisabeth and Adrian. Then she lay the deck face down and drew the first card.*

*The card on the table showed a woman, a queen by the crown on her head. She sat upon a throne, a flower sprout in one hand and a staff in the other. A black cat rested at her feet. On each side of the throne grew a flower like the sprout the queen held. There was nothing special about the card.*

*"The Queen of Wands tells me you create a powerful impression," the woman began.*

*Standing behind Elisabeth's chair, Adrian rolled his eyes. The woman reading the cards gave a half-smile.*

*"Do you not believe, boy?" the woman asked him.*

*"I think it rubbish," Adrian declared. Elisabeth's face turned up, and she scowled at him. But Adrian could not pretend to believe in something he did not, just because Elisabeth sat in the chair in front of him.*

*The woman's smile broadened before she turned back to the card. "You inspire confidence in others with your own courage and confidence." She lay a second card diagonally across the first. A tower on this cracked card was not much different than the one at Ravenshill. The lightning bolt that struck it set the structure to flame. "Chaos and destruction come," the woman said. Her voice was sad, and the words made the hair stand on the back of Adrian's neck. He could do nothing but stare at the card. Two figures plunged from the tower windows to their deaths.*

*"The seed has already been planted. There is no stopping what is to come. Change will tear you apart and destroy everything in its path."*

*Elisabeth shifted. Her posture was stiff. Adrian laid a hand on her shoulder, "We have to go home."*

*She brushed his hand away. "Not yet. Continue," Elisabeth said, perching on the edge of her seat.*

*The third card was laid down to the left of the other two. This one showed a man lying on the ground, ten swords in his back.*

*"The chaos will come from deceit. You will not see it coming. This betrayal will cut deep. It will make your world crumble around you."*

*"I think that is enough. You are scaring her," Adrian said, planting a firmer hand on Elisabeth's shoulder.*

*"The cards say what they will. I cannot control them." Then her eyes fell on Elisabeth.*

*"I am not afraid," she said. A slight quiver presented itself in her ten-year-old voice, telling him otherwise.*

*A fourth card was laid on the table to the right of the other cards. This depicted a wheel in the center of the card. On the left of the wheel descended a snake. Beneath the wheel was Anubis, the Egyptian god of the dead. On top sat a sphinx, and all four corners of the card held winged creatures. But unlike the others, this one fell upside down.*

*The woman's eyes glued to him. "Your fortune is to change, and it will not be for the better. You will fight against this, but you will lose. It is best when faced with this change that you accept it. To do otherwise will keep the wheel reversed."*

*Adrian's eyes returned to the table, and the fifth card was placed over the first and second cards. This one depicted a woman in robes holding two swords crossed over her chest. Her eyes were covered by a blindfold.*

*"You will try to correct your situation, but you will be powerless in the face of the forces against you. You will find that it does not matter the choice you make. It will be the wrong choice."*

*Elisabeth sat very still in front of him. Adrian's skin grew clammy, and a chill ran up his spine. The woman paused, studying them both.*

*The sixth card was laid below the first and second cards. On this card, a man held five swords over his shoulder. He looked back at two swords stabbed into the ground behind him. Adrian nearly scoffed at what the woman said, but a part of him worried the cards held some truth.*

*"You will doubt yourself over what is to come. You will keep secrets, and they will darken you."*

*The seventh card landed on the right of all the cards and closer to the woman. The card held a man suspended by one ankle from a post. Like the card with the wheel, this card lay upside down.*

*"You will lose all your skills when it comes to handling the situations I have laid out before you. As a result, you will lose confidence in yourself and fear you can make no positive changes to your circumstance. And indeed, you will not be able to."*

*Adrian held his breath, and the eighth card fell above the seventh.*

*This card depicted an armored knight riding a winged horse. The knight's sword was held aloft, and the horse charged forward. Dark clouds hovered over the knight's head, and the trees behind him blew.*

*"There is someone that will charge into the storm with you. The danger will not deter them."*

*The ninth card was placed above the eighth. A man and a woman held two cups with their arms intertwined.*

*"You will develop a close bond with your knight of swords and love him deeply. You will have a passion for him that cannot be extinguished."*

*The tenth card fell over the ninth. It depicted a man etching pentacle shapes into eight coins. Behind him stood a town.*

*"You will strive for perfection. You will be eager to prove yourself. You will strive to become a master with your skills." The tent fell silent.*

*Elisabeth straitened. "I do not understand."*

*"That is what the cards say," the woman said, reclining on her rickety chair. Her gaze slid from Elisabeth to Adrian. Adrian didn't meet her eyes.*

*"What happens? Will the turmoil end?"*

*"It depends on the path that is taken."*

*"But you said the seed was planted, and I could not change it."*

*"You cannot change it," she said, leaning forward. The wood of her chair protested with a creak. "But he can," she said, pointing at the seventh card with the knight painted on its surface. Then the woman pointed to the fourth card and the man holding the lantern. "When you are lost, you must look inside yourself for the answer."*

*"But," the woman said, pointing to Elisabeth and the first card she drew. "Do not forget this woman. You have great courage. You will lead men to great victories."*

*Elisabeth's head swiveled, and she looked at Adrian. She hesitated, unsure of what, if anything, she had learned here. Adrian was thankful it was over until Elisabeth jumped from her seat and grabbed Adrian by the arm.*

*"Now you," she said. She used her petite body to push him into the chair.*

*"No," he insisted, annoyed and a little uneasy.*

*"If you can help your friend when she needs a friend, do you not want to know if the cards wish to reveal this?"*

*"Do it," Elisabeth insisted.*

*The woman stood and went to a small basket. From it, she pulled another deck of cards. The crisp, new stack was not marked with stains or worn edges. It was not like the older, roughly painted cards of thin wood. Instead, these were printed on paper, thick and vibrant with their colors.*

*"This is for the higher-class customers," she said. Then, coming back, she shuffled the cards. "I was not going to waste them on two brats. But I want to see yours alongside hers."*

*Not knowing what she was talking about, he surmised he should keep it that way. So he dropped more coins into the woman's hand though all he wanted to do was leave.*

*She laid his first card down. "You are in a relationship that is creating deep connections and partnerships. This relationship is in its early stage, and you all have mutual respect and appreciation for each other."*

*The similarity between his first card and Elisabeth's ninth that told the story of her relationship with the Knight of Swords. "They speak the same, but their pictures are drawn by different people," the woman said. Adrian's card showed far more detail, created by a true artist with incredible talent. He knew why she wouldn't endanger the delicate creations with overuse.*

*The symbol of commerce, trade, and exchange came from the cup drawn on his card—Caduceus of Hermes. It consisted of a winged staff with two snakes wrapped around it. At the top of the caduceus was a lion's head. "This card represents the same but tells more in the picture that I know." She pointed to the lion's head. "This is fire and passion. It does not appear on her card, but it is the same."*

*Adrian fell silent. She turned the second card over, laying it diagonally across his first in the same pattern as Elisabeth's. This card showed a woman and a child in a boat. With them stands six swords. The water around the boat was tumultuous, but ahead it lay quiet. "You will enter a state of transition."*

*She placed the third card. A king sat on his throne, holding a wand with a blossoming flower. His throne and cape were decorated with lions and salamanders, the latter biting their own tails.*

*"You have been highly ambitious. You feel you are a leader but are not yet ready to lead."*

*The fourth card turned, and a woman knelt by a pool. She held two water containers, one she poured into the pool, the other onto dry ground. One foot, the woman planted in water, and the other on the earth.*

*"Your faith will be tested."*

*The fifth card was laid out. The cards fell, repeating Elisabeth's display. A king sat on a throne adorned with four rams' heads. His robe was red over his suit of armor, and he sported a long white beard with a gold crown on his head. Behind his throne was a mountain range with a river running beneath them.*

*"You desire to be a powerful man. An honorable and chivalrous man."*

*She laid the sixth card down, and it copied another of Elisabeth's. It was the card with the man and the ten swords in his back.*

*"You will not be untouched by the betrayal that destroys her," she said, nodding at Elisabeth standing beside Adrian.*

*Card seven came out, the knight on the horse. The same card was drawn for Elisabeth. The card that told the fortune-teller someone would charge into the storm with her, who would comfort her, now lay in front of him. Adrian leaned forward, but he would still deny any interest.*

*"Move forward," the woman said, pointing to the card. She lay a finger upon his card and then upon Elisabeth's. Adrian noticed the order in the cards on the table held a significance of their own to the woman.*

*She tapped Elisabeth's knight card. "This man will give her the strength to go with her courage." She pointed at Adrian. "This tells me you have strength. The obstacles ahead will not faze you. I cannot be sure this," she said, pointing again at Elisabeth's knight card, "is you. But if you want it, it may be. You must lay the path to follow. What is to come for her is already on its way."*

*The eighth card was laid on the table. The woman's hand paused, laying it down slowly, making Adrian want to yank it from her. "Choose your path well." She pointed at Elisabeth's first card. The one she lay upon the table for him mirrored Elisabeth's first card. His card had more color and details but was the same as Elisabeth's card, telling of her great influence.*

*"As the Knight of Swords will be a great influence and guide to your friend. So shall someone of great courage and confidence be a great influence to you."*

*The ninth card fell on the table. It was the same as the last card laid down for Elisabeth. "Though it is the same," she said, pointing at Elisabeth's card with the man etching eight coins. "This represents differently. You want to be a master of your skills. You wish to be a great knight. But you have the fear you cannot be."*

*The woman paused and drew the last card from the deck. Adrian grew inexplicably afraid. The cards told a terrifying tale, though Adrian knew they said nothing at all.*

*A man stood before seven cups, studying their contents. Some cups held jewels and a wreath of victory. Others, a snake or a dragon. Clouds settled around the man.*

*"You will face many choices. Be careful. The choices may look as if they will bring you what you seek. But each choice will have a good side and a bad. You must choose even if you feel paralyzed by your options."*

*The woman tapped Elisabeth's first card, then the card laid out for Adrian that matched it. "Remember your courage. Do not let it falter, and do not relinquish it."*

*Thunder rocked the tent, and Adrian shot to his feet. He grabbed Elisabeth's hand, pulling her toward the entrance. "We have to get home."*

*"You cannot choose your knight's path for him," the woman said, standing and following. "Your only choice will be to hold on to your courage so you will not be defeated. Be mindful of time. It can quickly run out."*

*Adrian yanked Elisabeth from the tent and beneath black clouds, annoyed they had wasted precious time listening to the woman's fairytales and dark fiction.*

# Chapter 6

**Monday, May 22, 1447, Aberdeen, Scotland**

Mist rose before them, and Elisabeth shuffled, keeping her feet moving. The shoes she left Ravenshill with provided inadequate protection against the rocks and earth she treads across. Blisters formed, and when she complained, James yanked the shoes from her feet and threw them away from her, forbidding her to retrieve them. Her feet became bloodied, and yet she was driven on. That was days ago. She could not track how long ago she fled through the pouring rain. The men forced her to do their chores, and she became intimately acquainted with fear and exhaustion with no reprieve. Nothing beyond that reached into her mind and filled her heart.

"They wait for us," Dwayne said. As Elisabeth's tired legs propelled her up the hill toward Dwayne.

The column picked up speed, and Elisabeth forced her legs to do the same. Nothing angered Dwayne more than her falling behind. She reached the summit spreading out with the men, and her mouth dropped open. She knew her father would never find her across an ocean so vast it concealed secret places, a sundry of countries and cities where she would disappear. Her knees buckled beneath her.

The ocean spread out before her. The waves roared and crashed, and the taste of ocean salt permeated the air around her, prickling her skin. Perhaps, it was beautiful, but Elisabeth could not see it in such terms. A ship lay at anchor, and two smaller boats sat on the shore, waiting for their passengers. The ocean would take her, and she would never find her way back.

Each time she cried, the men beat her. Now they ignored her. The expanse of water was terrifying in the eleven-year-old's eyes. Did monsters lie beneath the surface? Would they toss her over and feed her to them? Would a storm take the ship? Would that not be better? The question of their destination was farthest from her mind. All that mattered was they were taking her away. *Please, God,* she pleaded. *Save me.*

"Please let me go home." Her voice had dwindled, becoming something smaller, more desperate than she ever thought she would be. She drew a steadying breath through the flowing tears and collecting snot.

She bolted to her feet and raced back along the trail the way they came. She knew her attempt was futile. Laughter came from behind her, and for a moment, she did not think anyone would give chase. Hoofbeats came for her, the thunder growing. A terrifying sound escaped her throat, and she forced her legs faster. The small pebbles cut the soles of her feet and the days of walking dragged at her.

The rope landed over her, falling across her shoulders, yanking tight. The air crushed from her chest. Her flight was halted as she was simultaneously yanked backward. No sooner than she landed, the rope slackened, and the rider turned his horse. She stumbled up, keeping her feet beneath her as the man moved his horse slowly back up the hill and down the other side. The horse's hooves hit the sand, and he spurred the animal. Elisabeth flew off her feet.

Landing in the deep sand did not nock her breath from her, but the noose tightened around her chest and took it. The sand cut at her, burned her, and the animal flew across the earth. She wanted to cry out, to let them know she was dying. But no one here would care. Instead, she could hear them laughing, the other horses running behind her. If the rope was released, she would be trampled by those following.

Then the animal's stride changed, and it raced into the surf. Water exploded around her and ripped at her. The waves dragged against her, pulling her deep, the water settling over her, and the horse went deeper. Salt exploded up her nose. If she could draw a breath, it would enter her lungs and drown her. She did not want to die, but, at the same time, she did not want to go on the ship. Was this what God sent for her? Was he saving her from the ship by killing her in the surf? Perhaps God abandoned her altogether. Finally, the animal came to a stop, and she was hauled to her feet.

She fought for breath as the rope lifted from her. Her chest ached, and her lungs dragged in great gulps of air, choking from the sand, water, and pain. She wobbled on her feet from shock. One of the men lifted and then tossed her. She landed hard in the bottom of one of the boats, but she still could not breathe. By the time her panic settled, and she knew she would not die of affixation, the small boat moved away from shore. The men rowed with terrifying speed. Her chance of escape died. She knew she would never get an opportunity again.

She lay on the floor of the boat. It shifted, and the oars slapped down into the water. The wood groaned and quaked beneath her. Her teeth chattered, and she could not control her shivers. The small craft scraped against the hull of the big ship. It loomed over her. Men stood on the deck above her, appearing far away. The vessel was giant and intimidating, with the men standing and making the small boat shift violently.

A different fear joined all the rest. The jostling men threatened to tip the boat. She could swim but couldn't catch her breath now and would drown if she fell into the water. Then she was lifted and slung over a warm and solid shoulder. The man climbed the swaying ladder that shifted against the swaying ship. Elisabeth thought she might puke for a moment, but her stomach was too empty.

The man stepped onto the ship rising and falling beneath him. His long strides carried him across the deck toward the scrape of old hinges and muted voices. The voices froze her, and she lifted her head, wishing everything to still so she could hear the voices. They pleaded desperately, hopelessly. Dozens of terrified voices just like hers. Then her body was shifted and pulled off the shoulder. The man held one arm and one leg, suspending her. The darkness beneath her loomed deep. Then, from that darkness appeared pale hands, reaching upward. Below the hands glowed faces, gaunt terrified faces pleading, hands reaching for her. Elisabeth cried out and grabbed for the man suspending her. The man released her, and she shrieked. Elisabeth kept a tight grip on his arm for a moment, but he shook her off, and she could not keep hold of his skin, slick by the same water soaking her and weighing down her dress and cloak. The hands reached for her, and the light above receded. She flailed, frantic and terrified, seeking something to cling to, but her hands met empty air.

A hand touched her, and a scream tore loose from her throat. Like monsters, they would tear her apart in the darkness. There would be nothing left of her by the time they finished. She closed her eyes tight, and the hands grabbed her, plucking her from the air, catching her. She was cradled there for a moment. Then, growing courage, she opened her eyes. Two men held her. One spoke, and she did not understand him. She looked into his brown eyes. Then the overhead door slammed, and she plunged into absolute and suffocating darkness. Then the men sat her on her feet, and the hands left her. They did not hurt her, but they were the only faces she knew inside this darkness. She reached for them, but someone bumped into her. The people shifted, and she dropped her hands to her sides. Those men were gone, and she became awash in a sea of faceless bodies.

Then hands landed on her, striking her head. Large, strong hands. They trailed down her head, along her face, and her shoulders. The hands felt at her as if this person was familiar with her and could do such a thing. Then the hands fell on her cloak and yanked it. They persisted, pulling Elisabeth to the floor, and continued ripping until the cloak tore from her with mercy. Freed, she scrambled onto her feet and moved backward, bumping into bodies, stepping on them, tripping and falling. People shoved at her and grumbled. She understood none of the words they spoke. She continued moving backward until a solid wall pressed against her back. She crouched there, drew her knees to her chest, and wrapped her quivering arms around them.

Elisabeth learned how immeasurable time became in the thick darkness. People moved about. Their whispers spread through the darkness, not carrying far. Weighed down by the heaviness of the air pressing on them. The stench and heat of the bodies in the hold made it hard to breathe. There was a shifting and movement of a different kind aboard the ship. Calls came from above, and she understood the ship was leaving its anchor. She screamed, jumping to her feet. She called, pleaded, and then she was shoved hard against the wall. A cacophony of "Shh" rose around her. The sound was terrifying in the darkness, and she fell silent.

Elisabeth retook her place against the wall, crouching there, listening as the whispering began. No one close spoke, and if they did, she did not understand their language.

Time rolled by with each wave beneath the ship, the floor rising and falling. She understood there was no privacy here among the press of bodies. The darkness shrouded her, and eventually, she added to the stench of human waste with no other option. Elisabeth could feel a difference in the ship's pitch when they came to anchor. Not long after, the hold doors opened, and men came spilling into the hole she was slung into. The hatch overhead was closed once again, and the men began screaming. Elisabeth understood a few of the words. The barbarians' dialect could be compatible enough with her own to communicate, but she remained silent. Bodies pressed against her, pinning and crushing her against the wall as the others tried to silence the men. The door overhead opened again, and a man stood silhouetted against the sun and slung contents from the bucket he held in his hand. The stench filled the hold before the hatch was closed, plunging them into blackness once again. Bodies shifted, and Elisabeth understood why they whispered and stopped her screams. Some of the crew saved their excrement for silencing their prisoners. Most effective because the men fell quiet, and the darkness settled again.

Later, long after her stomach grew tight and sick with hunger, the hatch opened again, and food was thrown down. Dried fish and tough bread filled with maggots. Someone shoved a piece of fish at her. She did not know who gave her food while others fought for it.

The ship moved. It bounced across the seas, pitching and groaning. People starved, and people died within the hold. Horrible things happened to those who could not get up from the floor. The hunger turned others desperate, and those who fell became their prey in the absolute darkness. She heard it all in the dark, including the old and young whimpers. Survivors, Elisabeth could call them nothing else here. The weak fell, and the strong lived, however they could, within the cloaking darkness. Elisabeth did not know if she was weak or a survivor. She prayed, wished, and then demanded guidance, but none came. Elisabeth starved and listened. Sometimes she got some of the food thrown to them, and sometimes she did not. But the one constant she could depend on here was the ship's movement and the stench of feces, urine, and rotting corpses.

Misery lived among them, called for them, claiming their souls. Elisabeth remained on the pitching floor, huddled against the wall. She was often shifted along it, but there was a comfort in having it at her back, holding her up. She could not bury her face in it but could rest her head against it. She reassured herself that one day she would again stand on solid ground. She prayed for this and lost faith in it while the ship continued rolling and tossing beneath them.

### ***Sunday, June 18, 1447, Klaipeda, Lithuania***

The ship anchored again, just like each time before the hatch above opened. But no men or women joined their numbers this time, and no little girls were tossed into the horrors. Instead, a wooden ladder was slipped down.

Elisabeth pressed herself against the wall. What lay for her out there? She could hear the noises, the men yelling back and forth. Those she suffered with began climbing. She knew there wasn't a choice. She stepped to the ladder, watching them rise into the sun. Inevitably, she, too, climbed. But what lay out there could be more horrific than what the light from above showed as it washed away the darkness. The noise from overhead was no longer muffled. The light cast down showed the horrors of what lay in the dark. Elisabeth could not scramble up the ladder fast enough.

Elisabeth dragged herself from the hold with the rest of the skeletons. She could not help but wonder if the lucky ones died below. Stepping onto the deck, she drew in her first breath of fresh air, freed from one nightmare, leaving her contemplating what hell would come next. The air was different here, terrifyingly so. No one would ever come looking for Lady Elisabeth Kirkham of Ravenshill here. She knew this in her gut.

As they filed out of the hold, they shivered and winced in the bright light of day. The stench of unwashed bodies, death, and bodily functions coated them all. The captors threw them overboard into the churning waters, offended by their smell. Most could not swim and thrashed about, panicked before being hauled into the smaller boats taking them ashore.

Screams echoed around Elisabeth. Grown men and women cried and begged as they were grabbed, slung, or pushed over the rails. The harder they cried, the louder the men laughed. The people shifted, pressing backward while the men shoved, and the crack of a whip echoed. People surged forward as the strap began landing. Elisabeth pushed with them, afraid of getting lashed or trampled more than going into the water. They would all go over the side.

Elisabeth stepped to the men reaching and grabbing arms from the crush of people.

One man laughed at her standing alone, frightened and waiting her turn. Her exhausted mind recognized him. He was the horseman that threw the rope over her and dragged her. He did not look like an evil man. His hair was a golden hue like hers, his eyes dark green like a summer meadow. His oval face was young and appeared kind. But it was deceiving. The men doing the throwing ignored her for a moment, so she waited, and the man found humor. Finally, the horseman stepped forward. She raised her eyes to his face, and he smacked her. She forgot she wasn't supposed to look at any of them. Her first captors taught her that.

She straightened, the wind whipping the seawater, beating at her, tangling the filth of her clothes and hair. She shivered and hunched her shoulders, looking down on the deck's boards.

"You think you are better than the rest of them, don't you?" the man asked with a jeering tone.

Elisabeth shook her head no. She did not like this man noticing her, and the question frightened her. How could she answer such a thing? The man laughed. It was a sound that made fear creep up her spine. "You'll learn soon enough."

Elisabeth was afraid of what she would learn. He might take great satisfaction watching the lessons served to her.

"Throw this one next," the man said. Hands seized her, and she was slung. Fear made her hold her breath before she even hit the water. It rushed up and swallowed her. The cold severity of it froze her chest driving its shards of sharp fingers into her skull. She kicked toward the surface and broke through with a gasp before the waves sucked her back under. She kicked her exhausted legs again, and her head broke the surface. The boat hauling people from the water floated far away.

Her clothes dragged at her, the water weighing them down. She fought against the tide and pulled herself toward the boat. But the current made the effort a battle, and she feared she would lose it before the boat turned her way. Finally, she was hauled from the water and dropped into the bottom with others. Some of the prisoners rowed them toward shore while the rest huddled together, seeking reprieve from the wind and warmth from their emaciated bodies pressed together. She had grown accustomed to the heat of the cargo hold, but here the wind blew a chill from the north.

The boats landed against solid ground, and their captors forced them into the angry surf again. Elisabeth stumbled over the edge. Her exhausted legs could not hold her, and she fell. The water nearly swept her away, but Elisabeth grabbed the end of one of the oars. She gained her feet, becoming aware the man at the other end of the oar was staring at her. She fought against the pull and push of the tide. The man leaped from the boat, splashing down beside her. He screamed at her, grabbed her head, and shoved her beneath the water. He pressed down on her, holding her beneath the surface. She struggled and panicked. The weight of her attacker's body pressed her down to the bottom. Just as she thought all was lost, the weight shifted, and someone grabbed and yanked her upward. She coughed and sputtered. Someone hoisted her by an arm and leg and threw her onto the sand. The exhaustion was too heavy, dragging at her, more bitter than the cold wind.

"Get moving!" the voice ordered over top of her.

Elisabeth rolled to her hands and knees. She lifted her head, and the horror of what was happening around her sank in. Three ships sat anchored offshore, all unloading their cargo of people. Not all thrown into the water made it to the surface. Instead, their bodies floated, washing up on shore, or the current grabbed them and pulled them out to sea. The corpse of the man who tried to drown her was one of those. The water turned red around him. His cut throat had freed him from his crazed mind and saved her from drowning. Slowly, the current washed him away from the land to be lost in the depths of the vast sea.

As she gawked, a foot came out and kicked her shoulder. She sprawled. "Get up," the man growled at her. So she did, her shoulder throbbing, her chest ached, and her legs dragged their way up the sand. All the while, the men behind her screamed and cracked their vicious whips. Would there ever be a moment in her future she wouldn't be terrified? She wanted to curl up on the sand and cry until her heart healed. She wanted an opportunity for her mind to process what happened, was happening, and would happen to her. But she was not permitted even that tiny level of grief, and numbly her body forced itself to move.

The prisoners were separated. The children were placed inside a pen, such as that would hold goats and sheep. The children were hunched on the ground together, crying and shivering. Elisabeth hesitated, but the man behind her gave her a mighty shove that sent her sprawling. The hands of a child helped her up.

Elisabeth looked into the face of another girl. She was small, with pale porcelain skin surrounded by vibrant red hair and large brown eyes set inside her gaunt face. "You are English?" the girl asked.

A sob escaped Elisabeth. She could understand the language of someone other than her captors. Elisabeth grabbed the other girl and clung to her, crying. Elisabeth was unfamiliar with the girl's accent. But it did not matter. The girl helped guide her into the huddle of children.

"I am Edith," the girl said.

"I am Elisabeth," she said through the chattering of her teeth. The shivers took over where the exhaustion left off.

The children remained in their pens. A burly, terrifying-looking man guarded them. He did not seem to understand their fear and exhaustion would keep them from trying to climb over the small walls of their cage. They received bread and some kind of slop that tasted foul but helped fill the empty crater that had become her stomach. The captors began settling and began their entertainment. The children were held safely, their guard warning away any man coming near, looking for amusement. Edith and Elisabeth huddled together, hearing the screams of the women and the cries of agony from the men whose torture became entertainment after they tired of the women.

Despite the fear and cold, it was better than the ship. She curled into a ball and let her exhausted mind recall a memory of home, hoping it would lull her to sleep.

**_Thursday, June 2, 1446, Ravenshill_**

*Elisabeth's breaths labored, trying to keep up with Adrian on their race to Ravenshill. The sky opened overhead, dumping torrents of water onto the earth. The wind whipped, and the saturated ground turned to slop beneath their feet. Her shoes soaked up the water, her clothes drug at her, and her tired legs.*

*"Hurry," Adrian said, pausing for her. Then, reaching him, he seized her hand and dragged her behind him. She struggled to keep up, slipping in the mud, but Adrian's hand kept her upright. Lightning crashed and shook the ground, and a squeak of fright escaped Elisabeth.*

*Adrian's grip tightened, and he picked up his pace. They were not prepared for what greeted them at the bridge. Adrian stopped suddenly, pulling Elisabeth up beside him.*

*"Oh no," she said, watching the water rushing across the top of it. Earlier, the water threatened to take over the bottom of the bridge. Now the tumultuous waters churned across it, swallowing it with fury.*

*"Come on," he said, tugging her hand again.*

*Elisabeth planted her feet and refused to move. "We can't cross it," she declared.*

*"Then what do you think we should do?" Adrian asked. His dark hair was plastered against his head, and the rivulets of water ran down his face. He raised his voice to be heard over the din of the storm and furious river.*

*Elisabeth's eyes fell on Adrian, then to the bridge, before offering a slight shake of her head. Her eyes rolled franticly, a mirror of her torment. What could they do? This was the only bridge for miles, and the storm raged relentlessly.*

*Adrian tugged her hand again. The card with the knight invaded her mind, and she took a hesitant step forward and then another. The water swirled around their legs, swallowing their feet in the brown churning river. Adrian's hand was strong, and he placed himself on the downriver side of her. She could feel the water pressing her against his solid body, keeping it from sweeping her away.*

*"We're almost there," Adrian called. Then, another bolt of lightning split the sky overhead.*

*Terror threatened to make Elisabeth weep. They were not even halfway across.*

*"Watch out," Adrian warned. He grabbed her, and her feet lost purchase on the saturated wood. He hauled her against him and placed himself on the upriver side. A giant tree churned its way toward the bridge. It was upon them. The branches reached, the trunk bobbed and swirled, its roots ripped from the ground by terrifying violence. A twisting mass of death came for them.*

*The tree crashed into the bridge, the anchored structure moved, and Adrian fell. His arms tightened around her, and they plunged into the water with the bridge's splintering wood and the swirling tree. The force of the water swept them away and hammered at them.*

*Their bodies were pulled beneath the surface before she could draw a breath. Elisabeth knew she would drown by the water dumped from the sky or what churned around them.*

*Adrian fought against the water. One hand remained clamped around her waist while the other reached and fought toward the surface. Elisabeth drew in a quick breath before the water churned them again, and they plunged back into the depths of the river.*

*Again, Adrian fought back to the surface, dragging Elisabeth with him. They broke the surface as the tree swept by them. She could feel the branches reaching for them before the impact of one slammed into Adrian. His hand released her.*

*Suddenly Elisabeth found herself alone in the murderous flow. She swam, fought against the pull, and searched madly for Adrian. Her head was forced under again, and a branch caught her hair. She jerked, feeling the tendrils pull free from her scalp, and the tree corkscrewed and released her hair, but another branch tangled in her tunic. It plunged her down, and she fought against the tree and the cloying waves of madness.*

*She grabbed a branch, using it to pull herself toward the surface. The tree corkscrewed again, and Adrian disappeared beneath the surface, tangled among the roots. Elisabeth pulled herself toward the trunk and the root ball that held Adrian prisoner. She struggled to keep the churning tree from taking her under as it corkscrewed its way down the river. Branches dragged at her. One caught her, and the tree lurched. It flung her over it. The tree pushed her, threatening to pull her beneath it. She fought and turned, grabbing a branch and pulling herself back toward the trunk before the limb ripped from her hand, and the tree turned again.*

*The trunk of the tree pushed against her, and she wished she could get back upriver from it, but it churned and twisted. Then the tree slammed to a sudden stop. A branch grabbed her while the river pushed her on. It tangled with her. She fought, and then the tree lurched again. She grabbed one of the roots and pulled herself toward the churning mass. Adrian resurfaced next to her.*

*Elisabeth grabbed his tunic, refusing to let him go as the tree corkscrewed, dragging them under. She pulled herself into Adrian, wrapping her legs around him, gripping him with all her strength. One hand held him while she searched for the root keeping him trapped. She freed him from one of the roots, but the tree twisted and entangled them again. She fought the current and the tree, struggling, clinging to the motionless boy, the river driving them on.*

*The tree caught on something else, nearly dislodging Elisabeth from Adrian. She worked fast, knowing she could not hold her breath or Adrian much longer. She freed the one root wrapped around his leg, tangling with the sword sheath still strapped to his side. She freed him of the root holding his shoulder wedged against the earth, still clinging to the tree. Then they were free. His body almost slipped from her, but she grasped him tighter, fighting harder against his weight to keep them above the surface. The water pushed, and Elisabeth pulled them toward the riverbank. What lay on the river's edge before was overtaken by the raging river. The water surged through the tree line, submerging trees and threatening to rip them away.*

*Her hand shot out, and she grabbed a branch. The current pulled her free. She fought again to get a firm grip on Adrian, the river threatening to take him away. Then she slammed into the trunk of another tree. She wedged herself there, pulling Adrian in front of her. His body pinned her against the tree, the strong current pressed on them, keeping them pinned, giving Elisabeth a chance to breathe and take stock of their surroundings.*

*They rested not far from the bank of the raging river. She reached for the river bottom, but it was too far away. She dove from the tree toward the shore, but the river carried them further downstream. She grabbed for another tree, wrapping an arm around Adrian's chest and lunging again. The water caught them and forced them beneath the surface. The tree she aimed for flew past her shoulder, the water pulling them along. She fought for the surface, and her foot kicked the trunk of another tree. She used her leg to grab for it, wrapping around it. She clung there for a minute but was no match for the raging water.*

*Her leg slipped free, and she reached, swimming and fighting toward the next tree. She slammed into it, and the force of Adrian's body pressing on her from the current forced the breath from her. Closer to shore, she reached for the river bottom again and almost cried, not feeling it. She needed to move. The weight of Adrian and the force of the water crushed her.*

*Elisabeth pushed off, plunging toward the next tree. This one she caught with her shoulder, letting the current push her forward until her body wedged there. She paused, catching her breath while readjusting her grip on Adrian. Testing for the bottom again, she wanted to scream or cry. It was not there.*

*She moved, letting the water take them into the current again. It swirled them. She reached for tree after tree. And then the current swept them back out. She fought and tired, and then her foot scraped against something. She fought to grab it with her legs—a tree. It fell long before this storm, its trunk now as stuck to the ground as its roots once were. She caught it and grappled with it, the current still trying to pull Adrian from her.*

*She gritted her teeth and used the last of her strength to pull them along the tree until she found the river bottom beneath her. She pulled and tugged until she could drag Adrian onto the solid ground so only his legs rested in the water. She knelt beside him, her chest heaving and exhaustion threatening to collapse her.*

*"Adrian," she cried. She shook him, and tears flowed from her eyes, mixing with the rain saturating her and everything around them. "Please, Adrian," she said. "Adrian." She shook him, slapped him, and continued calling his name.*

*Adrian's hand twitched. Elisabeth seized it, pulling it to her chest, squeezing it with all her strength and will. "Adrian." In his name was the plea he open his eyes.*

*His eyelids fluttered, and he was looking at her. "Elisabeth?" He stared at her, clinging to his hand.*

*Knowledge settled in his gray-blue eyes, and he sat up with a groan. Elisabeth moved closer, touching him, feeling for bumps on his head or broken bones. Adrian coughed, and still, Elisabeth touched him, reassuring herself he lived.*

*He tried slapping her hand away, but she seized it. The water beat against his legs, and he drew them out of the river. He turned to her, the rain pelting down on them.*

*"Elisabeth." his voice was quiet, and there was a note of disbelief that they sat safely on the bank of the river and not drowned in its evil depths. He dragged her against him and enveloped her, crushing her, and she began to cry.*

*"We're okay," he said, stroking a hand down her wet hair. His other arm held her caged against him, and*

*he buried his head in her neck. "Oh, Elisabeth," he said. "You are my Knight of Swords," he said, awed.*

*Elisabeth sat another moment in his arms before she pulled back. "Does that make you my queen?" she asked with a giggle.*

*He scowled at her before he began laughing too. The relief of their survival washed over them. It escaped through the hysterical laughter that consumed them as they clung to one another. Then, just as abruptly, Adrian's laughter stopped. He gripped her hand tight and pulled it to his chest. "That makes me forever in your debt. I will always choose the path that will bring me to you." He hugged her again for several long breaths. Pulling away, tears shone in his eyes.*

*"If you are going to cry on me, I will forever call you my queen," she warned him. He smiled before wiping a soaked sleeve across his eyes.*

*"Come on," he said, climbing to shaking legs and dragging Elisabeth up beside him. They stood by the river, watching it churn and twist. Elisabeth's heart sank. They stood on the wrong side of the river.*

*Adrian led her through the trees, and soon they stepped back onto the muddy road. He did not release her hand in the downpour but kept it firmly within his grasp. Finally, they reached the next bridge, and Elisabeth's legs wobbled. Did the exhaustion increase her fear or the water churning beneath the bridge? The rain had slowed, turning into a steady sprinkle.*

*"I'm scared," Elisabeth whispered.*

*Adrian chuckled and patted her hand. "You're my knight of swords? Or Jeanne d'Arc?"*

*"Jeanne died."*

*"I told you," Adrian began. His voice sounded confident. "I will always be your knight of swords. So*

*when you are afraid, hold to my hand, and I will carry us through. And when I am afraid, I will hold on to you."*

*Tears filled Elisabeth's eyes, and she nodded. Unfortunately, they had no choice. They had to cross the bridge to return to Ravenshill before Lincoln and her father returned.*

*"We'll run," Adrian said. "I will watch for danger. You keep your eyes ahead and run," Adrian said with all the confidence that they would make it safely to the other side.*

*Elisabeth nodded, Adrian gave her hand a tug, and they sprinted across the bridge. Finally, they reached the other side, and Elisabeth released a long breath.*

# Chapter 7

**Thursday, July 20, 1447, Aberdeen, Scotland**

She was gone. They put Elisabeth on a ship, and now she was out there somewhere. No longer could they track her through England and Scotland. Where did they take her? How would they follow her now? They were far behind that ship. How much farther behind would they be after landing in each port? How far would they take her?

Lincoln took the news far better than Adrian could have. Adrian could not talk to Lincoln about his worries. Lincoln's feathers remained unruffled. His mind flowed smoothly from one track to another. He took this ordeal as he would take a typical day.

Lincoln bought them passage on the next ship bound for ports in Norway, Denmark, and several others all the way to Lithuania, where the ship carrying Elisabeth was bound. Days could be spent in these places, loading and unloading cargo. How much farther behind would they fall? Elisabeth's ship stopped at ports too. What if Elisabeth didn't go as far as her ship was going? What if she was taken off at a port they too would stop in, and they wouldn't know? She was part of the cargo bound for the slave market in Klaipeda. If she made it there, how would they ever find her after that?

The news came to Adrian two days before, and hysterical worry threatened. This came between bouts of sorrow so deep that he sometimes turned from Lincoln to hide his tears. Apprehension filled Adrian. He bled fear climbing aboard the rocking ship. He became ill the instant he planted two feet on the deck. The rise and fall beneath him turned his stomach into pandemonium.

"You'll be okay, Young Adrian," Lincoln said. He led the way down the steep set of steps that led below deck. He nudged Adrian toward the bunks made of ropes. They swung with the rise and fall of the ship. Adrian felt himself sway, as they did, in perfect unison with the rolling ship. Three bunks stacked one over the other. Lincoln put his bag on the one suspended over Adrian's. Adrian clung to the ropes. He spread his feet, attempting to steady himself and the role of his stomach. "You will grow used to the rocking."

Adrian doubted it. After a few minutes, the space beneath the deck became suffocating. He raced for the steps and the precious air above. Back on deck, he leaned over the side and launched his lunch into the ocean. He lifted his head to see the ropes pulled from the port. The ship drifted from the coast. Night fell upon the ship, and Adrian sought sleep. But the rocking of the ropes proved far worse than the rocking of the vessel alone. He sat on the deck. Each time he laid his head down or even closed his eyes, everything in him lurched.

The sun rose over the ocean. The surface shone like glass, but the boat did not skim smoothly across it. A spectacular display of colors exploded over the horizon, heralding a new day. But it, too, sickened his stomach with the ship rolling and bucking beneath him. Everything he lay his eyes on rocked with him. The only thing that didn't rock was the horizon. That messed with his equilibrium, making him greener. Lincoln brought him food. His stomach bit with hunger, but Adrian knew he could keep nothing down after one bite. The day wore on, and the sky darkened. By noon ominous clouds rolled in, and the sails whipped ferociously, snapping and popping with the rising wind.

The night took over the day, and the ship bucked. Great torrents of rain fell, soaking Adrian. Before the rain began, he tried taking refuge below. But his stomach immediately whirled and twisted, his head threatening to explode with each crash of the ship riding down waves before climbing up the other side. He felt as if he might pass out. The anticipation of the falling ship debilitated him. It came with the fear they would shatter apart when they landed at each wave's bottom. He crawled to the upper deck to see something beyond the spinning walls.

The bow crashed into the sea, and the ocean sprayed over the side. He clung to a rope that secured crates to the deck. He wrapped his arms and legs around it, holding on for dear life. The storm crashed, and the water sloshed on the deck around him. He feared the storm would never end. Weak and exhausted, he feared it would sweep him away into the tumultuous sea any minute. He prayed, and he cried. He thought of his parents and worried he never made them proud. His brother would make a good Baron of Stokesley and Earl of Helmsley, or so he hoped. He could never imagine he would ever die this way. His mind screamed for Elisabeth. He wished for an invisible connection, so she would know he tried to reach her. He wanted her to know he tried.

From above came a tremendous explosion. Wood cracked, and the rope grew slack in his hand as the world shattered around him. Darkness followed.

## ***Sunday, September 5, 1445, Ravenshill***

*"Who is that?" Elisabeth called, peering over the stones in front of her and Walter. The rocks created Elisabeth's fortress that Adrian tried knocking down with the sticks he launched at them from his own fort. The extra hands of Walter helped keep their rocks from tumbling, and their sticks carved away at Adrian's wall ever so slowly. He could not defend and repair at the same time. Adrian had not launched an attack in a few minutes and knew Elisabeth readied for his charge. Adrian stood from behind his stones. His father approached on foot, and Adrian dropped his sticks, Elisabeth's fortress safe for the moment.*

*He was ready for his father to disapprove of him playing with Elisabeth. Hagan de Ros sent his son to Ravenshill to be a squire, not launch sticks at the nine-year-old and four-year-old heirs of Ravenshill. They had played at their fortress all afternoon, and all three were filthy. None of them bothered slipping shoes on before racing to the river. The river's shore was plentiful with rock to make their fortresses. When they overheated, they swam, and the nearby soft fields gave them a place to play any number of games. Both he and Elisabeth knew she should not be playing at such things with the boys, but there were no little girls here.*

*She preferred the boy's games to dolls and ruffles. Perhaps she would enjoy her doll Priscilla more and do more lady-like things if she had a female friend. But*

*Adrian and Walter never wanted to play with the doll. Adrian had gone so far as to almost run the doll through with his wooden sword. Elisabeth had stopped bringing Priscilla into the game, filling Adrian with guilt. He prepared for his father's displeasure. Hoping he would never find out about the baby doll.*

*Elisabeth took Walter by the hand and followed with steps that trudged behind him. She would not be happy meeting his father for the first time with bare feet and a filthy torn dress.*

*"Father." Adrian greeted his dad, staring up at him. He was always filled with awe when he looked at the large stature of his father. A big man, broad of chest, thick of arms and legs, and intelligent. Adrian remembered his manners, "This is The Honorable Elisabeth and Walter," Adrian said, introducing them.*

*Elisabeth curtsied to him. Adrian almost laughed at her in her old brown dress, a little too short for her with her filthy bare feet and legs disappearing beneath it. Her frazzled blond hair and dirty cheeks lent her an air of comedy. Walter stood beside her, his hand resting in hers, staring up at the big man with adoration filling his blue eyes. His mouth gaped open, and Adrian was proud his father could evoke such a reaction from the child.*

*"This is Earl Hagan de Ros of Helmsley, my father." Pride filled Adrian's voice. Elisabeth stared at his father. His father held his own title as a legend, just like Sir Lincoln. His father earned his title for his dedication and prowess on French battlefields before age twenty. Then his right hand was crushed on one of those battlefields, and he never fought again. The fingers twisted haphazardly, and the skin on the back of his hand protruded in two places where the bones snapped. After all the time that passed, any hand movement still*

*pained him. Sometimes his fingers jerked uncontrollably, leaving him groaning and sweating. No one understood why he did not remove the offending appendage, but he was adamant his hand remained attached.*

*Elisabeth nudged Walter from his stupor. He looked like an imbecile staring at the man. Walter offered Adrian's father a deep bow. Then, straightening, his face transformed from her kid brother's to that of someone stronger.*

*"I have heard much about the both of you. I am forever grateful that you befriended my son. I see he is in good hands here."*

*"Have you seen Sir Lincoln?" Adrian asked, snatching his father's attention.*

*"I have." His father's tone was always sour whenever the subject of Lincoln Victers arose. Even more when Lord Thomas's name was mentioned. Yet Adrian was at Ravenshill training with one, under the lordship of the other. Whatever the trouble between the three grown men, it did not affect Adrian.*

*Fear seeped into Adrian. "Is all well?" he asked. This was the first time in four years his father came to Ravenshill.*

*"All is well, son," his father reassured him. "I have brought you a gift."*

*"A gift?" Adrian asked. "What is it?" A gift that brought his father so far from Helmsley had to be grand.*

*The man laughed a deep, rolling sound that funneled from the man's ample chest. "I did not carry it out here. Come."*

*His father walked toward the keep, but Elisabeth and Walter did not follow. Adrian raced the two steps back to her, seizing her hand and dragging her and Walter behind him. Elisabeth would be embarrassed by her attire and try to correct it. She once asked him what kind of lady ran about with bare feet. He had no answer. He knew his mother didn't go about shoeless, nor did any of his female cousins, though they weren't titled. But what did it matter at Ravenshill? Only he and the Kirkhams held titles of consequence. If they ran about in bare feet, who would care? But he knew Elisabeth was afraid his father would care. He also knew it would not end with finding a pair of slippers. She would need a clean dress and cloak only after washing, including her tangled hair. His father would be long gone by the time Elisabeth felt presentable. Reaching the inner bailey, it was too late for her to flee. Adrian relinquished his hold on her.*

*His father walked to his horse, waiting patiently. Then, from his saddle, he pulled a sheathed sword. "If you are to be a knight, it is time you have a real sword to fight with."*

*His father laid the weapon in his son's hands. It was heavier than the one Adrian carried. Adrian knew his father's sword well. He admired it for years. He did not need to pull the two-handed sword to remember every detail. Adrian did not know if there was another sword like it. Made of wootz steel, the blade was forged by an expert craftsman from India. The grainy pattern of his father's was not haphazard as the two other wootz swords Adrian had seen. Instead, the contrasting luster of the high-carbon and low-carbon steel melded and forged together with great care. Thus, a blade of still water was created. The metal water was interrupted by a few raindrops. The dark, fine-haired crystal patterns rippled out from the raindrops, creating swirls and the flow of steel down the blade.*

*The rain guard and cross guard were made of the same steel, but the patterns were gilded. The gold created a contrasting effect to the darker pattern of the blade. This design flowed into the sword's grip, bound tightly by leather strips. The leather was undyed and aged into a deep brown through the years. Hagan could not guess how many hands held the sword before he took it from a dead knight's hand in France. The end of the pommel was a simple triangle, with the gilding reaching the very end.*

*Adrian fought tears, words failing him. His father wrapped an arm around his shoulders and pulled him into a hug against his chest. There Adrian took the opportunity to wipe away the two stray tears. The tears came from pride, holding his father's sword, and love for the man who honored him with such a gift.*

*Then his father stepped back, kneeling beside him and removing Adrian's old sword from his belt. Freeing it, he handed Walter the smaller sword with slight hesitation. "You will be a big knight one day, too," he said. Walter took the sheathed weapon. It was large for the boy, but Adrian remembered a day, not long ago, that his father's sword was much too large for him. Now, his father strapped it onto his belt, the tip resting not far above his ankles. When Adrian was a child, his father strapped the sword around Adrian's waist and let him feel its weight. Then, it was too long and rested against the floor, so he never felt its weight on his hips. Now feeling its weight, he thought he might explode with the pride of it.*

*He turned to Elisabeth and smiled at her. He could not read her expression, no matter how he ached to know her thoughts. When his father asked Adrian and Walter to show him where they might catch some fish for the evening meal, Adrian hung back. He seized Elisabeth's hand again before she could disperse with the rest of the household. He pulled her into one of the stalls that stood open.*

*"Is something the matter?" he asked her.*

*She shook her head no, studying him, her eyes roving over his face, locking on them for an uncomfortable amount of time before traveling on.*

*"Why do you look at me like that?" he asked her.*

*"Because, today, you don't look like a boy," she said. "When you stood beside your father, and he put his sword on you, you looked like a man. I don't know how, but this morning you were a boy like Walter, but now, you seem taller and older."*

*Adrian smiled at her, then bowed, "I am your knight in shining armor now," he said, winking at her. She laughed and hesitated momentarily when he straightened and presented his arm to her. She slid her hand onto his forearm, and he guided her toward the tower as a knight would his lady.*

**Saturday, July 22, 1447, northern coast of Germany**

The hand on his arm tightened. "Adrian." His name came from far away. His mind slogged through the mire of confusion, swimming upward. Then, finally, his eyes snapped open, staring into the dark brown eyes of the knight who began this nightmare. But, no, he couldn't blame Lincoln. That horse went off track long before Lincoln rid Ravenshill of witnesses.

"Adrian." Lincoln's calloused hand rested on his cheek. It was a hand that killed but that he knew could be gentle. When Adrian was younger and was thrown from his horse, spraining his wrist, Lincoln wrapped it with gentleness and great concern that had etched his brow.

"What happened?" Adrian croaked out.

Relief filled the man's face, and his fingers jerked, tightening for a moment. Then, a sound akin to a sob escaped the man before he straightened from Adrian.

"The mast snapped in the storm," Lincoln informed him.

Suddenly the ship lurched beneath him. The swing of the ropes he lay upon made his empty stomach swell and flip. Adrian struggled up, swinging his legs over the side of the netting, falling to his knees. But he stumbled back up, heading for the deck. Lincoln followed close behind. The storm abated, and a clear blue sky greeted him. The ship lay at anchor near a coast, boats ferrying back and forth.

"We were blown off course and missed the passage over Denmark."

Adrian gripped the rail and heaved his empty stomach, but nothing came out but the spittle he launched over the side. A boat moved away, and he wished he was on it to plant his feet on solid ground.

"We have landed south of Denmark and must travel across land."

Adrian turned to Lincoln. The deck rose and fell beneath his feet. He wanted to hang over the side again but knew there was nothing in his stomach and hadn't been for days. "Congratulations," Lincoln said. He slapped Adrian on the shoulder. "This ship's misfortune is your blessing. Stay here, and I will retrieve our horses."

Adrian scowled at Lincoln's retreat and turned, looking again at the land. It rose and fell with the ship, and he felt his stomach churn. He could not wait to climb into one of the smaller boats. He closed his eyes, but they snapped back open. He would save his prayer for the shore.

# Chapter 8

**Tuesday, August 15, 1447, Ural Mountains, Lithuania**

Dawn brought more men. At first, Elisabeth did not understand what was happening. In her naïve mind, she thought their rescue might be imminent. Hope bloomed.

"Are they here for us?" Elisabeth whispered. They moved from one group to another.

"Someone is," Edith told her. Whispering was the only way to communicate. Each time anyone's voice rose for the guards to hear, a whip snaked out and cracked across their backs, faces, arms, or legs. It did not matter. Only the silence of the prisoners mattered.

"Really?" Elisabeth asked.

Something on her face prompted Edith to say, "They're here to buy us."

The hope in Elisabeth's chest shattered. Elisabeth stared. The men moved closer and closer. How many times could a person be sold? For her, this would be the second time. She was too naïve to know what fate could befall a little girl, now a slave. All she knew was that she was brought here the last time she was sold. So far from home, there was little chance anyone would come for her. And now, she feared she would be pulled farther still.

The pens emptied. Some men dropped from the group, purchasing the slaves they came for. Then the group stood over the fence holding the children. The guard called for them to all stand.

Elisabeth did so, clinching her chilled hands while her knees shook, and she couldn't breathe. The men began circling as a monetary value was levied on each of them. Then the men stood before Elisabeth and Edith. One of those men seemed to take particular enjoyment in tormenting her.

"That one, there is a lady." It was the horseman who had dragged her across the beach before embarking on the ship. The man who stood on the ship's deck, knowing she and so many others rotted below. Now he stood over her in the heavy fur cloak that made him look like a bear while she froze. The knowledge made her grow colder than the freezing wind that whipped. The other men chuckle, a terrifying sound that warned her of things to come she could not fathom.

"Oh, a lady," a man said, mocking her. By his accent, Elisabeth could tell he was not English. He was a small man. His face held a harsh coldness with sharp angles and a hawk-like nose. His skin was leathered, his dark hair graying and thinning.

"Those two are small enough for the tunnels. I will also take those two strong-looking boys and that older girl there," the horseman said.

Elisabeth, Edith, and the other three were forced together. Elisabeth could not stop shaking, even when Edith slipped her hand into Elisabeth's. Then, a man came forward with a rope and tied the boy's hands together. She wanted to bolt. But they stood on open ground. The grown men on horses would not let her get far.

Then the man was standing over Elisabeth and Edith. He grabbed Edith, yanking her hand from Elisabeth's grip. Edith was crying, and Elisabeth became even more frightened. Her tears told Elisabeth the next place would be no better than this one.

The man grabbed her hands, pulling her forward. A frightening sound escaped her. One she had never heard come from herself because she had never been so terrified. Her hands were tied with the other children, a rope stringing them together. She could not stop the trembling of her hands and body. The man's grip holding her was painful. He met her eyes, and she knew he did not care. No one here cared about their terror. Despite the fact that a piece of Elisabeth already knew no one here cared, it was still horrifying to see.

The older girl was left free and standing alone. She was confused and terrified. Horses gathered, and their riders leered at her. Some touched her, making her shrink from their groping hands. Then the horseman stepped forward.

"I am Master. You are my property now and will work my mines. You girls will be sold again when you are old enough to have your innocence bid for. You boys will work for me until you die of old age if you are so lucky." Then the man turned to the older girl, grabbed her by the arm, and pulled her against him. "And you will warm our blankets on the long journey." The girl tried pulling away, but his iron grip held her tight.

Days rolled by, twining and joining with the nights. The children trudged, unsheltered from the blazing sun and chilling torrential rains, while the older girl rode with the men. After the first evening, the girl's screams and cries fell silent. After that night, her face changed. It was the face of a girl lost. The face of a girl who knew nothing good was left for her. Elisabeth and Edith could only stare at their future selves. They saw how the men could transform the souls of their prisoners and crush them.

The journey was long on foot. They ate a slop of grain and salted fish once a day, enough to keep them moving but never enough to fill their bellies. Talking was not permitted. Anyone caught talking brought the whip across their backs. Elisabeth found it increasingly difficult to move her feet, keep her eyes open, and not let the exhaustion have her.

No privacy was afforded them. They were always on the move or huddled together. Edith stumbled once, and the whip ripped across her back. She cried out with shock and pain.

The land here was steep, and the heat of late summer days zapped any additional strength from the children. At night the chill of the oncoming season whipped across the land. The journey stretched, and the nights grew colder, hinting at harsh winters. During their trek, Elisabeth hoped things would improve once they arrived at the mines. But she should know no comforts were coming. This journey should have prepared her for that, but she was only a child and did not know.

A small house and a barn sat on the property, where the men finally stopped. Elisabeth lost track of time from when she left her home. How long had passed since she killed her brother? The storm she fled into that night seemed so long ago. It was an entire lifetime that had passed.

She was placed with the other children in the barn. Some children were already huddled there beneath threadbare blankets, nothing more than moving corpses. Their skin was pale, and their bodies were emaciated. Edith cried at the sight of them. The man standing behind them raised his arm. Elisabeth seized Edith's hand and dragged her into the stall designated for the children. The girls moved to a corner sitting together, their arms intertwined, pressing against one another.

The men left them there, the darkness heavy. When Elisabeth's eyes adjusted to the dark, she crawled to a nearby blanket and pulled it over her and Edith. Elisabeth managed to sleep until the threadbare blanket was yanked off them. It brought Elisabeth awake with a jolt, and Edith sat up. A large boy gripped the blanket and turned away from them. Elisabeth sprang to her feet, stopping him.

The boy turned and shoved Elisabeth, and she stumbled, falling back onto the cold dirt floor. The boy spoke, his words Elisabeth did not understand, but the cold lilt left little to the imagination. The boy would fight for the blanket. Edith bent over her. There were not enough worn blankets for all the children, and the smaller ones, like Elisabeth and Edith, got none.

Exhaustion took them shuddering against one another, trying to sleep through the chilling night. Elisabeth was thankful for the drafty barn walls blocking the persistent wind. It wailed outside, banging against the brittle wood of the old structure.

Yells woke them before dawn lit the skies. A torch chased back the night and illuminated the small children brought in. Elisabeth and Edith sat together, watching them drag themselves into the stall. They were filthy, wretched-looking creatures. There was a hollowness about their eyes. Despite her tender years, Elisabeth knew where the emptiness came from. It was the emptiness that came when all hope was lost.

"You little ones," the man said. Pointing at them, Elisabeth's blood ran cold.

Edith jumped up and pulled Elisabeth with her. Elisabeth was still so tired and hungry, she did not know how much longer she could go on. Edith was doing no better. But Edith, Elisabeth surmised, was a peasant accustomed to a subservient role and Elisabeth decided to follow her lead.

"Get moving," the man growled. The walk was not a long one. Elisabeth never saw a mine before this place. The flickering lanterns disappeared into a gaping hole dug into the mountain. She knew why they were there. They needed her and Edith because they were small and could fit easier in the tunnels.

Master was there, and he laughed at Elisabeth. His stride carried him quickly to her. His hand touched the mass of her blonde hair, now caked with filth, and he smirked. It seemed as if years had passed since she ran her hand through hair that was silky, soft, and clean.

"You are here to mine my jewels," Master said. "I know you know what they look like, my lady," the man said with a mocking sneer and a bow. Born to something better, Elisabeth was ashamed among these children. Edith watched her and Master, uneasy.

"Mining anything is dangerous work. Gas can build up inside those caves, and the candles can set it off. That's why I have you slaves do it."

He tossed two small tools down at their feet and two buckets. "Four buckets apiece, and then you can eat and rest." The man laughed and walked away. His laugh told Elisabeth those four buckets would be hard to fill.

A man shoved them toward the tunnel. A younger man, who appeared to be a slave, took control of them at the entrance. He carried a small whip, the one long strap replaced by several shorter ones. It was a whip the boy could still wield in the confines of the tunnel.

"Go," he ordered. By his accent, Elisabeth could tell English was not his language. But he knew what "go" meant.

Elisabeth followed Edith, and the boy came behind them. They moved past numerous other tunnels carved into the mountain. The main tunnel was large, the ceiling supported with wood beams leaving Elisabeth wary of their ability to hold up a mountain. Two of the intersecting tunnels were likewise carved out and reinforced. But the boy pushed them toward an array of smaller tunnels.

"How long have you been here?" Elisabeth asked the boy.

He did not reply but drew his hand back and lay the whip across her back. She fell to her knees with a gasp. Edith turned, but the boy barked at them to "go." So, Edith did, and Elisabeth stumbled up and followed, her back stinging and bleeding.

The boy finally stopped, pointing to the precious lavender quartz seam, showing them how to chip it out with no words spoken. The piece he pulled loose he tossed into the bucket Edith held. For the effort put forth, the payout in the size of that piece of quartz was small. Then the boy pointed to the three holes leading deeper into the mountain. The tunnels were small, and they would be forced to crawl. “Go,” the boy snapped. The girls hesitated, and the boy raised the hand with the whip.

Edith scrambled into her tunnel while Elisabeth moved a little slower. His hand holding the whip gave her time to come to terms with what she had to do. Her hand shaking, she took up the small lantern and crawled into the hole. It closed around her, suffocating her. It became so small that she could not crawl on her hands and knees but instead pulled herself through on her stomach, pushing the lantern ahead and dragging the bucket behind. The ground scraped against her skin. The dark, quiet pounded at her, echoing and suffocating. She crawled, strangled, and shook, reaching the end. She stared at the dirt before her, and she cried. She forgot to look for the gems in the walls while she crawled. She sobbed, her knees and hands hurting. She could not see the quartz the boy showed them. But she mostly cried because she was lost. There was no way out and no way she could stop being cold and hungry. Though the heat of the days getting here baked her, something inside had frozen.

Eventually, she crawled backward, searching the walls. It created its own agony with the dirt and rock scraping the opposite way, pulling up her skirt, and rubbing across her thighs. Finally, she found where the last child had stopped digging at the rock. She would have saved herself a lot of time and scrapes if she had remained focused and not let her fear blind her. The rock was gauged and chiseled away here, and she wondered about the child before her. A shallow hole appeared here, and, in its depth, she saw the glint of the gem she was looking for. She surmised the hole was created by the last child pulling a piece of the treasure away. She began digging out the rock from around the amethyst. Filling her bucket was only a slight dilemma. The biggest problem was the debris that filled the small tunnel. The rubble piled up around her. The falling debris stung her eyes and choked her, making her breathing difficult in such a small space. She could only make so many trips in and out of the tunnel, and she had to carry out the debris with the quartz. Her skin grew raw, and always the amount of effort for the yield was disproportionate. Everything was mixed in the bucket, and she crawled it out of the hole. The boy waited and pointed, indicating she would dump it onto the ground. This she did, and he moved forward, waving her back into the tunnel.

Crawling on her stomach, her arms and legs grew raw from scraping through the rock and dirt. She tried rolling onto her back, but the whip's lash marks screamed at her.

The boy separated the debris from the quartz and amethyst crystals using a bucket and measuring their efforts. They filled slower than she could ever guess. Hours and hours stacked on top of each other. Finally, the boy changed for another boy, who spoke English but was cruel. It did not matter that she, Edith, and the little boy in the third hole worked for hours. He eagerly laid the whip across their back or legs if they faltered coming out of their tunnels. In Elisabeth's exhausted, pain-filled mind, she knew this new boy was messing with the little boy in the other tunnel. He placed some of the boy's yield in Elisabeth and Edith's buckets.

Elisabeth wanted to say something. She knew it wasn't fair. But she remained silent because she was getting out sooner. Her instinct told her that her treasures would go into another kid's bucket if she protested the injustice. The tunnel became a nightmare of agony. Her flesh was scraped from her bones and was left raw and bleeding. She said nothing.

The boy was still working when Elisabeth crawled from her hole for the last time. Her heart dropped seeing Edith still in her tunnel. She paused, and the boy moved toward her. He was big. He wasn't just one of the taller boys but near the size of a man. His muscles were thickly corded across his chest, arms, and neck. He was an intimidating boy, and his eagerness to use the whip was even more so.

He thrust her against the wall, leaning over her, pinning her with his putrid-smelling body and breath. "I could protect you if you made it worth my while."

"Why do I need your protection?" Her instinct told her not to take anything from this boy though she trembled in fear of his wrath. Something inside her told her she would rather scrape her skin from her bones inside that tunnel.

"I can ensure your bucket is filled the fastest," he said. He used the whip's handle, drawing it down the side of her cheek. "I can't take your maidenhead, but you can pleasure me in other ways." He pressed his groin into her, grinding her hard against the wall.

She grabbed the whip's handle, and for an instant, she thought she might win this battle she had no idea how to wage. But it was only his surprise that gave him pause. He ripped the whip back from her hand and landed blow after blow of the handle on her. She fell, and he continued striking her head, shoulders, back, and legs. Finally, expending his rage, he stepped back. She lay on her side, her knees drawn to her chest, her arms covering her head, and she sobbed. Her body was broken, and the fear of the vicious attack left her paralyzed.

"I can just as easily empty one or all of your buckets into someone else's," he warned. "But I will give you time to think about this. Go back to the barn."

Outside the tunnel, she was given a bowl with grain and salted fish before being taken back to the barn. She could barely walk by the time she started that way. Once there, she curled onto the floor and continued sobbing until she fell into an exhausted sleep.

# Chapter 9

**Wednesday, September 27, 1447, Turza Wilcza, Poland**

The road stretched forever. Adrian missed his bed, hot meals, Ravenshill, and everything that did not involve the road and the back of his horse. The horse was a constant, and meals were not. They stopped, rested the horses, and grabbed a couple hours of sleep before resuming the journey. Day after day.

Adrian's shoulders sat lower, his back not as straight, and his confidence wavered. His eyes trailed from Lincoln's back to the blue lake on his left. It beckoned him to its shores, begged him to slip his feet into its cool water, and lured him to swim in its depths. He paused for a minute, turning toward it slightly. A soft breeze cooled his face, heated by the sun that flamed in the cloudless sky.

Today was a reprieve from the last couple that bit through their clothes with icy fingers. Winter was coming. Adrian exhaled slowly, and a prick behind his eyes warned him his mind should not stray in the direction it suddenly turned. But he could not help himself. Elisabeth was still out there, lost and afraid. He wondered now if she was hungry. When it was cold, he wondered if she was warm. Every minute he felt safe, he knew she was not. And now he sat on his horse, dreaming of swimming in a lake. *How can you forget so fast, you selfish boy? What kind of knight would abandon hope on the side of a lake for his own pleasure?* The pressure behind his eyes eased, and his heartbeat quickened. He was wasting time they did not have.

Adrian turned back to the road, startled by Lincoln watching him. Adrian nudged his horse forward. Her hooves seemed as tired as his soul. He was losing his courage quickly, his hope fleeing even faster.

This journey began with Adrian asking himself who Lincoln was, convincing himself he was not the man he respected. But approaching him now, Adrian knew he respected the knight more. He was the guardian of Ravenshill, the protector of its people. One of those people was gone, and he was doing more than any other knight would do. He turned a blind eye to the innocent lives he took. It was his loyalty to Ravenshill that mattered.

Adrian reached Lincoln, and they sat silently. Lincoln's eyes went to the lake, and Adrian searched his stern face. Adrian did not know how man servants Lincoln to keep the darkness of that night hidden. But, for the servants left to live attested to the knight's trust in them. Lincoln killed those people for Thomas, for Ravenshill. Lincoln made the journey to London for the first time to find a Walter to replace the dead one for Thomas. Lincoln sent Adrian to retrieve the second Walter while he cleaned up another mess for Ravenshill. But Adrian knew this journey was not for Ravenshill. It was not for Thomas. It was for Elisabeth. Ravenshill could stand without the little girl. The Kirkham name would survive with the son. Thomas sent them, but it was for Elisabeth Lincoln continued. For Lord Thomas, Lincoln sent the message letting him know his daughter still lived, and they had to leave English shores to continue. It was for Elisabeth that he did not send the message until the day they sailed from the English port. Far too late for Thomas to order them to abandon hope. Adrian would like to think the baron would not give up on his daughter. But it was a risk Lincoln so obviously did not want to take. For Elisabeth.

"A journey without faith is difficult," Lincoln said, his eyes remaining on the lake. Adrian turned to it. The ripples across its glassy surface heralded the caressing breeze that promised to quench thirst or soul. The lake did not care.

"How can you be sure we'll find her."

Lincoln's gaze returned to Adrian. "I am not sure, Adrian," Lincoln said. Adrian's heart seized in his throat, and his eyes dashed back to him.

Adrian shook his head. Everything in him wanted to scream for Lincoln to take it back. He never wanted to hear that statement from Lincoln. The knight was supposed to always be sure and know what to do and where to lead, and Adrian would follow.

"How can you be sure we will?"

The question took Adrian back. His brows furrowed, and he looked down at his horse's neck. "We have to."

"No, Adrian, we do not have to. We can return to Ravenshill at any time. You can go to Helmsley, or we can embark on a new journey together."

"I am following you."

Lincoln's lips twisted in a grimace. He lifted himself in the saddle, stretching his hips before settling again. "After you learned secrets and saw the side of me I never wished you to see, you still follow. You can return to your father. He will be glad you have severed the tie with Ravenshill. You know this. Yet you have not posed the first question to me. Why?"

Adrian struggled to understand, confused and fearful.

"I have little faith we can find her. I am no more foolish than you. We both know the odds."

Lincoln's words confused Adrien. "Then why did you bring us here? Why did we travel all this way?"

"For the same reason, you did not ask me questions, faith. You had faith in me when we rode from Ravenshill. You had faith I had a plan when we stepped onto that ship. Faith wavers. It grows tired. It wavers for us both the harder and longer this journey grows. When your faith wavers in Him and me," he said with a gesture toward the sky, "have faith in yourself. Faith is in truth. You find faith and strength where you can. If you cannot see His favor in that lake, feel it in the breeze. I understand it is hard to have faith in a god who allowed Elisabeth to be taken in the first place. It is hard not to rage and want to turn your back. Never do that. Find another truth to put your faith in."

"What would that truth be?"

"Your soul will never rest until you know here," he placed his hand over his heart, "she is gone. The truth is you will spend a lifetime regretting not going another mile because you grew tired. So I go, and you follow because we know the truth. We are not yet ready to let her go. From that, we can gain faith He is not ready for us to let her go. Despite what we are taught, He does not control everything. Evil abounded that night. It gave and took, unmindful of God's will. But if you want it, listen to the spark, and as long as it lives, He will let you know beyond a doubt when to push on and when to fall back. See the truth in what will fill your soul. Evil took her, and now He drives us to get her back."

Lincoln turned his horse as the weightlessness, far more powerful than the water of the lake, lifted his shoulders and straightened his back with new resolve. The spark of faith jumped into an inferno. He understood now. He saw the evil that pulled a little boy to his death with his own eyes. It upturned everything and brought more evil. Evil was the truth. It wanted to suck everyone at Ravenshill into a quagmire of bitterness, regret, rage, and sorrow. That was the truth. He could not wait for the divine hand of God to save Elisabeth. If he allowed the seed of darkness into his soul, evil would win, and the truth was he would never see Elisabeth again.

"How do you decide which way to go? Is there something guiding you to these decisions?"

Lincoln laughed as he set his horse to a walk. "Nothing like that. I chose the road I know and traveled in my past."

Further faith lifted Adrian's shoulders. How could he have forgotten? This was the land of the Teutonic Knights. This was the place where Lincoln became a legend.

They arrived at the Polish town of Turza Wilcza. Lincoln left Adrian with the horses several times, searching for someone, but he did not say who. They stopped at a tavern, and Lincoln finally signaled Adrian to join him. They drank ale, listening to the chatter around them. They sat at the bar with Lincoln scanning the small number of patrons scattered about the room. Adrian asked Lincoln who he searched for, but the man only said, "Someone," without explanation.

A woman came to Adrian. She spoke to him, but Adrian did not understand. She trailed a hand down the back of Adrian's neck, and he suppressed a shiver of delight. She said something else, wrapping her hand around the back of his neck. Leaning over him, her voice dropped.

Adrian's gaze sought Lincoln's, but the man stood and moved across the room toward a woman who entered. Nervousness filled Adrian while the woman's breath fanned across his ear. How to tell the whore he had no coin or interest eluded him. Until this journey, he did not feel like a man. But things change. This woman's hands stroked his neck as if she knew the secrets of men. Her warm breath sent a tingling sensation to his crotch, fanning across his ear with her whisper.

Her tongue teased the back of his earlobe. Her hand slid down his neck to his shoulder, draping it across his chest and pinning him to his seat. She rubbed her hand across his chest, and her smallness made him feel more of a man than his twelve years. Her hand moved lower, and by God's mercy, Lincoln returned. He spoke to her and sent her slinking away to lurk nearby.

"This journey and the secrets you honor make you a man," Lincoln grabbed Adrian's hand and slapped coins into his palm. "Your date of birth passed on this journey without celebration." He held to Adrian's wrist and called to the girl. "Go with her now," he said, releasing Adrian. The girl moved their way. "She will make you a man."

With that, Lincoln turned and walked back to the woman who had entered a moment ago, and together they left the tavern. Adrian sat a moment, feeling the weight of the coins. On his hip hung his father's sword. In his heart, he missed his home. Lincoln was correct. He was a man now. His age might still be a little shy, but this journey made him realize his strength and resilience. It made him understand how to be a man. The woman stared at him with heat in her brown eyes, burning him.

Adrian slipped from his seat and walked to the woman. She was older than himself by several years. Her attractiveness included a sultry appeal that oozed from her knowledge of men and what her eyes promised. Speechless, he held his hand with the coins out, palm up. The woman's gaze fixed on them before sliding to Adrian. A feline smile spread across her face. Then she reached out a hand, closed his fingers around his coin, took his arm, and led him from the tavern. She took him to the livery where Adrian and Lincoln had left their horses. She knocked on the door in the back of the livery. It opened, and she motioned for Adrian to give her access to the coin in his hand. He opened his fingers, and she gave the man in the doorway one of the coins. The man said something to her before walking down the livery aisle and leaving the building altogether.

The woman said something and indicated he would precede her into the room. Adrian entered a clean room, a tidy bed in the corner, out of place in the back of the stable. The earthy scent of horse mixed with the sweet odor of wood crackling in the warm hearth. The woman took Adrian's hand and pulled him to the bed. She pressed him down, slipped the coin from his hand, and lay it on the table next to the bed. She then selected one, held it up for him to see, tucked it into her pouch tied at her waist, and began to undress with a smile.

The woman bared herself to him. She was not the first woman he saw naked. He even saw Elisabeth—accidentally. But this woman was not like Elisabeth, just a child. This woman possessed a mature and developed body with plump breasts. She had hips that flared and an ass that made a yearning build he did not understand. Standing naked, she turned for him to see all of her. Unclothed, she walked forward, pulled him from the bed, and began to untie his doublet. As she did so, she began to suckle his neck until a groan escaped him. Baring his chest, her teeth grazed their way down to his abdomen.

When she freed him from his braies, she spoke again before shoving him onto the bed. Once seated, she took him into her mouth. The first orgasm he experienced changed much of his outlook on life. He assumed it might be so for any boy who transitioned to a man in such a way. Then the woman lingered, and after a few moments, she stood, went to the table, picked up another coin, held it for him to see, and slipped it into the pouch lying on the floor. Then she came back to him.

Each coin paid for a different service from the whore that night. Adrian missed an entire night's sleep, but to say he missed it was like saying a prisoner missed the gallows. By the time he stepped into the aisle of the livery, his legs were jelly, but the world seemed different, smaller, and conquerable. Lincoln soon arrived, and they saddled their horses with no words spoken between them. Adrian expected Lincoln to question him, even offer a comment, but the man said no word about the coin or the whore.

**Sunday, October 1, 1447, Turza Wilcza, Poland**

The riders stretched across the road, blocking their path. Adrian knew they were a threat. If Lincoln had been a dog, his hackles would rise, and his lips would pull back in a snarl. Lincoln straightened, took his reins in one hand, and pulled his sword with the other. He accomplished his action with stealth and laid his weapon across his lap. Adrian began to follow suit and draw his sword. What Lincoln said shot terror through him. "Be ready to run." Then he nudged his horse and cast over his shoulder, "Stay back. You do not engage these men. You run." Lincoln walked his horse forward, closing the distance with the men.

Adrian moved closer but kept his horse a few paces behind.

"We have waited a long time for your return," one man said, his accent heavily French.

Another man spoke a language unfamiliar to Adrian. Lincoln turned to the man and responded in kind. The other men laughed, but the man who had spoken scowled.

"Have you been waiting on this road all these years?" Lincoln asked. He leaned forward, an elbow resting on the flat of his sword. By all appearances, the man was bored. However, the amusement in his voice made it clear he baited these men.

The man speaking English frowned and spat in Lincoln's direction. "There are many who wish to see your head off your shoulders."

"You weren't men enough to do it twenty years ago," Lincoln replied. "What makes you think you can do it now?"

The leader smiled. “Because you do not have an army at your flank. Only one boy.”

Adrian’s horse shifted beneath him. So many things in Adrian’s life and training prepared him for battles but did not prepare him for the fear he found in the current situation. Was he to run if Lincoln raised his blade? But then what? What did Lincoln expect him to do after that? And these men did not look like professional fighters. Perhaps farmers, but not soldiers.

“How did you know I had even come?” Lincoln questioned, giving the men his attention again.

“Your favorite whore, of course. I knew you would find her. You spent too much time with her. I knew one day you would be back.” Then the man tsked. “You are such a fool. Whores have no loyalty but to money. All these years, we paid her. She came running to us as soon as you came to her again.” The man smiled. “I did not think it would be this long.” Then he shrugged. “But justice has come to us this day.”

Lincoln laughed. “Justice,” he scoffed. “You wish to murder me.”

“You know about murder more than the rest of us.” The leader began to walk his horse forward, and Lincoln straightened, palming his sword, waiting to lay the first strike.

The leader paused, and despite the superior numbers, Adrian read the uncertainty on his face. He was a big man, stout enough to pull a plow faster than the strongest horses. His eyes were of a dark color Adrian could not discern at a distance. His long, light brown hair faded and greyed with his age. “For sure you do not wish to fight us?”

“For sure,” Lincoln replied. His tone mocked him. “For sure, I wish to kill you.”

Apparent unease settled over the men's faces.

"But I see you are too big of a coward as you were then." Then, with contempt, Lincoln said something in the other language.

Fury raced across the man's face, and he raised his sword with a cry of rage. Lincoln spurred his horse forward with a fury that matched the other man's. The others were moving forward too. Adrian swung his horse, urging it away from the crash of the swords. Adrian raced a short distance back along the road, out of sight. Then he turned his horse around and listened, waiting for pursuers. There were none. His mind returned to the question of what he was to do now.

Lincoln had not spoken much of his time as a Teutonic Knight. He would grow quiet when Adrian asked and put him off for another day. Until those days rolled into months, becoming years. Adrian always sensed something dark happened while Lincoln fought for the Catholic Church.

But what did the man mean by justice? Adrian rode back toward the men, listening carefully. Lincoln knew the encounter would lead to this from the very beginning. Perhaps with Adrian fighting, too, they could have defeated the men. But if Lincoln believed that, he would not have sent Adrian away.

As he returned to find Lincoln, the men were gone. Lincoln was gone. Blood flecked the ground churned beneath horses' hooves. Adrian did not take long to catch up to the group of men. He stayed a distance away, but the men knew he trailed them. Every head turned his way. They turned forward again and continued along their path, seeing him as no threat. They led Lincoln on his horse, hands tied behind his back. Adrian breathed a sigh of relief, seeing he still lived. Justice—the word worried Adrian.

The town came into sight a short time later. Justice? Would he get a trial? The men entered the town, and Adrian spurred his horse faster. People came to gape at the procession surrounding them. The men pulled their horses to a stop outside a large structure. The building rose three stories and felt intimidating as it loomed over them.

Adrian dismounted, tied his horse to a post, and moved into the crowd surrounding the men dragging Lincoln from his horse. Lincoln stumbled but landed on his feet. They pushed him up the steps before turning Lincoln halfway up. The leader said something to the gathered crowd, raising a cheer. Adrian's blood chilled.

After a small speech, the men who gathered with Lincoln on the steps turned him and led him into the structure. The crowd dispersed around Adrian. He stood wondering what he could do in a land alone, unable to understand their language. He paused before advancing. At least two men inside could communicate and tell him what was happening. He climbed the steps, opened the door, and froze. All eyes turned to him.

One set of those eyes was Lincoln's, and he scowled. "What is happening that you have Sir Lincoln prisoner?" Adrian asked with false bravado.

The man who spoke English on the road stepped forward. "You are the boy who ran like a coward," the man taunted.

"I am following the orders given to me by my master," Adrian replied, refusing to let this man see how offended his accusation made him.

The man turned to Lincoln, then swung back to Adrian. "This man led the army that destroyed this land.

He and his men brought hell upon us, and it is time he pays for that."

"He was a Crusader. He fought for the Church," Adrian declared.

"He was known here as Żniwiarza, The Reaper, and he will die for the torture and murder of our people."

"It was war," Adrian declared.

The man stalked forward. Adrian read the anger on his face but refused to give his ground. He would not show himself a coward again. "It was his war, not ours. That was murder. He did not give us a chance to fight."

"I do not understand. What requires justice for a man who passes through your land?" Adrian persisted.

"For sure, if you had been here, you would not dare ask such a question as that." The man turned and moved away, ordering the men holding Lincoln between them.

"You cannot take him," Adrian said, following them with determination.

Lincoln drew to a stop, and the men let him turn to Adrian. "Get yourself home," Lincoln said.

Adrian studied Lincoln.

"But they will kill you," Adrian said.

Lincoln shrugged, and again, Adrian feared the man he put upon the pedestal so long ago might not be the man he thought. He bowed to their call for justice. The only way Lincoln would do such a thing was if he was guilty.

"What of Elisabeth?" Adrian asked. His heart constricted with panic.

"The search for her is over. Get yourself home and forget her and me."

Adrian shook his head. Lincoln turned away and allowed them to lead him through another door. Hysteria threatened to overtake Adrian. Go home? How could he go home? Lincoln vowed they would bring Elisabeth home. But how many months had it been that they searched? Finally, they had a direction, and now he had to stop the search and let Lincoln die? Justice? Would they give him justice if anything could be said for Lincoln's innocence? Adrian knew Lincoln would never acquiesce without a fight if he possessed any.

Several people stared at Adrian. "English?" he asked. *Someone here had to speak it.* "Can someone understand me?" He asked the question again. Desperation filled him.

A woman stepped forward, lay a hand on his forearm, and tugged on him. Lost and afraid, he followed her. She led him through the corridors and up the stairs until she stood before a door she knocked softly at. A voice from inside called out. The woman stepped back and motioned him toward the closed door. Adrian hesitated, realizing the woman had not understood him at all. Perhaps this man who had called out could. He opened the door and stepped inside.

The man said something to him.

Adrian shook his head. "I do not understand."

"You are lucky," the man said in English. "I understand. I am Oskar. What do you need help with?"

Adrian swallowed and took the seat the man offered amidst the stacks of books. The piles made the room look like a shamble filling every surface. The table beside him held books towering over his head. "My master has been arrested for murder. He cannot be guilty. He was a soldier for God."

The middle-aged man studied Adrian for some time. The diminutive man, Oskar, had been wise to turn to scholarly pursuits instead of the blade. He kept his long blonde hair pulled back, snug at the base of his skull. His brown eyes stood out, stark against his pale and gaunt face.

"Crusaders are not friends here," Oskar said. "But to charge one for a murder, I do not understand. Did they give a time frame he was supposed to commit these murders?"

"Sir Lincoln asked the man if he had been waiting twenty years for him to return."

The man nodded after giving this information some thought. "What is his name? The Teutonic Knights caused a great deal of destruction twenty years ago."

"Sir Lincoln Victers."

Oskar was quiet for a moment, his face thoughtful, before shaking his head. "I have never heard of this man."

Adrian swallowed. "One of the men said he was known as The Reaper."

"Żniwiarza," Oskar said, and the tone of his voice chilled Adrian. "Justice would have been if he died in his mother's wound and never breathed air. There is no help for your friend here."

"Is there nothing I can do?" Adrian asked. He hated the way his voice sounded. A sad, lost tone that trembled with each word. It made him sound like the coward the man had accused him of being.

"Pray for a merciful death and leave here before they find you guilty by association."

Adrian left Oskar, but he lingered outside the building. How could he leave Lincoln to face a trial alone? A trial where his guilt was already decided. What if he was guilty? But that had been war, and war was different. There was no murder in war—only war. But the man had said he didn't give them a chance to fight. What did that mean? Did it mean Lincoln's army had outnumbered theirs, cheating them of a fight? That was not murder.

Tomorrow the trial would begin. But Adrian knew it would be quick. Who here would stand for Lincoln? Of course, Adrian would, but he did not bear witness. To make matters worse, as if they could be, he could not even speak the language. Frustrated, Adrian stood outside the tiny structure no bigger than a box. They had moved Lincoln to the confines, and he did not want to leave its sight. Iron bars covered the windows of the thick wood door. One man guarded it and kept Adrian away, along with Lincoln's commands from inside ordering Adrian to go home.

# Chapter 10

**Monday, October 2, 1447, Ural Mountains, Lithuania**

All too soon, her day began again. It was worse on the second day. Her skin was raw, and the scabs tore away to bleed. With her aching body, it seemed to take twice as long to fill her buckets. She did not see the cruel boy, but one of those sent to do his job laid the whip across her twice because she lingered too long before folding herself back inside her tomb.

And so, the days went. Elisabeth's skin grew raw, ripping away and growing infected. Liquid drained from the wounds, drying and caking to be pulled away daily. It was a relief to push the flaming skin into the snow to cool it. But nothing offered any relief. With the cooling of the skin came the bite of the freeze. The chill of the harsh winter was something that never left. Instead, it settled into her bones, as did the fear.

Every waking moment was filled with fear. When she lay down exhausted, she dreamed of her fears. There was no way to free herself and no way to escape. Despite how poorly she was doing, Edith and many others were far weaker. She feared the day she would turn skeletal and pale like them.

Then an illness began sweeping amongst the children, taking the lives the hard work and tunnels did not. Elisabeth woke one morning with her head pounding, unable to draw breath into her aching chest. The men were there, and she stumbled to her feet and shuffled into the cold with Edith helping her across the yard, Elisabeth's arm draped across her shoulder. Then she worked. But her work was slow. Her body ached beyond what the tunnels had created. She knew a fever raged inside her.

It was late into the night before Elisabeth gathered enough quartz. She collapsed inside the barn and felt all the damage done to her body with great intensity. The pain made her feel like writhing on the ground, but she was too exhausted, and her eyes felt as if they blazed with fire in her pale face.

***Sunday, October 23, 1446, Ravenshill***

*"Do you know that you give yourself away?" Elisabeth asked as she entered the stable behind Adrian*

*"What?" he snapped. Elisabeth knew he would be in a foul mood. She had been watching Lincoln take Adrian down repeatedly with the staff. Even though Lincoln was who he was, Adrian still thought he would beat him one day. Not at the age of ten, Elisabeth always wanted to tell him. But she never did because that would not help Adrian's mood.*

*She scowled. "You are the most impatient person I have ever seen. Lincoln knows what you are going to do because your face gives away everything." Elisabeth did not know how often she had seen Lincoln and Adrian sparring, but this was the first time she had noticed*

*Adrian and Lincoln's faces. Lincoln's was empty, not a brow furrowed or lips tightened, but his eyes were continuously shifting with his feet.*

*On the other hand, Adrian's face gave every anticipated move away. His eyes remained on his opponent right before Adrian would move. Then, the instant before he did, his eyes would shift in that direction.*

*"Don't be absurd," Adrian snapped again.*

*She shrugged and began to walk away. She had better things to do than to help someone who thought they did not need it from her. Adrian had started to take on the attitude that chivalry included treating her like she was some kind of idiot. He could bow to her and offer his hand, but that did not mean she needed him to sit her on her horse or ride slower because she would not have to struggle to keep up with his larger horse. He knew she was as capable as he at most anything, and the lines between lord and lady were blurred.*

*"Tell me," he said to stop her.*

*She felt herself smile before she turned and crossed her arms over her chest and waited. "I'm sorry, my lady," he said with a halfhearted bow. Then, when she still did not speak, he bowed in front of her. His bow was deep, mocking. "My sincerest apologies, my lady."*

*"You are so impatient for the next move that some part of you is already moving there before you do."*

*"That's ridiculous." But he stopped her as she began to turn away. "Pray continue."*

*"When you are going to lift your sword, you shift your right foot first and look in the direction you are going to strike."*

*"Show me." He thrust a staff at her. "Please," he said when she did not immediately take the practice weapon. She smirked at him before taking the staff.*

*It did not take her long to prove her point. She first blocked his staff on a downward stroke. The force of his strike reverberated down the staff and stung her palms, but she kept her grip. She stopped an upward thrust because his shoulders warned her it was coming. She whacked him on the back of his legs in that move.*

*"Hey," he said in surprise with an admonishing tone.*

*Elisabeth shrugged and twirled her stick for good measure. "If you do not wish to be a great knight, that is your decision to make."*

*Elisabeth knew his attack was coming because his blue-gray eyes told her. She raised the staff, but Adrian intended to take it from her hands. His weapon snapped against hers, and she was astonished at the power behind his strike. She had seen he was fast, nearly as quick as Lincoln, but she did not know the men struck each other with such force. Her palms stung, and she took two steps back.*

*"Lord Adrian," Presley's rasping voice came to them. They heard the admonishment in it. The man was as old as the stable he worked in if Elisabeth had to guess. The stable was built with the keep centuries before, but his leathered face and snow-white hair showed she could be correct. He was a tall man, and his thinness made him look frail, but she saw how he handled the horses, and he was strong. "A lord does not play staffs with a lady. Return them to the armory. Immediately."*

*Adrian's eyes darted, full of guilt and regret, as he stepped to her and plucked the staff from her hands.*

*"Sorry," he mumbled as Presley began to tell Elisabeth how a lady should not even be spending time in the stable. He told her she was spooking the horses. She guessed it was playing with the staffs near them, but she did not listen to much of what Presley said. He was like some of the others and tried to keep Elisabeth within the keep of Ravenshill, where they thought she belonged. But there was not enough to do inside the small castle to fill her days. There were no day-long preparations to feed a large number of people. She did not have to mend a large family's clothing, nor did she have the cloth and thread to make some.*

*Once Presley excused her, she raced toward the armory.*

*"Go to the Great Forest?" she asked, making it just inside the door as Adrian turned from the wall where he had placed the staffs. He smiled at her, snatched the staffs, and they raced to the place just outside the walls they called the Great Forest because of the make-believe games they would play while in reality, it was a small glade of ash and oak trees.*

*As they stepped beneath the trees with their skeletal arms reaching toward the sky, the leaves crunched underfoot, making a pleasant sound as they rustled. Adrian handed her the staff and patted her on the shoulder to show his gratitude that she continued with him. The breeze brought a threat of winter with its chilling bite. As Elisabeth moved, she was disconcerted that her blowing cloak provided a hindrance, but Adrian was likewise handicapped.*

*They sparred. Sometimes their staff's tips would end up tangled in each other or their own cloaks. Once Adrian's staff tangled in her hair, she hit him twice as payback once he freed it. By the time the dinner bell rang, Elisabeth was exhausted. Her hands had grown numb, leaving her grateful for the bell's loud peal on the wall that once rang to bring many from afar. The children knew it rang just for them now.*

*Elisabeth felt her face flush from the exhilaration of the battle with Adrian. She knew she had proved two points to Adrian. First, she was correct, and he gave himself away. The second was that she was perfectly capable of doing things and knowing things Adrian did. Despite the exhaustion, she felt a spring in her step. Her shoulders felt straighter as she and Adrian returned to the keep. Elisabeth lingered outside the armory, feeling the breeze blowing across her heated face through the open gates. She held her hands out so the cool breeze could provide some comfort.*

*She heard Adrian step out of the armory and saw her standing there. He paused briefly before asking, "What are you doing?"*

*"It feels good," she said, not moving from her position with her head thrown back and her arms spread from her body.*

*"You are a strange individual," Adrian scoffed.*

*"You judge me when you have not even seen what I speak of?" then Elisabeth tsked at him, "Does not sound like the actions of a fair knight."*

*She heard a sigh explode from Adrian, and a smile crept across her face. She fought it because the breeze felt better with it relaxed.*

*"What?" he asked, impatient.*

*She glanced from the corner of her eye. "For one, you must let the breeze caress your palms. Then you must tilt your head to feel it against your throat and relax your face."*

*Elisabeth closed her eyes again, and within a minute, she heard Adrian's grunt, which told her he appreciated the sensation. They stood a moment longer before Lincoln snapped at them from the hall's doorway. Giggling, Elisabeth and Adrian ran into the hall with the smells of meats, bread, and vegetables permeating the space. Her mouth watered, and her stomach grumbled as she took her seat.*

*The hall seemed to glow. Its walls were bathed in the late evening light, making the rocks glow red. Never before had she seen it so vibrant, so alive. It made love bite at her heart for this place of her birth. It was Ravenshill. It was splendid as she looked around at the high ceiling of old wooden rafters. The roof was two floors high. Great windows lined each side of the upper level, opening to the hall below. These windows looked into an abyss in the wall that glowed red. A haunting yet content feeling filled her. The only memory of her mother was upon the upper walkway. Her mother was looking down on her from one of the portals above. Elisabeth had no idea how old she was. It was before she was four, before Walter was born.*

*Something about Ravenshill in her dream seemed more intense, the sights, smells, food, tables, voices, and laughter of those few who gathered. It was warm within the safety of its walls as if Ravenshill needed no hearths because it lived and breathed for them. As long as its walls stood, the Kirkham family would stand.*

**Monday, October 2, 1447, Ural Mountains, Lithuania**

She did not know how she made it to the barn. She knew nothing for two days until her fever abated. She remembered Edith caring for her, at least bringing her water and using the corner of a blanket to wipe it across her brow to fight the fever. As Elisabeth lay on the cold dirt floor, she could not help but think Edith's mother must have done the same for her.

Once Elisabeth could move again, the men forced her to the tunnels when she wanted nothing more than to rest and recover some strength. Edith helped her across the yard, and they worked. The work never stopped. If the guards suspected she could dig during those two days, they would have dragged her to the tunnels. She felt she did not fully recover from the illness, but Elisabeth did not know how to judge such a thing. Her health, along with every child here, was failing. So many died of the same thing that had struck Elisabeth. But she survived because she had Edith to care for her and about her.

**Monday, October 2, 1447, Turza Wilcza, Poland**

"You are persistent," Oskar said as he climbed the steps to the three-story building the following morning. "Why are you here, boy?"

"They are to try Sir Lincoln today. I cannot help him if I do not speak the language."

Oskar sighed and turned. "I tell you, there is no help for the bastard. Has he told you what occurred those years ago?"

Adrian shook his head. The man advanced on him and turned him so he faced out onto the street. "Do you see that building there next to the bakery? Go knock on the door. If that man wishes to help, bring him to me."

Adrian took two tentative steps down the street. "Who is he?" he asked.

"He is Howard, your master's squire." The world tilted. It did not make sense. Why was Lincoln's old squire here, and why would he choose not to help Lincoln? Squires had a duty to their knights. What had happened here? He swallowed the lump of fear in his throat before darting for the small structure. He did not mean to bang on the door, but his heart pounded, knowing he was running out of time.

The man who opened the door did not look as he thought a knight should. Indeed, Howard appeared a little crazed with wild eyes when he opened the flimsy door. He said something in Polish, but Adrian recognized his English accent.

"I need your help," Adrian said, hoping to push past the man.

But the man was not welcoming and placed an arm on the door frame as a barrier. "It is a matter of life and death," Adrian said, attempting again to enter the man's structure. What Adrian did not expect from the small man was for Howard to grab his arm, turn him and, with his foot, take Adrian's legs from beneath him. Then Howard was on top of Adrian's back as the younger squire sprawled flat on his stomach. Then Howard pulled Adrian's arm back. He refused to cry out against the pain.

"The last people who wanted my help and spoke English left me to die. I do not wish to help you."

"They have Sir Lincoln," Adrian said between clenched teeth because the man was not easing the twisting of his arm. But with those words, Howard let him go and sprang to his feet.

Adrian rolled onto his back, sitting up and looking at the man. Howard had dismissed him and was staring toward the building Adrian had just come from. He realized the man was missing his right hand. He was staring at the stump when he felt Howard's steely eyes on him. "Why are you still here?"

"You have to help me," Adrian persisted.

"I don't help the English," Howard spat and turned to go back inside. Adrian scrambled, lurching forward and launching himself into the door frame as the man tried to shut the door. Adrian rolled over the threshold and came to rest in the room's darkness. That was all it was, one room lit by one window. The air was stagnant with the heat of the hearth trapped inside the small structure.

"Please," Adrian said, climbing to his feet. "They will kill him."

"Good," Howard said, turning from Adrian and going to the rickety chair sitting next to the rumpled bed. It appeared to be the only furniture in the room save a leaning table next to the chair with a candle close to extinguishing itself. It seemed as if the candle had not been lit in many months. It was covered in dust, as everything in the room was. At the foot of the bed was a small chest.

Adrian went to the chest and sat on it. To Howard, it indicated he would not leave. "I am Baron Adrian de Ros of Stokesley, squire sworn to Sir Lincoln. At least tell me why they want him dead." Adrian was aware of the plea that sounded in his voice, but he was beyond caring.

Howard scowled at him, studying him before giving a slight nod. "He was to lead an army to take back control of the Vistula. The Order was supposed to take control of three rivers they held a century ago." The man's voice was bitter as he spoke.

When the confusion must have registered on Adrian's face, Howard sighed. "The Order of Teutonic Knights lost the war with Poland and signed a treaty in 1422. But the Knights did not wish to let the matter rest. They grew desperate because they suffered economically from the wars they fought and the ground lost. So, the leaders decided they would take the rivers

Neman, Vistula, and Daugava. The Order once controlled them all and the trade vessels that traversed their waters."

"They?" Adrian asked. When Howard looked at him, Adrian said. "You keep saying they. Why?"

"Because I was not a part of the Order. The Order's numbers had fallen with the wars and defeats, and recruiting had become difficult. So, they had to turn to mercenaries, and that is when I joined Lincoln."

"I thought Lincoln was a knight of the Order."

"He was, but after they promised him, he would rise within their ranks. Lincoln was not Sir Lincoln then. He was a foot soldier along with me. But they promised him glory, so he stayed, and I thought we were friends, so I stayed. He proved himself formidable, and he did become a high-ranking knight. So high he was to lead the army to take over Vistula River at sixteen." Howard laughed at that. "We knew nothing. Nothing that we thought we did. They recruited us with the idealism of chivalry and honor. The Order's motto had been 'Help, Defend, Heal,' but that was when they protected Christians on pilgrimage to the Holy Land. That is not what the Order was 20 years ago. Then they wanted power back. I will give Lincoln one allowance. Because we were not from Poland. We did not know what we were against."

"We took the castle of Gdańsk. We did not know what had happened there a hundred years before. How could we? The Knights slaughtered the people there when they took control of the castle. We took the castle back as you expect we would, with battle and bloodshed, then we began moving south. Lincoln heard an army was mustering in Plock, so we prepared to meet them there. But the information was false, and there was no army. I will give Lincoln another allowance. He had been betrayed and was yet to realize this. We followed what we thought was the army here to Turza Wilcza. However, what we followed were supply wagons carrying cargo from the river. When the people of Turza heard of the army coming, they gathered. I was taken hostage in the battle, but Lincoln was to hold the river at all costs. The cost was me because he would not relent, not even when they took my hand. He thought he was fighting the army coming to push us away from the river. So, he did not stop the slaughter. Whether that was what he should have done, who is to say. We were once friends, and he left me here to die. He may have thought me dead. I do not know. But the army was gone when I awoke in a strange bed. I lived, but I had no desire to go home or do anything."

"I guess the dead got their revenge in a way. Of the three commanders sent to take the rivers, Lincoln was successful. The slaughter did bring forth a Polish army, and most of Lincoln's army was wiped out. Lincoln was taken prisoner for some time and was to be tried, but somehow, he escaped his justice."

"Why do you say justice? He was fighting a war," Adrian persisted.

"No, he did not fight a war. He fought a small contingent of armed men, and then his bloodlust and the rest of his army turned on the innocent. Legend says blood ran in the streets, and it is the truth. Lincoln's place in the Order lasted throughout the campaign and his defeat. But his actions were sufficient to be called a hero in his homeland but the Reaper here."

"Sir Lincoln would never let that happen to the innocent, as you say. On the contrary, he is a chivalrous knight of the highest standing."

Howard guffawed and leaned toward Adrian. "He not only let that happen, but he led it. He was the first to cut down a villager. I still remember I was standing at his side. Some of the villagers had come to care for their wounded men. One of them ran at her fallen loved one at Lincoln's feet. He ran her through as she was throwing herself down next to him. She died before her husband. With that one action, the army fell on them. They didn't stand a chance."

"No," Adrian said, shaking his head. "I do not believe what you say."

Howard shrugged. "That is your choice, but it is the truth."

"Who betrayed him?"

"Who's to say," the man said as he jumped to his feet. "I have wasted enough time with the memory of that man." Howard stood over Adrian now. Adrian felt cold inside. How could Lincoln do such things and then leave his squire behind? Allow him to lose a hand just to hold the river.

"But they are trying him now," Adrian insisted, even drawing back when Howard reached for him. But Adrian was not here to fight a battle with the former squire. He had to save Lincoln, and he would not find help here. So, Adrian stood and fled back to Oskar. He exploded into the corridor of the second floor to see Lincoln surrounded by men. They all paused at the intrusion.

"Why are you still here?" Lincoln asked with hesitation edging his voice.

"I am here to help you."

“No, Young Adrian,” Lincoln said, and his voice sounded desolate. “You cannot help me. Go home.”

Adrian scowled at his knight and then turned to Oskar as Lincoln was led into the room filled with people. He heard the murmurs as the door closed behind them.

“He was betrayed,” Adrian said.

Oskar looked at him, confused.

“Lincoln was betrayed. That was why he led his army here, to begin with.”

“That does not matter. It does not change his actions.”

“But he was just a child leading an army. He was only sixteen.”

“And how old are you?”

“I am twelve.”

“We are to dismiss the slaughter of our people because you say he was a child? That boy was old enough to marry, father children, and lead an army. I fear you would love to lead an army at the tender age of twelve to free your master. But that my boy would be as foolish as him butchering the innocent,” Oskar said.

“He was only here because someone told him he was to face an army, but you did not have an army. That is what he thought he found.”

“As he said, let it go, Young Adrian, and go home.” Oskar turned from him then and entered the room.

Adrian stood staring at the closed door before him, knowing they were trying the man, and he knew what the verdict would be. Adrian turned and fled back down the stairs and out the door. Reaching Howard’s hut, he burst in, but the man was not there. The room stood empty. Adrian almost left the room, but his eyes landed on the chest at the foot of the bed. He looked around himself, knowing what he was about to do was wrong, he did not understand what he even looked for, but he had to find something.

As soon as he opened the chest, he saw the white cloak with the black crosses adorning it. Beneath that was the man's tunic with the black cross on a white background. Just the day before, he would have touched the Order's uniform with reverence, but now he shoved it aside, feeling as if it was tainted, at least his idea of it was. Other items were held in the trunk, but the most interesting was the gold coins that lay deep in the bottom of the chest, along with some jewels and silver. He was staring at this when the door opened again. Howard stood in the doorway, looking nothing like the man who would have such treasures.

"What are you doing here?" Howard demanded.

The man came at him fast, but Adrian had already fought with him once and was prepared to defend himself better. He drew his sword, placed it at Howard's throat, and brought him up short. "You're a thief," Adrian surmised.

Howard scowled. Adrian walked forward, guiding the old squire from the door and pushing him further into the room. Until Adrian stood as a barrier between Howard and the door.

"What else do you expect me to do?"

Adrian felt confused. The man could have gone home. Howard could still provide an honest living for himself despite not having a hand. "Why did you never go home?"

"I told you," Howard growled. "I didn't want to."

Adrian studied him, and he began to see a contradiction before him. "Why is that?" Adrian asked him.

"I did not want to," the man persisted.

"Why?" Adrian pressed on with the question and pushed Howard against the wall with the tip of his sword.

"I did not want to," the man said again, angrier.

"I think I know why," Adrian said. "You didn't go home because you knew Lincoln would find you. You knew he would find you because you are the one who betrayed him."

"You do not know," Howard said as he tried to shove the sword away.

Adrian refused to yield, and the old squire received a cut across his hand for his efforts. "Why did you betray him?"

"Get out of my house," Howard roared, and he ducked beneath the sword, dodging the slice and aiming for Adrian's legs. But Adrian knew the move well, stepped to the side, and brought the pommel down on the back of Howard's neck. He dropped heavy and limp on the floor.

Adrian studied the man a moment. Not sure what to do now. Yes, he was confident Lincoln's squire had betrayed him and got the army to attack the villagers. Still, he did not know why and did not think the people in that room, deciding Lincoln's fate, would care. But Adrian surmised he had to try.

He tied Howard's arms behind his back, using his elbows to hold the bindings since he lacked a wrist. The only liquid he saw in the house was the chamber pot. Adrian dumped the contents over the man's head, which brought him up, sputtering and glaring. He plucked the man off the floor, avoiding touching the wet spots of Howard's clothing, and pulled him from the hut. Howard was still addled until Adrian thrust the court door open and pushed him inside. All eyes turned to them, then Lincoln shot to his feet.

"You!" Lincoln barked. He shoved one of the guards away as he advanced like a bull through those gathered. Men tried to stop him, but Lincoln was intent on the prey in Adrian's hands. He seized his old squire by the lapel of his ragged tunic and dragged him close to his face, ignoring the stench of piss. "Why are you still alive?"

Lincoln was not relieved to see his old squire but furious. Howard was terrified as he looked up into the knight's face. "Tell me, why do you still live?" Lincoln shook Howard with a violence that left the smaller man addled further.

Men had come to separate them, but once done, they stepped back to watch the unfolding of what happened next. "Tell them what happened," Adrian demanded of Lincoln.

"Go home, Young Adrian," Lincoln bellowed at him.

Adrian drew his dagger and placed it at Howard's throat, oblivious that the man's pee was now soaking into his own clothes. Then Adrian's eyes fell on Oskar.

"This is the man who betrayed Sir Lincoln, so he would lead his army here. I do not know why, but he is the one."

Adrian was aware his body was shaking. He had never held a knife to a man's throat before. He had never killed a man, but he felt confident he could kill this one. He shoved Howard forward, who fell on his knees in front of Lincoln. The squire looked up at the knight's scowling face, and then fresh urine darkened Howard's tunic. The men surrounding the three stepped back. Howard's fear had given them pause.

"This man told me his hand was cut from him to stop Sir Lincoln's army. Is this true?" Adrian asked.

"For sure, he lies," one of the men who had captured Lincoln said, pushing his way forward. "Howard lost his hand because he was stealing Rafal's chickens. He was caught stealing before."

"If he is a thief and part of the army that butchered you people, why is he alive?" Lincoln asked. Adrian heard the angry bite of his words. It was cold as ice, and its edge was sharp.

All eyes turned to the man who had captured Lincoln. "Corvin is the one who gave mercy to Howard after the fact."

"For sure," the man with the heavy French accent said. "Howard said he tried to stop The Reaper. He had an injury he said he did not receive in the battle but from their commander when he tried to stop the carnage."

Lincoln stood, glaring at the man still on his knees. "Is this the truth, Lincoln?" Adrian asked. When Lincoln said nothing, Adrian stepped closer. "Tell these people what happened," Adrian ground out to him, looking up at the man. For the first time, he did not feel the respect mixed with the awe and fear he always felt when looking upon the great knight. Instead, Adrian felt desperation tightening his chest, making it ache. "If not to save yourself but to save Elisabeth. You know she is lost without you."

Lincoln's eyes fell on Adrian, then on Corvin. "Please, Lincoln, for Elisabeth." The boy felt himself shaking. It was the end of his hope and respect for Lincoln if he did not speak.

When Lincoln spoke, it was Polish, so Adrian could not understand, but Oskar stepped closer and interpreted the words in a low tone. Lincoln sent him a scathing look.

"I am guilty of leading that army here. I am guilty of so many things that created the man I am. I know now what dozens of wagon tracks look like compared to an army. Today, I know when I have been lied to and when a snake lurks. As I have been lied to, so have you. Squire Howard told me the scouts had spotted an army, so I was prepared to fight an army."

Lincoln paused a moment. "I was not prepared for half my army to turn on me when we reached your garrison. His lies were a trap for me that half the mercenaries at my back laid in place. I reached your garrison alone because the men I thought were at my back were fighting each other."

Then Lincoln was looking at Adrian. "To say it was a horrendous battle would not give all those deaths justice. I killed the innocent, but my men and I did not know who were friends or enemies. Howard and his men hid among the villagers. We couldn't stop. We were flanked on all sides. In the terror of that instance, the question of friend or foe in the heat of battle is not easily answered. I know I killed friends. I knew then, but we did not have time to ask. None of us did. That is what I am guilty of."

Adrian wrapped his fist around his dagger, then raised it and slammed it into the old squire's jaw. The man staggered a minute. "Why would you do such a thing?" Adrian asked him. Rage filled the boy with an incredible intensity that made him quake. This was not the chivalry of squires and knights. Many lessons slammed into Adrian at that moment. The biggest was the faint line between right and wrong, and he worried it was not as clear for a knight as Adrian believed a short time ago.

Howard looked at Lincoln without speaking, so Adrian hit him again. It was the first blood he ever drew that was not an accident at practice. He saw as he drew his fist away from the punch that it had opened a small cut across Howard's cheekbone. "Why?" Adrian demanded again.

Howard looked to the men surrounding him instead of answering, so Adrian hit him twice more. Howard weaved a little on his knees afterward. "Tell me," Adrian demanded in a voice that did not sound as weak as a twelve-year-old boy who was scared out of his wits. The story Lincoln told did not pardon him at all. As a matter of fact, he had admitted to killing the innocent.

The squire turned his head, looked at Adrian, then spit the bloody fluid from his mouth at Adrian's face. It fell short, but Adrian did not hesitate to land several blows to Howard that drove him to the floor, with Adrian following. Finally, someone grabbed Adrian's arms and pulled him off. His hand hurt and his knuckles split open, but it was nothing to what Howard's face looked like, and Adrian was not remorseful.

One of the men said something to Howard as he groaned on the floor. When he said nothing, the man kicked him.

"He was a foot soldier," Howard said before the boot could strike him in the ribs again. "I should have been knighted to lead that army, not Lincoln. He was a peasant. I, at least, came from good stock. If my father's title was not taken, I would have been a true knight, not reduced to some mercenary to serve a peasant." Adrian could hear the contempt dripping from Howard's voice.

"You were a foolish boy to not see this man's hate for you," the Frenchman said. "For sure, I do not understand why you protected him when you were captured at Wloclawek."

"Because I did injure Howard in the battle, but I did not have a chance to finish the job. But I swore to him I would one day. If I told my story, I would not get to kill him myself. I never found him, so I assumed he died after all." Lincoln's eyes were cold, and his hard-to-read face was now a kaleidoscope of fury as he looked at the man lying on the floor.

"I demand he dies for his part next to me," Lincoln said, having switched back to Polish. "I ask humbly that I see his death before mine so that maybe my soul can rest." Oskar translated to Adrian. Lincoln glared at Oskar.

Howard tried to jump to his feet, but men grabbed him, and orders were called out.

"They are arresting Howard, they will make their judgment soon, but you must leave the room," Oskar informed Adrian.

Adrian felt as if he was sweating, and he shook his head. The man lay a hand on his arm. "I will come for you," Oskar assured him, and for the first time, Adrian felt as if he was not alone.

It did not take long before Adrian was called back into the room. Oskar stood beside him and spoke every word to Adrian that the judge said to the room. "Sir Lincoln Victers is charged with the deaths of 52 women and children. Because of what was learned here today, he will no longer be charged with their murders, but he is still responsible. Howard is charged with the murder of those fifty-two. He will be executed by beheading to be carried out in the square." The room waited as the guards suppressed Howard's heated words.

"Because Sir Lincoln's actions were guided by deceit, and thus his punishment, it will be Sir Lincoln's sword that will take Howard's head." The man began screaming and was dragged from the room before the judgment could continue.

"For every life lost, Sir Lincoln will receive one lash of the whip to be carried out after Howard's execution. Then, once his punishment is carried out, Sir Lincoln will be free to go. This will be done immediately to end this ugly affair."

Adrian felt cold from his head to his toes. He had never seen a whip laid across a man, but could Lincoln survive 52 lashes? He had seen the unfortunate horse of a cloth peddler that had had the lash laid across him so hard that he carried the scars. Could a human survive that? The entire room began to shift, and Oskar pulled Adrian along. Howard was already on his knees when the crowd converged on the square. The walls of the buildings pressed in on them from all sides. Adrian always imagined if he witnessed a beheading, it would happen upon the gallows, some distance away. It was apparent this was not something that ever occurred in the town. There was no permanent place for capital punishment. Lincoln was pushed forward, and someone handed him the sword taken from him when the men had first subdued him on the road. He took the belt and placed it carefully about his waist before pulling the sword. Lincoln studied it for a moment. Turned his stance so that he had the full swing of his arms, then, with no further hesitation, he took Howard's head from his shoulders. He slipped the sword back into its sheath and then nodded to his jailers.

They gave him the dignity of walking under his own power to the post they indicated. Lincoln began removing his shirt as Adrian walked to stand before him. But he did not know what to say. What if Lincoln did not survive? What choice did he have? So Adrian said nothing as they retied his hands to the post. He winced at the tightness, but no one but Adrian watched the man with such intensity. Before the first strike landed, Lincoln looked at Adrian, straightening a little against the post, and gave him a slight nod that told Adrian all would be well. Adrian did not feel it would be so.

The first crack of the whip was like thunder, and the lightning raked across Lincoln's back. Despite the pain, he kept his eyes trained on Adrian. A man next to the one wielding the whip counted out each strike. By the fifteenth, a groan of pain escaped with each strike—by the twenty-fifth, it was a whimper. When the fifty-second strike landed, Lincoln was unconscious. Someone stuffed Lincoln's tunic into Adrian's hands, leaving them there. Howard's body was taken away at some point and those who gathered to witness the punishments lost interest. Adrian did not know what to do, and as he stood looking at his knight suspended on the post, he began to cry. He fought it. He was supposed to be a man. He had taken his first woman and saved Sir Lincoln. He was a man now who was not supposed to cry. But seeing Lincoln as he was and knowing what had led up to it, what Lincoln had already suffered here once, it did not seem right. Adrian was glad Lincoln's sword hung from his hips now. It seemed fitting that a warrior like him had his sword if he died.

Adrian tried to show Lincoln his strong, brave side. Still, as Lincoln's eyes began to flutter open,

Adrian knew he could not stop the tears that flowed harder from relief. Lincoln's head rested against the post, and Adrian watched him struggling to get his legs beneath him. He had to clear his throat once before the words came in a croak, "Untie me."

Adrian did not hesitate, pulling his dagger and slicing through the ropes holding Lincoln. He felt Lincoln shaking from the effort and saw the strain and pain written across his face as he tried to stand with his own strength.

"Get the horses," Lincoln said as he leaned his weight on the post.

Adrian didn't want to release his hand. It did not seem like he could stand alone, even if a post held him up. "But..." Adrian began to protest.

"For Elisabeth," Lincoln said as his eyes fluttered. "We must go now."

Perhaps those were the only words Lincoln could say to him that would make Adrian release his hands and flee for the horses. As he ran, his mind took up the beat of his feet. *We're coming for you, Elisabeth.*

# Chapter 12

**Tuesday, November 28, 1447, Ural Mountains, Lithuania**

One evening, long after Elisabeth returned from the tunnels, she lay awake waiting for Edith. Finally, long into the morning hours, Edith stumbled into the barn. Few words were ever spoken in the barn. All the children lived in a constant state of exhaustion, and if that did not keep them quiet, the fear did. As Edith lay down beside Elisabeth with great care of her battered body, she began crying. Elisabeth wrapped her arms around her as best she could, trying not to cause undue pain on flesh forever raw.

"He's taking my stones," she whispered to Elisabeth. "I filled my buckets two times over." Edith cried until she fell asleep.

They came for Edith before Elisabeth. But Elisabeth went in her place. The cruel boy was unhappy because he knew he was close to breaking Edith for his lecherous demands. So today, Elisabeth paid Edith's price, and each bucket she filled outside her tunnel would be lighter when she returned with the next.

The guards were aware Elisabeth had taken Edith's place. They, too, were aware this was a part of the cruel boy's attempt to get what he wanted. But they were all slaves. As long as the boy played the Master's game wisely, how he chose to punish the slaves was his business. Master, however, saw things differently. When he heard of Elisabeth's sacrifice, he was waiting when she dragged herself back to the barn.

She came up short as she stumbled inside, seeing the man there. It had been days since she last saw him.

"My lady," he said, offering her a bow. The hair on the back of her neck bristled, and she began to shake. He straightened and strolled to her. "You are such a mite," he said. He reached for her chin and forced her face to look up at him. She learned her lessons and never looked any of the men in the eyes. "Do you know what is lower than a slave?"

She did not pretend to want to answer that.

"A female slave." His cold fingers bit into her. "You are property. They are property," he said, pointing to the children in the stall. "Property has no opinions, nor does it have a concern for other property. You weaken yourself with your actions. By doing so, you take from me." He released her chin and then backhanded her.

She fell with a grunt and gasp.

"Both will go to the tunnels and give me six buckets. I will not have you thinking you are something more than property."

The other children woke and now sat staring at the exchange. Edith sat amongst them, shaking her head with tears in her eyes. She did not ask Elisabeth for her sacrifice, and now she, too, was being punished.

Elisabeth did not know how long it took them to gather six buckets of precious rock. She went well beyond exhaustion. The boys who came took some pity on them and only beat their exhausted, broken bodies with the whip handle instead of opening more of their skin and making them bleed. That was the most mercy Elisabeth had seen since arriving. The realization shattered her. And that she was grateful for it made the pieces so much smaller that they would be impossible to gather back together.

Then Elisabeth came from her tunnel with her bucket to find her six buckets were filled. Edith's had been emptied, and there stood the cruel boy, smiling a most satisfied smile as she looked at Edith's empty buckets.

"Go on with you now, back to the barn," he said.

Feeling exhausted, Elisabeth went to her bucket and picked up the first one. She felt numb, aware of the folly she was making. But she could not stop herself as she could not stop the life that whirled about her but was stagnant at the same time. Her arms were raw, her hands even more so. She had to muster her strength to carry the bucket. Her mind cried, but her heart was furious and moved her feet. She sat her full bucket with Edith's, taking one of Edith's empty ones back to her tunnel. As she lowered herself to begin her crawl, she heard the tails of the whip coming through the air toward her, but she did not care. Elisabeth could not leave Edith to the cruel boy. She braced as it fell across her shoulders, raking down her back. Elisabeth screamed. She did not think she would be able to feel so much of the whip's bite through her exhaustion, but she was wrong. The tails ripped open flesh that had already been opened. It raked across the skin made raw by the floor of the tunnels.

Elisabeth still held the empty bucket in her hand and swung with it, striking the cruel boy in the head. He was not used to attacks and dropped the whip, falling backward. She grabbed the lost whip and advanced on him. She struck him repeatedly until the small, frightened voice behind her gave her pause.

"What have you done?"

Elisabeth looked down at the boy. He held his arms over his head to give his face protection, but his forearms had been lashed raw by his own whip. Blood covered both of them.

"Get to the barn, both of you," he screamed at them.

Elisabeth dropped the whip, and Edith, sobs flowing, took Elisabeth's hand and led her back to the barn. Elisabeth was healthy when she was brought here. But she was no longer, and she knew a punishment was coming, and she feared the unknown. How big was her offense? Edith, who knew a little more about these things, told her it could be her death.

It was evening before Master filled the door. He allowed his eyes to adjust to the gloom of the barn before advancing. Two other severe-looking men flanked him.

"Those two," he said, pointing to Elisabeth and Edith.

The men did not call them out but entered the pen with exhausted and terrified children scrambling from their path. Elisabeth stood. She was shaking from her failing body and her rising fear. But she held her ground while Edith tried to dash from one of the men's reaching grasp. It was a half-hearted attempt both girls knew was futile. One of the guards had Edith by the arm, and her sobs were terrifying. Elisabeth followed them out of the barn to stand in front of Master.

She felt close to breaking as she stared at the man's boots. The snow fell in a light and steady shower of large flakes, and the wind whipped across the land. There was a time such a wintery landscape would appeal to Elisabeth. She remembered watching many a snowstorm pass over the walls of Ravenshill. How beautiful and fresh the air felt. Here, this winter was nothing like those. At least in the tunnels, there were no cracks for the wind to whip through. The warmth of the lanterns did not escape into the open space of the barn. Here there was no protection from it, and her tattered dress was no longer any source of warmth.

Master waited on Elisabeth to raise her eyes to him. She had already learned she was not to look any of the men in the eyes. She was hit or kicked each time she did because they were more than she was. An easy matter because she was nothing, and she felt like nothing as she stood before the waiting man. But she knew what he wanted and feared what he would do when she complied. She stood quaking, doing her best not to sob with fear. Slowly she raised her eyes to meet his. He smirked.

"You constantly disappoint slave," he sneered at her. "I have had grown men who have not fought their place as much as you. I would kill you for what you have done, but the bidding has begun on your virtue. An enslaved noble is quite lucrative when bartering such a thing." He studied her, letting that sink in. Then he backhanded her. She felt the blow knock her sideways, and she stumbled, going down hard. Then Master crouched over her, flipping her to her stomach and placing his knees on her back. The pressure made her scream. "Quiet," he ordered her.

She fell silent as she looked at Edith lying on the ground in the same manner. One of the men stood over her, knife in hand.

"Sometimes, my lady," Master mocked. "The peasants must take the punishment." He paused before his order split across the frozen ground. "Take her tongue."

"No!" Elisabeth ordered, but Master's knees bit into her back, cutting the demand short. Her spine felt as if it shattered with her struggles.

As the men bent over Edith, the one on her back held her hair tight in one hand, forcing her head back while his knee brought out her scream. Elisabeth tried to turn her head away, but Master took a handful of her hair and twisted her head back around.

"You will watch your punishment."

Tears streamed, and she inhaled the frigid snow beneath her as Edith's screams rolled across the ground. Then those screams ended, and she heard Edith gagging before the girl fell silent.

"It is done," the men said, straightening.

Master rose from Elisabeth, but she could not move.

"You will still learn your place, slave," the man declared. "Until she heals, you will bring me eight buckets. If she does not heal, you will bring me eight until your time to make me a rich man." The words were ominous as the men turned and walked away.

Elisabeth lay on the ground sobbing, waiting for Edith to move, but the other girl did not. Finally, Elisabeth rose. Her aches and hunger were forgotten as she approached her friend. She crouched beside her, pulling her filthy and matted red hair back from her face. Blood oozed from her mouth, but the girl still breathed. Elisabeth tried to wake her, but she remained still. Elisabeth couldn't move her alone, and left in the snow, Edith would freeze to death. Elisabeth went to the barn. There was no help because they had already learned what she was finding difficult. They were only property, and property did not matter, not even to each other.

Edith and Elisabeth now had threadbare and filthy blankets, claiming those of the children who had died. Now, there were more than enough blankets. She took one of these to the yard and rolled Edith's still body onto it. Then she began to drag her toward the barn. Elisabeth sobbed and dug her feet into the frozen soil beneath the deepening snow as she worked backward. She had no strength left to do what she was doing. Food came after leaving the tunnel with their quotas for the day. Elisabeth could not remember a time she was not hungry, a time she had what her body needed. Even now, her stomach bit at her with hunger. The girl had not eaten because Elisabeth had taken her place in the tunnels, and Elisabeth knew no food would come to the barn unless she brought it herself. To feed Edith, Elisabeth would have to share her own food. That thought made her think about leaving Edith in the snow. But she knew she could not survive it. It would be merciful to leave her to freeze to death while she was unaware it was happening. She cried as her morals fought with her will to survive.

Elisabeth stumbled to her knees and sat on them. The pain was diminished by desperate exhaustion as her tears fell onto the blanket, mixing with Edith's blood as the nasty, smelling cloth absorbed both. When finally, she pulled Edith unconscious into the stall. She fell beside her and did not move for some time. Then one of the men roused her, and her day to gather eight buckets began.

To say Elisabeth suffered was giving a new definition to the word. The girl had not known what it was to suffer until she dug for two, ate for half, and prayed for her friend in between. Master warned her not to let Edith die, or Elisabeth would have to do the work of two until she was sold. Until she was sold as a whore. He found joy in telling her it would only end when her death came. Because that was how it was with slaves.

Then one day, Edith was sitting up on her own. Elisabeth could no longer move without her starving and exhausted muscles shaking. Weakness prevailed, and she had been able to do little to keep her friend from meeting the same fate. The food was not enough for one, let alone two. More than a month passed with Edith recovering, and each time Elisabeth stumbled back to the barn, she collapsed in tears that had long since dried. The crying took too much energy, so she lay tearless, letting her soul cry and rage for her.

One day, Elisabeth dragged herself into the barn and gave little notice to Edith propped against one of the stall's posts. Elisabeth crossed to her, dropped the dried fish in her hand, and lay beside her. Immediately the other girl's arms were around her. They were nothing but bones. Their ribs dug into one another, and their pelvises jutted. They had little body heat between them, but together they slept until the men came for Elisabeth again.

Two more days passed before Edith stood when the men came for Elisabeth. She did not know if Edith was strong enough for the work, but she would have only four buckets to fill today. That was all that mattered, and it was Elisabeth's lesson learned. Together they shuffled to the tunnels. Time rolled forward as it wanted to do. The girls clung to one another in the barn, desperate to chase away the knowledge this was their life. Despite being together, they were alone.

One morning, before dawn, Elisabeth felt Edith jerk awake. Then the girl spoke. The sound was garbled and strange sounding to both their ears. Edith clamped her hand over her mouth, her eyes huge in the glow of the setting moon casting its light through the cracks of the boards. Massive tears began to fall from the girl's brown eyes. "Elisabeth," the girl tried to say. It sounded nothing like Elisabeth, but she knew it was a plea to her to give her back the speech she had once had. As Edith curled into a ball, Elisabeth wrapped her arms around her. She wanted to cry for her friend, but what did such things matter. Perhaps it was best Edith could not speak. She would be less likely to get herself in trouble. She would be less likely to get a friend's tongue cut from their head.

**Sunday, December 3, 1447, Ural Mountains, Lithuania**

Edith pulled Elisabeth from her exhausted stupor. Elisabeth opened her eyes to boots and bolted up, her head swimming and pounding. Edith did what Edith always did after discovering she could not speak. She crouched behind Elisabeth. Edith could fold her skeletal body so tight into Elisabeth's back that she did not know where she ended, and the other girl began. Edith did so now. Her knees were drawn to her chest while pressing those knees into Elisabeth's back. But, perhaps, the most disturbing of all was Edith's fingers that came out to grip Elisabeth's collar, holding to her for dear life. They were bony fingers and always cold, like death had hold of Elisabeth and would not let her go.

Elisabeth sat on the stall floor, staring at Master's boots. She knew his shoes better than she knew his face, for she no longer lifted her gaze from them. Elisabeth couldn't. She wouldn't. Her body shook, and she felt Edith quivering behind her. She wanted to scream at Edith that she couldn't protect her. She was not a lifeline. But she could not bring herself to stop Edith's behavior because Elisabeth created it. She made all Edith's suffering beyond what the mines built in the children that worked them. Edith was why Elisabeth no longer raised her head to look into her captors' faces.

"My lady," Master said. The timbre of his voice and the shifting of his boots told her he bowed to her. When he did this, it terrified her with its mocking disdain. "I thought you might want to know I am at the highest bid I have ever received for one of my slaves. Although I did get an excellent price on a young prince of some obscure place, I do not remember. Poor boy," the man said with no remorse in his voice. "People love to buy and sell the nobility. But, of course, they will also like a young virgin without a tongue. It might be a trend I start. Imagine the fortune I can make providing mute virgins who can tell no tales," he declared. "Do not fret. We will have you two out of here before you starve."

The boots turned away, but they stopped before exiting the stall. "Four buckets today, slave," the man sneered at her.

Elisabeth did not care if it was four, eight, or twelve. Numbness crept in to take hold of Elisabeth's body and her will. Nothing made it through the shell. Nothing that was except Edith's knees pressed into her back and a grip so tight Elisabeth knew Edith depended on Elisabeth for survival. Elisabeth was Edith's hope, and some of her hated the girl for this because long ago, Elisabeth lost her own hope someone would come. It had been too long, months. She knew it had not been the eternity it felt like.

Time stretched on and on. The cold of winter set in, and it pulled from the children all the warmth the threadbare blankets could provide. Elisabeth felt she had passed over the brink of humanity when she felt grateful there were so many extra blankets. Each extra blanket was the death of a child. Death here was not mourned. No one cared when another body was pulled from the tunnels.

Elisabeth was sickened with herself when her mind went to the day she would become a whore. It was no longer a thought that filled her with dread but a longing for real food, warmth, clothes, and rest. Lying on her back on a bed would be far better than this. Her body was no longer hers, it belonged to Master, and soon it would belong to a new master.

Work went on, long, excruciating hours that wore each down and killed their souls. More kids would be brought in the spring, fresh children, fresh slaves, and bodies that had not yet grown cold. The only thing Elisabeth could think of when she thought of this was she was too weak to fight over her blankets. She knew she could not keep one for her and Edith when stronger children were brought. But something in Elisabeth's head warned her that it would not matter because she and Edith would both be gone by then.

**Friday, January 5, 1448, Ural Mountains, Lithuania**

The day of her fate came on a bitingly cold day, but it was no different for Elisabeth than any other. Each one was filled with a cold so deep it would be forever trapped inside her bones. Elisabeth and Edith staggered together from the tunnels. Boots on the ground in front of her brought Elisabeth to a stop. Edith pressed herself into Elisabeth's back, and the grip of her icy fingers sent a chill racing down Elisabeth's spine, claiming a little more of her strength.

"Someone has come to get a look at you," Master's voice cut through the haze that existed around Elisabeth.

Edith gripped and pressed harder. Elisabeth tried halfheartedly to free herself. She did not have the strength or will to make it so. She stood staring down at the boots, accepting what was to come.

Steps advanced on her, and Elisabeth did not know whether she shook more or if the relentless wind struck her harder. Edith pressed into her. She reminded herself it would be a blessing to be sold. Even if Elisabeth became a whore, she would not be here in this frozen hell. She had been here so long she forgot what real food tasted like or what it was to have a full belly.

"Elisabeth?" the voice finally said her name. It was a gentle voice. The Master's boots were gone, and there were two sets, one smaller than the other, in their place. Next to the boots hung the tips of swords. "My dearest Elisabeth, is it truly you?" The gentle voice tickled at her memory, and she found comfort in the familiar tone. But she didn't dare hope. Her mind played tricks on her often here. Finally, the smaller feet shifted, and a face appeared before her as the squire sank to his knees.

"Elisabeth," he said. Slowly Elisabeth forced her head up and looked at the boy's shoulder. She was so petrified she could not stop quivering. Edith whimpered behind her. "Elisabeth," Adrian said, and in his voice, she heard that he saw everything she had become. She dropped her eyes and stepped forward, dragging Edith with her. Edith's hold on Elisabeth drove her to her knees. She fell in front of Adrian, staring now at his broad chest. He was still strong. She saw it the way his clothing had not grown loose, or his arms and chest had not sunk in on themselves. She could not look at his face. He was a baron, a landholder. He wasn't property, not like her.

"Adrian," she whispered. Her voice cracked, and she broke. She reached for him, and he was there, meeting her. She seized hold of his arm and pressed herself into it, clinging as tightly to his sleeve as Edith clung to her back. Elisabeth sobbed. Adrian's hand stroked her hair, pulling her into his embrace. "Did you not think we would come?" she heard the young man whisper in her ear. She cried harder, ashamed because she had given up that hope long ago.

"To the barn with you," Master's voice cut through her like ice. Elisabeth clung harder to Adrian, aware her fingers bit into him, and the effort made her entire body shake. It was not Elisabeth Master spoke to, but Edith. Relief washed over Elisabeth, and she cried harder because that was not the person she wanted to be. Master stripped her of who that girl was, as he had stripped her flesh with his work and whips.

She felt the grip of Edith turn desperate as someone tried to separate them. The struggle was more intense than Elisabeth would have guessed from a little girl whose strength had dwindled to nothing. She found herself folding against Adrian's strong arm, terrified the effort to pull Edith from her would tear her from Adrian. Shame flooded through Elisabeth as Edith's grip on her dress released. All Elisabeth could do was bury her head further against Adrian as Edith's sobs and screams began to move away.

"Save her," Elisabeth whispered.

She felt Adrian shifting, and Elisabeth could not keep her frightened whimper inside.

"How much for that girl too?" Lincoln's voice cut across the grounds. Edith's sobs stopped.

Elisabeth stilled as best she could to hear the answer. She clung to Adrian's strong arm, but it was not enough to stop the tremors as she held to her lifeline.

"We do not have enough," Adrian's voice next to her ear cut through the haze.

Elisabeth shook her head, pulling, begging in silence.

"We are purchasing two slaves. Do we not get a deal?"

"I gave you a deal for that one. The bid for her maidenhead is already near the amount you have paid. This one will be nearly as valuable without a tongue."

"Please," Elisabeth begged of Adrian, pressing against his chest. She felt Adrian shift, and then he was standing. Elisabeth sobbed, too weak to cling anymore or to stand without his strength. She feared she would never be able to stand from the ground biting into her raw knees if he left her now. She lifted her head, her body weaving as the emotional toll claimed more of her physical strength.

Adrian walked to Lincoln, and together they collected their coins. She watched Lincoln shake his head as she stared at the ground at their feet. They did not have enough to buy Edith as they had purchased her. Adrian's eyes fell on her. Elisabeth was so afraid. She knew what she needed to do. She needed to tell them to take Edith to purchase her instead. Because Edith could not speak. She could not tell anyone what was happening between her and the cruel boy. Instinctively, Elisabeth knew the nasty boy made Edith cling to her more than the grown men who held them all here. This was Elisabeth's fault, yet she felt herself remain quiet. Her body began to shake anew.

Then Adrian was pulling his sword from its belt. His most valued possession was his family's sword. It was an expensive weapon. He did not speak to Lincoln but stepped to Master and presented the weapon.

"For the girl," he said.

Master studied the craftsmanship before nodding and motioning for Edith's release. A great sob escaped the child, and she ran straight to Elisabeth. Edith fell to crouch behind her. Again, she pressed her knees into Elisabeth's back and grabbed a handful of her tattered dress. This time Elisabeth reached a hand behind her and pulled Edith even closer.

They huddled together on the ground. Elisabeth was aware Lincoln and Adrian looked down on them as the rest of the children at the mines continued their day. Both girls quaked with the tears labored and beaten from them. The reality of the moments was bitter. Two of the three most influential people from her old life saw what she was now. They saw she was no more than a horse or one of the buckets she gathered the stones in.

# Chapter 13

**Friday, January 5, 1448, Ural Mountains, Lithuania**

Adrian and Lincoln watched the two girls crouch in the yard as the magnitude of chance became terrifyingly apparent. The blond girl holding the smaller one against her back was not Elisabeth Kirkham of Ravenshill. Adrian did not know what to expect as they searched for her. It took months of following leads for them to learn of the man who bought small children to work in his mines. Until then, Lincoln had searched for households and brothels that purchased children off the last ship. A great deal of relief filled Adrian when they learned the mines were the likeliest place she was taken. He could not picture her being passed around in a brothel. But this image before him was much worse.

These were not even children he watched, but animals. He hated that he had to leave this place and leave so many children here to die. But he had given his family's sword. Other than his life, he had nothing else to offer.

Lincoln went to his horse and stood next to it. He adjusted the straps and the stirrup with slow and deliberate movement. Adrian had come to know the man well, more so on this long journey together, and he recognized his stance as someone enraged. Was it because Adrian had given up his sword?

Adrian gave a hesitant step toward the girls, who somehow appeared to be one as they huddled on the ground before turning and going to Lincoln's side.

"Sir?" Adrian asked hesitantly. He glanced back at the girls, who did not move as snow began to fall, catching in their filthy hair. The white flakes stood out against the red hair of the one. The flakes landing on Elisabeth disappeared in her blonde hair, much like the girl had disappeared. "What do we do?"

"We leave here." The man's deep voice was pitched low as he said it.

"But you know these children will die."

"Leave it, Young Adrian. We can do nothing for them. We have found Elisabeth, and we leave here with her now." Lincoln turned from the horse and went to the girls. He loomed over them, a terrifying-looking man, but he loved one of those girls huddled on the ground as much as Adrian. That's why they had to leave here. They had to get Elisabeth away. They had to get her to safety, away from these poor souls that shuffled, froze, and starved.

Adrian saw how the knight's jaw clenched, and his eyes held a fury each time he looked at the men who kept the mines running. But those eyes softened when they fell on the girls quaking at his feet.

Adrian pulled the horses closer. The other girl had her head buried in Elisabeth's back. In contrast, Elisabeth's head was bowed, and together the girls swayed back and forth while their tiny, malnourished bodies quaked. Lincoln hesitated as he stood over them, then bent and took Elisabeth's hand that was not holding to the other child. Elisabeth raised her head but did not look at Lincoln. Instead, she looked at nothing but the ground. Obediently she stood, and the other child rose as if they were one. Adrian saw Lincoln had the same trouble he had, where to touch Elisabeth without causing her pain. Her flesh was ripped raw, and there was evidence of a whip. Adrian spared a moment to pray to God they would be away from this place before the fury he felt and lurked behind Lincoln's brown eyes exploded from them.

Lincoln looked to Adrian for guidance. Adrian dropped his head to look at the ground. He did not know what to do. How did one fix a child? Finally, Lincoln made a decision and reached for Elisabeth. The other girl allowed him to pull her from her grasp. Adrian lifted his head in time to see Lincon's lips flatten as her weight settled in the knight's arms. She would weigh nothing, for nothing was left on her frail bones. Lincoln sat Elisabeth on Adrian's horse, and she reached forward to grasp the horse's mane. Adrian looked up at her, but Elisabeth still looked to the ground. He saw the raw knuckles of her hands and the blisters on her palms. The scabs of her legs extended from ankles to thighs. Her feet were bare, and they had the skin stripped from them time and again. The filth that came from crawling beneath the earth was caked to her.

Lincoln held the horse while Adrian mounted behind Elisabeth. His hand came around her, steadying her as he sank into the saddle. Mounted on the horse in front of him, placed Elisabeth in his lap, and she weighed nothing. He had sparred with this girl with wooden swords on many occasions. She always had strength behind her thrusts. This girl whose waist he wrapped his hand around was nothing more than a battered skeleton. Once he had his arm around her, he could not pull it away. He kept hold of her, taking the reins in his free hand. She was so small. He wanted to cry for her and all she must have gone through. Adrian couldn't help but speculate both he and Elisabeth were no longer children. They had both seen things and done things children should not have to. But they had, and now they would go home and heal together. His arm around Elisabeth assured him of that.

Lincoln reached for the other girl. As he lifted her, she whimpered like an injured and frightened puppy. As he settled the girl on his horse, Lincoln shook his head, mumbled, and cast a brutal look in the slave owner's direction. The horse shifted beneath the girl, and Lincoln's hands came to rest on the animal's sides. They looked enormous next to the girl's thin legs. Then, he watched the little girl he gave his sword for, reach a raw hand to touch Lincoln's. Lincoln looked up at her, and the girl's brown eyes skittered across his before she cast her eyes down again and withdrew her hand.

They made camp long before dark to give the girls a chance to eat and rest. "What do we do with them?" Adrian asked Lincoln in a quiet voice. The one girl had eaten like one would expect of someone long deprived of basic nourishment. But Elisabeth had eaten little to nothing. Now, despite the exhaustion drawing Elisabeth down, she sat still, staring into the flames of the fire. The other girl fell asleep several minutes ago, pressed against Elisabeth's back. Both girls were wrapped in the men's blankets.

"It will be a long time before we get her to her father," Lincoln stated.

"They need to be cleaned," Adrian said.

"What do we put them in? We have no money for food, let alone clothes."

As a wolf howled, Adrian pointed in the direction of the sound. "A couple of their carcasses could be traded for a couple little girls' dresses, I would think."

"Yes, but taking a couple wolves is far easier than it sounds," Lincoln warned.

"Trading a sword for a girl sounds far easier than what it was," Adrian said, casting a glance at the sleeping girl.

Lincoln nodded. The man's sword was not worth as much as Adrian's. It was rather plain. After all, the Order did take a vow of poverty, and the sword was a mark of those knights. Its blade was average in appearance, as was the entire sword. The crossguard was steel, the handle wrapped in black leather for grip, and a black cross was etched onto the top of the pommel. The sword's real value was the value Lincoln put into it, the wealth of a past. It was a past filled with fighting but helping and healing Christians as they traveled to and from the Holy Land. The Order's motto was to help, defend, and heal, and Lincoln had done it all. Even that which was unholy.

"Do you think Elisabeth would have let us take her without her friend?"

"No, and I don't know why. She knows what I gave for her friend. That this child has that much value to Elisabeth makes me feel we, too, should value her as much."

Lincoln nodded. As another howl echoed through the night, Adrian stood. "Then, I shall begin by trading wolves for clothes."

The night was lit with the glow of a three-quarter moon. The wind beat against him with a force that chilled and bit. As he moved, his vision kept filling with Elisabeth, and the girl pressed into her back. Had they arrived in time to save them? It looked as if she had been shattered into a million pieces. Adrian wanted nothing more than to be able to scoop her up and put her back together, but it would not be that simple. Nothing was ever that simple.

As the night wore on and he found a wolf track, he wondered if he would ever hear her laughter again. Would she ever be the Elisabeth he knew because he did not see that girl in the blue eyes that refused to look at him? Nothing resided in her beautiful eyes, and that was terrifying to him. Had they been too late to save her? He pushed the dire thought from his mind and remembered the day she had gone hunting with him and Walter.

***Wednesday, November 2, 1446, Ravenshill***

*"Psst," the voice stopped him as he followed Walter out of the stable, leading their horses. Adrian turned to find Elisabeth lurking near the door. "Take me with you."*

*"Sir Lincoln said we should not take so much of your time from what girls should do," Adrian informed her. He was unsure what the nine-year-old girl was supposed to do, but he guessed it was not swordplay and fortress defense.*

*"But the kitchens are so boring. Katy and Annabelle just talk and talk about nothing interesting. So please take me with you, Adrian."*

*"All right," he relented. "But slip out on your own. We'll meet you at the bridge. I don't want Lincoln mad at me."*

*"Will he make you cry," she teased him.*

*"Shut up, Elisabeth," Adrian replied, but there was a smile on his face when he said it.*

*"Why do we have to wait on her," Walter complained a few minutes later as they stood beneath the giant willow that grew next to the river. Walter's docile pony stood next to Adrian. The well-behaved animal was trained well before the Ravenshill heir was ever put into his saddle. From the age of two, Walter was led on the pony. Then, finally, the toddler showed a connection to the horse, and he took the reins for the first time. Since then, Walter had become impatient with any delay related to the horses and riding them. He wanted to run, and his animal always wanted to run with him, for him. He never laid a whip on any animal, but their hearts seemed to pump and labor for the boy.*

*"She wants to go," Adrian replied, looking toward the keep with irritation flattening his lips. What was keeping her?*

*"So," Walter challenged.*

*Just then, Elisabeth's bobbing head came into view. She was running and was out of breath when she reached them.*

*"I brought food," she said, holding up the sack, beaming with pride.*

*Adrian relaxed, and a broad smile split his face as his heart leaped with relief. He took the sack from her and tossed it to Walter. Adrian did not mind when Elisabeth came. She was just as capable as any boy he had played with at Helmsley. "That is why we wait on Elisabeth," Adrian said as he reached down and let Elisabeth put her foot in his hand without a word. He boosted her into his saddle with a grunt of effort. She scooted back to the horse's rump. Her excitement made her eyes glow, and her cheeks redden in an enchanting way that made Adrian want to be absorbed by the light. He almost laughed out loud when he realized he was staring at her. He mounted as Walter tied the sack to his saddle.*

*The wind was chilly, trying to drive through their warm cloaks. Walter and Adrian had been on many hunts with Lincoln and Lord Thomas but never on their own. Lord Thomas had granted him that honor this morning, telling him to take Walter and find something to hunt for the table. He said it was one of the many things both boys would have to grow adept at. Adrian had not hesitated. He loved hunting since he brought his first stag down with a well-placed arrow.*

*The persistent wind whipped, and he felt Elisabeth bury her head into his back. The girl never failed to make him feel more of a man than he was, stronger even. Unless she was beating him at swordplay, but even then, her smile always made it okay.*

*They left the horses tied next to a glade and, on silent feet, slipped into the forest together. The land climbed and rolled, unlike the steep mountains just a little farther north. Finally, the forest opened to a small field of wild grasses. Protected by the woods, a lot of game sought refuge here, where Adrian always successfully hunted.*

*Today was no different. One footstep onto the field and a pheasant took flight. Adrian raised his bow and shot it out of the air with fast reflexes. Then, feeling giddy, Adrian led the way to the fallen bird.*

*Elisabeth poked her foot at the carcass. "It's not very big, is it?" she asked. Walter said nothing, so Elisabeth pressed, "You'll have to kill twenty at this size."*

*Walter laughed.*

*"I didn't see you shoot it," Adrian growled at Walter.*

*"I doubt anyone saw you shoot it. It's so small," Elisabeth declared.*

*"Then you try," Adrian said, thrusting his bow at her. She straightened to her full height, which Adrian had long surpassed.*

*"I will." Her face grew imperialistic, and she thrust her chin in the air as she took Adrian's bow.*

*"Good. If you get something, you can gut it too." He knew Elisabeth hated gutting the chickens when they were brought into the kitchen. She did it once and fled the kitchen to throw up in the yard.*

*"I will," she said. Adrian rolled his eyes at her and turned to prepare the carcass to take back home.*

*She moved into the brush with Walter trailing her. He almost called her back to place the arrow from the bird back into the quiver, but he told himself she would not even use one of his arrows. But it was not long before her calls rang back to him. "I got one! I shot it!"*

*As Adrian cleaned the blood from his knife, he couldn't hold back his grin. He wanted her to fail because she had teased him, but hearing the enthusiasm in her voice made him very glad she had not. Adrian tied the little pheasant to his saddle and waited. He waited. It seemed like hours. He was growing fearful and berating himself for letting them go out alone. He was a squire. Adrian was the most skilled of the three of them, and he let them go on their own. He was also annoyed because it was getting late, and he would have no more time to hunt with the sun racing from the sky. All they would have to show for their outing was his tiny pheasant and whatever it was that Elisabeth shot. He worked himself up into a near panic when he heard the branches crashing a moment before Elisabeth came into sight.*

*"We won't be able to get anything else with all the noise you two are making," Adrian admonished.*

*"We don't have to," Walter said from behind her. Elisabeth carried both the boys' bows in her hands, and when she stepped to the side, he saw the numerous pheasants that Walter had.*

*Adrian was aware he stood with his mouth hanging open, but he could not close it. There had to be fifteen if there was one in Walter's hands.*

*"Walter?" Adrian questioned. He could not believe the boy had killed that many. He was not a very good bowman. Perhaps adequate would be a stretch for his skill level.*

*"It wasn't me," Walter said. "It was all Elisabeth."*

*Adrian swung to the girl, and she stood beaming at him. He wanted to be petty, to not give her her victory because none of hers looked as small as the one he shot. But he could not squash the joy he saw written across every line of her perfect face. So, he moved forward and hugged Elisabeth realizing he was proud of her. He was the one that taught her to shoot a bow. They practiced a couple of times together, but he did not know her extraordinary skill.*

**Friday, January 5, 1448, Ural Mountains, Lithuania**

As Adrian stalked the wolf, the vision of her beaming face that day haunted him. He couldn't even recognize that girl now. They might look similar, but their souls looked different. He saw it in her eyes as she refused to look at him.

The howling of the wolves drew him to the prey they were ripping into. He crouched downwind from them, watching as they growled and the stronger ran the weaker ones away. He wondered if that was what it was like for Elisabeth. Had she felt like one of those vulnerable wolves, or had she felt like their prey as it was being hunted?

He watched the alpha male as he devoured the meat. His jowls were red with fresh blood, and he snarled and snapped at the ones who came near. He even jumped on one of the pups who came too close, and whether it was his intention or just his power, the giant wolf killed it with one snap of its jaws. As Adrian watched, he began to hate that wolf and how he treated the others in his pack. Why couldn't he share the carcass? It was large enough to feed them all, but that was not the way of wolves. That was not the way of slave owners.

His first shot was clean, driving deep into the chest of one of the animals that lurked nearby. The wolf came close enough to catch the scent of Adrian and scatter the pack with a warning. The dog dropped where it stood and did not move. Some pack members took notice as they all circled and waited their turn. But the one Adrian wanted was the alpha.

The second shot was not clean. It was as if the wolf had sensed him and moved from the path of his arrow—the tip embedded in the dog's shoulder before it yelped and dashed away. Adrian gave chase. The animal was easy to track in the wilderness, following the bloody pawprints. Soon sweat poured from Adrian despite the cold wind whipping against him.

He recalled the evening after their hunt and how Lincoln and Lord Thomas kept bragging about Walter and Adrian's hunting skills. Elisabeth remained silent, her mouth flat, and Adrian wanted so much to tell them that Elisabeth was the one who filled their plates with meat. She was the great hunter, the great bringer of death to the pheasants. But she swore both he and Walter to secrecy. Her reason was sound, and he knew she was right. Had the animals been brought with the truth that Elisabeth was the one to kill them, it might get Adrian in trouble. After all, he let her shoot the bow, let her out of his sight, and let her go on the hunt in the first place. But he knew it was hard for her to sit at the table and listen to praise that should have been hers. But she remained quiet as they all had. So, no one but Walter and Adrian knew of her prowess. And now Adrian alone, because the new Walter would never be told that secret. There was no need. He would need to know so many other things to slip into his role that one tiny secret would not matter.

He found the wolf floundering amongst the root ball of a fallen tree where it sought safety, entangling itself. It stood snarling and shaking from its rage and fear. Its wild instinct told the animal his death was upon him. Adrian knocked an arrow, raised the bow, and was ready to shoot the arrow through its chest as it crouched and snarled. It would be a clean shot that would end it quickly for the animal, but something inside Adrian made him lower the bow. He sank into a crouch and hesitated to sit the bow at his feet. He slid his dagger from the sheath on his belt when he stood. He paused, knowing what he was about to do was foolish, but he needed to draw the wolf's blood. He felt the craving build in his chest. He had wanted to make the man at the mine suffer. It was the first time Adrian felt rage as acute as what he felt after the shock of seeing Elisabeth wore off. It had returned as he watched the dying animal prepare to fight. For a fleeting moment, he wondered if the wolf knew it would die, whether it fought or not. But that wolf was the man who took Elisabeth. He was the one who laid a whip across her tender flesh. He was the one who did not feed her. He was the one who had not kept her safe.

He screamed a sound of rage as he moved in on the wolf. It fought Adrian, and he was glad for it. He never thought he would ever relinquish his family's sword. It was meant to be ripped from his cold, dead hand somewhere on a battlefield, or he would present it to his son one day. He never dreamed he would buy a little girl with it. That became the wolf's fault as its fangs sunk into Adrian's arm and held on.

It was the wolf's final attempt at survival and its last act as Adrian sliced his blade across its throat. The light faded from the wolf's eyes, and Adrian felt regret pour in. The great jaws relaxed, and the fangs fell from his arm. Adrian cried then with the bloody dagger in his hands. He smelled the blood heavily, felt it on himself, and his stomach lurched at thinking of what he had just done. The animal might have suffered less had he used the arrow. But he would not have the deep marks of its teeth in his arm. He would not feel a small part of Elisabeth's pain.

Adrian gutted the animal and retrieved the second one, doing the same. By morning he returned to his horse, found a river, and cleaned the worst of the blood from himself. A hare flushed out of its hole on the path back to camp, and Adrian brought it down, gutting it and strapping it to his saddle. It would make a fine breakfast for the girls.

Arriving back at the camp, he left his horse some distance away. It seemed important not to let the girls see the dead wolves.

Lincoln sat by a fire with both girls still sleeping. They were wrapped together beneath as many blankets and clothes as Adrian and Lincoln had brought. Lincoln's eyes fell on Adrian, assessing him, seeing the fatigue of a night on the move. Adrian thought he would feel proud for bringing down two wolves, but he took that victory from himself in the way he killed the alpha.

Lincoln stood, came closer, and asked, "Where are they?" It occurred to Adrian he did not ask if he took down any wolves. Lincoln asked him where they were. Did the man have that much faith in Adrian? It made his chest swell with pride at the thought.

Adrian pointed to where he had left his horse out of sight. Lincoln nodded, "I will see what I can do."

Adrian went to the fire and heard Lincoln riding away within a moment. He sat by the fire, feeling like he could sleep. Still, Adrian had to keep watch over Elisabeth and the other girl. For the other girl, Adrian gave up the possession that was most valuable to him. He would keep her safe as he would Elisabeth so that his sacrifice would not be in vain.

# Chapter 14

**Saturday, January 6, 1448, road to Ravenshill**

The water was cold. Elisabeth sat on the edge of the creek bank, shivering. The babbling of the water as it flowed was soothing. It was a simplistic sound. There were so many sounds Elisabeth thought she would never hear again, though she was unaware of them at the time. But the simple sound of flowing water had been absent in the mine tunnels and barn.

Lincoln was a few paces away with Edith. Elisabeth heard him talking to her, coaxing her to remove the filthy clothing that hung from her. The care in Lincoln's voice for her friend made her want to cry. Elisabeth heard them talking last night as she sat by the warmth of the fire. Despite the heat on her face and Edith pressed into her back, she still felt cold. Not her body, but herself, her soul. Her mind kept taking her back to the times she begged, to the times she feared far beyond anything she ever thought existed. Eventually, she laid down where she sat and closed her eyes. When she dozed, her nightmares swarmed in to attack, but

Adrian was there, and he vanquished each, and she slept.

It was late in the morning when they were awakened and brought here. Elisabeth knew from the conversation she heard that Adrian hunted wolves so they would have something to trade for clothes. She saw the clothes, the warm cloaks, the shoes, and her heart wept that Adrian was such a generous man. And Lincoln did not buy Elisabeth a piece of clothing he did not also purchase for Edith.

Elisabeth stood. The barn was still fresh in her mind. A place where modesty was not permitted. Her mind and body were numb, so she let Adrian pull the filthy and worn dress over her head. She did not care that he would see her naked. She knew she was only a skeleton with skin stretched across it. With the clothes, a salve for wounds was also purchased and spread across their raw skin. Elisabeth stood throughout it all and uttered no sound. She felt the constant pool of tears in her eyes as Adrian worked with great care and light hands. Then Elisabeth sat in the sun as Adrian worked the knots from her clean hair.

"Your father sent me to London to find a new brother for you," she heard Adrian say. She was aware the men remained quiet around her and Edith. Elisabeth felt their discomfort, and it left her with a level of unease. They had never treated her in such a way, which made her ashamed.

"I have found a child who will never be seen as anyone but Lord Walter Kirkham."

His touch was gentle as his fingertips raked against the back of her neck from time to time as he regathered her hair. His strokes were unhurried as if he had the rest of his life to sit with her thus. She closed her eyes.

"Why do you not speak to Lincoln or to me?" he asked after a moment.

Elisabeth opened her eyes. She was unsure what to say to the men, so she chose to say nothing.

"You need to eat to regain strength," Adrian continued. She heard the concern in his voice, wrapped still in his shock at her condition. Then, when Elisabeth did not reply, he slipped around to kneel in front of her. He moved his head to put himself in the path of her gaze, but she shifted hers away.

"You have yet to look me in the eyes," Adrian said. She still feared to look anyone in the eyes, especially these men, because they would see she was empty.

"The girl does not speak," Adrian continued.

"Because she does not have a tongue," Elisabeth whispered. Swallowing was difficult.

She was aware of Adrian's intense stare. She could feel the softness of his gaze. She felt uncomfortable, and she plucked at the hem of the cloak.

"Do you know her name?" Adrian asked in the softest of voices. He reached out a hand to push a blonde strand of hair behind her ear. His face moved toward her field of vision. She looked away.

"Edith." Elisabeth felt the tears, but they did not fall. "She told me before they took it."

"Why do you refuse to look me in the eye?" Adrian asked.

"I'm ashamed of what I became," she whispered.

Adrian fell quiet for a moment before he asked, "What did you become?"

"Property."

Adrian moved on her, grabbed her face, and pulled it around, forcing her startled eyes to fall on his. "You are not property," Adrian snarled.

"I am the reason she does not have a tongue." Elisabeth held his gaze, waiting to see judgment, possibly even hate, in the dark blue-gray eyes looking at her. But she did not see it. Instead, he placed a hand on the back of her head, pulling her forward so their foreheads rested together.

"You are the reason she is free, Sweet Elisabeth." His fingers bit into her scalp, refusing to let her gaze leave his. "Where would she be without you? Where would I be without you?" Adrian's gray eyes held hers. They were steady and sad with their plea that Elisabeth returns to him. She did not think she could ever be that girl again. His hand on the back of her neck gripped tightly yet gently. Then his other hand found hers, and his fingers were strong as they grasped it.

"Come back to us, Elisabeth," he whispered.

She tried to shake her head. "I do not know if I am that girl anymore."

"Of course, you aren't. I am not that boy you left behind. We are a man and a woman now. Experience has made us so. We will never be children again." He fell silent, holding her hand, cupping the back of her neck, his forehead resting against hers. Her eyes fell to their intertwined hands. Hers had grown so frail while his had grown stronger.

"I remember on the riverbank," he whispered. "I remember how you held my hand as we readied to run across the bridge, and I told you that when you are afraid to hold to my hand, I will carry us through. Do you remember?" he asked. Elisabeth did not speak or nod but grew still. She swallowed. "Hold to my hand

Elisabeth," he begged her. "Hold to my hand, and don't ever let it go."

Suddenly her fingers wrapped around his as a sob escaped her. She clung to it as fiercely as she clung to him at the mines. She remembered how desperate she felt, how he was her lifeline, and she clung to him as such. But she felt a considerable chasm had opened between them. She had experienced something without Adrian. She had been cold while he was warm. She had been alone when he had Lincoln. She had starved while he had eaten. It was a chasm she was unsure she would ever cross back to him.

Elisabeth nodded slightly against Adrian's forehead, and his hand slid from her neck. She wiped the tears from her eyes. Then she looked up into Adrian's face and saw one tear slip from his eye as she did so. She reached for it and touched his cheek where it rested.

Adrian's hand was gentle when he touched hers. When he pulled it from his face, he looked down at the delicate hands that had become raw and work-worn. He studied them for a moment before bending and kissing them. His lips were soft. "I am sorry I did not make it to you sooner." Something in his voice drew her eyes to his. She saw more tears mixed with such regret her heart ached for him. How was that possible that she suffered, but she sat beside him now, wishing to ease his pain more than anything. Adrian closed his eyes and murmured, "I will always come for you, Elisabeth."

They sat together on the bank, clinging to each other's hands and remembering another time. A time when the storm now seemed no threat at all. A time when their fear had been no match for the fear they had just survived.

"I love you, Elisabeth," Adrian whispered.

"I love you too, Adrian," she whispered back. She felt a piece of something heavy lift from her as if a chain weighed her down, still binding her to the mine.

**Sunday, January 7, 1448, road to Ravenshill**

The next day as they rode, the memory of the night she ran returned to her. She gave it no thought after the men took her. Her fear had made it impossible to think of something insignificant by then. She kept glancing at Lincoln, who led them with Edith perched on his horse's rump. Her arms stayed wrapped around him, which made Elisabeth feel a measure of relief. She witnessed what Lincoln would do and what lengths he would go to to protect the Kirkhams. He could defend Edith far better than Elisabeth. Elisabeth was unable to protect her at all. But Lincoln could, and she was grateful she knew this with certainty.

Her mind bounced back and forth between the fear for Edith and the worry over Ravenshill's finances. It sounded dire that night. Alarming enough for Lincoln to kill the witnesses that could take away the Kirkham heir. Was a little boy by the name of Walter Kirkham so important it did not matter the boy, only the name?

"Do you know how bad the finances are?" she asked Adrian.

She was capable of riding behind him now. She had enough strength to balance and keep hold of Adrian, but he preferred her in front of him, where he could hold her. He told her this, and she did not protest because she felt safest in his arms.

"Lincoln has said they are terrible. So bad Ravenshill may be lost."

"Why?"

She felt Adrian shrug. "Lincoln has said the only thing keeping Ravenshill running is my fee for living at Ravenshill."

Adrian was rescuing her again just by being at Ravenshill. He set that in motion the first time he stepped inside the bailey of the keep.

"We have you, and we have another Walter. We will save it," he declared.

Elisabeth wished she had the confidence of the squire that guided the horse. He could protect her from any danger, she had no doubt. But the fate that waited for her around the corner was frightening, and Adrian could not stop it. Did that mean she no longer had a dowery? She was betrothed, and the family of Blackpool was a wealthy one. If she could marry soon, she could help Ravenshill. But how long would that help go? Had her father managed Ravenshill poorly? Was he the reason the people had left over the years?

If Adrian could trade wolves for clothes for two little girls, there must be things at Ravenshill of value. Whether in physical form or service, they could raise money for the debts her father might owe. She was educated, more so than her father. Would he let her manage the finances? Could she? She was well-educated in mathematics, and reading had always been a breeze. Adrian's father wanted Adrian educated, and since there was no one at Ravenshill to do it, they sent Clayton. He was a harsh taskmaster and was initially reluctant to allow her to sit in on the lessons. He relented once he found she was listening at the door and helping Adrian later with those lessons. She made it a point not to disappoint him for his generosity. Most did not care if a woman was educated, and many did not think they should be. But Clayton fed her all she would devour. When the old man passed away in his sleep, the de Ros's decided what Adrian already knew would allow him to educate himself. They sent books after that. Many books came to Ravenshill, and Elisabeth read each one even if Adrian didn't. Her father turned the small chamber on the third floor into a library. It was a place where Elisabeth often buried herself.

As the days rolled by and they made their way closer to Ravenshill, the men set a pace that allowed the girls to regain their strength. But Elisabeth began chafing at the bit, deciding she would take over Ravenshill's finances. She had little choice if she wanted things to proceed as they should for her marriage. If she had no dowery, she would have no husband. Surely that would be the answer until Walter could take over as heir. At least at Ravenshill, they were far from court. Perhaps he could always remain at Ravenshill, but she knew the chances of that were slim. Eventually, he would have to present himself at court and serve the King. One did not carry the title without performing some service to the monarch.

**Sunday, January 21, 1448, *road to Ravenshill***

"Elisabeth," Lincoln said. His voice was soft and hesitant.

Elisabeth felt herself stiffen as she looked up at the man. She hated that a sliver of fear ran through her now when she heard his voice. She sometimes felt closer to the knight than she did to her father. Her father never took her up in front of him on a saddle and galloped it just for her. Just so she could feel the wind in her hair and shout with joy from the thrill of the fear. The giant destrier of Lincoln's was a massive beast, and it felt like thunder rolled beneath its hooves, and it was also fast for such a big animal. So fast it stole her breath and made her heart drum with madness. Her father never did anything like that with her. Nor had he given her a wooden sword and play fought with her. Her father did not fall to the ground as if she slew him. He did not lay still so convincingly for such a time, with his tongue hanging from his mouth, that she thought for a moment she had. He never leaped from the floor and dragged her into his lap, tickling her while she shrieked. Lincoln did those things and far more that made her who she was. Despite his reputation, she could never see him as a man of war. Now it was hard for her to look at him as anything but.

When she said nothing, he took a seat on the log next to her with hesitation. She was sleeping well each night until tonight. Edith clinging to her felt too much like suffocation, and Adrian's snores nearby did not help soothe her as they had along the way. Tomorrow they would reach the channel and sail back to England. Something about that scared her and made her restless. She couldn't stop thinking about the finances and how bad she could mess them up and doom them. But she knew she had to try. No one else would care so much and try as hard to fix things. Because now, no one at Ravenshill knew the things she knew.

Lincoln sat beside her for a while, absently picking apart a stick and throwing it into the fire. "I will not allow you to hurt Edith," she said.

He paused a moment before continuing to toss the fragments. "I do not wish to hurt Edith."

"No matter what she knows or will know, she is as loyal to me as you are."

"Elisabeth," Lincoln said, turning to face her. "Edith loves you more than Adrian or me. I did not think that was possible, but you are her sun and moon."

In her heart, Elisabeth knew Lincoln did not wish to hurt Edith. She knew he did not want to hurt anyone.

"That scares me," Elisabeth whispered.

"It is a heavy burden to carry. But one that is well worth the effort."

"Sir Lincoln?" Elisabeth asked.

"Yes, Elisabeth."

She sighed. "I am sorry for being the reason you had to do what you did that night."

"You are not the reason," Lincoln said, digging his stick in the dirt next to him. "Your father made the decisions that placed us where we are. What you did was an accident." The stick stopped moving, "What I did was not."

"Is this the way of it then?" Elisabeth asked.

Lincoln did not ask what she meant, but the stick started digging at the dirt again. "We do things we do not wish to do, so we have the burden of regret for the rest of our days." Lincoln's voice had a sad lilt to it.

"My lady," Lincoln began, lifting the stick and stroking it as if it would give him the words he wanted to say to her. "Life is not easy. We will always have trials, and the answers may seem like no answer at all, but it is all we can do. You are strong. These burdens may slow you, and they might weigh you down, but they will not break you. Of that, I am sure."

He swirled the stick in his hand thoughtfully for a moment. Then, he spoke as if he had made a decision, and Lincoln wanted to get the words out before he changed his mind. "I know they used a whip on you. I will not ask all of what was done to you because it may make me turn around and do what I knew I could not do then and kill those men. I was taken prisoner once. Those men hated me. There was no moment when they did not stand before me, and I did not feel pain. The pain and hunger leave their own scars. Those marks on your skin may fade, but the pain and hunger will stay with you. While a prisoner, I went to dark places inside my head. My experience as a prisoner was nothing to the terror I could find in my own head, in my nightmares. But that has made me the man who rages against the injustice I saw at the mines. It is the reason I did not pull you from Edith and ride away without a thought for her. It is the reason you will always have my respect."

"Why? I feel afraid of everything. Even you."

Lincoln shifted, and his gaze went to the fire. "That will fade too. You will realize your strength." He paused for a long time, "As for fearing me, I will pray that that too will fade."

Lincoln pointed his stick in Adrian's direction. "But if it does not, know that he will always protect you, even from me."

# Chapter 15

**Friday, February 2, 1448, Ravenshill**

As they neared Ravenshill, Adrian could feel Elisabeth's grip tighten on him. He could guess why. After all they had been through to bring her back, Elisabeth still had to face her father. The men had accomplished their task. After all the time spent searching, they returned the oldest and true Kirkham to Ravenshill, where she belonged. It was Elisabeth who had fled, Elisabeth who had killed her brother no matter that it was accidental, and Elisabeth who would stand before her father after all this time.

Throughout the journey, Adrian could not imagine the tiny castle of Ravenshill would be as important as it once was to him. But as they came ever closer to its walls, he knew he was wrong. It did not matter how far Adrian had traveled or what he had done along the way, Ravenshill called him back. He felt the relief and the breath he did not know he held all these months, release.

They feared snow would fall as the dark clouds threatened overhead throughout the last day on the road. But the sun broke through when the small party came within sight of River North Tyne. Now, as their horses reached the summit of the limestone knoll upon which Ravenshill sat, the weak light struck the stone walls. The hornfels rock that made up the walls, tower, and all other buildings inside the keep glowed beneath the soft light. The light gray stones held fragments of brown that turned the stones pink when the sun struck them. Depending on the sun's level and intensity, the stone of Ravenshill turned from a light gray that would sparkle as white as snow to a red that glowed like fire. Now the sun brought out a cacophony of all its colors, from dark gray to silver and pink to deep browns and reds. They were home.

Presley stepped to the closed gate and did not hesitate to open it at the sight of Lincoln. Lincoln led them forward with the silent Edith clinging to his back, taking in Ravenshill with avid interest. If the emptiness of the courtyard was disturbing, it did not show on her face. Adrian pulled his horse to a stop as Lincoln slipped a leg over his horse's neck and slid off. He reached for Edith, who reached for him so he could sit her on the ground.

The girl waited for Elisabeth as Adrian slipped from his horse. When he reached for Elisabeth, she glanced down at him. She looked about the silent courtyard with unease before she leaned toward him. She was so small. He had an overwhelming urge to wrap his arms around her, which he did, and hugged her fiercely.

Lincoln gazed at him with his unreadable expression as he gathered the horses' reins. "I'll tend them. Take Lady Elisabeth and Edith inside," Lincoln said.

Adrian heard Elisabeth draw in a deep breath to steady herself. He presented his elbow to her, and her blue-eyed gaze met his. With all the girl had faced, she was now facing perhaps her greatest fear—her father's wrath. It was something she saw on that one night, the night her nightmare began. She looked away, down at herself, and took a moment to smooth her hands down the front of her clothes. With that accomplished, she raised her head and set her jaw before laying a gentle hand on Adrian's arm.

Adrian led them to the hall first in search of Thomas.

"Lady Elisabeth," Katy said, peeking from the kitchen as the door banged behind the trio. Katy had not had a family to leave with throughout the decline of Ravenshill. She was one of the lucky few trusted by Lincoln to protect the secrets of Ravenshill. Adrian was not sure Katy would have gone even if she had a choice. Like everyone else in its walls, the woman served Ravenshill with loyalty.

The woman rushed toward Elisabeth, arms extended. "How are you, Katy?" Elisabeth asked, dropping her hand from Adrian to embrace the woman.

"I am relieved now to see you," Katy said, enveloping Elisabeth for a moment in her arms. "You are skin and bones, and so is your friend," the woman declared, turning away. "Sit, and I will get you some food."

"Edith will eat. At the moment, I must find my father."

Gone was the scared child he had pulled from his horse moments ago. Instead, at the age of twelve, Elisabeth stood as a queen would, outwardly confident and in control. She stood straight. Her left hand rested against her waist. Her right hand rested overtop her left. But her thumb gave her away as her left stroked back and forth over her right. Though she kept her hands hidden in the folds of fabric, it did not go unnoticed by Adrian.

From the corner of his eye, he watched Edith shake her head and take a step closer to Elisabeth. Elisabeth turned her head, but Edith refused to meet her gaze, her eyes now trained on the floor.

"You are safe here. I will return," Elisabeth reassured her. Her voice was gentle and kind, with a tone Adrian had never heard from her before. But Edith shook her head, not lifting her gaze, taking another step closer to Elisabeth.

"Your father is in the library," Katy said. "I will have food for you all when you return." Katy looked to Adrian, who offered her a thank you before presenting an arm to Elisabeth again.

"Yes, thank you," Elisabeth said, drawing another ounce of dignity from her dwindled supply. She smoothed her hands over the front of her dress, then laid a hand on Adrian again.

Adrian guided her from the hall, hearing Edith follow behind them. The trio hunched their shoulders and ducked their heads against the freezing wind. The arctic blast whipped through the gate, across the bailey, and swirled beneath the roof leading to the tower. It seemed much more chilling and deadly out there now that they were within the walls of Ravenshill with its warm hearths and blankets.

Adrian slipped his hand free of Elisabeth's, indicating she would proceed him across the plank of the small draw bridge that crossed the security ditch. The bridge was the last defense. They could take refuge in the tower and draw the wooden planks closed if the walls were breached. It would not make the tower impenetrable, but it might buy them some time if needed. Many of Elisabeth's ancestors perished in the tower two centuries before. They starved in a siege, along with many servants who took refuge with them, or so the story goes.

Elisabeth paused as they reached the bottom of the steps. Adrian felt her sigh. Then she was on the narrow spiral stairs, and he felt relief that he followed behind. He would never see the steep staircase as anything but deadly again as they twisted clockwise up four floors. He knew he could not follow Elisabeth up or lead her down each time she stepped foot on them to catch her if she slipped. He did not think she would appreciate the request that he do so.

Adrian felt Elisabeth's hesitation as she gained the last wood step of the staircase. She drew a long, steadying breath before she stepped out from behind the short wall that kept all the heat from the hearth escaping from the room and into the stairs. This was where all the books went that his parents sent him. It had turned from a cluttered storage space to a disorganized library. Though Lord Thomas was not educated, he was proud to educate his children. He was the one that declared the garret become the library, as many other manor houses and castles had begun to acquire the same.

Elisabeth smoothed her hands down the front of the tunic Adrian had bought her, and he wanted to tell her it could not get much smoother. Then she tugged at the belt at her waist before placing one hand over the other and settled. Her head raised, and she gave a slight nod before taking the three strides that carried her around the wall and within sight of her father.

Lord Thomas sat behind the desk in a high-backed, plush chair. His head was turned, staring across space he was not a part of in his faraway gaze. It took him a moment to realize he was no longer alone with his thoughts. His blue eyes widened. "Elisabeth?" he asked in quiet disbelief. Then the man shot to his feet and rushed around the desk to seize his daughter in his arms. Adrian heard the breath whoosh from Elisabeth's chest as her father grabbed her with solid arms and drew her against himself, crushing her. "Thank God for his mercy. You have returned," he whispered.

Then Lord Thomas released Elisabeth and reached for Adrian, drawing him into a similar hug that forced the air from his chest. When he released Adrian, he was going for Edith but paused. "Who is this?" he asked the other two, deciding not to embrace her.

"This is Edith," Elisabeth said. "She will stay with us."

"Whatever you want, my child. We will find a way to feed her," Lord Thomas said, pulling Elisabeth back into his arms. Adrian saw the tears that filled the man's eyes and Elisabeth's. It was like looking into identical mirrors of blue. Walter's eyes were once the same, but now Adrian knew Walter's had unexplainable gold flecks in them. He hadn't seen the boy yet. He wondered and worried the boy was no longer at Ravenshill.

Then Lord Thomas was holding Elisabeth at arm's length and studying her. "What happened to you?" her father asked with profound sadness because he knew his daughter had suffered to return to him in the condition she was in. It would not do to tell him her appearance had improved on the journey. Not waiting for an answer, the older man dropped onto his knees in front of her. "Forgive me. I did not mean to strike you."

Her father clung to Elisabeth's hands, gripping them as a father would hold to the child he thought he would never see again. Then his brow furrowed, and he looked down at her hands, turning them with care to see the rough callouses that had developed on her palms. That was when the Lord of Ravenshill burst into tears and buried his head in his daughter's hands.

Elisabeth's face softened, and she closed her eyes and bowed her head over her father as he wept. Adrian felt he shouldn't be there, intruding on this moment. Edith appeared to find the wooden archway in the room fascinating. Adrian began to turn away, but he heard Lord Thomas shift as he did and struggle to his knees. Adrian had not realized how old Baron Thomas was until that moment. He looked grayer, thinner, and feebler as he stumbled off his knees.

"I must speak of my dowery with you," she said as Lord Thomas released her hands.

The man nodded, his expression somber, looking older still as his face fell even further in sorrow. "There is none," he said with sad remorse. "Please forgive me that as well," Adrian heard the man whisper.

Elisabeth turned to Adrian. "I will join you both in the hall soon." Adrian did not miss the opportunity to bow to her. He would never take that opportunity lightly again.

He turned and saw Edith hesitating. "Go," he ordered her but used a gentle voice.

She looked to Elisabeth, who offered the girl an encouraging nod, but still, Edith hesitated. Finally, Elisabeth walked to the girl, who began to tremble. "Adrian will keep you safe until I come for you," Elisabeth told her softly. Though she had lowered her voice, Adrian and Lord Thomas both heard.

Edith nodded, but her brown eyes held incredible trepidation as she turned away. Adrian led the redhead onto the steps but hesitated, remembering his thoughts as they had climbed them. When he reached the first turn on the stairs, he stopped and moved to the side to allow Edith to continue down. But she stopped when he stopped and now stood a step above him.

"I wish to wait on Lady Elisabeth to escort her to the hall," Adrian explained.

Edith hesitated before sinking down to sit on the step. Adrian felt a scowl creeping onto his face, but he forced it away. He stayed because he did not want Elisabeth to fall down the steps she had trod all her living years. Edith wanted to stay because she seemed to need Elisabeth. Adrian understood something had happened that made Elisabeth feel responsible for Edith losing her tongue. But Edith sought protection with Elisabeth, and he knew she must have provided it to Edith somewhere along the way.

Adrian took a step back to squeeze onto the same step as Edith. They could hear slight murmurs of the father and daughter from the room above.

After a long stretch of silence between them, Adrian said, "You are safe here, Edith." She did not look at him. "There is not a soul here who will hurt you."

Silence fell again, then he thought it necessary to say, "I am afraid to let her out of my sight too."

She turned to him and smiled. He saw more smiles from Edith on the journey home than from Elisabeth. She was recovering not just physically but emotionally. They grew together on the long journey back to Ravenshill. In that time, Adrian began to suspect Edith was once a bright and bubbly girl since her smiles and laughter returned quickly to her. Perhaps Elisabeth would find her laughter again and lose the serious twist of her lips and crease in her brow. Maybe one day, her eyes would light up again with her laughter.

When they heard Elisabeth's soft step on the stairs above them, they shot to their feet, unable to hide the guilt on their faces. She looked down at them with an expression that bordered more on annoyance than anger. Adrian cleared his throat. "We are here to escort you."

"I think I remember the way, Adrian," she said, but not unkindly.

He nodded his head once before turning and preceding her down the steps. As he stepped off the steps, he saw Walter standing in the middle of the lord's hall. His appearance in the room where he had died made his heart freeze for a moment.

"Welcome home, Baby Squire," the boy said with a cocky grin twisting his lips. He held his hands behind his back, straightening his posture. He held his head higher, almost imperialistic. Lord knew the boy did not need more confidence.

"Walter?" the sound came out strangled behind him. Adrian jumped to the side, realizing he stood where Walter's body lay months before. And yet, Walter stood before them now.

Elisabeth advanced as if she saw a ghost. "Sister?" Walter said. Relief was not in his voice but surprise at seeing her face after all this time. It must have been quite the mystery for him.

"Yes, brother," she choked with a bit of hesitation. She stopped an arm's length from him, and her eyes trailed up the boy who grew substantially in their absence and back down. "Incredible," she murmured. Then her eyes studied Walter's for a moment, and he saw her scowl. She saw the difference in the eyes, too, and Adrian worried again that others would as well.

"Katy has promised us food," Adrian blurted. The first meeting between the brother and the sister, who weren't, grew a little weird as they stood staring at one another.

"Escort your sister to the hall, please," Elisabeth said, offering her arm. Walter seemed to hesitate for a moment before locking his arm with Elisabeth's and guiding her toward the hall.

Adrian was starved, and true to her word, Katy had food sitting on one of the tables as they entered. Adrian was ready to sink onto the bench where it sat, but Elisabeth stopped and looked from their food to the head table.

"Come, we deserve to sit as the leaders of Ravenshill," Elisabeth said, taking two of the trenchers in her hands and leading them up onto the step. She set them down on the table, pulled her father's chair out, and motioned Walter. "Come," she encouraged him.

Walter joined her and sank into the seat Adrian had never seen anyone else sit in except Lord Thomas.

"Come, bring your food." She motioned to Adrian and Edith. Adrian hesitated. He never sat at the head table with the lord and his children. It was filled with other lords and ladies when knights were abundant here. But Sir Lincoln did not sit at the esteemed table, so Adrian did not.

"Adrian," Elisabeth said, motioning him to a chair next to her. "Edith," she ordered, directing her to the chair on the other side of her.

Edith looked from Adrian to Elisabeth. The smile Elisabeth presented to them was a wary one, but she raised her head, squared her shoulders, and took her seat as regal as any queen could. Adrian took his seat, and from the corner of his eye, he saw Edith do the same.

Elisabeth fell on the food with ravenous hunger. Adrian was starved, ready to attack it. But he hesitated. Lord Thomas's words about finding a way to feed Edith returned to him. He could never imagine things at

Ravenshill were so dire they may not be able to spare food for one more child.

Elisabeth paused and sighed. Adrian's eyes crossed Elisabeth's plate and her hand that held the chunk of bread dripping with gravy. She was hungry too, the bread already half consumed, the tips of her fingers she had plunged into the gravy with the bread. If Adrian had done that before all this, she would call him an animal. Beyond her, Edith sat, her hands folded in her lap, her head down, not touching her food.

"Eat," she snapped at them. He saw her drawn face soften before turning to Edith and then to him. "Eat. We will have food," she said with a nod.

"How?" he mouthed to her.

She shook her head and shrugged.

"It is here now, for all of us," she said, her face turning back to Edith. "Eat," she coaxed in the gentlest of voices.

Edith's eyes lifted to Elisabeth's. She stared at her for a moment before she flung herself from her chair, wrapping her arms around Elisabeth. Then Edith released her and sank back into her chair before attacking the food in front of her.

"Are you well?" Adrian asked, leaning over to Elisabeth. The lines seemed to etch deeper and deeper as she was left in the silence of her own thoughts while everyone ate.

"I have no dowery," Elisabeth said. She did not look at Adrian, but he recognized the significance. She was betrothed to a wealthy man. It was a circumstance that alleviated a significant amount of worry for Ravenshill since Elisabeth neared a marriageable age. But with no dowery, there would be no marriage.

Perhaps they were animals as they attacked the food. When Lincoln entered, more food was brought, and he took a seat on the other side of Walter at Elisabeth's bidding. The knight did not question Elisabeth when she bade him sit with them. But Adrian's mind was a whirlwind of questions. The biggest was how Lord Thomas could bring such ruination to his household.

# Chapter 16

**Sunday, February 4, 1448, Ravenshill**

Elisabeth studied the letter in her hand. She broke the wax seal on this one as she had all the others from the same recipient—five, in fact. The seal made her hands shake when she discovered the first one. Set in red wax, the ship was overlaid by a sword with a serpent wrapped around it. On the Marsdon coat of arms, the snake hissed and flicked its tongue between long fangs. Having been betrothed to Harris Marsdon for as long as she could remember, Elisabeth knew the family had gained wealth from the shipping trade. But seeing the wax seal of his father left her with a chill.

Ensconcing herself in the library, Elisabeth ransacked all the drawers, shelves, and cubby holes to locate all ledgers, contracts, and documents. Among those, she began to discover the unread correspondences. As she found the letters, she organized them by their seals. When she had them all collected, three letters with the ship and sword seal lay in a pile with five others that bore a variation of the seal.

Seven letters bore the seal of Darlene Marsdon, Harris's mother, while the eighth bore the seal of Harris himself.

The seals were not broken, leaving them rudely and possibly devastatingly unacknowledged. Lady Darlene was quite put out by the tone of her final letter that Elisabeth had not presented herself at Blackpool for her training with the family. She surmised as she went through the letters that Lord Harlyn was the first to request Elisabeth arrive at Blackpool for training as a wife there. The letter arrived before she was taken to the mines. The second letter from him bordered on malcontent that no word was received. The third letter from him questioned if Elisabeth and her father planned to honor the contract. Lady Darlene sent the fourth. The tone was warm and pleasant. She sent each one after that, and by the seventh, she was outraged. Lord Harlyn threatened her father for breaking the contract in the rest of his correspondence. The one letter from Harris stated he wished for a better bride than one who would ignore his parents.

But the seal of King Henry VI made her wait with fear to open those last. Lord and Lady Marsdon‘s outrage was nothing compared to King Henry‘s when her father did not send the required number of men for the fight in France. It did not matter. They did not have the four knights or even twenty-foot soldiers the King demanded from a small keep. Her father had ignored the King's command to serve him for more than a year. Added to direct threats from King Henry was the indignation of Hugh Fenn, one of the King's auditors, and the unpaid taxes of the Kirkham family for Ravenshill.

Their threats in the written words in front of her were terrifying. Hugh only wanted the money owed.

Though she did not know how to accomplish this, it was easier than the King's command. King Henry questioned her father's loyalty and even hinted at charges of treason. His words were the ones that echoed and terrified her.

The demands grew even more terrible after the initial readings. After looking over her father's financial ledgers, her heart was gripped by fear. There was no possible way they could pay that many men to send to France. They didn't even have that number of men to protect Ravenshill. But the King demanded his men, or he would give Ravenshill over to someone who could supply his army. As if that was not complicated enough, any hope for Ravenshill lay in her marriage to Harris. A wedding her father could no longer afford, and the Marsdons of Blackpool may no longer want.

She couldn't even afford the clothes she needed to go to Blackpool. One space in the ledger told the tale but, in reality, revealed nothing at all. What did her father believe Walter could do? What did she think her husband could do? Nothing, because without a dowery, she would have no husband.

The footfalls sounded in the archway, and Lincoln entered. He hesitated as Elisabeth's tired eyes connected with his. Then Elisabeth smiled at him. The gesture was warm and forgiving. As was her father and Adrian, this man was a constant in her life. His future was tied to Ravenshill as tightly as hers. His life, he was willing to give to her family. He spilled the blood of innocent people to protect her family. She did not like that, but what was done was done. She learned a lot of truths after running from that reality. Now it was up to her to tell Lincoln what a colossal mistake it was to pledge his sword to Thomas Kirkham.

"Is it bad?" he asked.

Elisabeth's nod was slight as her eyes dropped to the final letter from the King. She wanted to hand it to him, so he could see. She wanted to show him the ledgers so he, too, could see what a mess she was struggling to unravel over the last two days, but Lincoln could not read. So many times, over the previous days, she wished she, too, was ignorant of the numbers she stared at and the threats and promises of dire consequences revealed in the letters.

"The King requires an army of four knights, twenty-foot soldiers, and ten archers to be sent to France."

Lincoln remained standing like a giant oak in the middle of the room. But his devotion and strength could not help them now. He had protected their lands since he was a young man, but Elisabeth knew he could not protect them from what was to come.

"Lord Harlyn demands I come to foster at Blackpool so I can be prepared for marriage."

Elisabeth brushed her fingers across the neat pile of letters beside her. One pile was from the King, one from Blackpool. She hoped to see them organized and stacked would help her think better and harder. But, instead, the stacks did nothing but draw her eyes to them again and again.

"I cannot afford a dress, let alone a dowery. I know the Marsdons are wealthy. Perhaps they would show us favor and send the army of men for us." Elisabeth shook her head, "But I cannot even afford a dress to present myself in."

"I will buy your dress," Lincoln said. His voice was deep and as solid as his frame. Tears sprang to her eyes for his generosity, and her eyes darted away. Lincoln was their man. He was there serving them, and he served them well. He did his duty well, and that did not include buying her a dress.

"You are kind, Sir Lincoln," she said, tapping her finger on the edge of the open ledger. "It is not just the one dress that I need. I need a wardrobe of fine gowns to impress those at Blackpool. So I must find a better solution."

The room fell silent with their thoughts. Then Elisabeth broke it and asked, "Do you know what happened here?"

Lincoln shrugged but spoke. "Finances were stressed by the time we returned from France. The war cut into the coffers, and the steward stole the rest while Lord Thomas fought for the King. When he returned, your mother helped ease the situation because she could read. But your father had no help once she died because he could afford none."

"He can't read?" Elisabeth questioned. She had never known that about her father.

"Is that why the seals are unbroken from these letters?" Elisabeth asked.

Lincoln nodded his head with a great deal of sadness. Elisabeth wondered how different things would be at Ravenshill if her father could read and manage finances and correspondence. "Presley keeps the ledgers for him. For what help that is from a man who can read only a little and is poorly versed in mathematics."

"There are a few extra horses that can be sold."

Elisabeth nodded and made a note.

"How much do you think we can get for them?"

"There are three. We could get ten pounds apiece for two of them right away. Then, with fewer people to feed, we may be able to sell a horse or two kept for plowing and wagons."

Elisabeth made another note. "Will you find out how many horses can be sold without crippling us?"

"Yes, my lady," Lincoln said with a bow to her before he left the room.

Elisabeth tapped the edge of the ledger. If they could do with fewer horses, they would need less grain and less farrier time to make shoes. An entire list of things came to mind that would ease the Ravenshill burden. There were many other things around the castle they could do without. She began making notes of the things off the top of her head they might be able to sell. Along with those notes, she made more about where she could look to discover others.

She spent the remainder of her day accumulating a list. Fortunately, Ravenshill was once wealthy, and they still had many things purchased during such profitable years. Much of the fine furniture could go.

She and her father lived inside the tower. Adrian and Lincoln occupied the barracks, and Katy and Annabelle lived in the room attached to the kitchen. If Lincoln and Adrian moved from the barracks, they wouldn't have to heat it, and they could empty it of the furniture. The rest of the servants lived in their own homes outside the walls.

As far as the servants, they only needed to retain the cook and a maid for the house. They could no longer afford to keep men just standing on the parapets. She had to rid Ravenshill of the extra guards in order to keep the rest. The money they received from Adrian's family to foster him would help do that.

In the early hours of the morning, she climbed into her bed. Its ornately carved wood was deep mahogany, solid, and worth a small fortune. Sleep rushed toward her, and she felt her eyes grow heavy. She could not help but think it might be her last chance to sleep well for some time. For tomorrow she would begin to gather the furnishings they could do without. This, she had concluded, would include her own bed. She would take a cot from the barracks.

The next morning she had the unpleasant task of telling most of the servants and guards they would have to find employment elsewhere. At the end of the day, those who remained gathered in the courtyard as the light was beginning to wane.

"Times are hard for Ravenshill. At the moment, you are all we can afford to keep in employment." The group was a pitiful small lot, the cook Katy, the chambermaid Annabelle, the groom Presley, one knight, one squire, a little street urchin that was supposed to be a lord, one little girl who had no tongue, and her father who seemed to be aging rapidly since turning Ravenshill finances over to her. "I will soon go to Blackpool and plead for assistance for men to fight under Ravenshill in France. I will foster there, and hopefully, soon, we can grow Ravenshill again."

Elisabeth felt so frail as she looked grown men and women in their faces and told them they should not worry, that she could solve her father's problems. She saw the strain of their futures written on their faces—all except the children. Adrian, Edith, and Walter looked at her as if Elisabeth could save them and stitch a perfect tapestry afterward. She tugged on her belt, smoothed her tunic, and whispered to the Heavens that she did have this and would not let them fall.

**Wednesday, April 3, 1448, Ravenshill**

Elisabeth looked at the bolts and bolts of rich fabrics piled on the flat surfaces of the lord's hall on the first floor of the tower. After selling all she felt they could spare, she could not spend it all on a wardrobe of dresses made by a seamstress. By buying the fabric to sew herself, Elisabeth would save half of what she earned for things Ravenshill would need.

She had taken possession of her father's signet ring, with the outline of a raven carved into silver. It would leave the silhouette of a raven in the wax that sealed letters he could not write. She wrote to Blackpool first, and it seemed as if she held her breath waiting for a response. When it came, it was terse but confirmed the contract would still be honored. The problem she now faced was getting to Blackpool sooner than later. She still needed to beg them to send support to the King in their stead before he sent someone to take Ravenshill.

While Elisabeth studied the cloth, Edith studied her with a sparkle of humor in her brown eyes. She found the situation funny, no doubt. She had so many clothes to sew and only two weeks before she had to leave. She recognized it was impossible, but Elisabeth would make as many as she could. It might get her into a couple gowns and cloaks before she had to leave.

"Let's get to work," Elisabeth said, smoothing her dress and raising her head a notch. Suddenly she faltered. Could Edith sew? What if she had never been taught? What if it was only she who could do this? Could she even get one dress done? There was more required than placing the stitches into the materials. Her measurements needed to be taken, the fabric cut then pieced together.

"Can you sew?" Elisabeth asked. A knot rose and formed in her throat, nearly choking her with the fear she had just made a horrible decision that left Ravenshill even more destitute.

Edith nodded, reading the apprehension on Elisabeth's face. Edith reached for Elisabeth, patted her hand, and lifted one finger before fleeing the room. Elisabeth tried to encourage Edith to speak. She told her she would learn to understand her, that she was sure some words would not have changed without a tongue to form them if they had not required the tongue. But Edith refused to utter a single word and had not since she tried to say Elisabeth's name at the mine.

When they returned to Ravenshill, both she and Edith put on weight. Despite the girl's silence, Elisabeth came to appreciate Edith's sparkle. She bounced throughout the day. Elisabeth only knew her before as a slave, so she did not know if this was Edith's way or a new fondness for freedom and life out of the dirt. Elisabeth envied her and the girl's ability to still play childish games with Walter. While those played, Adrian and Elisabeth would look on, both too wise and burdened to know how to feel such simple joy.

Within a moment, Edith returned with Katy and Annabelle in tow.

"Can you sew?" she asked them.

"Yes, my lady," Katy said while Annabelle nodded.

"And cut patterns?" Elisabeth asked, daring to hope.

Both women nodded, and Elisabeth was awash with relief.

Edith dashed from the room again. When she returned this time, she brought Walter with her. Elisabeth had not thought of employing the men.

Indeed, they could do some stitching. If not stitching, maybe cutting the fabric or laying a pattern.

"Do you know how to sew?" Elisabeth asked.

"Some," he replied. "My..." he trailed off. "Remember, you taught me some. I remember what you taught me."

Elisabeth nodded. She suspected that the boy was about to identify someone from his past who taught him the skill. Elisabeth was learning the boy was bright, and Adrian was working with him on things he should already know. They taught him family stories and their ancestry from the long line of Kirkhams farther back than the Vikings and the name Kirkham. What Walter embraced the most was learning to read. Elisabeth guessed a part of it was knowing how devastating not being able to read could be.

The last three servants of Ravenshill also knew the great family secret. They could be trusted not to tell the world Walter Kirkham was an imposter. They were not present when Walter died, but the three proved loyal through the years and were spared.

"Get the other men," Elisabeth said as she began to organize the materials, and Annabelle started to take measurements.

By midday, all the women of Ravenshill were making dresses and cloaks. The men worked alongside making the clothing that would honor the Kirkham name. The men included her father. After standing in the doorway, he had come in silently, watching what the entire household was involved in. Then he stepped forward, took some pins from Lincoln, and began to help fold the seams of a cloak to be sewed.

Elisabeth learned Walter had a great stitch, putting Elisabeth to shame, not that she ever thought she was good at the mundane task. Lincoln was a Neanderthal and barely could make a straight cut, let alone stitch. Still, he became helpful in pinning patterns to the fabric and removing pins as the gowns came together.

That evening as her help dwindled to see to other tasks, Edith and Elisabeth were left to finish the final stitches before they were called to the last meal of the day. Elisabeth's fingers ached, and she knew she would have to get used to that. Despite all the help, they had a lot more sewing to do. As she tied off the thread and bit it off with her teeth, she looked up to see Edith's head bowed, and giant tears fell onto the fabric in her lap.

Elisabeth laid her work on the table. Then, she walked to her, sinking down next to her and placing a hand over the girl's still hands.

"What is wrong?" Elisabeth asked, but she knew Edith would not tell her. Not in words. Edith flung her work on the floor and wrapped her arms around Elisabeth's neck, clinging to her and sobbing.

"Oh, Edith," Elisabeth said. The feeling washed over her, reminding her of the mines. Of the terrified Edith, the way she clung to her and hid behind her. "It's okay. I will not leave you behind. I can take a servant, and Adrian will escort us."

Edith pulled back and studied Elisabeth. "I would never leave you behind. You should know that about me by now."

Edith nodded her head, then leaned forward and leaned her head on Elisabeth's shoulder. "It will be okay. You will see," Elisabeth said, stroking Edith's red hair. Elisabeth reassured her while having no way of knowing if it was true.

A few minutes later, Elisabeth entered the hall for the meal and saw everyone seated at the head table. Her father sat in his chair. But he did not look as regal and powerful to her as he once had. She sat next to him, and the hall remained silent.

"I have something to say," her father said at some length, standing from the table. "I must apologize to each of you. Decisions I made years ago have led to the demise of Ravenshill. I owe you all an apology, especially my daughter."

Her father turned to her then, and she saw sadness in his eyes. "I may have ruined your life with my foolishness, and I am so proud of your bravery and loyalty to Ravenshill. I hope that one day you can forgive me."

Elisabeth wanted to say she forgave him. She tried to rid herself of that burden of frustration she felt each time she looked at him or the ledgers that showed the extent of their debt. But she was unable to stop it from rolling through her. She offered him a smile and hoped that would do.

**Wednesday, April 17, 1448, Ravenshill**

The day came to leave Ravenshill. Five dresses were completed, along with two cloaks. Two other dresses and a cloak would be delivered to Blackpool upon completion. They even fashioned Edith a couple of dresses that would befit her place as Elisabeth's servant.

"Do you know what you are doing?" Lincoln asked her as he stood holding her horse. Ravenshill no longer had a carriage, but she loved to ride, and they had made a luxurious velvet riding habit. Elisabeth would wear that for the journey. There would be little question, with such riding clothes, as to why she arrived on horseback and not in a carriage. It was clothing designed for a horsewoman.

"If I do not, I shall figure it out in all due haste."

Lincoln gave her a nod before giving her her horse's head. "Let us go, Lady of Blackpool," Adrian said teasingly. Soon, she would marry the wealthy Harris with a lot of luck, and all their problems would fall into his purse. Elisabeth refused to cry as they rode out the gate. Therefore, she refused to look behind her at the stone walls, the stone tower that reached for the sun that peaked out from the morning clouds.

The ride south built the nerves in Elisabeth's breast to a complete frenzy of turmoil and self-doubt. She felt her hands shaking when she rode onto the cobblestones of Blackpool's expansive castle late the following evening.

"You are brave," Adrian reminded her, helping her to the ground. As soon as she was on firm ground, she thought she might vomit. She swallowed, tugging down on her high-waisted belt that sparkled with silver embroidery. She smoothed down the hem of the green velvet jacket and pulled her thin cloak together, hiding the hands that clinched it. She raised her head to look at those gathering on the steps of the giant castle of Blackpool.

The structure was beautiful and intimidating, sitting upon the rocky coastline with the waves crashing against the rocks below. When Elisabeth first heard the sound of the surf as they approached, she began to sweat. For her, the sound was not a pleasant one. It was a reminder of her past. She struggled daily to shed it, to push away the nightmare of life then. Until she conquered the daytime, she knew she could not banish the demons that woke her each night. The incessant sound of the ocean would not help soothe her in this place. But she had learned she could survive anything.

She advanced with Adrian and Edith trailing her. It was a struggle to keep her eyes looking up and ahead. She felt so cowed it was almost as if she were advancing on Master standing on the steps with the cruel boy waiting beside him.

“Elisabeth,” Darlene Marsdon said. Elisabeth detected the coldness in her tone. “It is about time you graced us with your presence.”

Elisabeth curtsied to her as Lady Darlene looked over her head with disdain at Edith and Adrian. “Come inside. Christen will see you settled.” The man who stood beside Darlene said nothing. Elisabeth guessed it was her future father-in-law, Baron Harlyn Marsdon. Her future husband was missing, and her stomach dropped even further. She wanted to speak to him first. Lord Harlyn looked intimidating, standing beside his wife. Still, she had to send news back with Adrian about whether Blackpool would give men to fight.

Elisabeth curtsied again and followed Lady Darlene inside. The castle of Blackpool was magnificent. Ravenshill was only a cold stone keep, with a hall added. Centuries old, Ravenshill did not have the improved luxuries as Blackpool did. It was warmer here, without the heat of the hearths leaching into the bare stones. The chambers were larger and plentiful. She and Edith would share a room with four other girls fostering at Blackpool. Now, the only thing left was to convince the Marsdons she was worth the soldiers she would request in her family’s name.

# Chapter 17

**Friday, April 19, 1448, Blackpool, England**

Adrian stood outside Lord Harlyn's office. Elisabeth waited before him, tugging at her belt, a nervous habit since returning from the mines. Finally, the voice bid them enter from inside, and Elisabeth opened the door, advancing with all outward appearances to the world she was confident. But she was terrified. Adrian saw it in every line on her face and the way she fidgeted. He was here because she was scared to face Lord Harlyn alone.

Adrian would leave soon, and Lord Harris had not made an appearance. A frustrated Elisabeth told him no one seemed to want to tell her whether her fiancé was even in residence. Adrian did not like these people, but Elisabeth reassured him she would be in exemplary care with them. But she didn't know he could see the fear raging inside her.

Her stride carried her forward to stand before her future father-in-law. Adrian was only slightly relieved to see Harlyn stand as a sign of respect for his future daughter-in-law. The man towered over Elisabeth, who

Adrian realized was still just a child. Despite everything, it was a child standing before Harlyn.

"I thank you for granting me an audience this morning," she said after making a deep curtsy to him.

"What is it, Elisabeth?" the man asked. Adrian did not know how the man could already be impatient with her, but his voice told them he was.

"It is of a financial matter," Elisabeth informed him.

"Oh, does your father know you are speaking of financial matters? That is best left to men."

Adrian felt Elisabeth tense. He was sure the statement would have been offensive to the spirited child before. But for her to have survived the mines and struggled to right Ravenshill's finances, he knew Elisabeth was deeply offended. For a moment, Adrian feared the man behind his desk would not survive. But Elisabeth was not the same impetuous girl she had once been.

"It is urgent. But unfortunately, Father could not make the journey. He has been in poor health. But he has asked me to speak with you on this matter."

"Oh," the man said.

"Ravenshill has had some crisis that left our military ranks minimal," she began, but the man interrupted her.

"Oh? What kind of crisis?"

"I am not sure," Elisabeth stammered. Adrian stared at her. She did not stammer even when she was terrified. "I only know what he has said to me. It is, as you said, financial matters are best left to men. But he has bid me request fighting men to send to France under the Ravenshill banner."

"Why would I do this?" Harlyn asked.

"I guess because it is something that is done?" Elisabeth stammered again with a shrug.

"Men are not cheap," the man said with a scowl. Adrian thought neither were little girls.

"Perhaps when I see your dowery, I will send troops."

"I think Father needs them as soon as possible, or there was some talk of another prospect for me."

"Another prospect?" the man hissed. "One better than my son?"

Elisabeth shrugged. "That is what was said." Her voice and face looked far more innocent than even a newborn babe could be.

Harlyn studied her for several moments, and she remained meek under the scrutiny. Adrian did not know how she did not quake. He was ready to, and he was not the one putting on such a brave charade.

"Your father would dare not break our contract. When it is the King demanding, I fear something must be done. Very well. You best produce us an heir for this. Send the message I will provide the troops he needs. How many?" he asked.

"Four knights, twenty foot soldiers, and ten archers," she informed him quickly. Almost too quickly, if the man's deepening scowl was any indication.

"It was twenty-five foot soldiers and fifteen archers," Adrian corrected her. He could tell Harris was skeptical Elisabeth had the brain capacity to remember the numbers correctly. Adrian realized they might need extra men, a buffer so they would not have to come begging this man for more soldiers when some perished. With the war and disease prevalent in the English camps, it was no surprise many men died.

Harlyn was blind to the evidence Elisabeth was not just the messenger. She was the one who sat and worried for months running the numbers around and around in her head until they would be a part of her memory forever. Adrian was sure she could recite them in her sleep. The baron's scowl eased.

"Fine," he said. "I will send them to France. Tell your father to send his steward the next time he has financial business to discuss. I do not like the witless prattling of you women," he said with a wave of his hand to dismiss them.

Obediently Elisabeth curtsied, and Adrian bowed before making their way from the room.

"I will miss you, Adrian," Elisabeth said as they walked to the stables together.

Adrian did not feel relieved Elisabeth did not bring up Harlyn's manner. Adrian wanted to punch the man for calling Elisabeth witless. He wished Harris knew what a treasure he was getting in her. If Harris could pull Ravenshill back together, she would never falter at his side. But Adrian knew it would gall her to be around a man like Harlyn and how he must treat every woman. She would not like lying with his cold-hearted son, who couldn't even be bothered to meet his soon-to-be bride. Adrian was sure of that.

"I will miss you, Elisabeth," he said as he took her hand. "But don't fret. You can visit Ravenshill soon." His hand squeezed hers, and he knew he could not know when they would see each other again. The fear he would never see her again nearly choked him. He stopped short and almost made the mistake of pulling her against him but remembered where they stood. His eyes bore into her, and it seemed as if her fears had melted. "Most of all, remember you are brave. Braver than anyone here, I will wager my horse on it."

Elisabeth began to say something when a woman's voice cut across the courtyard. "Elisabeth, you come with me." The tall woman's stride ate the ground up between them. Then, reaching Elisabeth's side, she grabbed her arm, yanking her so she stumbled before she was yanked from Adrian's grasp. "And you, young man, keep away from her. I don't care who you are."

Adrian watched the woman drag Elisabeth away. She cast a couple quick glances back before she was pulled inside the hall. He stood a moment, then rubbed his hands together, trying to push from his mind that feeling of her hand being removed from his. It left them on a troubling note. He went to the stable and prepared his horse.

The hand on his shoulder froze him as he tied off his girth. He turned to see Edith standing behind him. He hoped he could look at her one day and not see her that first time he lay eyes on her. Now her brown eyes held a spark of appreciation for life. She never spoke, but she hummed a great deal. Sometimes they were long, beautiful, and occasionally sad songs. Other times they were bright and almost amusing to watch her head become animated, sometimes her shoulders and face as she entrenched herself in the song. She was a far cry from the terrified child they found with Elisabeth. Seeing her now, knowing what she was, made him forget the regret of losing his sword.

She stood before him now with her face scrubbed, her simple dress fit to her. The light brown woolen fabric darkened the girl's eyes to black. Her red hair shone with good health, and her pale face had the light of life instead of the darkness of death.

"You will take care of her?" he asked.

Edith nodded and patted her chest over her heart.

"I will miss you both," he told her.

Edith grabbed him and pulled him into a fierce hug. As Edith hugged him, he wondered why she did not fit to him as well as Elisabeth. It did not seem as if there was that warmth that softened them and molded them so well together as when he took Elisabeth in his arms. When Adrian released her, tears were in Edith's eyes, and she fled from the structure.

He led his horse into the courtyard, mounted, and turned the animal. He searched every doorway and window for a glimpse of Elisabeth. He feared it would be his last. He did not see her before he rode from Blackpool.

# Chapter 18

**Monday, June 17, 1448, Blackpool, England**

It began innocently enough. Edith was humming when the girls entered the chamber from their dance lessons. Elisabeth fell in tune with her, and then Benedetta started adding the bawdy lyrics. By the time Mistress Reed entered and saw the result, Edith had led them into a dance that was nothing like the dances Elisabeth and the girls of good breeding were learning. This was the kind Elisabeth would expect to find in alehouses and taverns in the Irish countryside. Of course, Mistress Reed heard the raucous laughter coming from the solar down the corridor.

"That is enough!" Mistress Reed growled, her face turning red in the doorway. The woman was large and intimidating. Elisabeth supposed she had to be strict in raising the girls to take on adulthood and marriage responsibilities. But her raised voice never failed to make Elisabeth's heart jump into her throat. She towered over almost every woman at Blackpool except Lady Darlene and Lady Taylin, Harris's sister. They were tall, but where Mistress Reed was stout as a bull, the

Marsdon women were slender. But they were no less intimidating with their scowls that seemed to equal Mistress Reed's disappointment in Elisabeth.

Mistress Reed advanced to Edith. "I do not like this idiot around you girls. She is obviously a bad influence. She will go to the kitchens, and I shall send you a new maid," Mistress Reed said, reaching for Edith's arm.

Edith took a step back to avoid the woman's grasp. Thunder creased her brow.

"I will be fine, Edith," Elisabeth reassured her in the hopes of calming both.

Mistress Reed relaxed, and Edith gave a short nod she would comply. They left the room together, and the four other girls stared at Elisabeth.

"Why do you like her so much?" Ivy asked in her snide voice.

"She is nice," Elisabeth said.

"She doesn't even talk," Ivy continued to push. "How can someone be nice if they can't speak."

"She cares for me well," Elisabeth defended.

Alice scoffed. Of course, she would take Ivy's side. She took Ivy's side on anything, and both girls quickly followed Benedetta. Thankfully, Benedetta was not mean like the other two girls. Benedetta was Italian and spoke with a thick accent. The girls looked up to her because she was well-traveled and was promised to a powerful duke in France. "She doesn't do anything," Alice said.

"She does what your maids do," Elisabeth said.

"Barely," Ivy said. "She can't do any of it right."

"It doesn't matter now, does it," Elisabeth said, knowing the girls were just trying to irritate her. They were very good at it. Ivy and Alice took an instant dislike to Elisabeth. She knew it was because she was to marry Lord Harris, the most handsome and chivalrous knight in all Christendom, according to the other girls. But he was yet to make an appearance. Elisabeth resided at Blackpool for two months while her betrothed came and went but seemed uncaring to visit with his future bride. But Elisabeth told herself, again and again, not to take offense. She was pushing forward for one reason, and that reason was Ravenshill.

She watched the thirty-nine-man army march from Blackpool to serve in France. She did not need a husband who gave a whit about her. She just needed those men, and she required Lord Harris's money. Nothing else mattered because things could become much worse. They could always get worse.

**Tuesday, June 18, 1448, Blackpool**

Two mornings after Edith was banished to the kitchens, she ran into the girls' chamber as they dressed. She ran straight to Elisabeth and flung herself at her, clinging to her. The fingers biting into her clothing terrified Elisabeth for a moment. As quickly as the redhead burst through the door, Elisabeth was again in that cold place. They were not standing within Blackpool's warm, safe walls but in the cruel place, she knew they would never be able to escape. Elisabeth tried to pry Edith off as if this was not happening in front of the other girls. Still, Edith did not want to release Elisabeth. Finally, with a great deal of effort she could not hide, Elisabeth managed to get Edith to let her loose. Elisabeth was going to ask her what was wrong, but the words died on her lips. A large bruise marked her jaw with smaller ones along the girl's wrists. It took Elisabeth a moment to realize they were left by the tight grip of strong fingers. Elisabeth lifted the sobbing girl's hair and saw bruises left from the same fingerprints on her neck.

"Edith," Elisabeth whispered through the rising lump in her throat. She fought back her own tears. The girl cried harder, falling into Elisabeth, who wrapped her tight. She looked up to see the other girls watching. Alice and Ivy held smirks of satisfaction that this girl they did not like because she had had her tongue cut from her was suffering anew. Elisabeth did not care. They knew nothing of what could befall them. They were safe here for a moment. But that could change in a heartbeat.

"Who did this to you?"

Elisabeth had to pull Edith away again and shake her so her brown, red-rimmed eyes would focus on her. "Show me who did this." Then because her voice had sounded so urgent, she softened it, and taking Edith's face in her hands, feeling the tears on her cold cheeks, she coaxed, "Show me."

Edith nodded, and both girls heard the snickers that followed them out the door. The man was a huge barbaric knight. When Elisabeth laid eyes on him as Edith quaked behind her, she felt her blood run cold. This man had laid hands on Edith. Edith was still just a child. Elisabeth had begun her monthly flux, but Edith had not, yet this man had touched her. Had he done more than touch and bruise?

With a force of will, Elisabeth turned away. Edith trailed her. The man was unaware of their presence as he jousted with others on the field.

Once out of sight, Elisabeth grabbed Edith and pulled her tight. "I will not let you leave my sight again," she told Edith, but even as she said it, she knew it was out of her hands. Elisabeth either played by the rules of Blackpool, or she could leave the solution to Ravenshill's problems behind. At least if she addressed it to Lady Darlene, she would know the importance of allowing her to keep Edith close. She just had to speak to her.

"My lady, might I have a word with you?" Elisabeth asked Lady Darlene as she curtsied before her and two of her friends. They drank tea beneath the shade of the giant oaks growing along the back of the property. Of all of Blackpool, this was the place that reminded Elisabeth of home.

"Spit it out," Darlene said. Her impatience was evident in her harsh voice.

Elisabeth glanced at the other ladies. "It is of some delicacy," Elisabeth said, hoping to speak to her privately.

"If you cannot speak of it among us all, it does not need to be spoken of."

Elisabeth tugged forcibly at her belt. "Very well. One of your knights has violated my maid."

Lady Darlene's eyes shot from Elisabeth to Edith, who stood close behind Elisabeth. Then to Elisabeth's horror, the woman burst out laughing, and the other two ladies followed suit. "Is this her attempt to marry above her station?" the woman asked. Her words were cruel. She rose from her chair and advanced. Elisabeth tried to make herself a barrier between Lady Darlene and Edith. But the woman reached out and slung Elisabeth away. "I will not have you smear the good name of one of our knights. None of them would touch the likes of you. The idea is ludicrous. Leave here. You are no longer welcome."

The woman stood over Edith, and the girl cowered before her. "Lady Darlene," Elisabeth pleaded.

"Get to your room," the woman snapped.

"Please let her stay," Elisabeth pleaded, wringing her hands.

"You be quiet, or you can leave too. I know my husband has sent troops in your father's stead. I personally do not think you are worth it. Do you wish to go with her?"

In a quiet voice, Elisabeth said, "No."

"Then go to your chamber," the woman ground out between gritted teeth.

Edith clamped onto Elisabeth's arm and began to drag her away. "Might Lord Adrian come to escort her back?" Elisabeth asked.

The woman looked ready to argue but relented. "It will keep us from sparing even more men in your name. She will stay in the kitchen until he arrives."

Elisabeth did not understand how difficult it would be to watch her friend ride away from her. Adrian arrived four days later, and Lady Darlene immediately turned him around with Edith in tow. He cast a concerned look in her direction but complied, never dismounting or speaking to Elisabeth. Edith was positioned on the back of Adrian's horse, her arms wrapped around his waist. How Elisabeth envied them being able to ride away. Her heart felt shattered when the two were out of sight. It was the first time Edith had not been at her side since the mines.

The days that followed seemed to be a blur. Elisabeth did not feel like herself. She didn't feel complete. The other girls seemed to grow more intense in their hatred of her. Their baiting grew more precise and on the mark. Though she was never alone, she felt she was without Edith. It was the first time Elisabeth realized Edith was what made her strong. The silent Edith had to be protected, or men like the knight would rip her apart. Now Elisabeth felt she had nothing that moved her forward. What was worse was seeing the knight that had hurt Edith. He walked the halls of Blackpool without care, and hatred for him grew in Elisabeth until she could not bear to look at him. She ensconced herself in the girls' chamber as often as possible to avoid him and everyone else who seemed to look at her and judge her.

Life at Blackpool became more complicated when Ivy and Alice woke her one night because she was moaning in her sleep. They declared she disturbed them all. Together, the two girls tossed her out of bed, dragging her with all her bedclothes to the outer chamber. Benedetta watched the action with indifference.

Lady Darlene would not grant her another chamber, though chambers were available. She thought Elisabeth should try harder to get along with the other girls. As a result, Elisabeth slept on the floor, in the corner of the solar. The hard wooden floor was better than the hard settee with the hard cushion that angled forward and away from the high wooden back. It left her feeling like one roll was all it would take to dump her on the floor.

**Friday, January 3, 1449, Blackpool**

"This stitch will never do, Elisabeth," Mistress Reed said as the tall woman peered over her shoulder. "Lord Harris will not be pleased with a wife who cannot make a better stitch."

Elisabeth was startled, unaware the woman was hovering behind her. Ivy called her flighty on more than one occasion as if she was some sort of horse. The other girls took up the notion and called her "Unbalanced Beth." But, of course, those girls would never know what she knew. They would never know the fear of someone lurking near them, waiting for an excuse to hurt them, beat them, and make them suffer. Such knowledge made one jumpy, and though sometimes Elisabeth's mind wanted them to know how that felt, her heart did not. No matter how cruel they were, she did not think they could ever be harsh enough to deserve the life she had suffered.

"Pull it out and begin again," Mistress Reed said with a scowl as Elisabeth looked up at her.

Elisabeth looked down at the stitches she had placed. She concentrated all morning on putting the beige thread in the beige fabric. She made the stitches small and tight because that was the complaint from Mistress Reed yesterday—that she made her stitches too big, and they would pull free. She studied the stitching and was annoyed to see what Mistress Reed was seeing.

"You must make your stitches perfect. Perfect size, spacing, and in a perfect line," Mistress Reed said the last as if Elisabeth was some imbecile.

Then she clapped her hands together to draw the attention of the three other girls. As if they weren't watching Unbalanced Beth get it wrong again and smirking about it. "Ladies, while Elisabeth is redoing her sloppy work, we shall go for a ride."

Elisabeth's heart sank. Riding was her favorite thing, but she rarely got an opportunity here. As the other girls gathered their things, Elisabeth began to pull out her tiny stitches while trying not to cry.

By the time Mistress Reed returned, it appeared as if Elisabeth had made no progress because she made the stitches too big and had to pull them free again. The woman was unhappy with her progress and told Elisabeth she must complete the task before beginning another.

One of the other tasks the other girls participated in throughout the day, but she missed out on, was dance lessons. She would ten to one rather learn the intricate steps of a dance than place a perfect stitch. They also continued their project of making preparations for the spring feast. It was to be an elaborate affair worthy of a king. This, too, was preferable to stitching and restitching to achieve elusive perfection.

By the day's final meal, she pulled the stitches out for the fifth time. Each time they got better. Soon they would be perfect. Once she accomplished that, she would go find food. The light waned outside the high windows. Elisabeth set flame to the lantern next to her chair. The light illuminated her work, showing she made the tiny stitches a little askew. She cut a stitch away and began the painstaking task of pulling the thread free.

By now, her fingers began to grow tired, the skin burned, then numbed from holding the tiny needle and forcing it into the thread repeatedly. Despite struggling, her stitches were either too big, too little, too close, too far apart, or not straight. Grains of sand settled in her eyes, biting into them, blurring. When her fingers began to bleed, she was careful to keep them wiped away so as not to stain the fabric.

What would become of them if she could not make her stitches perfect, and Lord Harris did not wish to continue the betrothal? By marrying her, Harris gained little except Elisabeth's long pedigree attached to the Crown. It would be easy enough to find a higher-titled lady. Therefore, she had to present herself properly and better than any other girl Lord Harris might seek. She could not afford to lose him as a future husband. Who else would take on the woes that befell the House of Ravenshill? How else could she bring them out of the mess?

She was sure if Harris would allow her an opportunity and get to know her, he would not see her as an imbecile. Elisabeth needed him to see her value. He needed to see he could not live without her. After all, there was still the issue of the dowery she did not have.

**Saturday, January 4, 1449, Blackpool**

Mistress Reed entered the chamber soon after finishing the day's first meal. She was annoyed Elisabeth did not join them. Mistress Reed was further aggravated when she did not appear in time to join them for the morning sewing in the solar. She was not prepared for the vision before her when she stepped across the threshold into the solar. Elisabeth sat hunched over her fabric. On the floor next to her was the pile of wispy remains of the stitches she pulled. Elisabeth glanced up, and Mistress Reed gasped. She heard the girls filling the doorway behind her do the same. Dark circles marred the girl's porcelain skin beneath her eyes. The white of her eyes surrounding the blue was red as a demon's. But it was the look of panic and desolation that scared her. Then she saw Elisabeth's fingers.

Quickly, Mistress Reed turned and all but forced the girls out of the doorway before slamming it in their faces. She turned back to her young charge and felt guilt for what she knew was her doing. Cautiously she advanced as Elisabeth bent again, stitching and oblivious to her raw fingers as they bled.

She sank onto the floor and placed a hand over the girl's tiny ones to still her. Big blue tear-stained eyes raised to hers. "I can make it perfect," she assured Mistress Reed. "It's not right now, but it's getting better." Elisabeth held the blood-stained cloth out for her inspection.

"Oh, my child," Mistress Reed said. Her voice was kind and soft, unlike what Elisabeth was used to hearing from her. She began to take Elisabeth's hands in her own to comfort her. But the carnage of them made her pull back. Instead, Mistress Reed placed a gentle hand on Elisabeth's cold, damp cheek, forcing her darting eyes to her own. "There are truly no perfect stitches. There will always be one that mars. I truly did not expect perfection, only improvement."

Elisabeth shook her head. The motion was frantic. "I can make them perfect. I can."

"It's alright, truly," Mistress Reed began to pull the cloth away from Elisabeth.

The girl seized it in an iron grip, refusing to release it. "I can get it right. I promise I can get it perfect," she declared. Her hands returned to the needle and material, drawing it close to her red-blue eyes. She winced when she pressed the needlepoint into the fabric, but it did not slow her.

"You have done fine work, dear," Mistress Reed coaxed. "Come away now, and we shall clean you up and feed you."

But Elisabeth could not relinquish the fabric without completing the task to please Mistress Reed and

Lord Harris. She couldn't risk garnering Lord Harris's displeasure. Instead, she could show them a perfect stitch, and they would both be pleased with her. Elisabeth jumped to her feet as Mistress Reed tried to take the fabric from her again. She carried the material next to the window. Her stitches were too large and too sloppy. She began to rip at them as she cried because she could do better. She knew she could do better. If they would give her a chance.

Mistress Reed tried to take the fabric away again, and Elisabeth fought against her in earnest. Elisabeth shoved at her twice, then hit her in the head with her fist. Then she stared at Mistress Reed, confused when the tall woman began to yell for help. The woman stood an arm's length away. A trickle of blood ran down her cheek. Why couldn't she just let Elisabeth show them she could get it right?

When the guard came to take it from her, she fought him. She fought them all until the physician was called. He forced something down her throat, and she was plunged into peaceful oblivion. Her world became disjointed after that. Nothing made sense—no words, space, or time. It all whirled about in constant confusion, bliss, and nightmares.

**Thursday, January 9, 1449, Blackpool**

"Why are you here?" Elisabeth looked up into the face of Adrian. A cloud hung heavy over her mind, a fog so deep it took her some time to recognize the boy whose face she knew as well as her own reflection. She stared at his beautiful gray eyes as she tried to understand what was happening around her. She tried to grasp time and reality but came up empty-handed. Everything was disjointed, flowing forward and backward. She lifted a hand to touch him. The tip of her index finger came in contact with his chin. It was solid, and she marveled at how masculine he looked, how big he was growing. Did he always look so exhausted?

She smiled at him as she moved her hand to cup his cheek. She wanted to feel its power, the reality that she was okay. With Adrian here, she would be okay. His hand wrapped around hers. The strength and heat of it made her suck in her breath.

"I'm taking you home."

Adrian stood from where he was crouching in front of her. She sat on the edge of the bed, dressed down to her shoes. They were not alone in the room. But why would they be? It would be scandalous and her ruin. He still held her hand and was tugging her.

She came off the bed sluggishly. Her knees were weak as Adrian took her arm, lifting and steadying her.

"I can't go," she said. She tried to free herself from Adrian's grasp, but he kept hold of her as he used it to force her toward the door.

"You must," he said. Elisabeth was confused. She didn't know why she had to leave.

Then it dawned on her. Lord Harris was sending her away. Was it her stitches? It couldn't be that. She could make them perfect. "Does Lord Harris not want me anymore?" she asked. Her tongue felt huge in her head. She was not sure, but her words sounded slurred. Adrian still would not release her. She tried again, and just before her elbow came from his grasp, his grip tightened.

"Adrian," she pleaded, prying at his hands. "I must stay and show Lord Harris..."

"Stop," he hissed at her, fingers digging into her flesh.

"Ouch! Please...," Adrian yanked her again.

"Come with me quietly. Now," he ground out.

The fog was clearing a little at a time, and his words made her realize again they were not alone.

She looked up at him, into his gray eyes, and was ashamed. She couldn't remember what she had done. But she knew she had done something. And now, she was doing something else to bring shame down on her.

She swallowed and gave two small nods as she fought back the tears. Adrian turned and slipped her hand into the crook of his arm, enveloping her hand with his strong one. He towered over her, sheltering her from whatever was happening to her. He slipped through the door, pulling her with him. Outside, he pulled her closer so the length of her side pressed into his powerful body. She felt he could envelop her and protect her from everything if she asked him to. She opened her mouth to ask him when his words stopped her.

"Do not let them see you cry."

The words were whispered gently. Elisabeth swallowed and lifted her head. The fog remained, but she knew people were coming from the room behind them. They watched her. His hand patted hers, and they walked. Through the corridors, she wanted to know why she was leaving. But she remained silent, noting that every person they passed paused to watch, and it was not respect that made it so. It was difficult to keep her head high and her eyes ahead as if those who gathered did not exist. Adrian was right. She could not let them see her cry.

Elisabeth felt as if she could breathe a little easier when they stepped out into the open air of the courtyard. She walked beside her mountain as each breath came easier and easier the farther they moved away from those who stared. Then he was stopping her next to two saddled horses. He pulled free from her and gathered the reins of one. He led it to her, guiding her to its side.

"I cannot ride out of here with you on the same horse as me. You have had a moment of distress, but Lord Harris has assured me he does not wish to end the engagement. So put your foot in my hand, and I will boost you."

Elisabeth did as Adrian said. She felt unbalanced on the horse's back. Adrian's hand grabbed her leg. It darted beneath her skirt and gripped her just below the knee. It remained long enough for her to get as secure as the fog allowed. Then the reins were in her hands, and Adrian left her to mount his own horse.

She was an excellent rider, but as her horse moved beneath her, she pitched in the saddle. Each step jolted her and made her head feel as if it was shattering. Elisabeth knew she rode alone for some time. She felt exhausted, and her head lolled back and forth as she wobbled more and more in the saddle. Then she was on the horse with Adrian behind her. His arms wrapped around her. One hand held the reins while the other flattened across her abdomen, pressing her against him. Finally, she felt safe again and let her head fall against him. He was real, and she was safe.

# Chapter 19

**Thursday, January 9, 1449, Blackpool, England**

Adrian was enraged when he walked into Elisabeth's chamber at Blackpool and saw the state they had the girl in. Lord Harris brought Mistress Reed in to tell him what transpired the morning the physician was called. Since then, Elisabeth had been kept in an opium stupor. She could not even walk under her own power without stumbling. Not far from Blackpool, Adrian climbed up to ride behind her, seeing her unsteady balance atop her horse. As he held her against himself, he could not help but wonder how many times he would have to come to her rescue. Not much longer since Lord Harris still had plans to marry her. This saddened him. He thought of her as a friend, perhaps even more than that, a sister. He did love her. That was why he felt such anger that they sedated her and gave her no more thought in the time it took them to send a message to Ravenshill and for him to arrive. For days, she was kept in a state where she could do little more than drool. But Elisabeth did an admirable job keeping her dignity. Once he could get through to her mind, she had to.

He rode with her throughout the rest of the day with her cradled in his arms, sleeping. He had to shift her from time to time to get circulation back to his arms or legs with her weight resting on him. That night he stopped at an inn and rented a room for her with the last of his coin. His plan was to sleep in the stable with the horses, but Elisabeth was scared. She was not aware yet of what was happening and what had happened. So, he spent the night on the floor of her room. He, too, was exhausted. Terrified of what was happening to Elisabeth, he had left Ravenshill immediately when the letter had arrived. He had not slept in the two days.

He could not say he got much sleep on the floor of the inn. He lay on the hard floor listening to Elisabeth's gentle breaths and cried as she thrashed and mumbled in her sleep. He knew where she was in her dream. Though he did not understand what resided in that particular nightmare, he knew Elisabeth was again in the mines. She settled back down, and her breaths steadied. Adrian did not know how, but he had to protect her better.

The following day there was more of Elisabeth in her blue eyes when he woke her. Finally, she could ride on her own, and Adrian was saddened and, at the same time, relieved. He could defend her better if she was on her own horse. But somehow, he felt cold and lonely without her folded into him.

"Can we stop here for a few minutes?" Elisabeth's voice carried to him from where she trailed him.

When Adrian turned, he saw Elisabeth looked exhausted and did not hesitate to draw his horse to a stop. They were almost within sight of Ravenshill castle, but he saw something in her face that made him want to grant her this wish even though he was frozen and exhausted.

He dismounted and went to Elisabeth. She released herself from her stirrups and fell into his arms, and he slipped her gently onto her feet.

She turned from him, and he followed her to stand on the riverbank next to her. Adrian could not look at the river without feeling himself being carried away by it. He would have drowned that day had she not fought to save him. He would always do the same for her.

"Did Lord Harris truly say he would still honor the engagement?" Elisabeth's voice came to him in an apprehensive whisper.

"He did. Do not worry. They are quite understanding of the incident."

"The Incident," she grumbled. "I'm sure that is how everyone will remember it."

"What happened?" he asked her, his voice patient and gentle.

She gave a heaving sigh. "I am not sure." Her eyes remained riveted across the water that meandered by them. "I know what happened. I can now remember all of it." She shook her head. "But I do not know what happened to me. Why I did it."

"What did you do?" His voice was gentle in its prodding.

"Mistress Reed told me Lord Harris would not appreciate a wife that could not make a good stitch. I became afraid. Lord Harris is Ravenshill's only hope. If he stops providing his men, the King will give Ravenshill to someone who can."

She turned her head, and Adrian could feel the heat of her blue eyes, but he remained riveted to the blue water before him. He did not dare scare her, stop her. “I lost my mind when I could not make my stitches look perfect.” She looked down at her hands, turning her palms up. “I stitched all night and pulled them out to stitch them again. Even when my hands grew bloody, I could not stop because I had to show everyone I could do it.” She shook her head, “Despite that, I could not. I did not.” She dropped her hands to her sides.

Adrian edged a little closer so he could take her hand in his. He stood on the river, holding it. He marveled at how much stronger her hands were now than when she pulled him from the river. “It will be okay. I am here now,” he told her as he rubbed his thumb across her palm and the callouses.

She was such a strong woman. Lord Harris made the right decision to keep her. He hoped his wife would be such a woman Elisabeth was as a child. But no. Elisabeth was growing from her child’s body. He did not realize it until he climbed on the horse with her. During her time at Ravenshill and Blackpool, she regained her weight. He felt the curves of her hips developing beneath his hand as he held her against him. Elisabeth would soon be old enough to marry and have a child. The thought of a man taking pleasure with her made him feel unsettled. It was because they grew up together and were as close as any brother and sister. Closer, his mind told him.

Soon they would go on with their lives. Elisabeth would go back to Blackpool and Adrian to Helmsley. Walter would be left to take on Elisabeth’s turmoil and troubles of Ravenshill.

By the time they arrived at Ravenshill, the sky had darkened and released a torrential rain their cloaks could not shield them from. Presley rushed out into the courtyard to take their horses. The two entered the keep together to be greeted by Walter and Edith. Edith rushed at Elisabeth, unmindful of her wet clothing, and slung herself against her. Walter stepped forward, patted Adrian on the back, and then began to help him from his dripping cloak.

"There is food," Walter said, waiting to take the cloak from Edith as she helped Elisabeth from it.

"We should get dry clothes," Adrian said, extricating himself from the group. Elisabeth nodded, and they moved toward the tower where the men had moved, now sharing the second floor with the family.

It was heaven to shed off his soaked clothes. He shivered as they dropped to the floor. When dressed, he hung them on the line running the width of the men's chamber. He stared at them momentarily, watching the water drip away to splatter on the wooden floor. He mused at the lack of servants at Ravenshill compared to the vast numbers at Helmsley. Yet, Adrian did not want to go home. He never wanted to go home. He wanted to stay here. This was his home. Although he had to do menial chores like everyone else, this was where he belonged. At Elisabeth's side was where he belonged. How could either of them make it through life without the other? He gave a slight chuckle in the stillness of the barracks. He would have to figure it out because life would not be the same away from Ravenshill and Elisabeth.

Walter entered the chamber through the faded tapestry.

"Your food is getting cold, Baby Squire," Walter said.

Adrian felt the sudden irritation run through him at the nickname Walter persisted in calling him. "Why do you keep calling me that?" Adrian snapped.

Walter shrugged then, with a wicked gleam, said, "When you are knighted, I will give you a new name."

"That's not likely to happen," Adrian grumbled. One thing he had not anticipated in a place as remote as Ravenshill, it was impossible to earn spurs when few even knew of an ambitious squire's existence.

"What was that?" Walter asked, already turning away as Adrian moved to follow.

"Nothing," Adrian replied.

They stepped out into the drizzle. "Can I ask you something?" Walter asked as they walked.

"What?" Adrian asked, feeling peevish.

"Have you kissed a girl?"

Adrian stopped and turned to Walter. "Why do you ask?"

"I just wanted to know."

"Have you?" Adrian asked, walking again.

"Yes."

Adrian took another couple of steps and halted. He turned to Walter, "Who did you kiss?"

Walter was silent a moment and then whispered, "Edith."

Adrian expelled a sigh. Of all the girls for Walter to kiss, he chose Edith. But who else would Walter kiss, Elisabeth? At least he seemed to recognize that would be far worse since they were supposed to be siblings. What would Lord Thomas say if he knew? By Lincoln's and Lord Thomas's edicts, Walter's training was rigorous to catch him up to the other boys his age in his newfound status. Lord Thomas risked a lot, and to know Walter might be throwing it away on Edith would be hard for him to forgive.

Lord Thomas was not the only one who would lose in the relationship between Walter and Edith. Walter would suffer too. By Walter's standards, he had to be more than passable. He wanted what Adrian wanted, a name for himself, not given but earned. A young lord, even one who gained his spurs, would rise no higher than was allowed for a man who married beneath his station. Walter would be no help to himself or Ravenshill then. And all the work they put into creating Baron Walter Kirkham would be for nothing.

"I do not think it is appropriate to do such a thing," Adrian said.

"I know, and Edith agrees. But a little kiss now and then hurts no one."

Adrian did not know a good response, so instead went with a defensive suggestion. "Do not tell Elisabeth."

They started walking again, entering the hall.

"How many have you kissed? Is Edith the only one?" Adrian asked as he paused just inside the door.

"Two," Walter replied.

Elisabeth's voice startled them, "What are you two talking about?"

They did not realize Elisabeth had walked up behind them and did not know how long she had been there. "That I have kissed two girls."

Adrian groaned at the topic. How did Walter not realize this would lead to who he kissed?

"You have not, Walter Kirkham," Elisabeth declared.

"I have, too," Walter said.

"Who?" she challenged.

"A girl when I..." Walter trailed off. "When I was somewhere else," he said. They had warned him to never speak of London, even in private. Ears could be anywhere. Walter did well to protect the secret that could put him back with his father or worse.

"And?" Elisabeth asked with her arms crossed.

Walter almost did not speak. But looking from Elisabeth to Adrian, it was apparent he found no other choice. "Edith," he said.

Elisabeth's assault was so fast that it startled both squires. Elisabeth reached for Walter, a fist raised, ready to hit him in the face as Adrian had taught her. But, instead, Adrian grabbed her by her raised arm and about the waist and dragged her backward.

"You filthy son of a bitch," she screamed at him as she thrashed against Adrian. "You are not to lay a hand on her." Adrian's hand clamped over her mouth, and she tried to bite him, but he pressed harder to prevent it.

"Shhhh," he tried to soothe in her ear.

"I only kissed her," Walter insisted. "I did not hurt her or even frighten her."

When she did not stop writhing in Adrian's arms, he shook her. She realized she could not fight him and quieted. Adrian eased his arms from around her.

"I will talk to Edith about this," Elisabeth snapped at him. Then she turned and cast Adrian a scathing look for his part in it before whisking past them into the hall.

Adrian took his position at the table next to Elisabeth. He felt as if there was a strain on the room. Adrian feared Elisabeth would ask Edith at the table if she was a willing participant in the kiss. But she had better sense and did not bring it up in front of Lord

Thomas. The meal had not progressed far before Elisabeth asked, “Have you kissed anyone, Adrian?”

Adrian wanted to pretend he didn’t hear her but knew that would be pointless.

Adrian sighed and turned to her. “This is not appropriate,” he said.

Elisabeth met his gaze. “This is not appropriate,” Elisabeth mimicked him. That was his answer to everything. “You and Walter were talking about it.”

“That is different. We are men.”

“Walter is not,” she insisted.

“He will be soon enough. You are a lady, and it is inappropriate for you to participate.”

“You are inappropriate, Adrian de Ros,” Elisabeth said. Her voice had risen in indignation, but she kept it pitched low. “I asked you a question, and as the lady of the keep, I demand an answer.”

Adrian glared at her.

“Well?” Elisabeth prompted.

“I have kissed one woman.”

For some reason, Elisabeth looked like she had been slapped.

“Who?” Elisabeth asked.

“Now…” he stopped his protest when Elisabeth raised a brow at him. “Her name was Janine, and you do not know her.”

“Thank you for answering my question,” Elisabeth said.

Adrian watched her back straighten so she could tug at the bottom of her jacket. She smoothed the fabric of her gown against her thigh several times before her hand came to a rest.

His eyes remained riveted on those hands before they raised to her. She cast him a wary glance before looking away under his scrutiny. Her nervous hands told him what she didn't want him to know. She did not like that he kissed the other girl. He did not understand why she should care. Adrian was already married in name. But she did, and now he knew and was glad for it.

The small house continued their meal in silence. Adrian kept glancing toward Elisabeth. She seemed fine, but the story she told him, of her mind breaking for a moment, bothered him. He knew she was under a great deal of pressure and responsibility. Perhaps it was too much. Added to that, her nightmares of the mines, and he could not fault her for losing her head for a brief period. But it was his strong and brave Elisabeth. That fact made it disturbing.

There was a level of discomfort in the hall. It was a strain because everyone knew why Elisabeth had returned, but no one wanted to speak of it. But at the same time, no one knew how to be normal around her.

Adrian noticed the food swirled about plates, and no one was eating. It was a waste of precious reserves. But Adrian found little appetite as he sat worrying about Elisabeth and how he could save her from another episode.

Next to him, he heard the soft sounds of a hum. It began quiet and solemn, but it grew jovial by the time it had grown to reach the ears of those at the table. Edith's eyes darted to Elisabeth. He watched the girls smile at each other across the table before Elisabeth joined in. Then, finally, Katy's hum joined them. When Walter took up the lyrics, recognizing the tune, Edith jumped from her chair. She motioned at Annabelle with her hands to encourage her to pick up the pace as she clapped her hands to the rhythm. Soon Lincoln picked up the lyrics as Elisabeth stood and motioned to Adrian.

Adrian stood and looked at the faces of Elisabeth and Edith. There was a glow about them, joy as the hall grew louder with a cacophony of raised voices, stomps, and claps. Edith had begun to dance with Lincoln. Adrian recognized the man had never taken a dance lesson by his awkward steps. But the man danced, and Adrian's eyes fell on Elisabeth, who looked at him, her eyes eager. She stopped humming and now seemed suspended, waiting to see if he would put the yoke of worries back across her shoulders. Instead, he smiled at her, kicked up his heels, and she laughed as he made his dance steps look ludicrous as he moved toward her.

He linked his elbow with hers and spun her. She followed his lead, and soon the entire hall was filled with the shouts and songs of the oppressed let free, if for only a fleeting moment. The men spun the women, and the women did not hesitate to lead in the unchoreographed steps. When Adrian grabbed hold of Elisabeth again, he yanked her against him. His hand was a perfect fit against the small of her back. His other gripped hers, holding it aloft as they pranced their way across the hall floor. He spun her and dipped her. She was unprepared, and he was left holding her full weight as her feet slipped from beneath her. Her hands came up to lock around his neck.

Adrian lifted her and spun her in a wide circle. Her feet flew out in an arc around them, and her laughter rang across the hall. Adrian looked up at her, at the way her eyes sparkled with light. Her eyes made the sun seem like it shone through the ceiling overhead. The life on her face, the smile, and the color made him think of an angel looking down at him. Such a lovely creature, he thought as he spun her again, clinging to her.

Annabelle began another song, this one even more exuberant than the last. The laughter filled the hall, ricocheting from the stone walls and ringing in their ears. Adrian's laugh was booming, and he did not hold back as he lifted and twirled all the women as they passed near him. Lord Thomas's laugh boomed, too, deeper. Lord Thomas clapped and moved about, making his own dance he pulled his daughter into. They twirled, and it seemed like Elisabeth's high-pitched, childlike laughter lifted the weighty air. Katy had a deep, feminine quality to her laugh, almost sultry. Sir Lincoln laughed like he had held it in for a lifetime, and it came out almost in barks. Presley was a stoic man, but a chuckle could be heard every so often coming from him as he, Lincoln, and Walter formed a line. The women were twirled around as they moved through it, a slalom of spins and laughter. But it was Elisabeth's laugh that rang above them all, clean and so feminine the sound was like a harp from heaven. When she drifted from him, he wanted nothing more than to have her back in his arms or her hand in his. When the songs died on everyone's lips, the dancing ceased. Adrian was on the opposite end of the hall than Elisabeth standing with Walter and Katy.

She beamed at him and offered him a small curtsy. He smiled back and offered her a bow before she turned and went toward the kitchen. Adrian followed Lincoln to their chamber.

"You should have traveled with another," Lincoln said as they settled into the darkness of their cots.

"They did not offer."

"You should be mindful you and Lady Elisabeth are no longer children. She is a woman whose reputation can be spoiled."

Lincoln fell silent then, and Adrian lay in the dark, staring at the ceiling. He knew Lincoln was right. Adrian knew his relationship with Lincoln changed forever that fateful night he killed the servants to keep a secret. A part of him itched to get away from Lincoln because Adrian was disappointed to realize Lincoln was not the chivalrous knight the stories portrayed. Brave, yes, but he was not chivalrous. He was a cruel killer. The servants were innocent. But at the same time, he saw the need. The servants, innocent or not, could be the reason for the downfall of Ravenshill with just one word. They could not trust that they would remain silent, not even if they gave their word.

Adrian thought of Lincoln's words. Adrian knew they were no longer children. Thanks to Lincoln and the whore in Poland, Adrian was aware of desire and pleasure. He knew he desired her when he held Elisabeth on his horse, her hand on the riverbank, and in his arms in the hall. But it was different than what the whore made him feel. He did not have to fill her with himself to feel pleasure. The moments alone pleased him and made him wish they could last forever.

Unable to sleep, he rose and went outside the tower to stroll the bailey until his mind quieted.

# Chapter 20

**Friday, March 21, 1449, Ravenshill**

The gates stood open, and no guards stood upon the parapets to announce the messenger's arrival. The diminutive man rode into the courtyard. His bay horse went unnoticed in the light drizzle falling. He tied the animal to a post and looked about himself before making his way to the hall. He located the cook, who located Lincoln, who had to locate Adrian before the message could be delivered to Elisabeth and not Lord Thomas, as Lord Harris instructed him. The little man seemed put out. Adrian and the messenger stood beneath the roof overhang, outside the stable, as he handed the sealed letter to Elisabeth.

"Thank you," Elisabeth said, taking the letter in hand. "Edith will take you to the kitchens and arrange some food. Your horse will be seen to."

"Thank you," the man said with a grateful bow.

"Care for the horse," Elisabeth told Adrian, preoccupied as she looked down at the letter in her hand. It had the seal of Lord Harris. She recognized the seal, so much like Lord Harlyn's but included a dragon rising up from the waters behind the ship.

"What is it?" Walter asked.

"I don't know," she replied. Her chin raised, and she used her free hand to tug at her belt and smooth down the front of her worn gray tunic. "I will be in the library."

Elisabeth felt her body want to tremble. She did not know what the letter said. But she knew it was a man who usually couldn't be bothered to communicate with his future bride. The walk to the library seemed eternal. The stones seemed to press in on her with the coldness of winter clinging to them. Her heart hammered as she stepped across the threshold into the library. This room was her sanctuary as well as a dungeon. Today it felt like the dungeon as her hands trembled with the letter clamped tightly. She stepped forward and stood in front of the desk. She picked up a dirk from the top, next to the neat ledger that now held well-organized finances. She worked it around the edge of the seal, breaking its hold. She unfolded the page.

Lord Harris's script was not as elegant as his mother's. But she quickly recognized his hand from his previous correspondence demanding her presence.

*"My dearest Elisabeth,"* the letter began. She felt herself bristle at the term dearest. It set an ominous tone in her head for what was to follow, for Lord Harris never offered any endearment to her. In fact, she did not think he ever even used her name on the scant occasions they encountered one another.

*"It has come to my attention that you were witnessed having relations with Baron Adrian de Ros that should be reserved for the marriage bed."*

Her mind seemed to slow down. An affair with Adrian? How could the man think such a thing of her?

*"The squire was witnessed entering a room with you and not leaving until morning. I have been most gracious in forgiving you the weakness of your mind, but this cannot be forgiven. As a result of this, I remove myself from this engagement. Also, I will remove my troops and suspend the aid I have rendered to the House of Ravenshill."*

The letter was signed, but his signature blurred. Elisabeth's eyes flew back to the beginning, and she reread it slower to ensure she did not misunderstand. Then the page fluttered from her hand, and she braced herself with her hands on her desk.

What would she do now? King Henry VI would not tolerate Ravenshill sending troops for such a short time. She had to replace them quickly. Elisabeth remembered the threats in the letters. Elisabeth now found herself without a fiancé. If he was not quiet about his suspicions, she would never have another, and Ravenshill would be lost. Now, she was Ravenshill's only hope, even though Walter was Ravenshill's future.

Elisabeth walked to the window. Crossed her arms over her chest and looked out at the courtyard below. So much here needed to be repaired. The gate required new hinges, one side hanging askew. Lincoln warned if they did not replace the hinge soon, the gate would be rendered useless.

She could see the crumbled wall next to the stable from her position. It made the walkway treacherous and was avoided. She was thankful this could not be seen from the outside, unlike the stable roof that was in full view along with the hole in it. It began with a leak that rotted the wood, weakening the top. All because one of the stones fell from the wall above and went through the rotted wood. She did not have a man who knew how to repair such a hole without replacing the roof, which no one here could do.

There were many other things, crumbling stones, rotting wood, rusting hinges, overworn, and deteriorating with time. Ravenshill was falling. How could she raise money for the King's army when they could not manage such simple repairs? Adrian exited the stable and crossed the bailey. He stopped halfway, and his face turned up to her. The squire stood momentarily as if undecided about which path to take. Finally, he continued in the direction that carried him to the tower. She prepared herself because she knew Adrian was coming for her. Unfortunately, he could not save her from this as he had saved her from so many other things. The thought, that cold seed of dead hope, planted itself, so it pricked at the back of her eyes as tears threatened to fall.

She jumped when she heard his boot steps behind her. When she whirled around, he stood in the doorway, and she recognized the look on his chiseled face in his dark gray-blue eyes. Seeing her in the window, he came to save her again. But it was she who had to save him this time. She had to save them all with only a wish and a prayer to her name.

"What is it?" Adrian asked. He stepped further into the room.

Elisabeth tugged at her belt and smoothed it down. She pretended to pick a piece of lint, hair, it didn't matter, from the fabric of her dress before she felt she could raise her head and look him in the eye. "Lord Harris has called off the engagement."

"Why?" Adrian asked, stepping closer.

He stood tall before her, looking down on her and reminding her she was not as large as she was in her own mind.

*It has come to my attention that you were witnessed having relations with Squire Adrian de Ros that should be reserved for the marriage bed.* Elisabeth recalled the words on the paper still lying on her desk.

Adrian was a handsome man. In fact, more attractive than Lord Harris. But looking at Adrian, she knew she could never have an affair with him because she already loved him. Far deeper than she thought she could ever love Lord Harris or any husband. And Adrian was already married, at least in name. The marriage would become official when both were old enough to take their vows and consummate them.

The seclusion of Ravenshill helped keep the Kirkham family out of numerous conflicts but not so with Adrian's family. Again and again, the family would fall with a king only to rise again. They were a family of fighters and deep loyalties, while the Kirkhams had little to do with English politics. One day, Elisabeth knew these differences would sweep them from each other.

"Elisabeth," he prompted. She hated how kind and caring his voice sounded at the moment.

She realized she was staring at him. He reached for her elbow, and she pulled away, crossing to the front of the desk again, placing the barrier between them. "The Incident worried the family. He feels it best."

Perhaps that was the first time she ever lied to Adrian. How could she tell him it was because of that night at the inn? He would blame himself even though she had insisted he remained. She could barely feel her face that night, let alone have enough wits about her to realize the damage she was asking for. Nothing happened. But no one would ever believe her.

She almost sent him home then. To his family's safety and the security their wealth could give him. Now that Lord Harris had withdrawn his support, she did not know what Ravenshill faced. But she needed Adrian more now than ever before because she needed an army. Her heart did a sick flip. She did lay the groundwork for the mess they were now in. It began with the Incident. Looking back, there was something about her slip from reality that was more terrifying than anything, even the mine. She could not dwell on that now. She needed to get an army to France.

"I need to speak to Sir Lincoln. Please send him."

Elisabeth watched Adrian cast another gaze over her before offering an incline of his head before exiting the room. Sir Lincoln had to take Adrian and her father as the three knights. It wasn't the four demanded. They would have to recruit archers and ground troops from the villagers. She did not know how to pay them or even pay for passage to France for all those men. The wolves were growling and stalking at the doors of Ravenshill, waiting for it to fall. The one that could make it fall faster than any of those wolves was the King of England.

Elisabeth wrung her hands as she tried to think of more things they could sell. Perhaps she could sell some dresses, but they were still at Blackpool. She wore a simple woolen dress when she arrived back home, so she did not have even one of those they had all worked to create. She did not have time to decide which of her people to send would anger the House of Blackpool less to retrieve them. She could hope someone there would do the kind thing and send them at the earliest moment.

If her father was going to France, he would not need his bed. It was sure to bring more than her own had. Though their herds were already thin, they would have to give up more livestock. Katy had mentioned she needed only one of the two ovens since few now resided at Ravenshill. Elisabeth did not know how much an oven would bring, but it had to bring something.

"Lady Elisabeth," Sir Lincoln said, nudging her from her contemplation with his grave voice.

She spun from the window. She was prepared to receive the knight and tell him of the new situation, but she hesitated. She knew he could kill with cold proficiency, not soldiers but the innocent—women who were in the wrong place at the wrong time. Elisabeth respected, feared, and adored Sir Lincoln since he would walk the halls with her small hand in his. He was the one who taught her to ride and, unbeknownst to her father, where to cut a man with her small dagger that would take his life. She remembered her childhood infatuation, convinced she would marry him. He was wise in his counsel when he told her to hasten her wedding. It was sound counsel and had great potential until she and Adrian messed it up.

"Lord Harris has dissolved the engagement. He will recall the men he sent to serve under the Ravenshill banner."

Lincoln stood with his hands folded behind his back, his legs anchored him to the floor. Despite what she witnessed in the chapel, she felt guilt for sending him to war in France. It had been a long war, one many men never returned from. She searched for the proper words to ease the reality she was sending him, Adrian, and her father to die in the war with France that may never end. The words were on the tip of her tongue only moments ago. But now, as she looked at the man, she found they had fled. She could almost feel his big strong hand enveloping hers and how she knew in her five-year-old heart that Sir Lincoln Victors could never be defeated at anything.

Lincoln cleared his throat. “If I may, my Lady?” he asked. “I think we can raise the army here. Perhaps you can still find a husband to help pay. But for now, you have three knights, and I would be honored to serve King Henry under the Ravenshill banner.”

Elisabeth wanted to deny him. Even though he said it was an honor, she knew it was not true. She heard Lincoln and her father talk enough about war to know they had had enough of it. But she could not take that into consideration now. Instead, Elisabeth crossed her arms over her chest and gave Lincoln a nod. “You are the kindest and truest friend of Ravenshill.”

“It is war, and wealth can be found.” He said nothing about death.

Anger flared in Elisabeth because they were out of choices. Not too long ago, those choices seemed exponential, but that time was gone.

“I am not sure how it works. Must I pay for all the troops throughout the entire campaign?”

“No,” Lincoln said with a gentle smile. “We only need to raise them and get them to France. The King will pay you, and then you pay the men.”

“Would I have time to broker another marriage contract before you can raise the troops?”

Lincoln shrugged. “It depends on the eagerness of the man you speak of.”

“I don’t know who I speak of,” Elisabeth sighed. “I just thought if I could get a marriage contract in all due haste, perhaps I can get troops, and Ravenshill can still be protected."

"That is your choice, my lady," Lincoln said. There was such gentleness in his deep voice she wanted to cry. "I am willing to go to France for the Kirkhams and the King."

"And I am grateful," Elisabeth assured him. "Are you privy to men who have their own wealth and may need a wife who will ignore her financial circumstances?"

"Perhaps. But I warn you, most of the men I have been acquainted with are old codgers. You could make a better match with a younger man."

"I do not care. An older man may be more eager for someone who has not been touched." A look passed in the man's dark eyes that told her, until now, he was unsure if such horror was added to her suffering.

"Sir Knox Hallewell has been widowed for many years. He never had a child with his wife. He may be interested in a quick union."

Elisabeth went to the desk, pulled out a ledger, and recorded some of the names and information Lincoln gave her. Then, after a lengthy discussion on the attributes and shortcomings of the men they could think of, Elisabeth settled herself on Sir Knox. He gained great wealth fighting in the war with France. He was back in England, and Lincoln agreed to invite the man to Ravenshill before raising troops.

Long after Lincoln left the study, Elisabeth sat looking at the ledger of names. She began to add some of her own. Her focus was so riveted to the page she did not hear the footsteps that brought Adrian to stand on the other side of the desk until he cleared his throat. Her head shot up, and her eyes fell on her friend.

"Lincoln has told me your intent."

Elisabeth could tell by his demeanor Adrian was not happy about her intent. She stood and walked around the desk.

"You can do better," he said.

Elisabeth scowled at him. "I could if time allowed. If I can get a contract with Sir Knox, I can get men to send to France."

"Lincoln said we would go to France," Adrian said. The annoyance was heavy in his voice.

"I want to keep you and Lincoln here to protect Ravenshill if possible."

"Keep us here?" Adrian thundered at her, making her take a subconscious step back. "Here we have been while men come back laden with riches and glory. Lincoln has already had his time on the battlefield, and so has your father. What about my chance Elisabeth? I have no chance if you keep me here."

"Adrian," she said, drawing a deep breath through her nose. She began to tug at her belt and smooth down her tunic. Adrian stepped forward and took both her hands in his, stilling them.

"I can fix this," he told her. "I will simply ask for your hand. You know my family has money. I can pull myself from my marriage. I am sure of it. I will marry you and then go to France and bring great glory to our families."

"Yes, Elisabeth," he said, lifting one of her hands to kiss it. "I could think of no one who matches me as well as you. Let me make the request of my parents. I will refuse my right as an heir if they do not grant me this favor."

"You are truly my knight of swords," she said, pulling her hands away and flinging them around his neck. He laughed at her and put his arms around her, pulling her closer. She would much rather wed Adrian than Lord Knox. She could not imagine a more comfortable union, and Adrian sounded confident he could make it happen.

"I shall go at once to Helmsley and seek permission," Adrian said, pulling from her. Then he reached down and boldly kissed her on the lips. "Do not worry. I will always come to your rescue."

He dashed from the room, leaving Elisabeth feeling relieved and anxious about the union with Adrian. With the marriage, the financial struggle of Ravenshill would wash away. Better perhaps was the fact she would not have to wed the old Sir Knox. For the first time in a long while, Elisabeth lay down without a thousand thoughts whirling in her mind. What led her into a blissful sleep was the feeling of Adrian holding her and his words, *"I will always come to your rescue."*

# Chapter 21

**Saturday, March 22, 1449, Helmsley, England**

Riding into the bailey of Helmsley, Adrian had a feeling of unease wash over him. This was not like coming home. Ravenshill was his home. Or was it Elisabeth? Would he be content here with Elisabeth? He would find out soon. If not here, they could live at Ravenshill if that was where she chose. He would give her anything if he could take away her worries.

"Son, how was your journey, and what brings you for this unexpected visit?" his father, Earl Hagan de Ros, asked as he met him halfway to the stable.

Adrian's father was an imposing man. Adrian would likely one day outreach him. At thirteen, he was quickly gaining on him. Hagan had once been a great knight, but a battle injury left his hand crushed, and he could no longer wield a sword.

A boy came out and took Cosmo's reins. "It has been some time since I have been home."

"Your timing is impeccable. I just returned from a hunt, and I daresay we will be partaking of the biggest boar in all England," his father said with a laugh, chucking him on the arm. Together they walked to the open firepit and the wild pig roasting over the crackling flame.

"It is a beast," his father said, sounding proud, before bursting into laughter. "The men have said I stole a suckling from its mother," he said with a laugh.

The pig was less than a year old. Its girth and growth were both lacking.

"It is bound to be tender," Adrian speculated.

"Tender," his father laughed. "I shall tell the men that is the reasoning. Truth be told, I was getting desperate and did not want to wait for a larger boar because I had already been hunting for hours. I did not think I would get a better opportunity."

"I am sure it did not see its death coming," Adrian teased.

"Indeed not," his father said, clapping him on the shoulder and guiding him toward the hall.

"My dear son," his mother said, placing his face between her hands. "You have come home. Dare I hope it is to stay?"

"No, only for a day. I came to speak over a matter with you."

"Of course, son," his father said, moving him toward the table where they settled.

"I wish to take a different wife," Adrian said, getting to the point of the visit.

"What of Waverly?" his mother, Angeline, asked.

"It is impossible," his father said in a tone that said this would not change. "Who do you think is worth disgracing this family?" Hagan demanded. His mother looked apprehensive as she witnessed Hagan's temper begin to rise.

"Lady Elisabeth Kirkham."

"Absolutely not!" his mother exploded.

"Kirkham?" his father asked. "She would not do. She would not do at all."

"Why not?" Adrian asked, annoyed that neither of them gave it any consideration.

"You haven't compromised her?" his mother asked, grabbing hold of his arm with a level of urgency that grew Adrian's annoyance.

"No," he insisted.

"Then why Elisabeth?" his father asked.

"Do you know what fate awaits, Ravenshill?" his mother persisted.

"I know its fate if I do not marry Elisabeth," Adrian replied.

Hagan shook his head. Fury lurked beneath the surface. "Thomas Kirkham sat the wheels rolling years ago. No one can stop it now. If you are married to the Kirkham girl, you will fall with it. I have worked too hard to let that happen to you."

"We have a contract, and it will be honored," his mother said, climbing to her feet and leaving the hall altogether.

"We will not allow the marriage regardless of your reasons. Even if you leave her in a delicate position, you will honor your marriage."

"But she has an older title. One that should be preserved, not left beneath the rubble."

"She is Thomas Kirkham's daughter. That is all that matters. I wish to say no more on the matter. The answer is no, and it will always be no."

Adrian's stomach curdled when his father's pig was served in the family hall. His mother's persistence that he should soon set a date for his bride to come to

Helmsley and consummate their marriage made it feel like a giant stone pulled at him.

"If I cannot have Elisabeth, I do not wish to be wed to a child."

"Lady Waverly is a perfect match, as we knew she was when you were children. Moreover, she is the daughter of our most devoted ally," his father insisted.

"I do not wish to have her," Adrian persisted.

"If you do not set a date, your father and I will," his mother said.

"I will not do it until I am ready," Adrian insisted.

"To not honor the contract is to bring dishonor to the family," his father growled. "I care not to face that humiliation."

"And I care not to be wed to her."

"You have met her," his mother insisted as if that was the point and would make this all better.

Adrian glared at his parents. He could not conceal his anger. Lincoln often schooled him on keeping calm and impassive to hide his fear, anger, or sorrow. But it was Elisabeth that made the lessons stick.

Adrian tuned out his parents, who cut him from the conversation and discussed the assets of his future bride. He looked down at his plate and the meat and gravy congealing. The bread was harder and not as good as what Katy made at Ravenshill. He loved riding into the Ravenshill bailey when she was baking it. The aroma made him feel like he had arrived home and never failed to make his mouth water.

Adrian scooted the meat around on his plate and drove the edge into the gravy, swirling it about. He almost smirked when he remembered Elisabeth as his bully. If those men did not take her, she would still have a piece of that in her. That piece of her did not care what she said to him, how she hurt him, because that was the game. It was a game she was good at and one that aggravated him beyond all sound reasoning.

Had she outgrown those games that frustrated him, or was it those men who forced it from her? For the briefest of moments, he told himself he was glad she no longer teased him relentlessly. But it was a part of that childhood that she was robbed of. Adrian wanted to tell his parents about the terrible experience Elisabeth had. But that would lead to too many questions about why she ran in the first place. Plus, his mother could not keep a secret. Neither could his father when he was deep in his cups.

He let his mind visit one of his memories of Elisabeth before she was taken.

When she was the girl who teased him after a disastrous practice with Lincoln, which got him yelled at.

*"Are you going to cry about it?" Elisabeth's voice had demanded of him.*

The corner of Adrian's mouth rose with a tiny smile as his parents prattled on about something that did not bring on the same feelings of warmth.

*"Oh, Adrian."* The sarcasm in her sympathetic voice always turned him from wounded by her words to being angered by them. This she knew too. But it was her pooching lips and sad face as she wiped an imaginary tear from her eye and said the words that made him want to hit her. *"Did mean Sir Lincoln give you a bruise? You poor boy. Maybe you just weren't meant to be a brave knight."*

It wasn't Lincoln that always made him try harder. It was Elisabeth. He could take Lincoln's anger and discipline, but he did not like Elisabeth teasing him because it did make him want to cry. Every time.

When he was on his game at practice, she would cheer him on. But when it did not go as well, she remained silent, and he always felt or imagined her disappointment. He wished she wouldn't come to watch them when he and Lincoln practiced with the staff. But she was his driving force. Whether it was her barbs if he failed or her cheers when he succeeded, she made him fight until the sweat poured into his eyes, and his shoulders felt as if he could raise his weapon not once more.

Adrian went to bed that night, thinking of his mistake coming home. If he didn't try to be chivalrous, he would still have the naïve hope he could save Elisabeth. He remembered meeting Waverly and paid her no mind that one time. Why would he? She was a little girl running around playing with dolls while he was busy playing with swords. He did remember she seemed to cry a lot and might be a bit spoiled. He lay abed in turmoil for what seemed hours. He didn't want Waverly. He wanted Elisabeth. He knew Elisabeth, protected her, and knew she was as loyal to him as he was to her. In his mind, it would have been a perfect match. But his parents would never see it that way.

Why would they have such strong feelings toward the Kirkhams? They saw the Kirkhams as a few rungs lower on the ladder than the de Ros family. And they knew the Kirkhams were barely clinging to that rung. Perhaps he was naïve in thinking they still clung to it. Maybe they already fell to the bottom, and his parents were right, and he would be taken down with them if he married Elisabeth.

Adrian rode from Helmsley the following day feeling unrested and on edge. It ate at him that he weighed the importance of helping Elisabeth or doing as his family bid him. He had a long history of doing what was expected of him. One of those things was going to Ravenshill. Adrian wanted to foster at York with his long-time friend Benton Blake.

But Adrian's father insisted he fostered with Sir Lincoln Victers. Lincoln was a legend. He still was. The shine of the man's success as a military deity would long outlive him. Adrian wondered how he ended up at Ravenshill if his parents were against the Kirkhams. While Ravenshill was home to Adrian, he sat idle as a squire while Benton Blake had already been to France and knighted. He saw a battlefield and was back home while Adrian sat with his thumb up his ass. Perhaps it was a good thing in the end. He might yet get his chance in France.

But what of Elisabeth? What were her choices—Knox? He was older than her father and more hardened than even Lincoln. How would a man like that treat Elisabeth? She was still a virgin, after all. Would the man take that into account? Would Adrian take that into account with Waverly? He laid with a whore, and she showed him what to do. Adrian was concerned because he knew it caused women pain when their maidenheads were taken. He would have to hurt Waverly, and he did not like that thought even though it was his duty to do so. At the same time, he felt a measure of relief. It would be easier to bed Waverly than it would be Elisabeth. How could he do such a thing to little Elisabeth? She was so small, so frail. But then, he thought, she wasn't. She was a strong fighter. But a woman couldn't fight her husband. At least, they shouldn't. But some women might have to because their husbands did not respect and treat them like treasures.

His mind whirled back to Elisabeth. She had to find a husband, Knox, or someone else. She would fight them if they tried to hurt her. Or would she. She was a passionate creature, but she was also something else since returning to Ravenshill. There was a quietness about her now, and there were times when she went away. Slipping back to the nightmare inside her own mind. No other man would ever understand and know that was where she went. He would never understand when she got into a frenzy, it was because she felt desperation again, and he would need to step in and save her. Would her husband ever bother to save her?

What about his own wife? Would she have her own secrets? Were there things in her past that would come back to haunt her? There were secrets Adrian had to keep from his wife. Even if he fell in love with this woman and they led joyous lives together, there would always be secrets among the Kirkhams. The secret of a man who gambled everything on a boy who pretended to be someone he wasn't. Then there was Elisabeth's secret. If the world knew Elisabeth Kirkham was broken, it would shun her. He could never tell anyone these secrets because they would ruin all of them. On top of these secrets piled more secrets and lies. Perhaps it was best to get away and begin his life as executor of his own estates.

His mind was so involved in his thoughts he did not see the group of men until he had ridden upon them. They stood in a line across the road, arm in arm, blocking his path, staring him down when he halted the horse.

"I'd be getting off that horse if I were you," one of the men said.

"I don't see that happening, gentlemen," Adrian replied. He rested his hand on his sword, making it clear to the men his intention.

"You can't fight all four of us," the man informed him.

Adrian shrugged, his eyes gazing across their line and then back to the man who spoke to him. "I need only kill one, and then there will be three." Adrian drew his sword slowly, giving a practiced spin once it was unsheathed. His horse pranced as he knew she would do. Though not his destrier, Cosmo could likewise trample them beneath her spirited hooves. "So, which man is to be first?" Adrian asked.

But Adrian didn't give the men time to decide or even respond. As the mare gathered herself in agitation, Adrian dug his heels into her side, and she bolted. The animal plowed through the line of men as if they were not there. Whatever the men thought he would do with his sword had been wrong. One man was bold, however, and smart enough not to be distracted by the fear of the blade. He flung himself at Adrian's back, knife in hand, but he miscalculated the horse's height or speed, for he did not reach Adrian, but his knife did. He felt it rake across his collarbone and down his shoulder before the man fell away with it, and Cosmo was leaving them behind.

He slowed his horse long enough to sheath his sword and assess the damage. His shirt was soaked with blood around the wound, and it burned like fire, but he was not going to bleed to death before making it home. By the time he rode into the bailey of Ravenshill, the sun had set. Stabbing pain radiated down his chest and arm from the wound. Presley was there to take the horse.

"What happened?" Presley asked, seeing the blood-soaked shirt beneath the one torch that attempted to banish the darkness.

"Highwaymen," Adrian grumbled. His throat felt dry.

"Better let one of the women look at it," Presley informed him. "It looks nasty."

Adrian headed for the hall. Inside he lit a lantern to light his way along the length of it. The hearth had long since grown cold. To the kitchen, he went. His feet felt heavy, and his legs were exhausted. The lantern light bounced off the walls, forcing the shadows back. The kitchen was empty, so he trudged back through the hall and to the tower. He knew where he could find one person in the keep and was not surprised to see the weak light reaching the threshold as he gained the top step. It was as if it beckoned to him, pulled him to the room where she was. She might not be alone, but if there was light there this time of night, it was Elisabeth.

"Good lord!" Elisabeth exclaimed, jumping up from behind the desk. "What has happened?" she asked, flying around the desk at him. She grabbed the arm that wasn't injured and pulled him forward so he stood next to the desk. She took the lantern from his hand and sat that on the desk too. With the two lanterns casting their light, Adrian looked down at himself. It did indeed look bad. His shirt was sodden with his blood. Some of it was dried, most fresh.

Her fingers went to his doublet, unbuttoning the ruined short coat with the delicate gold embroidery his mother gave him just yesterday. She slipped it from his shoulders, then lifted the blue shirt beneath, over his head. She took care to place them on the back of a chair.

She studied the wound intently, her fingers feathered beneath it. "What did you do?" she asked, looking up at Adrian with her big blue eyes. He felt annoyed by her, her touch, and her look of concern.

"What makes you think I have done something. I am the one that is cut, after all."

"Well," Elisabeth said as she guided and pushed Adrian into the nearby chair. "I do not know of anyone else that has just had a wound spontaneously open."

"There is a reason for it. I just did not do it," Adrian ground out.

Elisabeth bent closer, and her head dipped next to his. He looked toward the wall as her breath fanned across his skin. "Ouch!" he cried when she touched him too close to the wound.

"Hold still," she admonished.

"I would if you would not touch it," he growled.

She rose from him. "How can I treat it if I do not touch it?" she snapped.

"Where is Edith?" he asked. "I feel this would be treated much faster by someone who did not speak."

"You sure are an angry cub when you get a booboo," she said with laughter as she turned away from him. "I'll be back," she said before he could growl at her again.

Adrian waited an excessive amount of time for Elisabeth to return. Then, agitated, he stood and went around the desk and looked down at what she was working on. The ledger on top of the pile lay open with the household numbers. It had daily entries and detailed finances of Ravenshill recorded for the first time in years. Without the money to pay someone to keep such records, Thomas had not done so. If the Kirkhams kept Ravenshill, it would not be because of Thomas or Walter but because of Elisabeth. Looking at the ledger, he marveled at her intelligence. There were so many things accounted for in her log that Adrian, or most anyone he imagined, would not think to consider.

Next was another ledger that held the information on the eligible men of some financial background. The data was laid out as meticulously as the household finances. Each man's attributes were aligned in columns, as well as his downfalls. He froze when he saw the heading of one of the columns. He picked up the ledger and brought it closer. "Intercourse" was the title of the column. There were two pages of men's names with columns headed "Family," "Finance," "Age," and so forth. Most of the other columns had answers, but there were no answers for men under "intercourse."

"What are you doing?" Elisabeth snapped. She stood in front of him and snatched the book from his hands. "You got blood on it," she said, looking down at the pages.

"I'm sorry," Adrian mumbled. Elisabeth pushed him back toward the chair, and he sat while thinking of that one column.

"This is going to hurt," Elisabeth warned him. She placed a cloth beneath his wound and held a bottle above it.

"Aren't you supposed to say this is going to hurt me more than it hurts—." His words were drawn from him as the fire consumed him, burning with an intensity that made him clench his jaw before exploding, "Holy Christ!"

"Stop being a baby," she admonished him. She moved the cloth. He prepared for the next dousing of the liquid, eating away at his skin. He writhed, jerking away as the next dose hit the wound. "It really is just a scratch," she tried to tell him.

"It is not just a scratch," he gritted out. "Get it finished and stop chatting."

As soon as the words were out of his mouth, he knew he would regret them. If Elisabeth's narrowed eyes did not tell him, his knowledge of her should have stopped him. "As you say." She turned the bottle up and poured it from one end of the gash to the other.

Adrian sucked in his breath and held it, closing his eyes against the pain. He would not give her the satisfaction of crying out again. When Adrian opened them, it was to see her staring at him. She offered him a bland smile as if to say it did not matter if he kept it in or let it out. He paid the price for speaking to her as he had. Not all of the Elisabeth he had once known was gone.

"Where is Edith?" he asked her again.

"Not here," she bit out. Adrian scored a point insinuating Edith would be better suited.

"She is gentler," Adrian said.

"Oh?" Elisabeth asked, bending to look at the wound again. He could smell her hair as it hovered just beneath his chin as she inspected it. "I think you require stitches," she said, straightening.

Adrian looked from her to the wound. It was deep and long. But did it need stitching? She retrieved the need she dipped into the fiery liquid she poured on him. She ran the thread through the needle head, knotted it, then ran the thread and needle back through the liquid. He nearly quivered, thinking about the soaked thread being pulled through his flesh. As she came closer, her needle appeared large. “Um, Elisabeth,” he began, clearing his throat and eyeing the needle.

“What?” she asked as she reached him and bent.

“That needle looks big.”

Elisabeth paused and held up the needle. “It is not so big,” she declared. But he knew they looked at the same needle, which was enormous.

“Do you know what you are doing?”

“I have sewn,” she said.

“I know you have sewn,” he snapped. “I have sewn. But have you ever sewn flesh back together?”

Elisabeth shrugged. “How difficult can it be? Stitches are not undoable,” she declared.

“What do you mean?” he asked as she bent toward him again.

She straightened as she said, “They can be pulled out and placed again if it does not look correct when I have finished.” She swooped back toward him, but he grabbed her hand, stilling it.

“If you are going to do this, you must do it right the first time,” he insisted.

“If it is not done properly, it will leave a larger scar,” she said, trying to pull her hand away.

A vision of her stitching, pulling out the stitches to restitch, repeatedly flashed in his mind. Was that not what had occurred during the Incident at Blackpool? “Um, Elisabeth,” he said, and he knew he was beyond concealing his fear. His voice shook, as did the hand he held her arm with. “I think I will be fine without stitches.”

“Of course you will, you imbecile,” Elisabeth said, laughing at him. She jerked her hand away and stepped back. “You just need some salve and dressing.”

Adrian sighed with relief and annoyance as she spread the salve across the wound. Her fingers were light. He knew whatever she did now, nothing could feel worse than what his imagination had created.

"My parents have said no to our marriage." His voice was soft in the silence. He saw her nod but said nothing. Then, just as softly, he asked, "Why do you play games with me?"

Her head shot up at him, and her sharp blue eyes softened as she studied his.

"Because you are fun to play games with. You get mad, and then you laugh."

He took her hand in his, stilling it over his chest. He did not take his grip from her but gave her the opportunity to pull away. "Must I become mad before I laugh?"

"No," she said, looking up at him. Mischievousness danced behind her eyes' blueness. Adrian felt a genuine desire for the blond girl he grew up with for the first time. He wondered if seizing her for a kiss would turn that spark to anger or something else. "But it is fun nonetheless," she said with her perfect pink lips twisting into a smile.

Adrian did not know what he would have done had Edith not entered the room then. Elisabeth moved from him. They had an audience, which saved Adrian from a colossal mistake he felt he was about to make. What was he thinking? Even after Elisabeth turned the wound's bandaging over to Edith, Adrian could not stop thinking about the mess he had almost made. There would be no going back after he kissed her. His instinct told him this. But he wanted to grab and silence her laughter with his lips on hers.

# Chapter 22

**Wednesday, September 3, 1449, Ravenshill**

Elisabeth tapped on the ledger before her. Her mind was in deep thought. She was unsure how she would continue to feed her household long-term. All her hope was shattered when Adrian brought the news he would not be able to marry her. She had not believed the de Ros's would agree to annul Adrian's marriage, but she had hoped. She had hoped she would not have to marry an old man.

Now financial ruin loomed. The only solution was to find a new husband. But who? She hoped for someone more appealing than Knox. The options diminished after the episode at Blackpool got out. Now she was considered a gamble, and her virginity was not guaranteed, but that could be proven. The question of the stability of her mind was the wild card. It could be years before another episode might occur. She knew she had to lower her expectations and find a man who also had to do the same quickly.

She had to put these on paper because what was right about one might outweigh another. It was impossible to keep up with it all in her head. She might have better luck with older men since she was still of childbearing years, and he would find her to be a virgin on their wedding night. She began to narrow down the search further. Perhaps a man with shallow bloodlines would want her deeper ones. She continued tapping.

Lord Cornell, she culled immediately. He was rumored to abuse his late wife. Elisabeth thought she might prefer to starve to that. Viscount of Marlowe, she remembered, had died not long ago. His son Benton was still unmarried. Elisabeth had met the boy, but they had been younger. She remembered him as goofy in appearance and personality. That left Sir Knox Hallewell. He spent a great deal of time at court, ass-kissing, her father had said on more than one occasion of the man. He was twice widowed and twice gained great wealth from his brides. There was no longer a need for him to seek a wife for financial gain. He was without children, so he would find her age appealing. His title was minor, but he would be raised higher with marriage to Elisabeth. It was not something any of his previous wives did for him. All her reasoning led her back to Knox.

Then Adrian was in front of her, looking down at her with a scowl.

"It is like you are trying to find a bull for yourself," Adrian said. Annoyance edged his voice.

"Do you have a better way?" she snapped at him as she slammed the book closed.

"No," he admitted.

Elisabeth sighed. "I have made a decision," she announced. "I will set a proposal before Sir Knox Hallewell." Just saying it felt as if it set the marriage in stone.

"Why him?" Adrian asked. The irritation seemed to have grown in his voice.

"Because I know him to be quite wealthy and without children. I could offer him children and a title in his later years."

"That is very noble of you," Adrian replied with great sarcasm.

"Adrian," she began with exasperation, but something else she did not like hearing sounded in her voice—defeat.

"There has to be a better choice," Adrian insisted.

Elisabeth slammed the book down. "What is the better choice?" she demanded, flipping it open.

"Is it Lord Cornell who beat his wife?" she asked, pointing to his name in the ledger. "Is it Lord Pearcy who is known to whore with whatever woman will spread her legs for him? Perhaps Lord Donegon, who would much prefer a union with you than me?"

"I'm just trying to be helpful," Adrian snapped at her.

"Well, you're not."

Adrian came around the desk and looked at the page as she pointed to the names in it. "Elisabeth?" he asked as they stared at the open book for a moment.

She looked up at him, towering over her. He was tall, and it seemed like he got broader daily with his hours on the practice field. He leaned over her and pointed to the column by Knox's name labeled "intercourse."

"Why are they all blank?" For a moment, she could not speak. He seemed so masculine, leaning next to her. He wasn't a boy, and she did not feel like a child as the warmth from his body invaded her senses.

Elisabeth shifted away from him. He felt too close, leaning over her shoulder, his head next to hers. She shrugged, and in a tiny voice she hated, she said, "I am afraid they will hurt me, or I will be too repulsed to carry out my wifely duty. So, I thought I would try to find information to go in that column."

Adrian straightened and paced away from her. "I do not know enough to judge such a thing," she said.

Adrian stood gazing out the window overlooking the bailey. "It is probably best you don't," Adrian mumbled.

"Why do you say that?" she asked. She went to stand beside Adrian. He was destined to be a big and strong man, she mused as she stared out the window. In the glass, Elisabeth could see a hint of their reflection. She was considering selling the glass window that was the only one added to the keep over the years. Her reflection looked so small next to his. It had not always been that way. When Adrian stepped into their keep for the first time, she remembered they were the same age and so close in size. They stood before each other and looked each other in the eye. Now the years were evident in more than their size differences.

"I suspect that is why some men insist on a virgin bride. So that they will not know if he is good or bad."

"Does it really matter?" Elisabeth asked.

Adrian sighed and glanced down at her. "This is turning toward an inappropriate conversation," he warned.

She scowled but said nothing. Then, after several moments of silence between them, she said, "I fear you are the only one I am comfortable speaking to about such matters." She would be embarrassed to admit that to anyone except Adrian. She had the servants and

Edith, or her father. She did not like her people to see her indecision and fears. But Adrian saw the worst of her, and he still stood next to her.

He remained quiet for another moment before he cleared his throat and asked, “Do you have questions?”

“What should I expect?”

She looked up at Adrian as he looked down at her. Then his eyes darted away, and he was looking out the window again. “Well,” he said, seeming to gather his courage. “A man can be gentle, he can be patient and slow, or he can be impatient and rough.”

Elisabeth sighed when he offered her nothing else. “Have you ever?”

She had to glance at him to see him offer a slight nod. She watched him swallow beneath her scrutiny. Elisabeth wasn’t sure why, but it felt as if her heart sank a little.

“With whom?” she asked after watching the empty bailey beneath them for several minutes.

His voice was low, and it was apparent he never intended to tell her. “In Poland, we stopped at a tavern along the way, and one of the whores presented herself, so Lincoln bought her for me.”

Elisabeth swallowed the lump in her throat. “What was it like?”

Adrian shook his head and shot her an annoyed look. “It is different for a man with a whore rather than a wife.”

“How do you know? You have not been with your wife.”

She could see while Adrian stared into the bailey that he was scowling. “This conversation is not appropriate,” he warned again.

"Oh, shut up, Adrian," she snapped at him. "You know that does not matter between us."

She heard his heavy sigh as if she had dashed his hope that he could extract himself from the conversation.

"The whore was coarse. She got me erect and did all the work."

"But did you know what to do?"

Adrian let out a bark of laughter, "I soon figured it out."

"Will I?" she asked.

She saw his jaw clench and his eyes narrow, but he said nothing.

"What will a man of Knox's experience expect of me?"

"Elisabeth," he said, and her name sounded like a warning as it came out strangled.

"Will he show me what he expects of me as the whore did for you?"

Elisabeth heard him mumble, "This is inappropriate." Adrian's breathing had picked up, and she saw his chest rising and falling with anger etched in every line of his face. Then, finally, he shook his head before saying, "You are a virgin. If you lie beneath him, he will do what he must."

"I just have to lay there. I walked upon Carly and Rodger a few years ago, and she was on top of him. I think he liked it. What if he expects that of me?"

Adrian shook his head again, and her name came from his lips again, sounding even more strangled.

"Please, Adrian," she said, placing a hand on his arm that clinched beneath hers.

His hand came to cover hers, but he did not turn his head from the window. "If you have an attraction to the man, you will figure it out. If you do not, it does not matter, and he will take it for himself."

She did not like the last scenario. She had had men take from her before, and she already felt the urge to fight at the thought of someone taking something else from her. But when she vowed herself to Knox, she would have no choice. "It will surely hurt the first time, will it not?"

His fingers wrapped around hers, but still, he did not look at her. "That is what I have heard."

She swallowed and looked out over the courtyard.

"What if it hurts so bad, I want him to stop, but he does not."

His fingers tightened painfully on hers. "Then you grab him by the balls and squeeze so hard he screams and begs your forgiveness."

She couldn't help the giggle that escaped her, but as she looked up at Adrian, she still saw his face etched in seriousness and anger. "Seriously, Adrian, what do I do?"

Adrian spun on her so quickly that she tried to step back. But his fingers tightened and pulled her closer, so her body crashed into his. She looked up at him in surprise. He stared down at her with his gray-blue eyes tearing into her, all the way to her soul. "I cannot tell you, Elisabeth. I cannot protect you from that." He shook his head, released her fingers, and pulled her into his arms. He buried his head in her neck and whispered, "It should be me."

He held her, and she did not fight the warmth and protection of his arms. Would Knox make her feel this way? Would he ever even hug her with affection? What if they didn't even like each other? But all the questions centered around herself. The most problematic question had already been answered. The answer had been Knox because he could save Ravenshill.

"Put your arms around my neck," Adrian whispered to her.

She did not question but slipped her arms free of Adrian and wrapped them around the back of his neck. He slowly brought his head up. His breath raked across the skin of her neck, her earlobe, and her cheek. Until he was staring softly into her eyes. "Whenever you take a man to your bed, make him kiss you," Adrian said. He swallowed, and his eyes gathered moisture as he spoke his following words. "Make him kiss you like this."

Adrian pulled her closer still. His action was slow and deliberate. Elisabeth had plenty of time to stop him. She knew he would kiss her, and she would not stop him for many reasons. The first was she was terrified of marrying the man she had yet to meet. She was curious about kissing and intercourse for some time, not just because she was of marriageable age. But the biggest reason she didn't stop Adrian was that she wanted to know what it was like to be kissed by him.

His lips touched her like the lightest of breaths. She felt his lips and the tip of his tongue as he caressed his way back and forth across them. When she sighed, his lips claimed hers, suckling at them, stroking them with his tongue. He moved deliberately. His hands appeared on both sides of her head, holding her in place as he continued.

Elisabeth watched him as he watched her, and then his eyes drifted closed. His lips were still soft, but there seemed to be an urgency lurking. She allowed her own eyes to drift closed. When one hand dropped from her face to go to the small of her back and pull her tighter against him, she sighed. His lips grew more urgent, his tongue stroked across her teeth, and he beckoned her own to join his. She began to move with him, tasting him. When she used her tongue to stroke his lips with her own tongue, he groaned, his hand tightened on her back, and the other moved into her hair. She felt his fingers dig into her hair against her scalp. She could not remove herself from his strong arms if she wanted to, and she did not.

His lips bruised hers, but she did not care. Instead, she slid her hands into his hair and demanded more from him, pulling him down to her. She opened her mouth wider for him, and he dove in deeper with a growl that half groaned. His grip tightened, and the hand in her hair tugged, bending her head back. His lips left hers, and as her eyes fluttered open, she saw his had darkened to near black as he gazed at her. She saw an intensity, and she knew he would dip to her neck and kiss her there, and she wanted him there. She wanted so much from him, and she did not understand.

She nearly cried out when his grip loosened on her. “Kiss him like that, Elisabeth,” he whispered. “But when you close your eyes, remember me.”

A sob ripped from her, and she pulled him to her and clung to him with all her strength. But he did not wrap her in his arms. Instead, he stood, his body stiff, until she released him and, wiping her eyes, stepped back, away from his warmth. He wiped his mouth as he straightened, and his gaze was locked somewhere over her head.

“Do you wish Lincoln to invite Knox here?” he asked. It was uncanny how his voice changed, how he spoke as if what just transpired had not.

She swallowed and croaked, “Yes.”

He took two steps away from her and bowed. “I will let him know.” Then Adrian turned and left Elisabeth in a whirling turmoil of needs that confused, frightened, and thrilled her.

# Chapter 23

**Monday, March 9, 1450, Ravenshill**

Adrian watched Lord Knox's people as they filed into Ravenshill's bailey. For months the man kept Lincoln waiting on his invitation to Ravenshill. When Adrian arrived for Knox, the man perked up hearing Elisabeth's title and age and began asking questions, not about Elisabeth. He never asked the first question about her. He was interested in Ravenshill and the family's long lineage rooted deep in English soil. Far longer than any current nobility. He agreed to go to Ravenshill, not to meet Elisabeth, but to see the castle and land.

Adrian's heart sank when they gathered the morning of the departure from Knox's castle. Everyone in his family waited. Even his niece and nephews planned to travel with Knox's sister and her husband. The man's steward insisted on coming. And all his servants. As Adrian rode with them from the walls of Alton, he was surprised there was anyone left to manage it.

But now, as they began to dismount in Ravenshill's small bailey, he wondered how Elisabeth would feed them all. Adrian rode like mad ahead of the large procession to warn Elisabeth on the last leg of the journey. But, as he stood by and watched the chaos Lord Knox brought with him, he knew inside the keep everyone was in a frenzy to supply accommodations for those who would expect them. Adrian wondered what an incredible feat Elisabeth would accomplish if she could house so many in the small tower.

Presley guided Knox's servants in the settling of the animals. Within a few moments, Elisabeth was standing beside him on the steps. Adrian glanced at her and then took another good look at her. She was stunning, wearing the blue gown with the long jeweled and embroidered sleeves and the matching kirtle visible beneath the gown's long scooped neck. The fabric was left over from the bolts, and Elisabeth and the other women made her one more dress. The wealthy pricks at Blackpool had not returned her clothes, Adrian thought irritably.

Elisabeth tugged at the silver and sapphire belt high on her waist. She smoothed her hands down the front of the dress again and again. Adrian placed his hand over hers for a second to still them, then he drew it away and waited.

Knox stood across the bailey, and Adrian could see his eyes moving about, taking in Ravenshill. His face declared he did not like what he saw. As Adrian looked from one face to another, he could tell none of them were impressed. Adrian glanced at Elisabeth when she began fidgeting again. She offered him a worried look that was almost a grimace. She, too, was reading the faces of those in her bailey.

"Are you ready for this?" Adrian asked.

Elisabeth began to smooth her gown but placed her hands over her waist, cupping one in the other before she nodded. As Adrian took a step, he saw Elisabeth's head raise a notch, and she followed.

"Sir Knox, this is Elisabeth Kirkham, Lady of Ravenshill."

The man did not offer her a bow. Instead, he sneered as he looked down on her over his long, thick aquiline nose. "It is rather small," he said.

For a moment, Adrian thought the comment was about Elisabeth before he included "and old" in the statement.

Elisabeth did not hesitate to offer the man a curtsy. "Ravenshill is an old keep that has stood here on the border with Scotland for generations under the Kirkham name."

"Hmmm," the man said, making it clear he was unimpressed.

"If you would, please come inside. We have a meal being prepared."

"I would like to see the land around this little hunk of stone," Knox said, ignoring her.

Elisabeth hesitated, and her eyes fell on Adrian.

"I would be happy to show you," Adrian declared.

"Why not her father?" Knox snapped at him.

"Forgive me, but my father is hunting at the moment. He should be back later if you wish to wait."

"No, I do not wish to wait," Knox said, his voice impatient. "I guess you'll do." Then the man turned and barked at the servant that always lurked nearby to bring back his horse.

When Adrian gave Knox a thorough tour of the property, the man had found a problem with everything.

He did not know why Ravenshill mattered to Knox because Ravenshill would be Walter's, not Elisabeth's, to inherit. Adrian decided he did not like the man, and it wasn't just because he was a grouch. Adrian became acquainted with him quickly, whether at Ravenshill or Alton. Nothing satisfied Knox. But more importantly, the man was too old for Elisabeth. He hoped she would realize this, but he feared she would never see Sir Knox as anything but a way to rescue her home.

Knox led the way into the hall as if he owned the place. Adrian faltered. The noise of all those people gathered startled him. It had been a long time since he saw Ravenshill's hall so filled. Every table was occupied, and small children played in a corner. Servants, far more than Ravenshill may have ever had, were serving wine, of all things. Where had Elisabeth gotten wine? And how?

Elisabeth sat next to her father. One chair was left at the table, and Adrian knew it was for Knox, who walked to it and sat in the chair next to Elisabeth. Adrian studied the pair as they sat next to each other. Elisabeth spoke to Knox, who scowled, not even looking at her. But Adrian found he could not stop looking at Elisabeth. She looked strained and annoyed, but she hid it well. Why wouldn't she be annoyed? He did not know how they got food to flow from the kitchens. Despite the enormous effort launched to make Ravenshill appear as a place of prosperity instead of poverty, it was not enough. Knox's family still looked down their noses at everything they laid their eyes on.

As Adrian took a seat among Knox's squires, he wondered why the knights and squires had to come for what had to be the hundredth time. Why did the majority of these people have to come? All Knox had to do was look at Elisabeth and decide if he wanted her as a wife. He did not have to move in with his entire household. Knox's sister, Eileen, was far worse than the old knight himself. He heard her complaints about the food long before his table received theirs. Adrian scarfed down the food, finding nothing wrong with the amount, flavor, or quality.

As the meal dragged on, the sun settled from the sky. Lanterns were lit with the precious fuel rationed like everything else at Ravenshill, but the gathering remained. He could hear Eileen's shrill voice above the den as she speculated if Elisabeth was hearty or intelligent enough to carry Knox's child.

Adrian found the atmosphere inside oppressive. He wanted to stand on a table and point out to everyone what an extraordinary miracle Elisabeth of Ravenshill created for them. But he could say nothing because the extravagant meal and ample lantern fuel were supposed to be regular and not irregular.

"Are they irritating to you too?" Lincoln asked, making Adrian's breath seize in his chest as he walked into the gatehouse. They needed space for the rest of the party, masters and servants alike, so the family decided to bunk together in the gatehouse, all but Elisabeth. The latter had to suffer sharing space with the females of Knox's family for propriety's sake.

"You do not even know how much I would love to shove my fist down that pompous ass's throat," Adrian declared.

"But soon, you will be free to go on your way. So do not make Elisabeth second guess herself just because you love the girl."

Adrian turned to glower at Lincoln. "Don't give me that look. I know you have loved her since the first day she gave you my horse and played with you."

"It wasn't that day," Adrian grumbled.

"For sure, it was that day," Lincoln said.

A smile pulled at Adrian's lips. Their inside joke was now the favorite words of the man who took Lincoln captive in Poland. It never failed to make the other smile in remembrance when one or the other said, "For sure."

"What was that day?" Walter asked, entering with Presley trailing him.

"The first day young Adrian came to Ravenshill was the day he fell in love with our lady Elisabeth."

"Aye, he did," Presley agreed.

"I do not know what you all are talking about," Adrian persisted.

"I have seen it," Walter said. Adrian started. When had Walter joined the conversation? "The way you follow her around."

"The way you look at her," Annabelle said, hearing enough of the conversation to chime in when she entered.

"For sure, the way you look at her," Lincoln agreed. Then, in the candlelight, he dared Adrian to smile at that. "You would follow her to the ends of the Earth."

"It is a shame you were not her betrothed," Annabelle said.

"Can we stop this conversation? It is inappropriate."

"What is inappropriate about it," Lincoln asked. "We are only pointing out the obvious."

Adrian was irritated. It seemed so evident to them all.

"Where is Edith?" Walter asked.

"She is serving as lady's maid," Annabelle told him.

"And you best keep your eyes to yourself over that one, Young Lord," Lincoln said, pointing the dagger he was sharpening at Walter. "You have less chance of marrying her than Adrian does of marrying Elisabeth. Young Man, you are of a different status altogether, so do not begin mooning over her."

Walter fell silent, but Adrian knew what everyone in the room knew. The boy that wasn't Walter was from a similar background as the mute girl. Adrian knew they were both peasants, both orphaned and had come to Ravenshill with a lot of luck and a guiding hand from God.

Adrian and Walter went to their blankets after that. Still, Adrian lay awake in his long after the others blew out the candles and found their own slumber. He could not help but think back to the first day he came to Ravenshill. Then, standing before the portcullises, he was terrified. Even more so, seeing Lincoln for the first time.

### *Friday, September 20, 1443, Ravenshill*

*He was big. Bigger than almost any man Adrian ever saw. He had robust Italian features with long black hair gathered at the nape of his neck. His body was broad and appeared to have no flesh, only muscle. His voice was deep and loud. When first his eyes fell on the knight, he was glad he had come to this place despite his fear. If anyone could train him to be a great knight whose name would forever hang on tongues, it would be Sir Lincoln Victers.*

*He had little recollection of the tour through the small keep of Ravenshill. Instead, he watched Lincoln, the fluid way he moved despite his size. He made Adrian think of a giant prowling cat. Yet, despite his efforts, Adrian never learned to move like him. Perhaps he was yet to gain the bulk, or it came with experience and victories.*

*Adrian noticed the stone of the walls and buildings. Lincoln told him it was an old keep built on the border to secure it from Scotland during William's reign. The population was smaller now than it once was. Lincoln knew the fall of Ravenshill was coming. Yet, he allowed Adrian to come anyway.*

*The hall was cool when he entered and so very empty. He thought if he shouted, it would echo within the empty silence. Only one person occupied the giant space. It was a girl with the blondest hair he had ever seen. It was flaxen in its paleness.*

*When Lincoln introduced them, he almost missed her name because he was so mesmerized by the amount of blue that greeted him in the little girl's eyes. They were like a cloudless summer day, and they shone as bright as her brilliant smile he knew he would carry with him for days to come. As empty as Ravenshill was, it now did not feel empty. On the contrary, it felt warm where the cold stones pressed in on him before. She curtsied to him, startling him because he was entranced by those eyes. It was a perfect curtsy, much like her little face. He wondered if she was going to be as beautiful as she was pretty now. He offered her a deep bow, wondering if it was too deep.*

*When she asked him to come to play, he was startled by the invitation. At Helmsley, the squires did not play with the ladies. They rarely saw each other outside the great hall. But Ravenshill was much smaller, he thought as he looked around. How would he not see this girl daily? He looked to Lincoln should it be forbidden here.*

*Then Elisabeth seized his hand in hers with a strength that surprised him. She tugged at him and promised him a gift if he went with her. He did not need the present, he thought. He wanted to follow her. He would play with her, even if she wanted to play with dolls, because he wanted to see her smile more. It put him at ease and made thoughts of home slip into the recesses of his mind. Seeing her made this feel a little like home, even as he was yet to lay his head upon his new bed for the first time.*

*He sat on the hearth and looked down at the wood carvings she scooted his way. He realized they were well carved with great detail as he picked up the dog. Details included the fur and nose he admired as he turned the dog over in his hands. He was taken with them and glad she offered to share them with him. Next to her, he saw a horse, and he wanted so much to play with the horse. A good knight was nothing without a good horse, after all. He could make her horse the best knight's horse ever imagined with wooden figures and a squire's imagination. Then she was holding another horse out to him.*

*This horse was thick in legs and wide in the chest. Adrian could see it even had feathered feet, a long mane, and a tail that swept the ground. Lincoln carved them, Elisabeth said, and the destrier was made just for Adrian. He picked up the horse, gripping it, wanting to hug it, but he was not a girl to give in to such things. So he did not hear what she said as she held up her own horse and pranced it in the air for him. He was too overwhelmed by the magnitude of such a gift. The gesture began long ahead of his arrival. The time put into the details was a testament to that. The thoughtfulness of it almost bowled him over, but not as much as the girl with the blue eyes smiling at him.*

*Sitting on the stone, he thought it would be harder to imagine a great destrier with his wooden friends if they were inside a hall. "Can we play with them in the stable?" Adrian asked her.*

*He would never forget her response, "Where else would we play horses?" She did not hesitate. When had any of the girls at Helmsley even gone into the stable to play? Then, while they played in one of the empty stalls, in the aisles, and in the loft, no one came to chase them away for being in the way. They played until the dinner bell rang. The entire household ate as one. There was no first seating for lords and ladies and a second for the peasants. When the stable hands were out of food, so was Lord Thomas in his seat at the head table.*

*But Adrian was disappointed when Lincoln took them to the tiltyard for the first time. Lincoln handed him a staff and not a sword. He loved the rasps and clanks the practice blades made against one another. They were not sharpened or used in battle, for the chipping and dulling on an actual edge would make it useless on a battlefield. Yet, despite his size and age, Adrian could heft one of those swords well enough to hold his own. Did Lincoln think he could not? He hadn't played with sticks since he was old enough to hold one of the swords.*

*Adrian quickly told Lincoln he had already learned to fight with a sword. Lincoln told him he had not. What began as an exercise Adrian thought was beneath his skill level ended in embarrassment because he could not anticipate the quick blows Lincoln thrust at him. The stick would smack him in the precise places he was taught to block a sword. Although he could beat any other squire on the practice field, the stick moved too quickly, and Lincoln kept him on the defensive, and he never got a chance to wield his own staff.*

*Adrian grew ashamed of how fast Lincoln could disarm him by whacking his knuckles. Adrian could not even defend against that.*

*"You are good," Lincoln told him as they walked back to the gate. Adrian felt a little confused. No one ever told him he was good despite knowing he was. "You will learn nothing important practicing with another man who pulls his thrusts and speeds to avoid causing too much injury to his friend. In a real battle, you must move faster. You do not have time to assess your enemy. So, you have to move fast and hard, which is how you will practice from this day on. I will teach you to get out of battles alive."*

*"I will be as great as you someday," Adrian declared.*

# Chapter 24

**Wednesday, March 11, 1450, Ravenshill**

Elisabeth steadied her breathing and planted an empty smile on her face. She practiced it this morning in the mirror. After Eileen pointed out Elisabeth did not smile as if she was glad to be getting her brother as a husband. But it was hard not to be insulted by this man who was yet to commit to a union after eating Ravenshill's food for two days. They were making a desperate situation worse.

He demanded she shows him the wall this evening. He barked the order at her as she crossed the bailey. This was after Adrian brought him back from a tour of the village grist mill. She did not hesitate to obey, and now she was stuck between Knox and a plunge to her death. If not for Ravenshill, she might have to consider option B, as the man would not shut up about his superiority over everything.

"You have nothing to offer but your title. This castle and property would bring me no more wealth." Elisabeth was aware of this, as well as Knox should be.

He spoke as if Ravenshill did not have a male heir. He spoke as if it was already his.

He turned to her and looked down at her. "Are you a virgin?" he asked.

"Yes," she said, a little uncomfortable and wondered if it was typical for a man to ask this directly of his prospective bride.

"Well, there is that," he said before turning and walking from her. She anticipated watching him go, but halfway across, he barked to her without even turning, "I have not dismissed you." She hurried to catch up, feeling much like a dog at heel since she did nothing more than walk in his step as he went back to the bailey and into the hall. He seemed satisfied with this.

The meal was being held for him and him alone. He settled into his seat. His posture was imperialistic. As the food was blessed, he looked across his plate with disdain. Elisabeth wanted to cram each bite down his throat and demand he respects the effort her household was going through to provide them all with food. For the first time, Elisabeth could remember they had to have first seating and a second because, in the end, there was not enough food to go around. Someone hunted from sunup to sundown, and no one wanted to tell the visitors that they had dined on rats the night before. Katy was a whiz with herbs and spices. She could make any dish into a delicacy. But that also was something these horrid people did not appreciate.

After the meal was eaten, Knox cleared his throat and stood. "After looking over Ravenshill, I have considered it not enough of an attraction to tie myself to the Kirkham name. But I will get a grander title, and she has assured me she is a virgin. So, with those two factors, I have decided I will wed Elisabeth."

Congratulations rippled through the hall, but Elisabeth felt as if it spun. Wasn't that what she wanted? Her eyes skittered across everyone to fall on Adrian. He scowled at her, then lifted his goblet to her in a gesture of a toast. His eyes glittered. Elisabeth wished she could run to him. She wished she did not have to lie beneath the old ass that sat next to her. After swallowing long from his cup, Adrian sat his drink down without breaking eye contact with her. Then he stood to stalk from the hall.

"Where are you going, young man?" Knox demanded. The man's voice was raised, and the hall fell silent.

Elisabeth watched Adrian pause, unsure who Knox was speaking to. It was apparent to her because Adrian was the only one on the move.

Adrian turned. "I have not dismissed you," Knox said, standing. "If you are part of my household, you will learn respect."

"He is Baron Adrian de Ros. He fosters with Sir Lincoln," Elisabeth explained in a rush.

"I am perfectly aware of who he is. You will shut your mouth before I slap your teeth from your face."

Knox turned to demonstrate he was ready to do as he threatened by raising his hand. But she saw Adrian moving toward her from the corner of her eye. Lincoln and Walter were standing, but Adrian reached them first.

"No, Adrian," Elisabeth commanded, fearing Knox's hand would fall on her for speaking.

Knox paused, and his eyes fell on Adrian before moving to Walter and Lincoln. "This woman is mine now, and you will not interfere."

"She is not yours yet," Adrian declared. "And if you lay a hand upon her, you will regret it."

"I will have you flogged," Knox declared, raising a hand to point toward Adrian.

Elisabeth jumped to her feet and seized Knox's arm. "Please, my lord, he only...." Whatever she was going to say was cut short as Knox's hand cracked across her cheek. She staggered beneath the blow.

"Adrian! Halt!" Lincoln's voice ripped across the hall. For a terrifying moment, Elisabeth thought the squire would not listen because his sword was already in his hand and murder in his eyes.

Knox's eyes fell on Lincoln, and then the man grew still. His breath caught in his chest, and he was unable to breathe. Then his body crashed downward, his chair flew backward, and the weight of his body upended the table before he came to land amongst the buttered bread and squirrel meat that joined him on the floor. Knox's people rushed toward him. Elisabeth and the rest of her household stood still, gazes searching for the answer to what they should do. Elisabeth felt like applauding.

It was not a moment to be applauded, for Knox was dead. He perhaps stopped breathing before he hit the floor. Elisabeth did not know. But she did know two things. The first was that Knox's household began packing immediately, which was a blessing. The second thing was that her reputation was ruined with that blessing because Eileen declared she would make it so as soon as they returned to "civilization." Moreover, she kept proclaiming Elisabeth's guilt because she was a siren who called men to her to break their hearts, destroy and kill them. Eileen carried this all the way to the bailey, where they threw their belongings into the wagons.

"He was a perfectly healthy man before he promised himself to you and ate at your table!" Eileen screamed at Elisabeth before turning and following Knox's men from the gates of Ravenshill.

"It's for the best," Lincoln said after the last horse's tail disappeared from sight.

Elisabeth clenched her hands at her sides. She had already swallowed her pride, something she had been doing for days. She withstood the repulsion of his hand, of his words, and convinced herself she could withstand a marriage to him. For Ravenshill, she was willing to do anything. But he died and made everything so much worse than her marriage to him could ever be.

What did Lincoln know of it anyway? He went where she told him to and did what she told him to. What responsibilities lay upon his shoulders? He did what she said or didn't. It all came back to her. She raised her head and saw everyone looking at her. They were always looking at her, waiting for her decision.

"It truly is," Katy said.

What does she know of it, Elisabeth wondered to herself. She was the same, waiting for her direction, always content to let Elisabeth lead. Elisabeth was tired of leading them through the never-ending storm. It seemed as if it picked up in intensity as they went, beating relentlessly at her.

"That was fate...." Adrian began, but Elisabeth spun on him.

"Fate?" she asked. She kept her voice low, at her standard pitch, but inside, she raged. She did not care what Adrian was going to say. She knew they said these things to ease her mind, but the words built the feeling of desperation eating away at her instead. “Is it fate that I have lost another fiancé so the tongues will continue to wag of my curse?”

Adrian dared to bark laughter at her. On his face was a look of ease. Obviously, he was content that he did not have to hold his tongue. Adrian would soon go running home, so it was no concern what state he left them in. He told her he didn’t want her to marry Knox. What business of it was his? “You are not cursed,” Adrian reassured her.

“I know I am not cursed!” she felt herself explode with those words. She felt a beast rise in her chest, and it was a nasty thing with claws and teeth ready to tear into something. She stepped to him, grabbed his shirt, and shook him while screaming in his face. “But that does not matter! I have spent so much to get us somewhere, and we are nowhere, only poorer.”

“It will be okay,” Adrian said. She unwrapped her hands and let her fist fly into his chest. His hand went to it as his other tried to catch her.

She backed away, yanking her hand from his grasp. “How do you know? You will go on your way.”

“We’re in this together,” Lincoln tried to console her in a voice that was far gentler than usual.

“No,” she said, shaking her head. “We are not. This is not your name. This is not your heritage.”

Edith came toward her and reached for her. Elisabeth slung out a hand and shoved her away. “Why do I even put the effort forth?” she screamed again. “No one volunteers to do anything without me telling you. Can you not gather wood or clean a stall without me having to think of it first? I am tired of fighting for this place!” she turned and stalked toward the tower. “You all would be better off going somewhere else!”

She plunged into the dim light of the lord's hall, slamming the door behind her. It did not shake the stone tower. On the contrary, it stood solid as Elisabeth felt herself crumbling. She climbed the steps to the family chamber on the second floor, then out into the stairway that led to the private garden. Elisabeth did not reach the bottom before collapsing onto a step, clinging to the rail as she wept. She had hit and screamed at Adrian. How could she do such a thing? She breathed heavily as the guilt fought for room in her chest with the beast of rage.

She heard the door above her open. "Leave me," she warned. She listened to the steps falter, heavy boots with a sure stride. It had to be Adrian because Lincoln would turn away. Slowly the steps came toward her. She could not move as her fingers fell from the rail, and she gripped them in her lap. Her entire body began to shake with her rage again. She did not want him near, waiting for her next decision. She was out. Ravenshill could crumble to the ground, and Adrian could return home with his perfect wife and live happily ever after. There were no happy endings for her. She knew this. She was okay if she could leave this place and let everyone else do what they would. But they wouldn't, and she could not. That was why the beast raged still as he sank onto the step two above hers. His boots came to rest beside her on her step. His leg was inches from her shoulder. If he sat next to her or spoke to her, the beast would be unleashed again. But he didn't.

Elisabeth bent forward over the clenched hands in her lap and peered at the weeds and struggling plants, not seeing them as the beast began to settle.

She let out a long sigh that came out as a sob. Adrian's hand landed on her shoulder, which remained there until she raised her hand to lay atop his. He slipped down to sit next to her on her step and dropped his arm around her shoulders.

"I am so sorry," she said as the tears flowed. She looked up at Adrian, at his firm, handsome features. She had struck him. He was her anchor, her knight of swords, and she had struck him and screamed in his face. She buried her head against his chest, and his arms tightened around her, pressing her against him.

"It is all right, Elisabeth. Truly. All is forgiven," he whispered to her as he used a hand to smooth down her hair.

She began to gather herself, reluctant to leave Adrian's arms, but she knew he would not always be able to wrap them around her. She knew this could be the last time she was held in them. Finally, after her sobbing ended, she felt Adrian shift, and then his fingers were on her chin, lifting her face to his. He bent and offered a gentle kiss on her lips. It was a kiss that did not linger, but it was a kiss that told her that he still loved her despite what she had just done.

When he released her, she straightened, and he withdrew his arms. His shoulder brushed against hers as they fell silent again for a few moments, staring over the garden.

"I am so afraid," she whispered to him.

"I know," he replied. "We all know." A few breaths passed between them before he continued. "We all love you, and you will never be alone. Even when I leave, I will not forget how I love you, Elisabeth. Those people in there are loyal to you to the end. Even if Ravenshill falls, they will be there to hold you up. They will never leave you as I must."

"I pushed Edith," she whispered, remembering the girl's widening brown eyes and confusion. Despite how Edith clung to her, Elisabeth had never pushed Edith away before.

"She does not speak, but she is not stupid. She will not let that one thing separate you."

"She can speak," Elisabeth said, wiping a tear from her cheek. "She hates how it sounds now with no tongue, so she chooses not to say anything."

She saw Adrian nod from the corner of her eye. "Do not fear for Walter," he said. "He is a good kid and bright. He is very generous to others. He will be a good lord when the time comes. You just have to keep things together until then, Elisabeth," he said, reaching for her hand. "Just a little while longer," he said, wrapping his big hand around hers. She looked down at them, joined together. It was hard to hold his hand and not remember her clinging to him when they were much younger. But they survived that, and she would survive this.

She fought away the thought of Adrian's hand not being there, and she squeezed it. His grip was firm, his strength flowed through her, and she closed her eyes. She wanted to remember everything about his hand and how it made her feel. How it made her feel as if she could face anything. She committed it to her memory, where his fingers fell between hers. Where the tips of his fingers came to rest on the back of her hand and hers his. How much his fingers spread hers to accommodate his size. Then he released her hand, and she felt like sobbing. She did not open her eyes, doing her best to ensure she would always be able to recall the feeling of him wrapped around her.

"I saw the woodpile in the hall needed filling," he said with an edge of humor. "I will take care of it, and Lincoln will keep an eye on the piles throughout the keep too."

Elisabeth nodded but did not speak. He stared down at her for a moment, but Elisabeth refused to open her eyes and look at him. Then, finally, the tread of his boots carried him up the steps. When she heard the door above her close, she dropped her head in her lap and sobbed. Just memorizing his hand on hers was not enough. The warmth and strength were missing. How could she even stand when he was gone from Ravenshill?

# Chapter 25

**Thursday, February 10, 1452, Ravenshill**

"He's no better off than we are," Lord Thomas said. The snowstorm was raging outside for a day. The household gathered in the hall to pass the time locked indoors. Elisabeth and Lord Thomas discussed the next possible husband for Elisabeth.

"Lord Benton Marlowe," Elisabeth said with great decisiveness.

Adrian looked up from his chess game with Annabelle and saw Elisabeth staring at one of her ledgers. He looked to Lincoln and then to her father. Edith got up and went to look over her shoulder, where Elisabeth lay a finger on the page. The ledger of possible husbands was expanded and now contained meticulous notes on family lineages and potential wealth and holdings.

"What are you looking at?" Lincoln's words directed at Edith had a teasing quality about them.

"Benton's family has held the Linnels title for a few generations," Katy offered, where she set darning a shirt for Presley.

"That doesn't mean there is enough money there," Lord Thomas warned.

"There has to be," Elisabeth insisted.

"What are you looking at?" Lincoln asked Edith again.

"She's reading," Elisabeth snapped at him, unable to not let the conversation going on over her head distract her.

"She can read?" Lincoln asked, almost incredulous.

"Yes," Elisabeth said as Edith shifted behind her. The girl stood a little taller. "I have been teaching her." Edith was very proud that she could read and write.

Lincoln nodded, studying Edith.

"Is it hard to teach someone who does not speak?" Lincoln asked when Elisabeth turned back to her father.

"It's easy, as a matter of fact," Elisabeth stood with annoyance written across her face. "She doesn't interrupt." Then, finally, she snapped her ledger closed and headed for the tower.

Adrian sprung to his feet and followed. He dashed with her through the driving snow whipping beneath the overhanging roof and into the dark tower. "Did you say you were looking to marry Marlowe?" Adrian asked, taking her arm to stop her headlong journey to the library and the privacy it offered to contemplate this new decision.

"Yes," she said, turning with the book tucked beneath her arm.

"But he is just a scrawny boy."

Elisabeth sighed. "A boy will not die at my table, and this terror of my presence will end," she snapped at him. Then Elisabeth lay a hand on his forearm. "I am sorry," she said. "But I heard talk in the village, and they believe me to be cursed. Between a long-standing betrothal broken and Knox dying at my feet, Eileen has fueled a great deal of talk and speculation."

"Don't let it worry you," Adrian said, taking her hand in his.

Elisabeth straightened in indignation. "Don't let it worry me? How can I not? I will soon run out of time. I must send an army to France and find a way to feed us all. Now I must marry before these rumors get out of hand, and I can find no one willing to risk an alliance with me."

"Shhh," he said, drawing her to him and wrapping his arms around her. He cradled her head against his chest and held her there.

He felt her breathing slow as her chest rose and fell against his, seaming to match his own rhythm. Her heart beat. He could feel it as he pressed her against himself. Finally, it slowed, and her entire frame relaxed. "It cannot be as bad as that," Adrian said, still holding her. As soon as he released her, he knew she would go into a frenzy for a husband search again. Adrian could see the burden weighing her down and the strain of such a responsibility that she carried etch across her brow. He did not like to see it. If his parents had not refused marriage with her, he could make it all better. But his parents had to look out for Helmsley and do what they felt was best, as Elisabeth did with Ravenshill. He didn't want to fault them for that. Though it was difficult not to, even on the best of days.

He slid his arms from around her shoulders that seemed so narrow and thin beneath the burdens she carried. She needed a strong man. She needed a warrior like himself to protect and warm her bed, not some scrawny fool like Benton. Adrian knew Elisabeth was right. He heard the accusations that Elisabeth's engagements were doomed. She did have to move quickly for many reasons. The reason most pressing in his mind was that he was beginning to grow fonder of her. Now that husbands and wives were being discussed, he knew he could not find a better wife than Elisabeth. She would be loyal, a caring mother, and intelligent. He would have no problems running his household with Elisabeth at his side. But what was worse was his growing desire. At sixteen, they were both of the age they should marry. Adrian was tired of his mother's messages, reminding him she needed a date for the consummation.

As soon as he released her, he watched her don her armor. Her back straightened until it was ramrod straight. Her head went up a notch, so she had the appearance of looking down upon everyone. Her blue eyes lost their softness, and unbreakable steel courage filled them. Her shoulders went back, and it appeared that no heavy weight was pulling at them. Now she was the woman who believed the strongest of storms could not take her down. But they both knew better. They had both been there. Adrian guessed that was why she put on her armor, so no one would dare try to put her there again.

"What do you think?" she asked, tapping the book beneath her arm.

Adrian wanted to tell her she couldn't go to Benton with every part of his being. Benton couldn't protect her as he could. Adrian wanted to tell her Benton couldn't love her as he could. But this wasn't about love. It was about family and duty. Adrian already took his vows, and Elisabeth had to be married to set things right at Ravenshill.

"I think I will ride to Linnels and extend an invitation to Benton for you," Adrian said. He felt her urgency seeping into him.

"You will?" she asked.

He would do it twenty times if her face lit up for him each time he offered. Then, grabbing his arm with her free hand, she pulled him into a quick hug, kissing his cheek as she stepped away.

As Adrian pulled away, he wanted to flee because he did not want to go to Linnels. Adrian didn't want to let Benton have her. He didn't want Waverly. He wanted Elisabeth and needed to get away before that feeling grew. "I'll leave at first light," he said, backing away. He spun and hurried back to the storm outside. It would not matter if it did not let up. He had to get Benton here.

Adrian's resolve fled by the following day. With the waning of the storm and Elisabeth not in his arms, he was unsure why he had made such a hasty decision. But he did tell her he would go, so he readied his horse by torchlight and exited the gates just as the first rays of the sun were washing the land on a new day.

The ride to Linnels took a day, and he was riding beneath the portcullis as the bell rang for the day's last meal. He was foolish and did not wait to break his fast or take anything with him to eat during the journey, so his stomach growled at the prospect of food going into it. One of the guards escorted him into the hall, filled with people and warmth—a good sign of the keep's prosperity. The guard presented him to Viscount Benton Marlowe and his mother, Lady Lesley Marlowe.

Adrian knew the boy was near the age of himself, maybe even his senior, by a year or two. The boy was as short as his mother, and his body was as tiny as birch was to an oak. He had to stop his head from shaking a refusal to take this boy back to Elisabeth. Adrian knew Benton because Lincoln took him to Linnels often to train with some of their knights since he was acquainted with Benton's father before his recent death. Benton was soft-spoken and timid back then. Looking at him now, Adrian knew that had not changed. Despite Adrian training with the knights and not Benton, they became friends of a sort. Adrian had little time for making friends when they came to Linnels. But the boy considered him a friend by the look on Benton's face as Adrian stood before him.

"What has brought you here, old friend?" Benton asked, rising as his mother looked confused at his appearance.

"I thought I might seek a warm bed for the night and invite an old friend to join me on my journey to Ravenshill."

"It would be a delight," Benton said, and it was all he could do to keep from rolling his eyes at the boy's naivety or stupidity. He wasn't sure. Adrian would prefer the boy refuse and send him on his way. Adrian wished he had because the messenger would not have caught up to him then. As it was, the rider arrived late into the evening, close on Adrian's heels when he left Ravenshill that morning. It was from his mother, demanding he presents himself at Helmsley. His wife had arrived, and he needed to seal their vows.

He pondered the situation and decided they would ride to Helmsley if Benton was willing. Having Benton with him would give him an excuse to get away from Waverly with all due haste. Hopefully, before they set a date for him to return to Helmsley and take a woman's virginity despite never even holding her hand.

Benton was a willing companion, and Adrian hated to admit he still liked the young man. Despite all Adrian saw was wrong with him, he was a good person. He knew he was honest and dependable, which eased his mind a little as they traveled.

"Son," his father greeted him as he dismounted at the steps of Helmsley. The sun shone in a cloudless sky, melting away all but the memory of the recent storm.

His mother was there too, and seizing a girl by the arm dragged her toward Adrian. "Adrian, this is Lady Waverly, your bride," she said, pushing the young woman forward.

Adrian wanted to take a step back. There was something unwelcoming in the green eyes that looked at him. It appeared as if disdain flattened her lips as she looked down her nose. It had to be his imagination. She had no reason to disdain or look down on him since this was their second time laying eyes on one another. Unless she, too, did not want this marriage. But what could either of them do if that was the case?

Adrian bowed before both women, took Waverly's hand in his, and kissed the back of her knuckles. He did not misread the look of disrespect that slid across her brow as she yanked her hand away with a small gasp. Adrian straightened and looked at his mother.

His mother ignored the action and turned away, guiding Waverly back into the keep. "Your bride-to-be is a lovely lady," Benton said, appearing at Adrian's shoulder.

Adrian grunted. Perhaps she was, but he did not like her. She seemed against the marriage. Maybe there was another man in her life. If there was someone else, perhaps he could convince her to go to him and leave their marriage. If she did, his parents might reconsider Elisabeth before he got Benton to Ravenshill.

Before the evening meal, Adrian found the woman alone in the garden sitting on his mother's favorite bench. His mother loved her garden and the flowers and small trees she put a great deal of time into so she could sit on the bench and enjoy the fruits of her labor. Perhaps if this woman took such joy, she would not be so deplorable after all. The evergreen plants were a vivid green against the bare earth, and well-groomed trees prepared to bear fruit in the summer.

"Might I join you?" Adrian asked, offering her a bow.

She did not answer, but agitation crossed her face, and she let out an exasperated sigh before moving her skirt off the bench so he could settle in beside her. "I can leave you to your solitude," he offered.

"No," she said. Her voice sounded irritating with that one nasty word. "Your mother insisted I sit here. I don't care what you do."

Adrian felt he should leave, but to leave would be a kind of surrender. He took a seat on the bench. "Why did my mother tell you to sit here?"

Again, that exasperated sound escaped her. "She said it was lovely here. I find it dull," she said with a wave of her hand, dismissing his mother's creation.

"I think she was just hoping to make you comfortable here."

Waverly expelled a breath as if that was an impossibility. Adrian held back his sigh.

"Can I speak to you about our arrangement," he asked. Waverly turned her milk-white face to him but waited with disdain and impatience filling her eyes. "I feel you are as unhappy with it as I am."

"Why do you feel that way?" she demanded. "Why are you unhappy with the arrangement?" she added. "Your family came to mine," she said with great resentment. "I would not be here if not for that."

Adrian paused. He didn't understand what she was saying. She wanted to go on with the marriage? Or he owed her for putting her out on an engagement he had not wanted? "You want to be wed to me?"

Waverly shrugged as she looked down her nose at him. "Your family is wealthy and titled. I could do worse."

"But you could do better," Adrian informed her.

Waverly's eyes narrowed. "But you can't," she said. Then she sighed again. "I assure you I am untouched by any man. I will do my duty to give you sons and daughters."

"Your duty?" he asked. Of course, he knew they both had duties to their family, but it left him feeling cold to state it so bluntly.

"Yes," she said, staring at him as if he were an idiot. "My duty. Did you expect me to swoon at your feet? I will do no such thing. I have to marry you and bed you. I think you people are barbarians. I will spend most of our marriage in London but will travel to you when you demand it."

"When I demand it?" he asked. He could not imagine demanding this woman to be anywhere near him.

"Yes. To plant your seed," Waverly clarified.

Plant his seed? He felt Elisabeth wrapped in his arms. He saw her smile with blue eyes full of life. Joy was lacking in this woman's eyes, and no light shone across her face. A stern countenance and a determination to do her duty were what he saw. Would she ever soften? Not if she saw him as a barbarian. How could she grow fond of him if she was only around him when he rutted between her legs?

Adrian felt ill.

"I hope we did not interrupt a tryst," his father's voice cut through the garden. His tone was full of hope that he was. He appeared with Adrian's mother walking on his arm.

"Oh, Hagan," his mother said, slapping his arm.

Adrian heard a sound of annoyance escape the woman next to him. "Hardly," she replied under her breath. "Is your mother such a whore she would ask that?"

Did she just insinuate his mother was a whore because his father was teasing them? Waverly shot to her feet. "I have become exhausted in this sun. I shall return to my chambers until the meal is served," Waverly said, her voice imperialistic.

Adrian found a slight amount of satisfaction when his mother faltered. "Of course, my dear," his mother said. Adrian could tell her smile was still plastered to her face for Adrian's benefit.

Waverly stood waiting as if she expected something from the three people now staring at her. "Would you show me the way?" the young woman snapped at his mother.

"Of course, my dear," his mother said with surprise and disappointment.

Adrian stood as the two women left the garden. "Really, Father?" Adrian asked.

Lord Hagan turned to his son and scowled. "She is a good match."

"She is a bitch," Adrian stated.

"Why is Benton Marlowe here? Why did our messenger find you at Linnels and not Ravenshill?"

"I hope to introduce Elisabeth to Benton. Unfortunately, she is still in need of a husband."

"It is good that you have a good match yourself," his father replied. "You should not be playing matchmaker and messenger for the Kirkhams. That is not why we pay them to train you."

"I am still training as a knight," Adrian said, annoyed that he was not looking at the critical thing. His parents wanted him to lay with that horrid girl.

"You should return to Helmsley and take on some of the duties here."

"It is not the time for that," Adrian replied, trying to ease his way from his father.

Thunder etched its way across his father's brow. "If you do not return home soon, the fall of the Kirkhams will take you down with them."

"The fall of the Kirkhams?" Adrian asked.

"It is bound to happen," Hagan replied as if he provided no information that Adrian should not already have.

"Rumors abound about Elisabeth and the broken betrothal with Harris. Then to have Lord Knox die at her table does not bode well for her. I will tell Benton as much when I see him," his father threatened.

"Do not," Adrian said with all the command he had learned from Lincoln in his voice. "Benton and Elisabeth are no concern of yours."

"I suppose if she were married to someone else, she would get her claws out of you."

"Her claws are not in me," Adrian replied, exasperated.

"Oh, no?" his father asked. "She has gotten you to ask us for our favor in marriage to her. You watch her. Next, she will try to trap you by claiming to carry your child."

"She could not claim to carry my child since I have never touched her."

His father scoffed. "A woman can change that. She is a witch, and you be careful of her."

Adrian sighed but refused to argue with a man who had no idea what he spoke of. Adrian turned and left the garden. His heart was heavy, knowing his time at Ravenshill was ticking away.

# Chapter 26

**Thursday, February 17, 1452, Ravenshill**

Elisabeth was relieved to see Adrian return with Benton in tow. As they dismounted and she was introduced to the young man, two significant differences between Benton and Knox Hallewell were evident. First, Benton was not as advanced in years. She was quite surprised at how young he did look. The second, the younger man, was immediately taken by her. She did not know much about courting and husband searching, but it was apparent when he looked at her that he had a great deal more interest in her than Knox did. His eyes didn't scan the bailey for something else.

She needed this boy for his family's wealth. The matter was as simple as that. Her "father" had sent excuse after excuse to King Henry, declaring he had to resolve the issue of his daughter's marriage before his men could rejoin the King's forces. It was a stalling tactic and an attempt to get the King involved in finding her a husband. But he took no interest in her or her marriage. The stalling was not well received. Not a patient man, Elisabeth had never heard of a king that was. He declared he would soon rain his wrath down on Ravenshill.

She offered Benton a smile and a curtsy. He offered her a gallant bow and a kiss on the back of her knuckles. She ignored the fact he looked like a puppy looking up at her with his inexperienced eyes. She supposed not all men her age could look as adult as Adrian. She admonished herself for even comparing the two. She knew no one could come out ahead with a comparison against Adrian.

"My lady, this is Lord Benton Marlowe of Linnels. Benton, this is Lady Elisabeth Kirkham."

"My lady," Benton began with a thin, squeaky voice. "The description Adrian has given of you pales compared to your true beauty," he said, clinging to her hand a moment longer than necessary.

"I worry how Lord Adrian has been describing me," Elisabeth replied, teasing him. She flashed him a brilliant smile he returned.

"I truly thought I would be meeting an angel," he assured her. "But you are far more beautiful than that. A goddess," he rushed out, then looked embarrassed.

"Oh, Lord Benton," she said, blushing while looking at him from beneath her lashes. Annabelle showed Elisabeth a few days before how to flirt and said this could help cinch the deal with Benton.

The boy's face reddened, and his smile grew even broader. "Please, my lady, just call me Benton."

"I most assuredly will," Elisabeth said, planting herself at Benton's side and placing a hand on his arm. "If you will, please call me Elisabeth."

"Elisabeth." He said her name as if he spoke the name of a goddess.

She blushed again before guiding him toward the hall.

Elisabeth put a great deal of effort into flattering Benton for two days. It was unnecessary but a precaution she felt was necessary. On the third day, the boy professed his love and asked permission to court and marry her. She played the surprised and flattered young girl and assured him she was already so fond of him that courting would be pointless. Benton agreed. He secured their engagement with her father's blessing by the fourth day and sent the messenger to his mother to spread the blessed news.

**Monday, February 21, 1452, Ravenshill**

"When is the big day?" Adrian asked, stepping into the small garden. It was once the private garden of the ladies of the keep. Elisabeth never tended it, but no lady of Ravenshill was ever saddled with the entire family's fate on her shoulders. She detected a teasing tone, but there was something else there too.

"No date is set. But the sooner, the better," Elisabeth said as she continued to look up at the night sky. It never failed to awe her at the vastness. "The banns were posted."

She saw Adrian nod from the corner of her eye. She also noticed that he was staring at her. "Well, spit it out," she snapped at him.

"Are you doing the right thing?" he asked her.

She turned her head, looked at him, and shook it. "I have no idea."

"Shouldn't you be?"

"Should I be doing the right thing?" she could not keep the astonishment from her voice. "Did I do the right thing when Knox died after announcing our engagement? Did I do the right thing because my father cannot manage Ravenshill? Did I do the right thing when Harris sent me away? Did I do the right thing when those men took me to the mine?" Then her voice dropped low, "Did I do the right thing when I spoke up, and Edith lost her tongue? I'll answer that for you, Adrian. I did not do the right thing, so I truly do not believe I am doing the right thing now. But it is a thing to do, so I am doing it."

She turned and went to the hall to escape Adrian. He was letting his family dictate he not help her. She guessed she could not blame him so much for that. There were dire consequences that were liable to negate the real reason she and Adrian should marry. She knew there would be more to a marriage with Adrian than his money. It was far more complicated than that.

Benton jumped to his feet when she entered the hall. He immediately came to her, resting her hand on his forearm and guiding her to one of the tables. "I had Katy fix this just for you. I know how you like apples." On the table sat an apple pie whose fragrance penetrated her senses and made her mouth water. "Benton, it looks delicious," she said, taking the spoon he offered her as he stood back proudly for her to take her seat.

She sank into the chair and looked at him bashfully. It was no trick this time. She was ready to tear into it with a ferocity that matched her raging taste buds. "Go ahead, my lady," he said with a smile of joy at his surprise.

She dug into the pie, piercing the crust and digging deep into the sweet filling. The innards still steamed. It was as delicious as all Katy's pies were, but none could compare to her apple. Edith appeared with another spoon she presented to Benton. Elisabeth pushed the chair next to her out, beckoning him to sit, then stuffed another mouthful in.

It only took Elisabeth a few bites before she began to feel guilty. No one else at Ravenshill had apple pie to eat. The number of apples stored since fall was few and diminishing with age. Elisabeth knew precisely how many apples were left. Sometimes the apples had to go to the animals to supplement the food they did not have. Sometimes it was what they had to chase hunger away when they were unsuccessful in hunting and their other stored food supplies were diminishing. Never did she even consider making one of the apples into a pie. Her stomach flopped, wondering how many apples went into the filling.

Elisabeth feigned a full stomach, sitting back and holding a hand up. "The meal was so satisfying, and to add pie to it. I just don't think I can eat another bite."

Benton beamed.

"If you have had your fill, we should take a walk," she said, clamoring to her feet. Elisabeth felt little guilt for taking him from the pie. Perhaps because he did not hesitate to get to his feet, accepting her invitation to walk with her. As they passed Edith, who lingered in the archway, Elisabeth said, "I would hate for such a delicious pie to go to waste. Would you see it is distributed?" Edith nodded, and Elisabeth could almost see Edith salivate.

Elisabeth stepped out into the night with her hand resting on his forearm. It felt frail. It felt nothing like Adrian's strong arm beneath her palm. But she walked beside him because he came from a house that did not put second thoughts into sparing important food reserves for a sweet delicacy.

"I am honored that you are taking me for a husband," Benton said at some length.

"The honor is mine," Elisabeth assured him.

"I thought with my family's financial crisis, I would be hard-pressed to find a wife. Especially one as beautiful and well-bred as you."

Elisabeth faltered. "Financial crisis?" she questioned, schooling away her surprise.

"Oh yes," Benton said as he continued to walk while Elisabeth felt each step was a struggle. "My father gambled it. Most do not know this, but he killed himself because of the mess he made."

"So, you are destitute?" Elisabeth asked.

"Not destitute," Benton said. "But we are struggling. This marriage will help our situation if I dare say such a forward thing."

Elisabeth stopped and turned Benton toward her. "The Kirkhams have no money," Elisabeth's words were slow, so he could not mistake her. She felt the earth tilting. They had already announced their engagement. What would another broken engagement cost her?

"How can that be? I always thought Ravenshill must have accumulated wealth all the time it has existed."

Elisabeth shrugged.

"This can't be," Benton said, taking a step back and staring at her as if she had grown two heads.

"I assure you it is."

"Lady Elisabeth, I do greatly admire you. If I could have my choice of anyone, I would choose you. But I must marry someone who can benefit my family."

"We can't stop the engagement now," Elisabeth said, indignant.

"I have no choice, Elisabeth. Do you even have the money for a dowery?"

Elisabeth scowled at him then her temper flared. "Do not break this engagement. You do not have to marry me, but this engagement must last longer than a week."

"But..."

"But nothing," she snapped at him. "My fiancés have provided troops or have promised to provide troops to King Henry under the Kirkham name. So, if you can provide me with that, I will ease myself from this arrangement as quickly as possible."

"We have no spare troops, my lady. They are already in France."

"Do you know how hard it will be to get a husband after having a betrothal broken, a fiancé died, and an engagement ended after only a week?"

"I'm sorry, my lady...."

"Sorry, is it? You have no idea what this will do to Ravenshill. I cannot finance the ground troops, let alone the four knights," Elisabeth said, devastated to her core.

"You have three, my lady," Benton said. "Sir Lincoln, your father, and Adrian."

"Adrian is a squire."

"But only for a short time. Adrian should have already earned his spurs. I did last year."

Elisabeth grabbed him. "Go to France under our banner." She felt her fingers gripping the boy's arms so tightly she might bruise him. But what was happening was madness. She had to stop this young man from taking her hope by walking out the door. "After one campaign, you can break the engagement. We can find a plausible and acceptable reason to all without tainting my name."

"But what of the foot soldiers?" he asked. "You said you can't finance them. What of your father? Should these not be his worries?"

Elisabeth scowled at him, and he did not pursue that thread.

"But what of squires and horses?"

"Walter is a squire," Elisabeth said. "I can get squires, foot soldiers, and horses. It is the knights I need, and you will make our fourth. Please, Benton. One campaign to appease the King, and that will buy me some time to get it straightened out."

Benton appeared to be on the cusp of wavering. "Please," she begged. Then, "I beg of you," she said, just to clarify.

Benton relented with a nod of his head. "Truly anything for you, my lady. I would be honored to have you as my wife if only my family's circumstances were different."

Elisabeth laid her hands on Benton's arm. "It is okay," she said. "Truly, it is, and I understand. I am just sorry we did not discuss this sooner."

"Maybe because we have both grown so desperate, we were fuller of hope than sense."

Elisabeth chuckled. "I think you might be correct in that."

"What do I do now?" Benton asked. Adrian would never ask what he was to do. He always seemed to know.

"Tomorrow, return to Linnels. I will send a message when I have the rest of the troops."

Benton gave a short nod, but his face looked saddened as he gave her a bow. "I can hope in the time I give you that my family might befall a fortune so that we may continue the engagement in truth."

Elisabeth smiled. "I wish the same." Elisabeth returned to the hall and was glad to find everyone still gathered, but the pie was long gone. She felt she had failed them again as she paused in the archway. Despite not being her real brother, Walter was her responsibility. She would rather have this Walter than no Walter. He was different from the Walter Elisabeth knew as her brother. At times she felt she was betraying her brother's memory. But she never knew her actual brother. In her mind, she made it seem right that there were three Walters, two brothers that got to be hers, two different personalities crammed into one. Because they had to teach some of the second Walter's traits to the third so that people would not see the deception. And with the loss of another husband, all their careful planning would be for nothing if anyone knew Walter's secret. He would return to being a street urchin. She would become one and die on some street, filthy and dirty—just another nameless, unimportant person to be tossed to the side.

Adrian would be okay, as Adrian always was. He was chomping at the bit to go to France and fight for the King. But Lincoln served at Ravenshill since returning from France with her father. As Elisabeth's eyes strayed to Lincoln, she felt her guilt. She knew Lincoln didn't want to go to war. And what of her father? He fought as a young man, but that was many years ago. She smoothed her gown, giving the belt a tug. Finally, she cleared her throat and stepped into the room.

"I have some news to share," she said as all eyes turned to her.

She clasped her hands together at her waist and squared her shoulders. "I feel foolish saying this, but Benton's family is facing its own financial crisis at the moment. With that coming to light, we have decided not to wed. First, however," she began drawing in a long, steadying breath. "We must get more troops to King Henry. Since the banns were already posted, we thought it prudent to let the engagement extend for some period. Lord Benton also agreed to serve as a knight for the Kirkham banner in France."

"And the other knights?" Lincoln asked.

"I have no choice but to send the three we have."

The men looked from one to the other. Her father cleared his throat as if he might protest, but he did not argue with the solutions Elisabeth came up with. She guessed it was because his answer seemed to have been to ignore the King. It was a solution that inevitably failed. Lincoln studied her father's face, and she saw his knowledge that Lord Thomas would be leading them to war without question. Therefore, Sir Lincoln would be going to fight, and he would say nothing against it. Adrian took it as Elisabeth expected, with eagerness. Finally, in France, he would get his chance at all the glory he had hoped would be his as a knight of King Henry.

"What of the foot soldiers and bowmen?" Lincoln asked. His tone sounded like he disapproved of her decision, but as long as her father accepted it, so would he.

"I hoped you and Father could help me. I don't know how to recruit foot soldiers and bowmen."

"It begins with money to pay these foot soldiers and bowmen," Lincoln replied. He looked contrite when her eyes fell on him and darted to her father.

"We need twenty foot soldiers and ten bowmen. How much would this cost?"

“We will assume you will want the cheapest archers and foot soldiers available,” Lincoln began.

“But those will be the untrained ones,” Walter grumbled.

“As are you,” Lincoln snapped at him. “Now, quiet.”

“I know I can get five archers at three pence a day. However, I have three experienced foot soldiers who require eightpence a day. Having them will pretty much guarantee we will get the other seventeen. We could hope to get the majority of the rest at two pence a day, but that price will go up based on experience.”

Elisabeth scribbled the numbers down and then added them together. It seemed everyone in the room sought to distract her with their chatter. Estimating the cost of sending the men to France would have staggered her if she was not already sitting. Getting her soldiers to France to fight in a war Ravenshill wanted nothing to do with would cost them dearly. The sale of five horses might bring them that amount. But they did not have five horses to spare. They had the sheep’s wool to get them twenty-eight stones, but February was not a time to shear sheep. Elisabeth could save that amount by sending Katy and Annabelle away. Then she would not have to pay their yearly wages. Soon she would not have the money to keep them anyway. But she and Edith could not keep up with the work Ravenshill required, and Elisabeth could not imagine the two women not there.

She closed the ledger, and no one took note until she stood with a sigh. “I think we need to gather everything that can be spared.” She tapped the top of the ledger. “This is the last chance to get troops to Henry. After this sweep, we will have nothing else to barter or sell. So first, we will get our army to France, then I will figure out how the rest of us survives until the first harvest." As she said it, she knew not starving to death before the first harvest was only a small part of it. Her father had few serfs now, and most of their food supplies came from the freemen. Once these men learned Ravenshill could not provide them with basic protection, they may choose to leave. Or sell their harvests to those more able to purchase them. The great exodus would be a great stampede if they knew how much more taxes Ravenshill owed the King than they received from the rents of the freemen they collected them from. But that was all tomorrow's problem.

When the time came to say goodbye to her men, it was not as easy as she thought. It was not the financial side she was thinking of when everyone gathered for the farewells at the gates. Elisabeth delayed as long as she could as she watched the men gathering from the library window. She shuffled her way down the steps and dragged her feet across the bridge and through the muddy bailey.

"My beautiful daughter," Thomas exclaimed, sweeping her into his arms. "I will miss seeing your smiling face."

"I'll miss you too," she said, giving him a long hug that was hard to break.

"We will be back soon," Lincoln said as her father passed her off for the knight's farewell.

"Promise?" she asked.

Lincoln squeezed her, "I cannot promise but will pray for it."

Elisabeth nodded, fighting back the tears as he and her father moved to their horses.

"We go to France," Walter said, nearly attacking her as he hugged her farewell.

"Make sure you listen to everything they tell you," Elisabeth said.

"I will," the ten-year-old boy insisted before wiggling away as Edith appeared. He swept the girl into his arms and kissed her lips. She laughed as Adrian saved her from the exuberant boy.

They held to each other for a long time as Edith cried. Then Adrian stood in front of Elisabeth.

"Don't cry for me, Elisabeth," Adrian said.

She replied with a laugh. She was glad he brought levity to the moment. It helped keep the tears at bay. "I don't cry for you, you fool."

"You should most definitely cry for me. I leave you a boy and return a seasoned man of war."

"War," Elisabeth said. His words were crushing. She was sending them to war. She had known it, but now it seemed different. Final. So many men did not return from war. It hit her hard.

"It's okay, Elisabeth. It is a good thing."

"But it is battles."

"Do you think anyone would dare strike the Great Adrian de Ros? They will run from the field as soon as I step onto it."

"Adrian," she said. Her tears started to fall.

He pulled her into his arms, pressed her head against his chest, and held her tightly. "I will be safe, Elisabeth," he whispered, kissing her on top of the head.

"Please come back to me."

Adrian leaned back and used a finger to lift her chin, so she looked at him. "I will always come back for you." He pulled her against him again and held her for another minute before slipping his arms from around her.

"See you soon," Elisabeth said as he began to walk away.

Adrian turned, smiled at her, and, with a nod, said, "See you soon."

# Chapter 27

**Thursday, October 19, 1452, Bordeaux, Aquitaine**

Adrian felt like the journey to French soil was a disaster thus far. Lincoln suggested numerous times they return to Ravenshill since they were already down to three knights before stepping foot in France. If Adrian was superstitious, he would agree, and a part of him was. But there was a more decisive part of Adrian that said he had already waited too long for his chance at battle.

The misfortune began when the small army retrieved Benton at Linnels and marched south. Soon after, Benton fell ill. Then as they crossed the Channel, Benton breathed his last as Adrian suffered, as he did each time he stepped foot on a ship. The roll and pitch were too much for his stomach. Adrian thought he would join Benton before they made it across the channel. He hoped the sail would be a quick journey across, but they sailed along the French coast to Bordeaux and the English army. Despite that, when Lincoln brought up the subject of going home, Adrian felt his heart drop because he didn't want to go home.

He didn't know if he would find his glory on the battlefields. But he knew he did not want to return home. At least on a campaign, his parents could not pressure him into consummating his marriage. It was beginning to weigh heavily on his mind.

Lord Thomas quickly shut down the discussion of returning to England. Adrian guessed he, too, was running. The man could not right the disaster he brought to Ravenshill. Now he had a purpose again and hoped to bring some good fortune to the Kirkham name. So, his step became more assured, and his head, he held a little higher when they reached England's army.

"Lord Thomas," a voice called across the grounds of pitched tents and soldiers within minutes of entering the vast camp.

"John Talbot, Earl of Shrewsbury," Lincoln whispered.

Adrian had heard of Shrewsbury, but he never thought he would have an opportunity to meet the army's chief commander. The man who approached was old. Older than Adrian thought a man leading an army on foreign soil should be. But looking at him, Adrian saw his face was etched with a fierceness trapped in the lines of age.

"I am honored to have you in my lines," the man said, stepping forward to embrace Thomas.

"John, this is my son Walter and Baron Adrian of Stokesley." John gave great consideration to Adrian as he looked him over.

"It is strong fighting men you have brought me. I heard you were coming. It has been some time since your banner has flown under Henry's. Come, share some wine, and catch up with me," John said, pulling him away. Adrian wanted to go with Thomas and John.

He could think of nothing he would rather do than sit down and take wine with the army's commander unless it was with King Henry himself. But Adrian was not invited. This was apparent to him when the two men turned and left him standing.

When Adrian swiveled around to follow Lincoln, the man had disappeared from sight. Alone Adrian and Walter made their way deeper into the massive camp. Adrian did not let Walter see how apprehensive he felt without Lincoln or Thomas with them. He marched through the camp as if he was an old hand at military life. He sure didn't want Walter to call him "Baby Squire" in front of all these fighting men. The truth was he had never even slept inside a tent, let alone been in a place so filled with them and so many warriors. It was a daunting task to find one knight among them. The ring of swords striking against each other caught their attention. The strikes were fast, and both boys were intrigued by the short time between the strikes. The swords created a constant ringing as if from a bell, but both young men knew the sound of sword against sword.

They pushed their way through the small crowd of men who gathered to find Lincoln was one of the combatants.

Lincoln and the other man wielded blunted swords. Until Adrian realized this, he was terrified that Poland was happening again. The two men looked as if they were intent on killing one another. The strokes were fast and powerful. Each time one man struck the other's sword, he could see the straining muscles of their iron grips. Both men kept moving, and despite the cool air, they fought with their shirts off. The other man looked bigger than Lincoln as they spun and parried.

Sweat rolled down them, yet neither faltered. A small group was rambunctious in their cheers for the men, and Adrian realized they were calling Lincoln by name. It did not seem like they rooted for anyone but yelled commands at them. But the men had to be oblivious in the face of such an intense battle.

The grunts of the men rose above the calls of those gathered. Bets were laid, and Walter and Adrian had to hold their ground so they were not pushed away. It became the swordplay that would never end, Adrian was convinced. Both men should have exhausted themselves, yet they kept up their attack. They were equally matched, each got as many strikes as the other, and no one was left on the defensive. There was no way Adrian could withstand such a battle. He thought he was good, if not great, at swords. He was fast and strong, but nothing like what he witnessed coming from Lincoln. He realized there were many levels of training Lincoln did not even reach with him. He wondered if Lincoln wanted to return home because he knew Adrian wasn't ready. Would there be French knights with the skills of the two men he watched? It made Adrian want to run home because he could not survive a battle like he witnessed with real sharpened swords.

Lincoln stumbled. This gave his opponent the upper hand and put Lincoln on the defensive. With the speed and power of the strikes raining down on Lincoln's sword as he blocked, Lincoln's sword shook, and Adrian did not think he would regain his position. But Lincoln ducked a blow, spun as he crouched, and brought a leg out to sweep the other man's from beneath him. The man went down with a grunt, and Lincoln lifted his arms in the air, his sword still in his hand, and let out a roar of triumph. Adrian had never heard the like. It was fierce and brutal in nature. Some of the men gathered took up the cry. It was terrifying and thrilling. It ran through Adrian's veins, and he wanted to join, but no one joined except the one small group who celebrated as if the victory was theirs. Adrian had the impression those men were somehow extraordinary in the eyes of everyone. Adrian turned and smiled at Walter, who also had a look of exhilaration and awe on his face. The legendary knight, Lincoln Victers, had arrived.

The crowd dispersed as Lincoln reached down and offered the man on the ground a hand up. The man came up with a fluid motion that contradicted the intense battle that would exhaust lesser men. Then the two men embraced, and the others stepped forward to do the same. Seven big men surrounded Lincoln. None were young, perhaps in their later 30s, as was Lincoln.

"They are impressive, are they not?" a man's deep voice drew Adrian's attention away.

The man was young, his height nearly equal to Adrian's. He was not a peasant, perhaps a low lord or knight by the man's appearance. His hair was black, his eyes dark pitch and set deep in his tanned, oblong face. He was stout, not as wide in the chest or thick in arms as Adrian, but he was a big man.

With him was another man, not as large, but he had a look of great strength about him like his companion. This man's hair was blonde, appearing soft as down. His close-set eyes were hazel, and their slight upturn at the corners softened him. He seemed to be thin and lean beneath his chainmail and greatcoat.

"That is Sir Lincoln Victors. I am his squire," Adrian said.

"I know. I have heard many stories about Lincoln. That's my father, Sir Martin," the tallest said, motioning to the man just defeated by Lincoln.

"And my father, Sir Frederic," the other said, motioning to one of the other men in the group growing loud with friendly insults.

"Who are they?" Walter asked. He was unable to tear his eyes from the warriors.

"They are what is left of Sir Lincoln's mercenary army," the more petite man offered.

"Do you have a name, squire of Sir Lincoln Victors?" the taller man asked.

"I am Adrian de Ros of Helmsley, and this is Walter Kirkham of Ravenshill."

"I am very pleased to see the Ravenshill banner flying with us. I am Osbert," the tall man said. "I have not heard kind words about its absence these last few months. So, you are aware," Osbert said. His voice did not sound unkind but helpful.

A strong hand fell on Adrian's shoulder. When he looked up, it was to see Martin, Osbert's father looking down on him. It appeared as if he was glowering, but Adrian suspected it was the man's usual hardened expression. The man before him was an older replica of his son. He retained the broad chest, dark brown eyes that did not seem to miss a thing, and a head full of dark, nearly black hair. They were replicas of each other's heights. Adrian realized the most significant distinction between the two was more perception than visual. Martin had a stern look about his face, and a coldness pulled at the corner of his eyes. However, Osbert had a softness to his eyes. He appeared as gentle as his father was harsh. "It is my pleasure to meet the boy who was able to get this fool to take another squire," he said in a resounding baritone voice that could make the earth quake.

"Young Adrian is loyal. I have no worries with him at my back," Lincoln assured Martin as he moved closer while donning his shirt.

"Loyalty will get you only so far. But I see he will be a big man," Martin said, pushing Adrian at arm's length with a hand still on his shoulder so he could study him.

Lincoln laughed. "He is already a big man."

"But how does he fight?" one of the other men asked, stepping forward to join the inspection of Lincoln's squire.

"Very well for a boy who has not seen battle," Lincoln said.

Martin scowled before releasing him. Adrian felt he should be offended by Martin‘s scowl and Lincoln's words. It did not sound as if he had any skill at all. Lincoln took him from a big man to a boy.

"Let's see," Martin said, thrusting his practice sword into Adrian's hands. "Osbert, let's see what this great squire of Sir Lincoln has."

The young man was there, taking the sword Lincoln handed to him. When Adrian caught Lincoln's eye, the man gave him one nod. Did that mean he had confidence in Adrian's ability? Or did it mean it was good to know Adrian before he died by the brutal swings he just witnessed Lincoln win against? Adrian swung the sword in his hand, moving it from left to right, then back again as he arched it about himself feeling its weight and balance. It was different than the sharpened sword of his own Adrian would use for battle and the light staffs he spent countless hours practicing with. As he settled with the weight of it, more cumbersome than his own, he saw Osbert's confidence in his skill relayed in his stillness as he watched Adrian.

Adrian stopped and took a stance, measuring Osbert. Lincoln taught him what to look for, the cut of a man's chest, the circumference of their arms, the stance they took, the thickness of their legs, and their eyes. Adrian sparred with others when he got the opportunity to visit other properties. It was with Elisabeth, Edith, and Walter in more recent years. As he studied Osbert's dark brown eyes, they appeared to be gentle, lazy even, but the press of his lips betrayed him. He was ready to fight, and he would fight hard. Adrian knew this from instinct alone.

"If you do not attack him soon, I fear we will die of boredom watching you stand there," Lincoln quipped at him. It reminded Adrian he was to make the first move and lay the first strike if he could. In a flash, Adrian had the sword tightened in his hand and flew at Osbert with two quick lightning strides. He watched as his sword rose. Osbert was spinning from its reach and raising his own. Adrian turned with him and had his sword in position to take Osbert's blow. But Adrian kept his feet moving. It was the way to keep on the attack. If Osbert made him go on the defensive, Adrian could already tell the man's speed and strength would defeat him.

Adrian moved out of Osbert's sword reach as he spun to face him and was greeted by Osbert in his space again, his sword rising from waist level. But his other arm was moving toward his chest. *The boy thought it would be that easy, did he*? Adrian thought. Osbert did not distract Adrian with a fake sword swipe but thrust him off balance with an elbow to his chest. Adrian brought his sword down on Osbert's with all his strength. It was a bold move. If Osbert saw it coming, he could defeat it easily enough, even throw Adrian off balance. But Osbert didn't see it coming because Adrian lifted a knee, ready to thrust Osbert back. Osbert drew his abdomen in, dodging the knee. Adrian's sword arched downward. The blow rang with a crack like thunder as sword struck sword. The sound rang in Adrian's ears before his elbow flew into Osbert's face. He did not put all his strength behind it, for he suspected it would break the man's nose, but it sent him staggering backward, and Adrian's sword, heavy on Osbert's, ripped it from the man's hands.

A roar rose from those surrounding him. Adrian looked first to Osbert, who recovered from his stagger and now felt his face for injury. Then Adrian looked to Lincoln, who gave him a nod with a proud look on his face. Then Osbert's father threw an arm around Adrian's shoulders, nearly driving him to the ground with its weight. "I have not seen anyone disarm my son with such speed," he declared. "I cannot wait to see what you do against me."

Adrian felt himself on a high altar with the first words. The last turned him cold, and it raced up his spine. He saw this man fight Lincoln, and though Adrian proved himself better than a mere boy untouched by battle, he was not a man who was as hardened and skilled as this one crushing him with just one arm. Then he gave Adrian two hard slaps to his shoulder before releasing him.

"Come on, Big Man," Osbert said, still fingering his lip as he came to Adrian's side. "I'll show you where you can put your things."

The mercenaries had been fighting under John Talbot since parting ways with Lincoln. They fought under him in Maine and at the Siege of Orléans. They spent their lifetimes fighting for England on French soil. Adrian watched them all, willing to sit and listen to them reminisce of battles won and those lost. They spoke of the fallen solemnly and remembered the war's bright side with raucous laughter. Adrian could not help but feel honored to have fallen into this group of warriors. He did not know if they would be with them when the battle came, but he could hope, for they had survived this long. Their stories proved these men were invincible.

# Chapter 28

**Friday, October 20, 1452, Ravenshill**

The empty hall was silent. Elisabeth sat at one of the lesser tables, her gaze upon her father's chair and the one her mother once sat in. Things were so different just a short time ago, she mused. Now she did not know where tomorrow's food would come from. Despite rationing and those absent, making fewer mouths to feed, they still struggled under another financial burden—paying the troops to get them to the King. Once there, their payments came from the King, but soldiers, whether trained or untrained, had to make it there. That burden was the Kirkham's, which devastated their already empty coffers.

There was now a new list of people owed real debts. Now it was because of Elisabeth and her inability to get a husband. Perhaps she was cursed. How else could Benton's death be explained? He was a healthy young man to take ill and die, placing another mark against her record and a great deal of guilt in her heart. Benton would never have been on that ship where he died if not for her. She wished she had broken the engagement and turned elsewhere. Her men were pushing on to the King, and at least that responsibility was being seen to. Elisabeth prayed daily for the rest of the men's safety to the lowliest foot soldier. They were there because she sent them. She did not want their deaths resting on her head. The death of Benton was heavy enough.

Elisabeth shivered, looking around the empty hall. Only the light from the night sky cast its puny glow inside. The long room looked so lonely this time of night. She couldn't sleep. Maybe it was because Edith was not wrapped around her. Elisabeth had not slept alone since first arriving at the mines. Even at Blackpool, she had two other girls sharing her bed. But Elisabeth had too much space even on the smaller framed bed she gave up her expensive one for. She would not dare ask Edith to give up her own chamber to come back and share one just because she felt there was too much room in the bed to sleep.

It was not that the bed felt too big. It was because the world seemed so vast, and she and the rest of the Kirkhams were such small players. The world would not miss them when they were gone. The land would not weep when Ravenshill was turned over to a different family. A family who did not squander wealth and were good custodians for the King. Nights like this one weighed especially heavy. The food to feed the tiny household tomorrow was not a certainty. In addition, Sir Henry Percy, Earl of Northumberland, was sending a representative to discuss the current debt owed him from his residence at Alnwick Castle. Debts owed for what she did not know. He was gracious enough to loan a little more when she sent her men away. A request that might have been unnecessary if she had asked

Adrian to pay for the passage of his horse. But he was going for Ravenshill, and even though she knew his family could easily afford transportation, Elisabeth did not feel right asking him to foot that bill. She knew he probably gave it no thought with his fervor for greatness. Then she had to replace Lincoln's destrier that had passed the age of usefulness on a battlefield. It had aged beyond its use in just about every task at Ravenshill. But she would never ask Lincoln to give up his horse. Elisabeth could not remember her father ever having a horse, so she had to purchase one for him. Walter learned to ride on the workhorses and Adrian's horses. So, he had to have an animal purchased for him as well. As well as Lincoln when they arrived in France. Three horses, they had to buy when they could barely afford the ones they already had.

She feared that debt would be called in when Percy's representative arrived. Now would be the perfect time when they were already on their knees. She would have to feed this representative and whatever number of men came with him. She would have to feed their horses. What if they chose to stay for days or weeks?

She could hope there was a hunter amongst them. Perhaps that was what she would do when this man or men arrived. She would suggest a grand hunt. Presley had been unsuccessful with his game searches. The man was too old to go into the wilderness and ramble about on the uneven ground. He could not give chase if his old eyes saw something. Which, so far, they had not. Or she could suggest they move along as soon as the matter was discussed. Of course, that would not be appreciated by those to who they owed an outstanding debt. Whatever that debt was.

Elisabeth looked about in the deep shadows. Her mind wandered back to the barn and the stall where she had once suffered. She remembered how threatening the shadows felt there. Everything was sinister in a place such as that. Not here. This was her home, and it broke her heart with her fear she would lose it. She knew what it was to not feel safe, and the very thought of feeling that way again terrified her. With the thought of the barn came the memory of seeing Adrian there. She remembered how he held her, wrapped his arms around her, and told her she would be okay. That struggle for survival now seemed like a lifetime ago.

What if Adrian didn't return? The thought entered her head, and her heart cried. What if Walter didn't return? The thought saddened her because she had grown very fond of Walter. It built a feeling of panic because the Kirkhams who lived on the land of Ravenshill generation after generation would die without him. Not many English families survived and kept their lands when William the Bastard claimed them. Especially lying as it did in the north. But somehow, they survived and flourished. Elisabeth knew there was a traitor somewhere in their bloodlines. After being defeated in war, the survival of Ravenshill could not be accomplished otherwise. She wished she had the opportunity to sell her loyalties. They would not be cheap, but her household would not go hungry.

She thought of the soothsayer who read her cards when she was a child. She wanted to return to her. Had she not been correct that destruction was coming? That everything she knew would change? She had killed Walter and been enslaved. Her world had shattered twice in such a short time. But her mind went back to what she said of the betrayal. Her father? He planted the seeds that were tearing away at Ravenshill. As was predicted, every choice she had made so far had been wrong. She felt the fear of losing Adrian, being the reason for his death, and all the others. What if her decision to appease the King was wrong? Hadn't it already proven itself to be wrong with Benton's death? How could it be the right choice if a man died?

When was her knight of swords coming to save her? Or had he already saved her? Was Adrian the one, or was there another? The woman had spoken of passion between them. Elisabeth knew nothing about passion but felt they would know if she and Adrian had it. But he saved her. He was not afraid, and she could not feel safer in another man's arms. But nothing of what was happening was about passion. It was about poverty and making the right decisions for everyone, not just herself.

The door to the outside opened. From the shadows, she heard the light tread of Edith's feet coming toward her. Elisabeth schooled her features. She didn't want to scare Edith. Elisabeth promised she would not let Edith go hungry a long time ago. Tomorrow she was afraid she would have to break that promise.

A kerchief was dropped onto the table in front of Elisabeth, startling her. She straightened and looked to Edith, who nodded at the folded fabric. Elisabeth turned back to it and unfolded one flap with care. Now she could see something beneath the next fold and dark rusty-brown hair poked from beneath the edge. She spread the other flap and shrieked, unprepared for what she was looking at.

Once the shock wore off, she realized it was a tail, not some weird and grotesque snake. Her eyes darted to

Edith, who stepped back into deeper shadows, but Elisabeth could see her waving her to get up. Elisabeth stood and followed the quiet tread of Edith out into the bailey. One of the horses stood with the travois attached to its harness, and on that lay a lifeless boar.

Joy overtook Elisabeth, and a bark of laughter escaped with relief. She turned to Edith. "Did you kill it?" she asked.

Edith nodded, and Elisabeth saw the proud smile that turned the girl's lips upward. But Edith wasn't a girl either. She was a woman who survived slavery and could add huntress to her vast array of practical purposes. But at the top of that list was Elisabeth's savior. She reached forward and hugged Edith with a ferocity that she always felt the other woman hugging her with. They would be okay tomorrow. The boar could feed them for days.

Her mind traveled back to the man who was coming from Alnwick—or men. One man could devastate the meat supply with his veracious ways. She had not seen a warrior yet who did not devour everything placed before him. But Percy wouldn't send a warrior, would he? She didn't know what the man was capable of or what lengths someone would go to for a debt owed.

Luckily her father was away on a campaign. That would make it understandable that they were late on a payment. Elisabeth could just claim ignorance. Men were always looking at women as if they did not have one thought inside their heads. She could use that to her advantage. By the time Percy's man left, she could have him convinced she was a total fool where her father's finances were concerned. No one would expect her to know anything. Knowing sums and details about who and what was given and owed would not be something a daughter would be privy to.

"You are our savior," Elisabeth declared, giving a final hard squeeze before releasing Edith. "Have you been out all night?"

Edith nodded with pride and triumph written across her delicate features. "I will take care of the rest before Katy and Annabelle rise and can do their part. You go find rest. We have a guest arriving today." Elisabeth's gut twisted as if she had let the night pass her by and the stranger's arrival was imminent.

Edith nodded. Elisabeth had not told her a man was coming that could take everything away. This was the first she mentioned it to any of them. But of course, Edith would know. Nothing could be kept from her. But Elisabeth saw no need to tell any of them of the impending arrival. They knew what the situation was as far as food supplies went. Presley was hunting for a week and had not had much success. But Edith had, and it was a grand kill.

Edith helped get the pig to the small hoist outside the kitchen. As Elisabeth lifted the pig up by its back legs to suspend it, Edith took the horse back to the stable before finding slumber. Elisabeth carved at the animal, gutting it. Its warm innards gushed out onto the cobblestones at her feet. The smell of death surrounded her. She hated that smell. It reminded her of the mines and the barn. Death had its own smell, whether a pig killed in the woods or a child who had starved.

With a small amount of meat, the broth was prepared for the noon meal. With the last flour made into bread, the thin soup would be a passable meal for those due to arrive. But the party did not. The day rolled by, and Elisabeth began to fret. He was supposed to come that morning. That was why they made the broth. To be able to feed numbers without sacrificing too much of the meat and still be generous and substantial enough with the meal. Therefore, Ravenshill would not be considered selfish.

The household waited for what seemed like an eternity, with the meal's fragrance filling the hall from the kitchen. Finally, long after the dinner should be served, Elisabeth declared they would wait no longer. The household gathered and began to eat the day's first meal, agreeing they would skip the first to ration and anticipate the noon meal.

The door to the outside banged open, and Elisabeth heard booted steps enter as she jumped to her feet. A single man strode forward. His eyes looked left to right, taking in the hall, the people gathered, and then they fell on Elisabeth. It was a knight who had come, of that Elisabeth had no doubt. Percy had sent a knight to ask her father to pay his debt. Or he sent a knight to make her father pay his debt. And she forgot to post someone at the gate to announce his arrival.

"Where is Lord Thomas?" the man asked without preamble. His eyes scanned the hall with intensity, logging every inch of Ravenshill in his mind. In his eyes, she saw that he was surprised by the lack of frivolities used to grace their hall. What would be said if Percy knew they had already sold everything of value except the land? He would take the land, of course, her mind said.

"It is customary for a guest to announce himself," Elisabeth said, raising her head a notch. She cleared her throat and tugged at the hem of her short jacket. She smoothed it out before clasping her hands at her waist and strolling around the table. Her heart pounded, and her palms sweated. Besides herself and one old man, three women were here to greet him. That was the extent of the numbers left to protect Ravenshill.

It appeared as if the man's dark brown eyes only focused on Elisabeth when she stood before him. His eyes were intelligent, sharp even as the corner of his lips lifted the slightest. His bow to her was deep. His dark brown hair was thick on top of his head. Like his beard and mustache, it was well-trimmed. He was a handsome man, but he was large, and she did not know why Percy was choosing now to send a man. A man who appeared to have a great deal of military prowess.

"My apologies," he said upon straightening. "I am Henry Beaufort, Earl of Dorset. I have come to speak to Lord Thomas of an urgent matter."

"My apologies, my lord, my father is on campaign in France for the King. Therefore, he will be unable to meet with you."

His eyes studied her for a moment. "How long has he been away?"

Elisabeth paused. Why was he asking? Was it not enough that her father was not here? She chuckled and pretended she had given this a great deal of thought. "I do not recall. It seems so long and lonely without my father. One month seems like twenty."

"Is that so?" Beaufort asked, still eyeing her with keen intelligence and amusement. She did not like how he was looking at her at all.

She nodded but schooled her face to look blank, impassive, stupid even.

Beaufort turned halfway to his left, then right, giving those watching him significant consideration in the sparse hall. She did not like the way he was looking over everything. No one spoke up for a long time, and his eyes fell back on her.

"May we walk?" he asked. His words were abrupt, impatient even. The way he worded it, it sounded like a polite request. But since she was looking into his dark eyes and features, she felt it was not a request at all.

"Very well," she said, feigning indifference when the reality was she did not want to leave the presence of her meager forces to walk with this stranger.

She faltered when he turned and presented his arm to her. Nothing about the man thus far would mark him as gentlemanly or chivalrous. She forced her hand not to shake as she lay it on him. He did not fold his arm into himself to draw her closer. He did not even place his hand over hers but left her to be the one to touch him. As they crossed the hall, Elisabeth became aware this was the case. As they stepped out onto the breezeway, she felt unsure when it would be appropriate to remove her hand. Too soon would leave him knowing he left her feeling uncomfortable. Too long, and he might get the wrong idea.

"Lord Thomas has been gone at least a month?" he asked her. She heard a level of amusement in his voice that made her prickle.

Elisabeth giggled. "As I said, I do not recall."

"Yes," he said with some level of impatience in his voice. "You mentioned you missed him. You must be incredibly close to your father if you do not know if he has been gone a month or over a year. Have the seasons not changed here in his absence?"

Elisabeth swallowed. She pegged him as an arrogant man. She did not like his questions. She felt like he was laying a trap, but a trap for what? Could he believe she was lying and her father wasn't in France?

She giggled again. “Forgive me,” she said. “I have a flair for the dramatics. I am a woman, after all.” She lifted her hand from his and swirled it a moment in a gesture to dismiss her silliness. She lay it again on his forearm. He held it at the exact angle he first offered it to her. He gave no indication he wanted her hand there. But he gave no clue as to whether it was unwanted either. Their eyes fell simultaneously to her hand. She saw the slight tilt of his lip again, and she wanted to withdraw from him. She also was aware they were not walking. He did not lead her beyond the breezeway. It made the entirety of the moment awkward.

“It has been more than a month?” Henry questioned.

“It must have been,” she said with another slight giggle that was cut off as she tried to pull her hand from his arm, but his big hand wrapped around it with lightning speed. She would have to struggle to free it. She felt fear, terrifying in its intensity, constricting her chest. He did not squeeze but pinned it beneath his hand. Little enough pressure was applied that it would not be a considerable struggle. But to remove it would convey he not only made her feel uncomfortable but had the power to frighten her.

She relaxed, even taking a small step closer. She looked up at Henry from beneath her lashes and smiled. “It must have been early summer, maybe even spring since he has been gone.”

“That is interesting, Elisabeth.” She was surprised at his boldness in using her name but not that he knew who she was. His voice sounded amused again. “Who has been bartering in his stead.”

"Bartering?" she asked as alarm bells rang in her head. She swallowed. She could not stop the flash of fear that crossed her face as the earl's smile broadened.

"That is what I said."

"He must be sending the correspondence from France."

"That must be a great financial burden to send a messenger all the way from France."

"Messen—?" It was too late, the earl's brow raised, and she saw the smile rise to light his eyes. She tried to pull away, and then his hand tightened. It was a gentle taking of her fingers in his, wrapping his hand around them so she no longer had the option to pull away.

"I knew within the first few letters. Your father never sent letters," Henry said. "I don't know if he feared the letter would be intercepted or used against him. His reasoning was sound." He leaned closer to her and, in a low voice, said, "The written word is harder to dispute than the spoken."

She attempted another giggle, but his hand-applied pressure to her fingers. It was not enough pressure to hurt but enough to give her pause.

"Please do not insult my intelligence, Elisabeth," he said. His voice was smooth, and the way he said her name sounded like a deep purr. "Or your own."

"I do not know what you mean." She stood, her body rigid now as he gripped her hand.

"I think you do. Lord Thomas has been in debt to the Percys for a long time. He has handled that debt the same all that time. He handled it in a way most unsatisfactory to Alnwick's steward. Then things changed. The steward was curious how someone could manipulate him so thoroughly in a letter that he did not mind the delay of the payments. But not only did your reassurance satisfy him, he believed Thomas was prepared to continue the payment of his debt. Despite bearing your father's seal, we knew it was from a different source, which is why I am here. Now I must admit I am intrigued."

Elisabeth's mouth worked, but no words came out, so she closed it. He looked down at her hand lying on his forearm and released her fingers. He flattened her hand onto his arm, then covered it with his own again. "Lord Henry Percy will not know it is you." He patted her hand and smiled. He dropped his arm away and turned her hand, so he bent and kissed the back of her knuckles. He paused, looked up at her with devilment in his brown eyes, and a smile planted on his lips. "You're a secret that is all mine, Elisabeth."

He straightened, dropped her hand, and turned to study his surroundings. He took a great deal of time to take it all in, the lack of anything, down to people and animals. "I'll see you," he said with a wink. The man strolled away, went to his horse, mounted, and rode away. He left Elisabeth feeling a little trapped that someone outside their small household now knew one secret of hers.

# Chapter 29

**Wednesday, November 29, 1452, Bordeaux, Aquitaine**

The sweat rolled from Adrian, and his heavy arms felt like dropping the sword in his hand. But he whirled away from the blade just before it sliced his head. But Martin's sword pommel landed against his head, making it ring. It felt as if the older man cracked a rib when the edge of his sword caught Adrian only a few seconds ago. But Adrian was holding his own much longer than he expected.

Adrian spent the last few months doing little fighting other than practicing swords against men who itched for battle. They secured lands around Bordeaux, but the experienced fighting men were on the front lines. Adrian was left to polish their armor. The greatest pastime for Adrian was sparring with the other men. Each day they gathered, challenging one another with big boasts and blunted swords. The men itched to get a piece of Adrian because he was determined, strong, and fast. So determined by the second match against Martin, Adrian fell unconscious from the blows and exertion he put into trying to take Martin down. Martin crowed about how challenging it was to take down the young squire, and Adrian gained a reputation.

After the first match, Martin refused to take on the boy, as he kept calling Adrian afterward to goad him. It was two months before Martin took on Adrian's challenge. Before then, the man always declared Adrian was not ready. Today, his answer had changed.

Adrian landed a few blows. He had grown strong since arriving, and his strikes were powerful enough to overcome Martin. Martin's blood flowed from his nose where the pommel of Adrian's sword struck him in the face. Another blow had caught Martin in his side. Now the big man protected that side of himself, and Adrian knew if he could get an opening, he could end it. He just had to keep his feet beneath him and move.

Martin‘s elbow came toward his head. As the months of practice, military rations, and life in the field rolled by, Adrian grew in height, his muscles thickened, and he grew lean. As an unofficial member of Lincoln's Men, as they were known, he developed a reputation among them and the entirety of the military. Few outside their circle waged challenges on Lincoln's Men because none could withstand their fury.

Martin tried to take Adrian's feet from beneath him, but he stepped away at the last moment and brought his arm around to bring his blade down on Martin‘s back. The blow staggered Martin, and Adrian spun again. Martin took two stumbling steps to keep his balance. In so doing, he dropped the defense of his injured side, and Adrian moved before he could recover it. He drove a knee upward, guiding it into Martin's abdomen, and using his hands, shoved them into the man's side. The blows threw Martin off balance, and he stumbled. He was like a great mountain tumbling. His hands came up to stop his forward plunger, and the sword dropped from his hands. But Adrian's victory did not end there. The man fell further, landing on a knee before plunging down onto his chest. His face landed in the dirt before he was prone. The great mountain of Martin had fallen under Adrian's sword. Adrian lifted his arms, sword aloft, and roared out his victory. It ripped from deep within his chest, and he felt the primal warrior overtake him.

The men roared with him, echoing across the grounds. Exhilaration ran through him as his cries grew silent.

"That was great, Big Man," Osbert said, stepping forward and pulling the sword from his hand. He passed it to Walter and offered Adrian a wineskin. Parched, Adrian drank. The wine was heaven as it eased its way down his dry throat. "No one but Lincoln can take Dad down," Osbert said with a level of awe.

By then, Martin was back on his feet. One of the men was inspecting his back, where Adrian struck him with the flat of his sword. "By God's mercy, Big Man has an arm like the drop of an anvil," he said, straightening. "I'll be wanting a rematch with you."

"I do not think you are ready for such a match," Adrian said. He echoed Martin's words when Adrian requested a challenge and was denied the satisfaction. A few of the men closest roared their laughter while Martin looked annoyed, but at the same time, Adrian saw respect in his brown eyes.

Winter here was tepid compared to northern England. It made the nearly six months of sitting idle even more excruciating if the winter was severe and the cold bit into his toes and fingers. It left him feeling as if they should be on the move somewhere, doing something. He did not long for England as he thought he would. The camaraderie of Lincoln's Men took the sting out of being so far from home. Close friendships were developing between Walter and the other young men. The new generation of fighting men. His desire for home was a yearning to see Elisabeth and know what was happening at Ravenshill.

The year rolled over into a new one. Lord Thomas resided with Talbot behind secure walls. This seemed to leave Lincoln with a level of freedom he passed on to the rest of the Ravenshill army.

Games were the only things that kept the thousands of men who were chafing at the bit in check. Wrestling became a great pastime, as well as football and chess. Almost anything around the camp could be turned into a competition, and competitions could be bet on. Gambling ran rampant in the camps. Adrian was most competitive with swords, but anything was better than watching the sun march day after day across the sky.

He passed the time with the squires and young knights. Patrick's twelve-year-old squire Tumas and Osbert's eleven-year-old squire Elyas were trained rigorously for what was to come. It was a combined effort to have the boys ready. Time was pushed ahead here, and the boys were a little young to be titled squires, but men and boys alike often died here. Whether from sickness or battle, armies struggled to fill the ranks.

"Block high, strike low," Osbert screamed at Elyas for the third time that day. Adrian knew it was fear for the child that made Osbert anxious. The boy would be expected to watch Osbert's back in a battle and supply him with fresh water, a horse, and whatever he would need. This meant he needed to know how to fight when he entered the battle lines.

"Let me," Adrian said as Osbert stepped forward.

"I have shown him a thousand times," Osbert grumbled.

Adrian approached Elyas, who swallowed nervously as he looked up at the tall squire. No one seemed concerned Adrian was yet to earn his spurs. He was skilled, and that wall to climb was all that mattered here.

Tumas stepped to the side as Adrian drew his sword. At first, his move was slow and casual, but then he struck with the speed of lightning. But Elyas brought his sword up from below, and Adrian was able to easily knock it from the boy's hand.

"Like this," Adrian said. He took the pommel of his sword in both hands and took half a step forward as he brought the sword over his head, his knees slightly bent.

"You have to absorb the shock of a blade coming down. You are small, men like me have an advantage, and you must know how to block. Now do it."

The boy accomplished the move, and with lightning speed, Adrian brought his sword down on it, and the boy's blade dropped.

"Hold tight. Let it flow down your shoulders and to your knees. Again."

Elyas didn't drop his sword on the third try though Adrian's blow made his arms waver.

"Now, from the block, you drop your shoulder before your opponent can pull away for another strike. Twist away, then swing low." Again, Adrian demonstrated, and Elyas attempted it. More than an hour Adrian spent on that move alone. Though the boy was still having difficulty judging speed and strength against Adrian, he was improving.

"I taught you today about defense, but it is best to always attack. Don't wait for your opponent because you are small. Attack. Attack. Attack. If you have to defend, your opponent is too close, and you must get out of his reach. Stay out his reach, in and out, fast, like the strike of a snake." Adrian patted the boy on the back and turned away.

"Adrian," Lincoln's irritated voice startled him.

"Did you not hear me calling you?" Lincoln demanded.

"I was a little busy."

"I got a message for you."

"Who has sent me a message all the way here?" Then fear took hold. Had something happened to Elisabeth?

"It is from your father," Lincoln said, shoving the unopened letter into Adrian's chest.

Adrian looked at Lincoln as if his face could reveal what lay in the sealed letter. But Lincoln knew no more than Adrian. Adrian turned the letter in his hand, recognizing his father's seal. He began walking toward the camp as he broke the seal.

*Son,*

*It has been pointed out to me that you and your wife are now of age. It has also been made clear that her reputation becomes tarnished for a woman aged past a certain point without becoming a wife officially. So it is, for this reason, you must return home and remedy the situation with all due haste. Her family tires of the wait and demands you handle your responsibility.*

*The Lordship of Helmsley depends on your marriage. If you refuse to return home for the union, your claim to Helmsley's title will be denounced, and the heir will become your brother. It saddens me this is the case. But our family requires strong ties and honor for our good faith promises.*

*I hope this letter finds you well, and it is with regret I must inform you of this. But it is out of my hands if you do not return in haste.*

*Keep the faith.*

Adrian crumpled the letter and slung it as far as it would fly with a great deal of malice. They threatened to take his title away because he did not want to lay with the woman he married before he knew the magnitude of marriage. Did they not understand he was part of an army and he could not just leave on a whim? If he left, Elisabeth's troops would be short, and while this could be excused, he did not think it prudent. He had responsibilities. He gave an oath to Lord Thomas and Sir Lincoln. But he also had an obligation to honor his family's wishes. It would be easy enough to say he was not returning, but he could get nowhere near his dreams of a great knight and lord if he did not have his birth title. He was the oldest son. The responsibility was his to carry forth the de Ros name. He had no choice in the matter, and it infuriated him.

He looked around the encampment. What kind of life would he have if having death hanging over his head was more appealing than returning home? He felt like he was suffocating, as if the entire army pressed in on him. He hurried to the corrals, where he saddled Achilles and rode away. He was on enough patrols and attacks to have a good sense of direction in these foreign lands, so he rode toward the west. When he reached the shore, he sat the horse looking across the ocean, not seeing it. He held his jaw so tight it ached. Achilles was agitated by the feel of Adrian's emotions through the reins.

He climbed down and allowed Achilles to nip at the grass while he sat nearby, seeing nothing but feeling all the rage and disappointment he felt. Could he come back here, or would he be caged there? His father was still overseer of everything at Helmsley, so he would have little to nothing to do. Except plow a wife he did not like, he thought with bitter disgust.

Hoofbeats sounded, and Adrian looked up to see Osbert bringing his horse to a walk. Adrian turned back to the rolling surf and heard his friend's boots land on the ground and his soft steps in the grass as he neared.

"I could not help but notice you dropped this," Osbert said, dropping the wadded note into Adrian's lap.

Adrian smirked, knowing Osbert saw him throw it away.

"I take it you are excited about this," Osbert's voice was dry.

"I foresee it being a miserable experience with a miserable creature," Adrian declared.

"You do not like the bride?"

"I do not. This was all set up by my parents when I was young."

"Perhaps you are being too harsh toward her?" Osbert questioned. "She may be a lovely creature when you get to know her."

Adrian scoffed, "I know better than that."

"Oh, so you have laid eyes upon the one you think will make all others pale?" Osbert asked.

Adrian offered a half-shrug but remained quiet.

Osbert fell silent, but Adrian could tell he gave considerable thought to his following words. "You are a man of great privilege and responsibilities. I have risen to a knight and earned a comfortable living through battles. You are already where I can never be. I have no land to settle on unless I choose to give my sword to another man and fight his battles. A man like you would be the kind of man I would consider fighting for. You are a good man Lord Adrian, and you can do good things. Perhaps it is a little unwise to declare such a privilege miserable."

"I need to fight," Adrian declared. "I have been here for months and have seen no battles, and now I must go home before I have even wet my sword with the enemy's blood. It is frustrating," Adrian growled. "It is all so frustrating."

Osbert's words were perhaps the most frustrating because he spoke the truth. He was away from Helmsley long enough. He did not know what kind of person his brother was. He could be a spiteful brat who would be cruel to his people and bring dishonor to the de Ros name. But, without the title of baron, what hope did Adrian have for any future? He would be like Osbert and forever fighting for a position, any position that would provide a living.

"Come," Osbert said, slapping Adrian on the leg. "Let's go fight."

Adrian scoffed at him, shifting slightly to let him know he was content where he was.

"Seriously, Lincoln said if I brought you back, he would fight you."

Adrian's eyes shot to Osbert's. Lincoln would spar with Adrian with the staff, but Lincoln was the only one who did not take up the practice swords with him. As of yet, Adrian had not witnessed Lincoln's defeat in any of these matches. But Adrian defeated every man Lincoln had. It was something he itched to do for a long time, but it was a fight Lincoln always denied Adrian.

Adrian sprung to his feet, and Osbert laughed at him as they raced to their horses, having to take an extra moment to catch the animals they spooked.

The challenge was the greatest yet to have bets placed. Despite the chilling drizzle that began before the two men faced off, the crowd grew larger and larger until half the army gathered to place their bets on the great Sir Lincoln or his squire. Adrian doubted anything was bet that day on him. Still, as he hoisted and spun the sword, loosening his arms and feeling its weight, he channeled his frustration into the metal in his hands. Lincoln watched him intensely, getting a feel for his weapon like he had taught Adrian.

Then Lincoln charged him. He did not give a warning but was just on the attack, and Adrian spun away. His heart began to hammer in his chest as he focused on Lincoln, on his entire body, hoping to anticipate the attacks before they came. But Lincoln was fast and vicious. Everything Lincoln had fought the other men with, he now put into the match with Adrian. Adrian's fury fled, and all he could do was focus that energy on his next move.

Lincoln spun, struck, spun, struck. It was a constant barrage and chase for Adrian. He tried to attack, but no one he matched with thus far moved like Lincoln. Martin had a much stronger strike, but in comparison, he was easy to fight against because Adrian could catch him. Not so with Lincoln. Each time Adrian's sword fell, there was nothing there to strike. On the opposite side of the coin, it was all Adrian could do to block Lincoln's blows. Lincoln's sword rang off Adrian's for long, stretched-out minutes that made the sweat roll from Adrian and mix with the cold mist falling.

Then Lincoln slipped. It was slight, an error the man recovered from, but Adrian took the opportunity and pressed his attack. He brought his sword down twice, striking Lincoln viciously until the man could spin away. But Adrian was there, ready to take Lincoln's next strike, but it did not come. Not from the direction he anticipated. The flat of Lincoln's sword slammed into Adrian's back, nearly knocking him to the ground.

Adrian took two stumbling steps, spun from beneath Lincoln's next blow, and was there, bringing his sword down as Lincoln tried to thrust his at Adrian's side. Adrian dealt Lincoln's sword a mighty blow that ricocheted up his arm and rang across the camp. Adrian tried to follow up with a kick, but Lincoln fought as Adrian did, and his feet were always moving. There was nothing there for his foot to come in contact with. Lincoln anticipated the move, knocking Adrian off balance with his pommel's thrust into the back of Adrian's shoulder. But Adrian kept his feet, turning in time to bring his sword up to protect his groin from Lincoln's incoming knee. He threw an arm up to thrust Lincoln away, but Lincoln also anticipated the move. He moved in closer, locking an arm with Adrian's. A wrestling match for the swords ensued for a moment as Lincoln's bent arm gained a tight hold on Adrian's, and the smaller man tried to force Adrian to trip over his foot. Adrian tripped, and Lincoln released his arm. Still, Adrian twisted, bringing his other foot onto the ground and catching himself before he fell. The crowd roared, having held their collective breaths with the move they thought would send the squire to the ground.

Lincoln's sword came down heavily onto Adrian's sword arm. The pain shot from just above his elbow in all directions. Adrian forced his grip tighter and spun toward Lincoln's back as Lincoln spun away. Both men's swords rose, clashing above their heads, ringing with the grunts of the men. Lincoln was on the move again, striking Adrian in the side, but the air was empty as Adrian retaliated.

He did not know if he fought for minutes or hours. He knew it was not days because the people remained, and the mist still fell. Then he made the move that he knew would cost him. He took a step forward, thrusting his sword, anticipating Lincoln spinning into it. Still, the man knew it was there, and his arm wrapped around it before the spin was completed. He tried to yank the weapon from Adrian, but he held to it with determined tenacity. In doing so, Lincoln created a pendulum from which to swing Adrian. He twisted his squire forward and back, bringing a leg out to trip him, but Adrian was determined to not go down. He danced across the outstretched foot, and his eyes had time to lock with Lincoln's. Lincoln watched him as if he were a cat and Adrian, the mouse he had been toying with all along. Lincoln twisted forward again with a hard thrust that would have sent Adrian sprawling if Lincoln had not whipped him back. His leg was still there. Adrian stumbled across it, clinging to his sword. It was what kept him up as he tried to regain his balance. Then a smirk crossed Lincoln's face, and Adrian knew the knight's next move. Adrian felt his eyes widen the instant Lincoln released Adrian's sword. Adrian tumbled backward and landed in the mud.

Shouts like none other rose from the crowd. Above him, Lincoln roared his victory. A great cry of barbarism carried and was picked up as the chant of Lincoln's name filled the mouths of many. Adrian sat in the mud panting, then collapsed back to let the mist wash over him. He was exhausted. Never before had an opponent taken everything from him. He breathed heavily, staring up at the faces who came to smile down at him. It felt like they blocked his air. They stopped the cooling mist for sure, but Adrian was too exhausted to care.

By evening, Adrian had Commander Talbot's leave to travel back to England with Walter, Patrick, Osbert, and their squires. It felt like a funeral procession leaving the army behind, and Adrian was not what he dreamed he would be when the time came to leave France.

# Chapter 30

**Monday, February 12, 1453, Ravenshill**

Apprehension flooded Elisabeth when Annabelle called her to the parapets. Then, just as the floor was dropping from beneath her feet, she heard Annabelle assure her the banner of Ravenshill flew over the riders' heads. Elisabeth propped the broom against the wall. Her worn leather shoes pounded down the steps and out into the bailey. She reached the gate out of breath and waited for the riders as the first came into sight.

Walter. Her body expelled a substantial amount of relief as she watched his horse rear at his command. It hung in the air for a breath of time as other riders began to form around him. Among these was Adrian and his Achilles. As soon as all four of his horse's hooves were on the ground, Walter spurred the animal forward, and he charged, thunder rolling. Elisabeth stepped back with a giggle as the horse and rider charged through the gates.

She sprinted toward him as he swung out of his saddle. Presley was there to take his horse. She flung herself at him, and he caught her. She marveled at how much he had grown. She saw how tall he had grown and how strong he was as he grabbed her and wrapped her in his arms. He squeezed her, laughing when she gasped before sitting her on her feet. His attention was caught by the riders now filing into the bailey. Apprehension filled Elisabeth because there were several riders, and it would take a lot of food to feed them.

Adrian led them, and Elisabeth felt immense relief he returned. He, too, had grown into a man while he was away. Handsome, as were Walter and the two knights who rode with Adrian. They were big men. She could not say which man was larger. One was as dark of hair as the other man was red.

She stood next to Walter. Her eyes kept straying to her brother as the riders settled their animals and dismounted. She marveled at his height, how broad his chest was now, how handsome his face was as he grew into a man. It had lengthened, the cheeks fuller, his chin squarer. It was disturbing because she would never know how the other two Walters would have looked had they survived. But this Walter, she knew, would make her family proud. Elisabeth had never asked Walter what his name was before. She didn't think she ever would. Then, as the two strangers approached, she felt her brother's hand land upon her back. It was intense, and a piece of worry slipped away from her with the knowledge her brother, who had twice died, was no longer frail.

"Elisabeth," Walter said in the voice that had deepened and strengthened in his time away. "These are friends of mine, Sir Osbert and Sir Patrick," he introduced the men. Osbert was the dark man. His features were chiseled, and he stood a couple inches shorter than Adrian. Next to him, Patrick was as tall and broad as Osbert. All four men stood like giant trees, towering over her. A piece of her relaxed, knowing that Ravenshill was protected once again.

“Welcome to Ravenshill,” Elisabeth said. Osbert stepped forward and gave a gallant bow before reaching for the hands she clasped at her waist. She released her grip, and he took her hand carefully. His big one swallowed hers as he bent and kissed the back of it. His soft brown eyes looked up at her, and he offered her a smile that soothed her. He held her for a moment more, but not an amount of time that made her feel uncomfortable.

Patrick offered her a bow as Osbert released her. In

“Can you feed us, sister? I fear we are famished.”

She turned with Walter and the other men falling into step behind her as they led the way to the hall. “Where is Father?” she asked when Walter slipped his hand into hers.

“He has stayed in France. We have come to partake in the feast for Adrian’s consummation.”

Elisabeth gripped his fingers. She knew Adrian was married, but it was long ago. Over the years, she gave little thought that Adrian would have to solidify their union. There was a big part of her that hoped it would not happen. In the cards, the woman might have predicted Adrian could be her knight of swords. She had a sinking feeling he would not be returning to Ravenshill. His commitment to Ravenshill had long since expired. He was free to move on but had thus far chosen not to. But he was to be married in all ways, a true man, and he would leave. What if he planned to bring his wife here? They could always use extra people, but they didn't have food to feed additional people. As it was, she feared how long these men would be staying at Ravenshill. They looked like they all could eat a great deal.

"He is not excited about this. I will warn you. On the contrary, he has been in quite a foul mood since his father demanded he returns. His father claimed his brother would be named heir, and Adrian would be left to his own devices."

Elisabeth saw the stern scowl on Adrian's face. The fact he did not come forward to greet her was telling.

"I do believe Osbert was taken by you," Walter whispered to her as he opened the door and guided them into the hall. The interior was cold. The hearth had not been lit since December. The wood was dwindling, and if it was to be a long winter, she did not need to waste it heating the ample space for a household that was now small enough to eat at the table in the kitchen.

Elisabeth did not reply. She didn't know how to respond because her mind was locked on Adrian and his impending ceremony. Walter went to build a fire, and Elisabeth wanted to protest for an instant. But she would include more wood with her wishes for more food once the men were gone. She left the men in the hall for the kitchen.

The women were frantic there, gathering supplies and putting them in some semblance of a hearty and tasty meal for the men who were gone so long from home. Time seemed insubstantial as the kitchen turned into a frenzy. The remaining stove they did not sell was warmed. Potatoes and onions were cut, and Elisabeth reluctantly sacrificed an entire slab of salted pork for the men.

"My apologies," the redheaded Patrick said as he stepped into the kitchen. The three women paused to look at the big man. He had had time to clean the road filth off himself, remove his chain mail, and even tidy and trim his red hair and beard. He looked ashamed to be stepping forward with his request. "I have not eaten in two days. Is there something that might quiet my growling belly and give me strength? The enticing smells you ladies are creating are too much for my control."

"Edith has porridge we were to have today," Elisabeth said, turning to bid Edith retrieve a bowl for him, but she was already on the task. The porridge sat at the edge of the hearth, now unneeded with the meal they were creating.

Edith filled the bowl and approached the big knight. He gave a warm smile, his blue eyes full of cheer, as he reached for the porridge she offered him.

"My gratitude, mistress," he said with a voice that always seemed to have a cheerful note. It was a tone that almost made her want to smile when he spoke, coupled with the sparkle of humor that lit his pale blue eyes.

Edith inclined her head in acknowledgment as her hand crept from beneath his. She smiled and gave him one last glance before turning away.

"Let us take them all porridge to hold them until we complete this," Elisabeth said. She worried that it was more food gone from the scarce winter supply.

"I will take it," Patrick said. He raked a hand across the back of his mouth and handed his empty bowl to Edith, who held the tray of full bowls for the men. She took his cup, and he took the tray, offering her a wink and a smile. To Elisabeth's surprise, the girl giggled, bringing a wider smile from Patrick as he paused to watch Edith turn away.

Katy offered Elisabeth a knowing look as Patrick headed for the hall with the tray. She felt herself bristling at the thought the big man had an attraction to Edith. Elisabeth did not know what kind of man Patrick was. He dared not think he had a right to her because he was a knight and she a servant. She would do her best to keep Edith within her sight.

The thought had just entered her mind when Edith left the kitchen with Patrick's refilled bowl in her hand. She sighed. She would have to trust Adrian, and Walter would not bring someone to Ravenshill that would hurt any of them.

Elisabeth took her meal with the men while Katy, Edith, and Annabelle served and ate in the kitchen. She sat beside Adrian, who did not speak. Only a grunt and a glare from time to time came from him. He sat hunched over, his arm resting alongside his trencher as he bent over it, giving it his full attention. But his focus rested somewhere deep in his own thoughts.

The other men carried the conversation, primarily amongst themselves, since Adrian acted as a barrier Elisabeth had to talk around. The act annoyed him and kept Elisabeth silent despite the efforts from the others to include her.

"Do not mind him," Patrick said at some length. "He's had a sword up his arse since his parents forced this upon him."

"It's not just about the wedding," Walter offered. "He will be leaving service here and taking it up for his own house. But, unlike here, where we are left to our own, he will answer every move to the House of York."

"Surely he knows he will be a man of his own house and will decide who his loyalties are for," Elisabeth said. This statement got Adrian's eyes on her, and what she saw there made her uneasy. Adrian might as well be in France for all the warmth she was getting from him.

Lincoln shook his head. "His father has already said York will have the support of Helmsley. Like the marriage, he is ready to disown Adrian if he does not consent," Osbert offered.

Elisabeth knew Adrian's father would never disown him, but he was a good enough son not to challenge the threat.

Adrian slammed his hand down on the table, rattling his and Elisabeth's plates. "I am sitting here and can very well speak for myself."

"Then speak," Osbert said with the motion of his hand to indicate he had everyone's attention.

Adrian sighed and almost turned back to his food but stopped.

"Many things weigh heavy," he admitted. "I do not like this woman they say I am too…" Adrian paused, his eyes flowing over Elisabeth for a moment. "There is concern over York's malcontent with King Henry. I know my responsibility to whatever cause York is supporting will increase tenfold." Then Adrian shrugged then fell quiet.

The conversation turned elsewhere, but all Elisabeth could think of was Adrian leaving them. She knew the day would come. But in all that time, she hoped it would not since the fortuneteller said he could choose the path to keep them together. He had said he would always choose that path. Now she feared their paths were separating and may never converge again.

He ate little of the meal and left the hall early with a moroseness that lay heavy.

As the evening wore on, as more wood was fed into the large hearth and more mead was consumed, Elisabeth worried, counting the numbers in her head. As soon as she found an opportunity, she fled to the library and the ledgers. As she rounded the corner into the chamber, she paused, seeing Adrian standing in the window. He had already begun a small fire to heat the room.

"I knew you would need to do a recount of your numbers. The room was cold when I came in," he said. He did not turn from the window as he looked at the darkness beyond. "We will cut some wood before we leave."

"Thank you," Elisabeth said. She moved to stand beside him, and they stared at the emptiness that was the darkness of night. The light behind them danced across the window before them. Below, the moonlight washed over the bailey.

After a long silence, Elisabeth exclaimed, "I thought you would not leave me."

Adrian drew in a long, deep breath. "I have no choice," he said with a shake of his head.

"You do. Tell them you will not, and you will stay here."

"Here?" Adrian said, turning from the window to face her. "How will that be, do you think? Our children will have nothing. My parents have already guaranteed me that. They have promised we will have nothing, not even Ravenshill."

Elisabeth shook her head. "But the fortuneteller said you were my knight of swords."

Adrian grabbed her roughly by the arms and shook her. "I am not your knight of swords. I cannot help you out of this mess. I have my own family responsibilities. My parents have made it clear Ravenshill is no longer my concern, or they will bring it to ruin."

Elisabeth felt the tears biting at the back of her eyes. There was no doubt in Elisabeth's mind that the House of Helmsley was powerful enough to bring Ravenshill, already on its knees, to rubble. The man standing before her had been her hope, her chance that she did not face this alone. She knew Adrian's parents were against marriage between them. He just hadn't told her how strongly they felt about it. They were taking Adrian away, leaving her with great hopelessness. She was foolish to think that he would still be at her side when she was married and Adrian was married.

"How can I be strong when I know you will not come for me?" she asked, fighting back her tears.

He released her arms and seized her by the hand with both his, enveloping it. "Because you are the one with the strength between us. You pulled me from that river and saved me that day. It is I who will feel weaker without your hand to hold. So do not fear for yourself, Lady Elisabeth Kirkham of Ravenshill. It is your courage I carry with me every day. It is your courage that will be with me in every battle. It is your courage I will always hold close to my heart." He released her hand and took two steps back. "Fear for me because I must hold the hand of someone I already know can never give that to me."

He gave her a slow bow, his gray eyes studying her as he did so. Then, finally, he straightened and left her alone in the room.

Elisabeth sank into her chair and opened the ledger. Tomorrow Adrian, Osbert, and Patrick would leave to journey to Helmsley. She studied the numbers, estimating where they would be after feeding the men in the morning before they left. How much wood had they consumed in the hall tonight, and they would use in their chamber? For the budget of both, these things were in danger of not stretching until spring. It looked far worse now.

Elisabeth's mind strayed to Lincoln, and her sadness grew. She saw what he did for Ravenshill. She now recognized the magnitude of his sacrifice for her family. He may have given his soul for her father to have an heir. Now he would be tasked as the only man left at Ravenshill to protect them. But it was not Lincoln's place to feed them. She was the one who had to do that. So, she had to find a husband.

Elisabeth rose from her seat and went to find Adrian.

"I will join you at the celebration?" she announced, finding him in the chamber he was sharing with the other men.

Adrian paused as he shuffled through his bag on the table. Osbert reclined on one of the beds, and Patrick sat cross-legged on the floor, polishing his sword. Walter already snored from his bed.

"Do you wish to?" Adrian asked, a little uneasy.

Elisabeth straightened and replied. "I do. I hope to find a husband."

Adrian studied her for just a moment before nodding. "You can travel with us. We leave in the morning."

Elisabeth turned and fled back to her chamber. She and Edith spent half the night preparing for the journey. All Elisabeth had from Blackpool was the one dress she had left in, which had not even been hers. Even simple, it was better than her own. She would wear that to the ceremony. She chose two more worn gowns, but she and Edith mended them to make them at least presentable. Then the women packed and prepared. Katy would travel with them to visit her sister, who resided at Helmsley.

# Chapter 31

**Thursday, February 15, 1453, Helmsley**

Adrian fidgeted as he stood between his parents. Then, finally, the door swept open, and his wife entered through the tall doorway into the hall. She was a tall and lithe creature. Her head was high, and he thought it obvious she looked down her nose at them all.

Adrian couldn't help but let his eyes shift to Elisabeth, who stood between Osbert and Marquess Adam of Corbridge. Finally, he forced the scowl from his face. It was challenging to watch Osbert fawn over Elisabeth on the journey to Helmsley. The man made it obvious he was swooning for her. It irritated Adrian because Osbert was a good man, and Elisabeth would be a good wife. The problem was, though Osbert was not in debt as the Kirkhams, he was not wealthy either.

Elisabeth was gracious with Osbert, kind and flirtatious even. He never saw the girl act that way. But at seventeen, she wasn't a girl, Adrian reminded himself. She hadn't been a girl in a long time. Admittedly he was jealous watching her giggle at Osbert, blushing prettily for him, looking up at him with her coy and vivid blue eyes from beneath her lashes. While the woman who was his wife would never be someone who would giggle at him, who would blush and smile at his flattery.

Adrian's eyes strayed back to the woman he would have children with. She moved as if she floated. She was not shy to be watched. From across the space, he got the feeling she relished the attention. His eyes fell back to Elisabeth and Lord Corbridge beside her. He was a cousin of his mother's, a man titled in two countries, which did not include the land he lost to England in France. Losing that had done little to reduce the coffers of his household. He never chose to wed, and Adrian knew Elisabeth hoped he was growing to an age when he may be developing a driving need for children. Adrian was sure the man sought one thing from women, and he warned Elisabeth of this. She scoffed at him, declaring Corbridge had no chance of that. But Osbert heard, and he and Patrick glued themselves to her side.

The woman that moved toward Adrian would never have two men voluntarily stand by her side. She was much too cold and uninviting. The frigidness flowed from her, and Adrian felt the floor beneath him melting like lava as Elisabeth's laughter reached him. He felt his entire being seeping away with each step closer Waverly came to him. When she got to him, there was no glow to her cheeks or light in her pale blue eyes.

Adrian bowed, and Waverly curtsied before offering her hand to him to press a chaste kiss to the back of her knuckles. They turned, and she did not lay a hand on his offered arm as he escorted her to her seat at the table.

He dropped his arm to his side and straightened his spine. He had the urge to smooth down the front of his shirt with his hands. Would it soothe him, give him the fortitude it seemed to provide Elisabeth?

Adrian drank heavily at the evening meal, trying to drown out his wife's voice and Elisabeth's. It was excruciating sitting at the table with both women. Knowing what he was leaving behind and what he was going to gain did not boost his spirits. He excused himself early and made it to the well in the center of the inner bailey. Though he made it, it was by a thin margin as the earth wobbled beneath him. He was unsure if he should have stayed in the hall for more wine or gone to seek his bed. But he made it to the well, where he had to wait for the time being if he did not want to lose his meal and all the wine.

"It is her, isn't it?" Osbert asked, coming to sit on the stone where Adrian leaned. Adrian was unsure if sitting would make everything spin faster.

"It is who? What are you talking about?" Adrian asked, and for a brief moment, he closed his eyes against the sharpness of his own voice. But that action made him wobble and want to vomit.

"Elisabeth. She is the one you would rather have," Osbert said.

"She is my friend. But, of course, I would rather wed a friend than that shrill creature," Adrian grouched. He did not want to talk about this. It made his head ring.

"But it is more than that, isn't it?" Osbert asked. When Adrian said nothing, Osbert said the words that made his heart sink. "I need to know, in all honesty, because I wish to ask for her."

Adrian gripped the post so he would not crumble beneath the blow. He knew Elisabeth would find someone, but he never considered she would find a man such as Osbert. A good one who already cherished her if his soft eyes said anything when they looked at her. She would be happy with him and he with her.

In all Adrian's wildest fantasies, this was not how he thought it would end for him and Elisabeth. He never thought he would be wiling away his better years with a woman he would disdain. At the same time, Elisabeth would live happily and have the children of the man she could love. A part of him thought if they were both unhappy, there was a chance they could still find their happiness together. He felt that door slam.

Adrian closed his eyes, planting his feet and telling himself the world wasn't spinning. "She is a friend who I care dearly for. It would be a blessing to have two of my favorite friends joined." Adrian straightened, releasing the post. He turned to Osbert. "I wish you all the luck in your conquest. As for me, I think I will find my bed and sleep this one off."

Osbert nodded but said nothing as Adrian passed him. *"I wish to ask for her,"* kept ringing in his pounding head the next day. Even as he stood before everyone, tugging and smoothing on his belt for a bit of Elisabeth's strength, he thought of Osbert's intentions. He vowed to honor Waverly as his wife that day, but the entire time his mind rested on another woman and the man who intended to marry her.

**Friday, February 16, 1453, Helmsley**

They feasted, and Adrian drank. The evening wore on with frightening speed. His wife did not look at him as a new bride should. There was no dreaminess in her eyes, just the same cold aloofness that made up her soul. In a surreptitious move, his father pushed his goblet from him before Adrian could make it as far into his drink as he had the night before. All too soon, the evening exhausted itself, and it was time for the couple to retire and join as man and wife.

Adrian dragged himself up the steps and to his chamber. His wife was already waiting. Her ladies prepared and placed her in a simple white gown on the bed. He saw her with her blonde hair loose and flowing past her shoulders for the first time. She was wrapped beneath the blankets, and with her head poking from beneath, he thought she could be an attractive woman. But it did not matter her look. She was not beautiful. She was too cold to be beautiful.

"Do you wish to talk first?" Adrian offered, sitting at the table and removing his boots.

"Why would we do that?" Waverly asked. "Why do you come to me as my husband when you are still nothing more than a squire?"

Adrian straightened. "Need I remind you that I am heir to Helmsley and Baron of Stokesley."

A scoffing sound was expelled from Waverly's nose. "That means nothing. It is humiliating to be married to a squire of your age."

"You find marriage to me humiliating?" Adrian questioned.

"In the extreme."

"Why are you doing this, then?" Adrian asked, thinking he should put his boots back on.

"It is what we are supposed to do."

"You expect me to make you my wife in truth after you have told me it is humiliating to be married to me?"

"Yes, because that is what you are to do. I am a virgin, and you will break through my maidenhead, so all will know I was chaste, and our son will be legitimate."

Adrian stared at her, swallowing. He remained quiet for the longest time while she waited, her scowl growing deeper. "How can you lay there for me when I humiliate you?"

She shrugged. Adrian dropped his head into his hands. How could this be happening to him? Then his wife's voice cut across the room. "I will go away each time you make me pregnant. Otherwise, I will come to you many days a month and expect you to make me so."

Adrian raised his head, hope filling him that he could survive this. "I hope to return to France."

She frowned at him. "Go to France. I do not care. You can die there as long as you give me a son first."

Duty, Adrian thought. So much weighed on duty. He wanted to scream because it bore him down, driving him to his knees. Instead, he stood undoing the tie at his waist. When he was in his underclothes, he moved toward the bed, pulling the blankets aside. He climbed in, lying on his back, staring at the ceiling. Waverly did not move. She lay silently, waiting for him to do his duty.

Adrian sighed, then rolled toward her. He lifted himself and wrestled her gown up high enough so her legs could spread, and he could settle between them. She lay beneath him, watching him with no emotion in her eyes. There was no love, no fear, no malice. Nothing would help him take her, whether with gentleness or rage. He took hold of himself, stroking, trying to make himself harden.

He pressed himself against her, hoping the feeling alone would help him do his duty. He positioned the head, ready to plunge in and get it done, but his body would not cooperate with his task. "The sooner you do this, the sooner it will be done," her voice said. He was thrown off kilter to have his wife chastise him while she lay beneath him. Her face was turned away from him, her eyes staring at the wall.

He stroked himself again, thinking of strangling her. He closed his eyes and thought of the woman he had been with, concentrating on the memory of how it felt, her eyes watching him. Even a whore's eyes had more anticipation for what was to come than Waverly's. The thought of them did not help. So, he thought of Elisabeth. He thought of her eyes as if she was the woman beneath him. She would always look at him with love, of that he did not doubt. She would always be happy to wrap her arms around his neck. She would always melt beneath his kisses. He thought of the fire he felt ignite in her when he first took her lips. He had told her to think of him, but it was he who thought of her. How she turned her entire being over to him when he kissed her. How well their lips fit together, how sweet she tasted. He imagined moving from her lips to her jaw, smelling and tasting her. He envisioned a moan from her as he kissed his way down her neck, licking and nibbling. He thought of how soft her skin would be beneath his lips, how the swell of her breasts would taste beneath his tongue. Then, as he imagined licking those perfect little orbs of hers, he plunged himself into his wife. She gasped and gripped the sheets beneath her. That was the only sound that came from his wife as he planted his seed.

She rose from the bed when he rolled from her, donned her robe, and left the room. How many more times would he have to do that? He closed his eyes, wondering if he could ever do it without imagining Elisabeth beneath him. He never imagined her that way. He thought of kissing her and continued thinking of it long after he had. But this was the first time he imagined his hands upon her, his body taking hers. Now he felt a yearning.

He jumped from the bed and cleaned his wife's blood from himself. He felt as if he was unfaithful to Elisabeth. He yanked the sheet off the mattress and lay it in the hallway, returning to his bed. All could see his wife was not a whore if they so desired. His duty was done for the night. He lay in the bed, his mind whirling with sad hopelessness. His mind was locked on his fate and his wife it was his duty to mount. His responsibility was for as long as it took to get her with a child. How many times would he be expected to get her with a child? How many times could he before Elisabeth faded from his mind?

# Chapter 32

**Friday, February 16, 1453, Helmsley**

Elisabeth tried to push the man away in protest again. Still, he leaned upon her with a heavy persistence, pinning her against the table. He bent her over it. The wall on the other side of the narrow top pressed into the back of her head. "Please," she said, trying to avoid his lips that swallowed her plea. Adrian had not kissed her like this. This was revolting.

She remained gentle despite her heart hammering wildly. She just came to talk with Adam of Corbridge, flirt with him, and maybe get him interested in marriage. He knew she was a lady of good breeding. He should know he could not handle her this way. But she feared if she screamed or shoved too hard, he would become angry and never consider a woman as defiant as she.

His mouth was rough on hers. His tongue dove into hers, and the force of his lips made her teeth bite into her flesh. One of his hands gripped the belt at her waist, helping pin her there. The other came to rest at the nape of her neck before it trailed down. A finger slipped into her bodice and began to dig its way downward. How far did this have to go before it was inappropriate without the swearing of vows? This seemed to have escalated quickly from proper and was frightening her.

"Lady Elisabeth."

She almost sobbed in relief, hearing the soft, deep voice of inquiry behind Adam. The man raised his head but did not release her.

"What is it?" Adam snapped at Osbert.

Adam blocked her view of Osbert, but she heard the big man clear his throat. "I was inquiring as to the Lady's willingness to be manhandled," he said. Osbert sounded as if he was trying to be diplomatic. But his words had a bite to them and the coldness of insult.

"Are you her protector now?" Adam asked, straightening from Elisabeth a little more so she saw Osbert.

Osbert's eyes did not rest on her, but on Adam, and in the brown eyes she thought held only softness was furious darkness as his jaw clenched and nostrils flared. "If she so chooses," Osbert replied. He did not remove his eyes from Adam, who turned his head to stare at Elisabeth.

She could not look at him. He hurt her and scared her. But she feared that Adam might be her one hope left. What was a little pain compared to no more days of sitting about hungry to make her numbers match to get them through winter? But she already knew if Adam did have any interest in marrying her, she would always just be a possession to him—property. Elisabeth did not answer because she knew what would come from her mouth. It would be the order for Osbert to go away. But her fear kept her silent until Adam growled and pushed away from her.

As soon as he turned the corner, relief washed over Elisabeth. She let out a sigh before she deflated beneath Osbert's soft gaze. He moved to her, and she could feel the heat of his body as his chest filled her vision. He was tentative as he touched her. His hand came to her elbow before his gentle fingers wrapped around it. She could resist the soft pull. But her feet shuffled, and then his strong arms wrapped around her and held her as she cried for the colossal mistake she had just made. Not from the terror, Osbert thought he saved her from. But from the knowledge, more hunger and turmoil were on the horizon. Another lousy choice foretold.

After a moment, Elisabeth became aware of how fully Osbert enveloped her. His body was pressed against her, his arm wrapped around her shoulders, securing her against his broad chest. The other held her head pinned against it, tucking it beneath his chin. *If only it was as easy as this*, she thought. He offered her such security, such comfort with his soothing voice and gentle hands. But he could not provide the protection she needed that would keep Ravenshill. She had no doubt that he could raise his sword and fight off an army. But a blade would not cut down debt. Not the debt Ravenshill struggled under—obligations to dangerous and influential people. Had her father not told her as much?

Feeling her settle, Osbert began to unwrap himself from her. Suddenly Elisabeth had an overwhelming fear that the man she would find who could save her family would not be able to save her. Adrian was gone from her, and she had come to know his touch, and it was nothing like Lord Adam's. Would a man who was kind and gentle kiss her as Adam had? Was that a warning of what was to come? How could she know?

As his arm slipped from her waist, she seized it, pinning it there, refusing to let him step away. He looked down at her, and she felt herself melt beneath the man's soft gaze. She reached for him, placing a hand on his chest for balance as she moved onto her tiptoes. His free hand was gentle as he put it on top of her hand flattened against his chest. He paused, his eyes staring into hers, giving her a chance to pull away. How could she pull away? Adam wasn't going to let her pull away. What if no man she married would ever let her pull away? But her instinct told her Osbert would yield to her.

Then Osbert's head was coming down to meet hers. His lips were firm and touched her as the gentlest whispers would caress the ear. She pressed her lips more firmly against him, inviting him to show her how a gentleman should be. His hands came to either side of her head, holding her in position. His eyes were looking into hers, but now they drifted closed, and his lips danced across hers. His tongue teased them. His breath warmed them. She felt his body pulling hers against it though his hands still rested against either side of her head. As they collided, his lips took on an urgency that invited Elisabeth to join. His lips consumed hers. His tongue licked across them and entered her mouth, suckling and bringing a soft moan from Elisabeth.

Suddenly she was out of Osbert's grasp. He stood away from her and let the cold corridor seep the warmth of his body from her. He cleared his throat as his gaze devoured her as his lips had. She wanted to call him back. She wanted to cross the space. But instead, she raised her head and smoothed down the front of her gown. She tugged at the bottom of her belt and pulled the edges of her cloak together. Then, boldly she stepped forward and passed by Osbert, who did not try to stop her.

Entering the chamber where Edith and Katy sat, both women looked at her. "And how is Lord Adam?" Katy asked.

"Not my fiancé," Elisabeth said. She saw Katy look at Edith. Edith studied Elisabeth with dark eyes that seemed to reach in and knew what had happened between her and Osbert. For perhaps the first time, Elisabeth was glad she could not ask.

That night, Elisabeth lay in the bed with Katy pressing in on her on one side and Edith on the other. Even in sleep, the women clung to her, sought her, and used her to keep their nightmares away. Yet, Elisabeth felt cold despite their warmth and the fire in the hearth. A hearth that did not have to be extinguished at night to conserve for another day.

Did she have any chance of finding a man she could be happy with as she was with Adrian? Would her husband look at her with the indifference Adrian's wife looked at him with? Or would he look at her as Osbert looked at her? The memory of his eyes when he broke the kiss, made her feel like melting into the bed.

But her mind was trapped by Adrian. He was with his bride tonight, making her his as a husband did. Elisabeth gave a great deal of thought to what marriage to Adrian would be like. Until Osbert kissed her, she never thought of Adrian as a lover, despite the close relationship they had already shared. But they had not shared that intimacy. She imagined how Adrian kissed her. She had been kissed twice tonight. Both were on two different ends of a spectrum. She knew Adrian's lips were firm like Osbert's, but they would not hurt her as Adam's. Osbert was tentative when he kissed her, but Adrian was bold and confident. The thought of Adrian handling her with a wild passion brought tears to Elisabeth's eyes. Despite what Adrian said, he would always be her knight of swords. She understood the desire the fortuneteller spoke of. She felt an ember of attraction with Osbert. She knew had she gone to him for a second kiss, that ember would become a fire. But deep down, her instinct told her it could never be the raging inferno it would be between her and Adrian. She was thankful this realization was only coming to her now. Knowing desire would have been her undoing if Adrian was still within her reach.

Feeling the women cling to her, she felt caged and overwhelmed. Finally, she crawled from between them and left the room. She was sure the gown she wore to bed was wrinkled, but she doubted it would matter this time of night. She needed air. She needed to think.

She stepped out into the solar, easing her way passed the sleeping servants. She stepped into the corridor and quietly closed the door behind her. She was startled to see the silhouette standing at the large picture window at the end, staring out into the night.

"Adrian?" Elisabeth asked, approaching him. He stood with his shoulders stooped, and his demeanor gave him the appearance of a child.

"Why are you here?" she asked, stepping closer. Hanging in the air between them was the real question, *Why aren't you with your wife?*

"I do not like that woman?" he said. "She is hateful and cold. She is rude to every servant she comes in contact with. She thinks herself a queen and is the most obnoxious creature I have ever been near."

"Oh, Adrian," Elisabeth said, stepping forward. She stood beside him and reached out and took his hand in hers. "I am sorry."

She felt him shrug. "It is what I must do." His voice was lost and resigned to it as he said those words.

She stood beside him, holding his hand. Was it true she gave him his strength? He needed it now. He needed all of it now because it saddened her to her very core to see him like this. She squeezed his hand. He turned to her then, enveloping her hand with both his. "I do not know how I will do this until we have a child."

"Oh, Adrian," she said again. Her heart broke because he was wasted on a woman who made him feel this way.

Then his hands dropped away from her, and he turned his head to look out the window. She saw his jaw working, tightening.

"It will be all right," she said, reaching her hand out to turn his head back to her. "Truly, it will be all right. It is only a small thing."

"But I do not want it to be a small thing," he said. He looked at her in the darkness, and she could feel his gaze change. He reached for her. His hand snaked to the small of her back, and he slammed her slim body against his. Her hands went to his chest to catch herself. Landing there, she felt her fingers grip his shirt. His head swooped down on her, and his lips covered hers. He was not as gentle as Osbert. He claimed her lips with confidence and branded her. They demanded she yield to him. His strength pounded away at her senses, so she could not deny him. His tongue dove into her mouth, devouring her, pulling her tight, crushing her. She felt a level of viciousness release from Adrian, ebbing and charging him as his grip became frantic.

She felt her arms wrap around his neck, into his hair, and she pulled him closer. Her fingers bit into his scalp as his strong hands clung to her waist, lodging her against him. She felt his manhood and pressed herself into it, wanting something deep within her core she could not identify, but she knew Adrian was the key. His lips trailed across her cheek, to her neck, where his lips burned, and his teeth grazed. She wanted his lips back on hers, but where they were and where they were going made her voice useless. He held her up, pressing her, supporting her as she clung to him.

His lips were at the tops of his breasts. His breath plunged between them as his tongue trailed across the skin. Then Elisabeth felt him pause, and she opened her eyes. They gazed at one another, both panting, feeling the heat. "Elisabeth," he whispered her name. It was sad and resolute. Then his arms wrapped around her. He was stronger than Osbert and fanned an inferno where Osbert had only created a spark. This man that held her owned her heart. He had for a long time. Perhaps before she clung to his hand on the bank of the river with a storm raging around them.

"I would ask you to be with me as my companion if I was that kind of man," he said. She felt she should be insulted. He would consider her a mistress. Instead, a part of her wished he was that kind of man.

Finally, Adrian lay a lingering kiss on the top of her head before releasing her.

He drew in a steadying breath. "It is time for me to return to my life. I think it wise if this is our farewell."

Elisabeth nodded. Her hand trembled, and her heart shattered. Of course, it was wise. Because if they held one another again, neither of them would be smart enough to let go. It would be the ruination of Elisabeth and Ravenshill with her. But, of course, Adrian would be forgiven. He was a man, after all. And she was grateful he was a good man because she did not have the strength to stop him when he held her.

Elisabeth could say nothing as Adrian studied her for a moment before bowing deeply to her, then turning walked away. Elisabeth stood in the corridor for a long time. She was unwilling to return to her bed. It was filled with women who would find her in their sleep and cling to her.

She returned to the room by dawn and gathered their things when the other women woke. The room was abuzz as a knock sounded on their chamber door. Elisabeth went to it with shaking hands, fearing it was Adrian, while it was also her greatest hope. Osbert stood on the other side and bowed to her as she opened it.

"A word, my lady?" he asked.

"Of course," Elisabeth said, ducking from the room.

In the hallway stood Patrick and their squires. "Allow us to join your party and escort you home."

"That is unnecessary," Elisabeth assured him, offering him and the other knight a gentle smile.

"Please, my lady," Osbert said. "It would give me great pleasure to see you safely home before I must return to France."

Stated in such a manner, Elisabeth could not deny him. She was the driving force that got the group moving from Helmsley's gates soon after the rising sun. Elisabeth took a moment as her horse cleared the wall and turned to look at Helmsley and Adrian's new home. He stood upon the wall. The wind whipped his dark cloak about his shoulders, and he watched her. They stared at one another across the space, then she whirled her horse and rode away before the tears came, and all would know of her turmoil.

**Tuesday, February 20, 1453, Ravenshill**

Ravenshill seemed colder to Elisabeth as she entered the hall and crossed through to the kitchen. She looked around herself. The same stone walls, hearths, and windows would no longer be the same because Adrian wasn't with her. She felt Ravenshill had emptied with him. It seemed full even when the numbers abandoned them, but that feeling was gone. Then Osbert was in the doorway behind her. She did not have to turn to know it was him. He was patient as he waited behind her. No man was as patient as Osbert.

"My lady," his voice finally called, soft in its lilt and volume.

Elisabeth turned to look up at the warrior that would be leaving Ravenshill too. It dawned on her that Adrian would not return to France under the banner of Ravenshill. She only had Walter to send to rejoin her father in France. But that was a problem for tomorrow, she told herself. She felt like screaming that all she could do was walk backward, never forward.

"I would like to speak to your father while in France, but I must ask your permission to do so," Osbert said. His voice came out as nervous and hesitant.

"You have my leave to speak to my father," Elisabeth said with a smile spreading across her face.

"No, my lady," Osbert said quickly. She watched him swallow, and his dark eyes softened even more if such a thing could be possible. "I wish to ask him for your hand."

This surprised Elisabeth, and she could not respond. She needed a husband but a wealthy one, and she knew Osbert was not.

Osbert's voice continued in its gentle and deep soothing way. "I pray you forgive me, but I spoke to Adrian of you. He did not wish to speak of it, but he told me a little about your family's situation." The man paused but gathered himself and rushed on. "I am merely a knight, a common man, but I am a great warrior. I joined the King's men in France as a mercenary and was knighted on a battlefield. I have gained some wealth there. I will strive to earn all I can to help your family. If you marry me, your debt will be mine. I will handle it thus and will do all in my power to save Ravenshill. I swear I will protect you and all you love with my life because I already love you, Elisabeth."

He began to say more when Patrick and Edith entered the kitchen. The pair entered with Edith's hand clasped in Patrick's. They made it halfway to the hearth when Patrick stopped in his tracks and yanked Edith, spinning her, so she turned and fell into the big man. Immediately Elisabeth stepped forward to stop him when Osbert's hand clamped to her elbow. Before she could protest, he had her back pressed against his front, a hand wrapped around her waist, holding her there, and his other hand was clamped over her mouth. She could have released herself if she wished. She knew this, and her mind was close to panic for the briefest moments. But she knew Osbert would not hurt her, even if he did not just profess those words.

There was great warmth and protection as Osbert held her still. They remained thus long enough to watch

Patrick reach out, take Edith's chin in his hand and gently tip her head up to look at him. From their position, Elisabeth saw Patrick's face transform. It went from alive with mirth to adoration and softness. That same softness Elisabeth saw in Osbert's eyes when he looked at her.

She realized what she would get with Osbert Adrian could not give her. It felt as if Osbert thought her fragile enough to break when he touched her. Then, like now, Osbert did not hold her about her waist with a grip like iron. He only rested his arm across her hips, flattening his hand against her abdomen. His hand was strong. She could feel its weight across her shoulder. He had a warrior's strong, calloused hand as it gently pressed her lips together beneath his palm. Adrian knew she was not fragile. He knew she would not break and handled her thusly. Osbert handled her as if she was frail enough to shatter.

Suddenly, Patrick grabbed Edith, lifted her, and with giant strides, carried her to one of the tables and sat her upon it as she straddled him. Both his hands that supported her and held her there pulled her roughly against his groin. Osbert's hand along Elisabeth's waist tightened as his fingers wrapped around her side, pulling her closer. Elisabeth wanted to protest, but Osbert's head dropped to her ear, and his breath fanned across her ear, "Shhh."

Osbert began to move her quietly toward the door.

"Push me away, and I will go," Patrick's voice carried to them.

Elisabeth didn't allow Osbert to move her further. She looked to Edith, waiting for her to push the big knight away, and Elisabeth was ready to tear loose from Osbert if the man did not yield. But Edith did not push

Patrick away. Instead, her legs wrapped around the man's waist, and her hands clamped around his neck as she lifted herself toward him. He seized the woman and enveloped her. His lips took her in a passionate moment, making Elisabeth's loins burn. She could see Patrick and Edith shared a passion like Adrian and herself, and she was glad for her friend.

She was aware again of Osbert. He slipped his hand from her mouth, scooped Elisabeth into his arms, and carried her from the kitchen. Once in the hall, he sat her gently on her feet. He released her, but he did not move away.

"I saw in Adrian's eyes this morning what a misery it would be to have a wife or husband you do not like. It frightens me to think a man will get you that does not deserve you. I doubt I deserve a woman as fine as you, but I love you, Elisabeth. No man can offer you that as he asks for your hand. And no man will fight as hard for you."

Elisabeth stared up at him. In his eyes was that gentleness she was growing accustomed to, but she also saw a spark within them. That desire as he looked at her and a burning ache began. Elisabeth could not tear her eyes from him. They felt as if they melted her as their heat grew. She nodded her head. She could not imagine letting a man she did not like have that piece of her only a husband should have. She did not want that sour look to become a permanent line on her face as it would be on Adrian's.

A smile began to spread across Osbert's face. Elisabeth couldn't look away from the boy she saw appear on the man's face. Then, the smile faltered and washed away. A flame ignited in his dark eyes, and he licked his lips, hesitating. He looked away, and

Elisabeth's mind told her to step away. But as she began to shift, his eyes fell back on her. The flame was banked, but it was like the coals of fire, full of heat and promise.

"Tell me no, Elisabeth, and I will not kiss you. Because if I do, I do not think my chivalry will stand."

Elisabeth looked into his eyes, and she wanted nothing more. Adrian was gone, and she needed happiness. She wanted no man like she wanted Osbert. She wanted no husband but Osbert. "Yes," she whispered.

Osbert licked his lips again, and then his hands were on her face. His eyes fell to her lips. One of his thumbs traced across her bottom lip before his eyes rose to hers. He hesitated, giving her ample opportunity to change her mind. Then, Osbert's head lowered, and his lips feathered gently across hers. As his arms slipped from her face and wrapped about her waist, they were light and gentle, but the way his hand gripped her, she felt it was a gentleness that he fought with. He was afraid to break her or scare her. Her heart grew more for him knowing this. That he placed her before his desire, before himself.

She pulled her lips from beneath his. He moved to follow, but his gentleness remained as he let them part. "Kiss me like you want," she said, looking into his eyes. "Ladies will not break."

Osbert's head dipped again, and a hand came up to tighten against the back of her head, and his other yanked her against him so she felt every corded muscle of his body. His firm, demanding lips brought a surprised gasp from her. At the sound, he released her, stepping back. The loss of being in his arms devastated her. She wanted so much more.

"Osbert?" she questioned. His eyes blazed, and his jaw was set.

He shook his head, his breaths coming fast.

"I was not done," she said. Done with what? Kissing? No, she was done kissing him on the lips. She wanted to feel his lips trailing down her neck, across her breasts like Adrian's had. She had thought of nothing else since. She needed this man to wipe that memory away. He was the only one that could let her release Adrian.

"You do not know what you are asking," Osbert said. "I have not always been a gentle man or a chivalrous one."

Elisabeth took a step forward and placed a hand on his chest. She stared at it for a moment. It was so small on his broad chest. She was aware he, too, stared down at it, waiting. She felt his chest rise and fall beneath it and his heart's strong, powerful beat. That heart beat for her. Keeping herself pure for her future husband had never been an arduous undertaking. She never felt a desire as she did now. Staring at her hand, she weighed the decision she was about to make. For the first time in a long time, she did not think of Ravenshill and how this decision would affect it and its people. Instead, she thought of what this meant for her. It meant she would have to search nowhere else for a husband. Even if Osbert could not save Ravenshill, he could save her.

She lifted her head, and he met her eyes, still waiting. She felt his breath still in his chest as she lifted herself on her tiptoes and took his lips with hers. He remained frozen, not touching her as she fanned her lips across his. She watched him as she flicked her tongue out to suckle his bottom lip. She felt a sigh escape him as if he had given up on a long-fought battle. He moved with the speed of a cat. One arm gripped her waist, and another went to the back of her head. He forced her backward until she felt her shoulders slam into the wall as his lips devoured her, devoured her soul. She melted into him as his hand released her head to brace against the wall. His other hand unwound from her waist, grabbed her bottom, and lifted her, settling her between the wall and himself so her weight pressed down on him, and she felt his arousal through their clothes. It stoked the fire exploding between them. His lips left hers, trailing down her neck, his breath hot against her skin. She groaned when he blazed a path with his tongue upward to clamp again onto her lips. He tightened himself against her.

"Tell me you will take me to your bed tonight, or I must stop now," his words pressed against her ear, followed by his lips.

"Take me to my bed, Osbert," she whispered, wrapping herself around him.

He pulled her into his arms, lifting her into them. She watched his face as he walked toward her room. It was set in granite, but she saw the fire banked in its orbs until he entered the room, letting the tapestry fall behind them. Slowly he slid her down the front of himself until her feet touched the floor. He removed his shirt, and his chest lay bare. He paused then, looking down at her.

Elisabeth had the distinct impression he was giving her yet another chance to stop. But she reached for him. Running her hands up over his chest. She reveled in the firmness, the strength held in check beneath the surface. She ran them up to his shoulders, stroking across their expanse. His lips met hers. He was gentle again, and she was grateful because she had feared this moment for so long. She did not like pain, but if anyone was going to be gentle, it was this man.

Slowly he undressed her. His lips caressed her, stroking as each item fell to the floor. When she was bare, he lifted her gently in his arms and carried her to sit on the edge of the bed. He began all over again, her lips, neck, shoulders, and then they seared her breasts.

What followed was surreal as her mind entered a thick haze of desire Osbert knew how to ignite. She felt his every touch, his every breath when it fanned across her. She was beneath him, but at the same time, she was far away in a place where sensations were intensified. He took her gently, slowly, and she never knew such a sharp pain could then lead the way to such pleasure.

Elisabeth sighed, a contented sound as Osbert settled onto the bed beside her. He pulled her into his arms, dropping her head onto his chest.

"I'm going to leave Patrick when we return to France," Osbert said.

"Can you not send him in your stead?"

"Next time, but I must go see my father and yours."

Elisabeth nodded against his bare skin.

His chest did not take long to rise and fall in a steady rhythm beneath her cheek. His masculine scent filled her nostrils. His strength soothed her, and feeling his warmth and love, she drifted to sleep with him.

# Chapter 33

**Wednesday, March 28, 1453, Bordeaux, Aquitaine**

It was a relief for Adrian to step foot back on French soil. For an entire month, he was caged at Helmsley with Waverly. He had to perform as her husband for a whole month despite growing to hate her. He did not think she had the emotional capacity to reciprocate that hatred. He spent much of the month on the edge of a drunken stupor. His mood became as foul as his wife's.

He felt odd serving under the Helmsley banner. A youth untested in battle now with his own army trailing him. Three hundred men rode with Adrian from Helmsley. They would join the other two hundred his father provided King Henry. His father, the military strategist, told Adrian the numbers would signify to King Henry that Adrian was to be a far greater lord than his father.

It was all for one king, but it felt like a betrayal to not have the raven on the banner over his head. Nevertheless, Lincoln's men had welcomed him back. He had earned his place with them.

“Is this how you spend your time now, Young Adrian?” Lincoln’s voice brought Adrian’s head up from the chess game, and he spun. With Lincoln stood Walter, Osbert, and Elyas. Adrian’s face split into a grin. Looking at his friends now returned, he thought of what he had lost and what he had gained. This was his home, his new home, and these men were it, and he was grateful for his place.

“I have to,” Adrian replied. “I have scared all my challengers in the physical games.” He smirked at his own cockiness.

“We will change that,” Walter declared.

Adrian smiled. He knew it was condescending in nature, unwilling to consider he might be dethroned of his reputation.

Then Osbert’s face grew sober. “Can I speak to you, Adrian?” Adrian paused and felt concerned because Osbert’s face was masked with stern determination.

Adrian stood and followed him from the others.

“I have asked Elisabeth to wed me, and she has agreed. I spoke to her father first thing upon our arrival, and he has given his blessing,” Osbert said.

Adrian felt the ground shift beneath him. She was gone. He could not help that his face fell, but he brought it back into a smile. “I am glad for you,” he said. “Truly, you two will have happiness together.” He reached an arm out, and Osbert locked his with it, and the two men nodded. Adrian felt he was turning Elisabeth over to him in that gesture, relinquishing his claim to her. But he knew it was a claim he never had.

Despite the news that greeted him on Osbert’s arrival and a date set in the summer for the wedding, Adrian was glad his friends had returned. With Walter and Lincoln there, it was as if he had a part of his family back.

**Wednesday, April 25, 1453, Fronsac, Aquitaine**

Adrian licked his lips. He looked across the army stretched out before Talbot's men. He swallowed a throat that had closed. He only knew he held his breath when he drew in a loud inhalation. It was a ragged sound. A sound that terrified him because it verified he was not prepared for what he was about to face.

Adrian's breath fell into rapid and shallow inhalations. Knowledge came to him at a rapidity that blindsided him. This was why Lincoln's men had that unidentifiable look about them. Why he always felt something dark and menacing lurking beneath Lincoln's surface. It was the mark Death left on them after they looked him in the eyes and cheated him of their souls.

Adrian fought the urge to turn to Lincoln and beg him to let him walk away from this. He would give up his title, his home, to anyone who could stare down the overwhelming army and not feel like wetting themselves. Any man who could stand in the front of a small battle line without sweaty palms. He wiped one palm and then the other on Achilles's neck. He felt the speckles of his black hair cling to the moisture on his skin.

Lincoln's big hand came down on his shoulder.

"You will be alright, Son," Lincoln said through his open visor.

As Adrian turned toward Lincoln, he wished he had lowered his visor because the knight would see no bravery in his eyes, only terror.

"You are ready for this, Adrian. You would not be here, despite Ravenshill. I would not have allowed you to come to France if I did not think you were ready. Just remember, don't be intimidated by your opponent, be unpredictable so he can't anticipate your next move."

Adrian nodded, but his eyes still stood wide with his fear. His breath still constricted inside his armor. He heard the call for the longbowmen to knock their arrows and prepare for the first volley. The call came forward, and the whoosh of the strings sounded as the deadly arrows were propelled forward.

Beside him, Lincoln lowered his visor to protect his face. Adrian did the same.

Adrian heard the cries as the armor-piercing bodkins fell upon them. Talbot held his infantry's charge as the French side roared their outrage and stormed forward. The archers sent four rapid volleys into the charging French infantry. Then, a surge of English foot soldiers was ordered forward. The armor and weapons sent up an echoing explosion of destruction. Finally, the horn sounded that ordered the cavalry's charge.

Adrian loosed Achilles as Lincoln's horse Xanthus shot forward. As he and his horse bore down on the French, his fear fled, and as Achilles reached the lines and ripped through them, he felt horror take hold.

With poleax in hand and shaking legs holding him upright in his saddle, the English forces hit the line of French hard. French soldiers were knocked to the ground. Adrian swung to the left and right, spinning his horse as the English knights broke through the lines already softened with the archers' attack. The knights moved deeper onto the ground the French were slowly retreating from. The foot soldiers were a swirling mass surrounding the cavalry. The press of men pushed foot soldiers and knights together. The goal—the walls of Fronsac.

His eyes had little time to take in the men Achilles knocked beneath his hooves and trampled. For only a frantic second or two, did he have the time to register the sounds of screams from the dying, the sound of bones breaking, the cries of the horses, and the sound of the horns and drums competing to rise above the cacophony of death.

Something inside Adrian changed at that moment. The frenzy was gone in his mind. He no longer thought of the trenches that lay ahead and feared the force of the army that stood there behind breastworks. His mind took in the strategy before him. The small number of the enemy army lined up for the first charge. The French troops had no intention of putting forth a real fight until the English made it across the trenches. That was where their numbers were amassed.

The small French army would take out the first wave. They would retreat with the English military charging after. The frenzy of chasing their enemies would lead men blindly into the ditch, where they would be at their weakest. Men would be cut down, and horses would fall. But Adrian had to be off Achilles by then. Lincoln had told him, again and again, he had to get off Achilles before reaching the trench. The spears on the opposite side would guarantee a horse's death if the trench did not do the trick. Lincoln warned that every cavalryman knew this, but the charge had a way of sweeping men with it blindly.

A French foot soldier, bolstered by Adrian's lack of fight, grabbed his plated leg. Without hesitation, Adrian's instinct took over the calamity of his mind. Adrian raised his poleaxe and brought it crashing down on the foot soldier's unprotected head. Adrian saw the splatter and felt the concussion of the collapsing skull beneath his weapon. Baron Adrian de Ros had killed his first man.

A horn blew and warned of the incoming French cavalry a moment before they reached their lines.

For just a moment, the fear returned when he saw the well-armored knights. Hulking figures atop their fierce horses. How many more were their numbers than Talbot‘s? Row after row, they had to defeat the French fortifications. The moment's desperation overrode the fear as the horsemen on both sides clashed, and weapons swept through the air.

Adrian took a blow to his shoulder, but it had little effect on Adrian’s seat. Adrian spun Achilles, and as the animal came around, Adrian swung his poleaxe and struck the other knight in the head with a force that tumbled him to the ground. The other knight was swallowed beneath the hooves and feet of the armies.

Adrian felt the hands of the foot soldiers reaching for him, trying to force him from his saddle or the animal from beneath him. He spun Achilles moving the men back as more knights from the opposing side reached them.

French cavalry and foot soldiers converged on the English knights, trying to cut down their animals. Adrian felt Achilles lash out, his head dipping and biting at those who came too close. Then hands gripped Adrian, yanking him from the saddle. He hit the ground hard. The metal of his armor did little to cushion his landing. He felt the poleaxe pulled from his hand, and then it was coming at his head. Adrian rolled, sweeping his leg out, taking two men down by his unexpected attack when he appeared ready to take his death blow. He was well used to the weight of his armor, and it did not slow his fight. He came off the ground with speed unexpected for a man of his size. As he rolled to his feet, he lowered his head and charged at three men rushing toward him. He threw his arms out and swept all three down onto the ground with him. He landed halfway across two of them, not taking a moment to recover before jumping to his feet. His sword cleared its scabbard, and he took a defensive stance among the men. None wore armor, all were unprepared foot soldiers, and he saw uncertainty in their eyes.

A force of English foot soldiers reached them, and the men who anticipated killing Adrian became otherwise occupied. Adrian moved to help finish them when a knight in full armor materialized in front of him. He was not as big as Adrian, and beneath the man's helm, he could see nothing of the man's fierceness, but he could feel it. The other knight did not hesitate. He lifted his poleax and brought it, singing toward Adrian. Adrian brought his blade up, blocking the man's first strike.

Adrian spun away, circling him as the man tried to follow. *Cumbersome*, Adrian thought, seeing the man could not keep up with Adrian. He used this to his advantage and attacked, thrusting the point of his sword forward, trying to find an opening before he had to defend against the deadly poleaxe. The weapon the other knight carried could drive straight through Adrian's armor. It could crush his skull despite the helm that was secure upon his head. It could crush his elbow or even his windpipe if it landed in the proper places. Adrian fought and moved in determination not to allow the knight a chance to land one blow. Adrian felt the tip of his sword slide beneath the knight's harness and into his side. He tore the sword out of the flesh to avoid the oncoming poleaxe. But the hammer found Adrian, crashing down onto his back. He staggered, knowing to lose his feet would be to lose his life.

Adrian took two stumbling steps forward as he turned and moved against the knight again. All Adrian's blow seemed to do was show the knight where he was vulnerable. He did not give Adrian the opportunity again. For a few moments, neither Adrian nor the French knight landed a blow to each other. Then the tide turned in the other knight's favor when a second knight came at Adrian's back. Adrian saw the movement as he spun, and he brought his sword up in time to block the spike coming at his head. The blow struck Adrian's sword like an explosion, flowing down his arms. He almost dropped the sword from the pain that reverberated into his hands. He stepped back and spun so the first knight's poleaxe fell on empty air.

Then Adrian faced both men. One knight's armor was polished. The other's armor was painted, mismatched pieces he must have scavenged from other battles. The one knight was of apparent high standing and wealth since he could pay someone just to keep his armor polished at such a substantial level. It flashed a moment in Adrian's mind how battle classes came together. Both men, despite their status, stood side by side, ready to fight him. But Adrian was sure he could kill the wealthy, as well as the poor man.

Adrian hefted his sword back and forth in his hands, loosening his grip for the briefest of moments so both hands would be strong again for the fight that came charging his way. Both men moved as one. It was as if there was some signal given to them. One raised his poleaxe, and the other aimed at his side. The polished knight was intent on driving the spike into his skull. At the same time, the other would be content to shatter his ribs and penetrate an organ. Adrian stepped toward the painted knight, spinning toward the incoming hammer. He brought his sword up, letting it take the blow, and his weapon's momentum died in the air.

Adrian did not stop the dance of his feet as he elbowed the man in the face. It did no damage, only snapped the helmed man's head back and forced him to take a step back. For a moment, it was Adrian and the polished knight again. He moved in on the knight as his weapon came at Adrian. Adrian ducked and stepped forward. He felt the handle of the weapon come in contact with his shoulder. The blow dropped him to his knees, but it was a strategic and misleading move on Adrian's part. For an instant, the knight thought he landed his blow as intended or, at the very least, took him off his feet. But as the man drew back to land a killing blow, Adrian rose from the ground, sword pointed upward, and drove the point between the man's helm and his collar. It was a sickening sound above the mayhem of battle. He yanked his sword free, and the blood exploded over him as the knight dropped to his knees.

But the painted knight was moving again. Raging as he lunged at Adrian, meeting him head-on. One strike, two strikes, he came at Adrian. Adrian blocked the strikes, remaining over the now-dead knight as the rest of the army pressed in. As the second strike came toward him, he took a step forward until the toe of his boot was stopped by the polished knight. Adrian blocked another blow, bending as the enemy's weapon arced down. He grabbed the ax the polished knight's dead hand had released.

Adrian swung the weapon, and his strong shoulders drove it. With strength he knew he could wield, he brought the spike down onto the crown of the man's head. At the same time, Adrian brought up the tip of the sword he still held in his other hand. He felt the weight of the painted knight fall on it. Adrian pulled his arm back, pulling the blade from deep within the man's skull.

Adrian breathed heavily, fighting the urge to double over to steady his breath. That would only paint a target on his back. Instead, he prepared for another attack. No more knights came toward him, and as his poleaxe claimed one more life and was ready to take another, the fortress of Fronsac began to surrender. Adrian stood amongst the army, looking at the dead lying about. He dropped his weapons. Exhaustion and the sadness of it became too much for his hands to grip them. He breathed in a long breath. Roars from the other men rose in the air, but Adrian did not partake. Yes, the victory was theirs, but he did not feel the triumph he did at the end of a match. Men died here, and Adrian had killed his share. He turned, his eyes traveling across them. Those men would not walk again. For this, he trained, and it was his desire throughout childhood. He found glory today on the battlefield, but it did not shine as brightly as he thought it would.

**Friday, April 27, 1453, Fronsac, Aquitaine**

"Are you about?" Lord Thomas's voice called from outside the tent.

Adrian stepped to the flap and exited into the afternoon's cool breeze. Soon it would be time to put on his armor. Adrian's time had finally come, and he would be knighted by Commander Talbot. Tonight was the moment he spent his life holding his breath for.

Adrian always assumed he would be adorned in his ceremonial armor tucked safely away at Helmsley. Not in the armor he fought in. But he did not mind, for it was a symbol that he earned this.

"I have brought you something for your ceremony." With a flourish, Thomas motioned to the men carrying the pieces of armor. They came nearer, and Adrian saw the blackened steel of the newly forged metal.

"What is this?" Adrian asked as one of the men offered him the helmet. Adrian studied it, turning it in his hands. It was beautifully crafted. The gold russet made the armor far more elegant than Adrian's at home. It was also far more expensive.

"It is my gift to you. I knew this day would come, and I had the opportunity in our adventures to acquire this suit along with one for Lincoln and myself. I am proud, and though you do not fight for Ravenshill now, I will always consider you a son."

Thomas embraced Adrian, giving him a hearty pat as they parted.

"This is far too generous," Adrian said, holding the helmet out to Thomas.

Thomas folded his arms across his chest and waved it away. "You saved my daughter. Nothing I could ever do for you is too generous."

Thomas remained and helped Adrian's men fit the armor onto him. The weight of it surprised Adrian, expecting it to be lighter than his battle armor. But this armor had thick plates of steel. It was built for war but far too beautiful. They must have belonged to a wealthy

French household Talbot, and Thomas ransacked on a foray.

As the dinner unfolded, the men who survived and excelled received honor. Adrian was unsure what he had done to excel, but he had survived. Lord Lisle presented him to Commander Talbot. The old lord did not move like a man of his age is like to do. He was straight-backed. His face still held hostile cruelty in its dark depths despite the lines of time etched in his leathered face. His light, reddish-brown hair had thinned and turned almost translucent.

He bid Adrian kneel. Adrian's breath caught in his throat for what he had sought the entirety of his life. Tears of pride threatened to fill his eyes. Lisle pulled Adrian's sword from its sheath and handed it to Talbot. As he was dubbed with the title of knight, far more valuable to him than the title of baron or earl, he was surprised by the weight of it. His newfound knowledge made it settle heavier than any armor.

"Do you step heavier now because your head has become so big?" Lincoln teased him as they moved back to their own camp.

Osbert laughed, and Adrian smiled. Despite the magnitude of the ceremony, he did step lighter because his chest was filled with pride. He had done it. After seeking it for so long, knighthood was his. It was not a title easily earned.

"Your family will be proud," Osbert said.

The smile faded from Adrian's face. He knew one person who would be very proud of him. Her eyes would shine with genuine joy, and her cheeks would light with color. But he could not share the news with her. She would be joined by another soon. The banns were posted in England, and they would exchange their vows as soon as Osbert could return to Ravenshill.

Adrian's mind went to his wife and how she was ashamed of his status as a squire. He would send a message informing her of his knighting. He did not think it would make his wife any happier.

The English army was on the move again, and the French arrived in mass force and laid siege against the town of Castillon. Thirty miles north, Talbot mustered the men. The army charged from Bordeaux. Adrian was unsure of the exact count of the English forces, but it was in the thousands. Moving like a giant serpent with its long stretch of infantry, knights, archers, and supplies. It became clear that as the army moved quickly, the mounted troops had an advantage and were putting distance between them and the infantry forces.

Lincoln was the one to point this out early in the march. That was one of Lincoln's numerous complaints about Talbot and how he ran his army. He felt the man was too rash and dealt with many a defeat because of it. But Adrian thought this was just Lincoln overthinking the strategy of one leader from his perspective as a leader of his own forces. But Adrian began to wonder about his friend's wisdom as the columns became more distanced. After a respite in Libourne for the night, by the following day, the foot soldiers were far behind. What started as an entire army of thousands was now in the hundreds made of mounted archers and men-at-arms. The advancing English forces hit a small garrison of men at a priory. The force was annihilated before Lincoln's men reached them.

Talbot sent men thundering ahead to Castillon to study the strength of the French forces. Adrian and the rest of Lincoln's men washed the dust and fatigue of the road away with wine as they rested and awaited news. Lincoln was relieved that they were now waiting for the rest of the English army to catch up. But that hope was dashed when they were called to arms before the infantry arrived.

**Tuesday, July 17, 1453, Castillon, Aquitaine**

Talbot rode among them. Lincoln's comments and the fact the men would not be charging in on horseback but on foot frayed at Adrian's confidence. They did not have enough men. He saw the wisdom of Lincoln's words as he looked at the deep trench. It extended a half-mile, running parallel with the Dordogne River a mile away. Giant earthworks ran behind the trench. From Adrian's position, he could see that it was fortified by massive tree trunks. Upon those earthworks was the first line of the French defense. It wasn't the ditch or the walls. It was firepower. Some were handheld, but other cannons were large and fixed to the battlements. The weapons took the advantage of the English archers away. They could cut down a foot soldier with deadly force, armored or not, before the enemy ever reached the lines. This was not the small number of French they had encountered thus far. There had to be hundreds of French stretching along the length of the town's fortifications.

As Adrian studied what they faced, he saw the breastworks were the French defense's first obstacle. The English forces had to make it across the trench, up the steep mound of earth and wall. Then they had to conquer the men defending it before crossing open terrain beneath the artillery barrage before reaching the gates. Here there would be more cannons, Adrian did not doubt. Finally, they had to climb the walls before they even began fighting for the town. They did not have enough men.

Talbot positioned his army with his experienced men-at-arms at the forefront of the assault. This put Lincoln and his men on the front lines. The rest of the army formed a tight column behind them. They charged in full armor, cries rose from Lincoln's men, and Adrian picked it up. Voices rang loud across the open ground before the French fired the first shot. Adrian saw the smoke. He heard the explosions and whistles as the cannons let loose up and down the lines. Martin was struck in front of Adrian. The man was lifted off his feet and thrown backward into him. Adrian staggered, which saved him from the incoming projectiles that decimated the front line.

Cries rose, commands came, and the men pushed on. The cannons reloaded as men began to climb the other side of the trench. Knights in armor were fired upon at point-blank range and rolled back into it. Lincoln was in front of Adrian, leading him to the top and ready to dive over the other side when a man with a handheld cannon appeared. He fired, then Lincoln fell. His body slammed into Adrian, driving him backward, and they rolled together back into the trench.

The breath erupted from Adrian's chest, and he lay a minute with the weight of Lincoln on top of him. The knight did not move. Upon this realization, Adrian scrambled from beneath him and bent over him. He lifted his visor, peering down into the still face of the man who was like a father to him. "Let's move," Osbert was there, trying to tug Adrian to his feet.

Adrian left Lincoln lying in the ditch and climbed the breastworks again, fighting past those staggering beneath the onslaught of cannon fire. As the men continued to fall, those behind used their bodies as shields, driving forward despite the blood that exploded, slickening the ground.

As they fought for ground, the gunfire drove them back, forcing them to give as much as it seemed they gained. The men above Osbert and Adrian fell, and it left them exposed. A cannon fired, and it ripped through Osbert. His armor was no defense as one of the balls struck him. Adrian reached for him but felt the pain of a ball tearing through his own armor. Then Adrian fell, tumbling as darkness took hold.

— TO BE CONTINUED —

Dear Reader,

I hope you enjoyed book one of the Snakes & Swords Trilogy. Check out book two, *In the Grass*, and continue the journey with Elisabeth and Adrian as the Wars of the Roses begins.

If you haven't signed up yet, my newsletter avarmsbooks.com offers free giveaways and series extras.

Find me on Instagram, Facebook, Twitter, and Pinterest, I'd love to hear from you.

A.V. Arms

**Snakes & Wolves Trilogy**

Book 1 - Snakes & Wolves

Book 2 - In the Grass

Book 3 - At the Door